'Racy legal thrillers lift the lid on sex and racial prejudice at the bar' – *Guardian*

'Murphy paints a trenchant picture of establishment cover-up, and cannily subverts the clichés of the legal genre in his all-too-topical narrative' – *Financial Times*

'Peter Murphy's novel is an excellent read from start to finish and highly recommended' – *Historical Novel Review*

'An intelligent amalgam of spy story and legal drama'– *Times*

'A gripping, enjoyable and informative read'
– *Promoting Crime Fiction*

'The ability of an author to create living characters is always dependent on his knowledge of what they would do and say in any given circumstances – a talent that Peter Murphy possesses in abundance' – *Crime Review UK*

'Murphy's clever legal thriller revels in the chicanery of the English law courts of the period' – *Independent*

'The forensic process is examined in a light touch, good-humoured style, which will evoke a constant stream of smiles, and chuckles from nonlawyers and lawyers alike'
– **Lord Judge**, *former Lord Chief Justice of England and Wales*

'A gripping page-turner. A compelling and disturbing tale of English law courts, lawyers, and their clients, told with the authenticity that only an insider like Murphy can deliver. The best read I've come across in a long time'
– **David Ambrose**

'If anyone's looking for the next big courtroom drama… look no further. Murphy is your man' – *ICLR*

ALSO BY PETER MURPHY

The American Novels

Removal
Test of Resolve
A Statue for Jacob

The Ben Schroeder Series

A Higher Duty
A Matter for the Jury
And Is There Honey Still for Tea?
The Heirs of Owain Glyndŵr
Calling Down the Storm
One Law for the Rest of Us
Verbal

The Walden Series

Walden of Bermondsey
Judge Walden: Back in Session
Judge Walden: Call the Next Case

TO BECOME AN OUTLAW

A BEN SCHROEDER NOVEL

PETER MURPHY

NO EXIT PRESS

First published in 2022 by No Exit Press,
an imprint of Oldcastle Books Ltd,
Harpenden, UK

noexit.co.uk
@noexitpress

ISBN
978-0-85730-466-7 (print)
978-0-85730-483-4 (epub)

2 4 6 8 10 9 7 5 3 1

Typeset in 11 on 14pt Minion Pro
by Avocet Typeset, Bideford, Devon, EX39 2BP
Printed in Great Britain by CPI Group (UK) Ltd, Croydon, CR0 4YY

For more information about Crime Fiction go to crimetime.co.uk

When a man is denied the right to live the life he believes in,
he has no choice but to become an outlaw.

Nelson Mandela

PART ONE

1

Danie du Plessis

I knew instantly that Nick Erasmus – or whatever his name may have been – was dead. I knew the moment his head hit the fender in front of the fireplace.

I knew because I'd heard that sound before – only once before, thank God, but that was enough. When I heard the sound before, I was on the East Campus at Witwatersrand, watching a student demonstration in progress right in front of the Great Hall, one of many such demonstrations that took place at the University in 1964. The students, several hundred of them, were confronting a phalanx of police officers wearing riot gear, carrying shields, and armed to the teeth, with everything from tear gas to live rounds. I saw a young white officer club a black student over the head, just the once – not because of any immediate threat to himself that I could see, but arbitrarily, almost casually, as if acting out of some sense of entitlement. I saw the student fall to the ground and lie perfectly still, while other students demonstrated, and the police postured threateningly, all around him.

I heard the sound of the clubbing, and I knew then that the student was dead, just as I knew today that Nick Erasmus was dead.

The student's death was widely reported in the press, but no action was taken against the officer. He was on duty, protecting the public against rioters, the authorities said. That seemed to conclude the matter. That was how things were then.

2

I was born in Bloemfontein, in the Free State, in 1942. My father was a lawyer, who would later become a judge. My mother was a schoolteacher, which I always thought was a strange profession for her, because it always seemed to me that she didn't like children very much. Neither did my father, come to that. I am an only child, and I have often wondered whether my arrival in this world was planned, or even desired. My parents delegated most of my upbringing to Hilda, our black house servant. I can't remember a time when Hilda wasn't in charge of my daily routine. It was Hilda who taught me how to get dressed, how to tie my shoelaces, and all the other essential practical lessons of early childhood. Hilda was a warm and wise woman. She could be strict when necessary, but never once was I in doubt of her love and care. Our relationship was always very close. As a child I thought of her as my real mother. She was certainly more of a mother to me than the formal, reserved woman I was taken to meet, dressed up in my best clothes, for dinner in the evenings – when I was finally deemed old enough for the privilege of eating politely in silence, and listening to two adults talking to each other intermittently over my head, as if I wasn't there.

I thought of Hilda as my real mother long before my parents, and the Dutch Reformed Church they attended assiduously every week, did their best to explain to me why a black woman could never be a mother to a white child. My parents believed implicitly in racial segregation on every level, and looked to their church for confirmation that God took the same view. Once, when I was fifteen or thereabouts, I pointed out to my parents that, if Jesus were to appear in Bloemfontein on the following Sunday, he wouldn't be allowed in our church because of the colour of his skin. It was not well received. I have only my closeness to Hilda to thank for my choice to reject the idea that people should be forced to live separate and apart from each other because of their colour. Without her influence in my life, who knows what I might have become? Inertia being the potent force it is, I might have drifted ever closer to the establishment into which I had been born, and become a part of it by default, without ever questioning what it stood for. But she was there in my life. In church and at school, I had little choice but to pay lip service to the relentless Afrikaner orthodoxy that was rammed down my throat day after day. But because of Hilda, it never took root.

One of Hilda's delegated tasks was to teach me to speak English. My parents, like most Afrikaners, claimed direct descent from the Voortrekkers. I was never shown any specific evidence of our ancestry, but then, none was expected. It was considered impolite in Afrikaner society to question a claim to Voortrekker ancestry. Just as all Welshmen are presumed to descend from Owain Glyndŵr, and all Scotsmen from Robert the Bruce, all Afrikaners are presumed to descend from the Voortrekkers – and in fairness, in the Free State or the Transvaal, the presumption wasn't totally unreasonable. In any case, whether we were, or were not the progeny of Voortrekkers, my parents were Afrikaners to the core. The only language permitted at meals and social gatherings was Afrikaans. When I was about twelve, a great-aunt, whose word I am inclined to credit, confided in me that as a younger woman, my mother could carry on a pretty decent conversation in isiXhosa. How my mother had acquired that facility, my great aunt either didn't know, or chose not to reveal to me. When I questioned her about it some years later, my mother, in the tone of voice she might have used to deny an allegation of shoplifting, indignantly denied knowing so much as a single word of isiXhosa.

My parents were, of course, perfectly aware that, to build any kind of life for oneself, to participate in any kind of professional or commercial activity in the modern South Africa, it was necessary to speak English to the same standard as Afrikaans. It became Hilda's responsibility to teach me this necessary foreign language. Fortunately, she started without delay, so I spoke English from an early age and grew up bilingual, as is the rule in South Africa generally. But Hilda also had something of a subversive streak in her, and when I reached the age of nine or ten, and she felt she could trust me not to talk about it to anyone else, she covertly taught me the basics of isiZulu. Hilda hailed from Pietermaritzburg. I never heard the full story of how and why she left Natal to be with us in the Free State. My parents whispered that she had been taken from home to a charity run by the Dutch Reformed Church to take her out of the range of some nameless abuse, and that they had agreed to provide her with a home at the request of the charity. Hilda never spoke of her history to me, and I never asked her. But isiZulu was her language, and she was proud of it. She taught me enough to share some basic conversation, all of it under the strict condition that my parents should never know about it. They never did. I could probably manage a few sentences in isiZulu even today, though it's been a long time since I tried; and sadly, my short, secretive talks with Hilda never brought me close to my proficiency in English or Afrikaans.

I knew by the time I was twelve that I could not continue to live in the sinister, claustrophobic atmosphere of my parents' circle. I worked hard at school, but it's probably true to say that I had no real say in the matter. My father took charge of that area of my life, and as the son of a workaholic lawyer, there would be no truancy, or lack of attention to teachers, or slacking off, for me. Homework would be done immediately on arriving home, and would be done well, however long it took. Criticism was the rule, and praise rare. Marks in exams were usually discussed, not in terms of the marks obtained, but of those inexplicably lost. Many children, I suspect, would not have coped well with the regime to which I was subjected. But it's surprising what you can adapt to when you have no choice; and besides, I had come to realise that high achievement in school, leading to a place at university, was my only route out. For good measure, I also risked life and limb playing rugby and cricket, and was good enough to represent my school at both.

On leaving school, I was offered a place to read law at WITS, the University of the Witwatersrand, in Johannesburg. The decision to read law pleased my father, needless to say, but it wasn't made for the reasons he probably assumed.

It had nothing to do with following in his footsteps. By then, in 1961, it was already becoming clear that the apartheid regime of Hendrik Verwoerd was determined to destroy anyone and anything that stood in its path, and that only recourse to the rule of law could provide any hope of survival, if indeed there were any such hope left at all.

3

As a student at WITS, I followed much the same routine as I had at school. I was determined that, when I graduated and was ready to look for work as a lawyer, I would have a clear alternative to returning to Bloemfontein. My father could have found me a job as an attorney or an advocate in any of the city's leading firms or chambers, just by picking up the phone. He was a man of considerable influence, even before he was appointed to the bench. He was also a man unlikely to take kindly to any suggestion that I would prefer him not to use that influence, that I had something else of my own in mind – especially if that something else were to involve my living somewhere other than Bloemfontein. To have any chance of a smooth break with home, I would have to land a position so impressive that even my father would be hard pressed to argue against it. That meant hard work and discipline throughout the three years it would take me to earn my law degree.

The only real regret I had about leaving Bloemfontein was the inevitable separation from Hilda. It was a wrench for both of us when I first left home to go to Johannesburg. For some weeks I was genuinely homesick, but it had nothing to do with our house or my parents. I simply couldn't get used to being away from the woman who had been such an integral part of my life for as long as I had memory. Leaving Hilda behind caused me pain that has never really gone away, and I know it caused her pain too. Towards the end of my third year at WITS, she left her position with my parents, returned to Pietermaritzburg, and found a job as a live-in cook and companion to a rich, elderly white lady, from which she eventually retired in reasonable circumstances. We kept in touch by means of letters, Christmas cards, photographs, and the like, until she died. She gave every impression of being content with her life, but I know the pain of our inevitable separation, now that I had left behind the childhood that had bound us together, lingered, as it did with me. I think she understood that there was no way back home for me. I hope so. But that thought has never made it any easier.

I did venture out of the library for the odd game of rugby or cricket, and I'm glad I did, because it was through cricket that I met Pieter, who became, and remains to this day my closest friend. Pieter is not his real name. I'm not going to disclose his name, because of the extraordinary act of kindness he performed for me late in 1964, when I had allowed myself to drift into a very dangerous situation. Had that act of kindness become known to the authorities then, there would have been serious consequences for Pieter as well as for me; and although that danger has passed now, and although, I daresay, many people will have no difficulty in guessing his identity, I'm going to do what I can to preserve his anonymity in my story.

Pieter was the son of a very wealthy, socially liberal industrialist. The family was made of money, and because the source of that money was the manufacture of specialised items essential to the country's defence industry, even Verwoerd and Vorster turned a deaf ear on the not infrequent occasions when Pieter's father was uncomfortably outspoken about his contempt for apartheid. The old man practised what he preached. The firm's workforce included staff from each of the racial categories then recognised in South Africa – White, Cape Coloured, Asian, and Black – but no one in the firm talked about racial categories. They were colleagues who worked together harmoniously, and nothing else mattered. Pieter took the company over after his father's death and ran it with great success, but when I knew him, his only passion in life was cricket. He was an astonishing cricketer, a brilliant opening batsman who made centuries effortlessly, and an acrobatic fielder who never put down a catch in the slips. If it had not been for the embargo on South African cricket in the wake of the D'Oliveira affair, he would undoubtedly have played for South Africa, and would probably have been a leading light in the world of test cricket. Pieter knew that, and he felt his loss acutely. But he supported the sporting embargos as a matter of principle, and led the move towards racially integrated cricket in South Africa.

The other diversion from work I permitted myself was the occasional girlfriend, four in all, before Amy. All four were fellow law students. I'd convinced myself that I couldn't afford the time, or the energy, to develop a wider social life outside the University, or even, it seemed, outside the Law Faculty. All four, needless to say, were white. Sexual relations across racial lines had been illegal in South Africa since 1950, as was marriage between people with differently coloured skin. Not only that, but I suppose I unconsciously gravitated to girls who turned out to have a similar family background to my own. When my first partner, Anna, talked to me about her home life in Cape Town over coffee one afternoon, after we had sat together through an interminable lecture on liability for misconduct by slaves in Roman law, it sounded depressingly familiar.

But we were attracted to each other, and as she was just as inexperienced in sexual matters as I was, it was inevitable that we would learn together. We would get together, in my room or hers, and learn from each other the basic skills of undressing, kissing, and satisfying each other, which would never have been the subject of discussion in my family, or hers. Sex in any guise was taboo as far as my parents were concerned, and not even Hilda would have talked to me about the kind of details I needed to know when I was with Anna, although she had explained to me in outline how babies were made. No, I learned the practical side of things from Anna, as she did from me. I learned other things, too.

During our pillow talk, I came to know things about her that I probably wouldn't have learned over a hundred cups of post-lecture coffee. The most startling of these was that she approved wholeheartedly of apartheid, and was a huge admirer of Verwoerd, which she made clear when, in all innocence, I asked her whether she had ever fancied a man who wasn't white. The question genuinely shocked her. Alone in my room after she had left, I asked myself how I could have missed it. Somehow, I had convinced myself that, despite her conservative upbringing, she must have found a path similar to mine, and emerged with at least some liberal instincts intact. But she hadn't had a Hilda in her life. I suddenly had a terrible notion that she might one day start screaming 'Hendrik' over and over again when she came. I find that image rather funny now, but at the time it really spooked me. In fairness to her, the only name Anna ever spoke when she came was mine, and she whispered it rather than screaming it. But somehow, things were never the same for me again, and we broke up soon afterwards. Anna married a fellow student, a man we both knew quite well, just after she graduated. After a couple of years of legal practice, her husband got himself elected to Parliament, and rose to a position of some importance in the National Party.

None of my other three girlfriends had any sympathy for apartheid. Indeed two of them joined in the protests, when they became more and more frequent during our third year. So, from that point of view, I suppose, we were more compatible. We were still very discreet about sex, but far more relaxed once we were alone behind closed doors. We had mastered the basics of contraception, and had no inhibitions about 'going all the way'; and with salacious fragments of news becoming available about the sexual revolution going on in America, we had as much inspiration as we needed to experiment with new and daring ways to satisfy each other. But much as I look back on those days with great affection, none of my girlfriends made me want to spend the rest of my life with her, and I'm quite sure they felt the same way about me.

Then, just before my graduation in July 1964, I met Amy Coetzee. Amy had just finished her first year of law study, and we met at a reception for a judge of the Supreme Court, who had presided over a seminar on the future of international law. After my experiences with my girlfriends, I flattered myself that I understood about attraction, and indeed, about lust. But I wasn't prepared for the effect Amy had on me, which was of a different order from that of any other woman I have ever met, before or since. As we shook hands and introduced ourselves, I went hot and cold, and I am not embarrassed to confess that I wanted to take her, there and then, on the floor, allowing the reception to continue around us.

A few days later, we took each other in my room, by common consent, violently, tearing off clothes, gasping for breath, and finally collapsing side by side. She was slim, very pretty, with jet-black hair and the most seductive dark eyes I've ever seen; and I had no sooner come than I was feeling the desire rising again. I set out to kiss her all over, starting with her beautiful feet. When I finished by kissing her on the lips, she took my hand.

'Danie,' she said, 'can I ask you something?'

'Of course: anything.'

'You have noticed that I'm Coloured, haven't you?'

4

My reward for all the hard work I had put into my studies was an offer to join the Law Faculty at WITS as a junior lecturer. The offer came out of the blue. I was amazed, and only too delighted to accept. For one thing, a lectureship at a prestigious university immediately after graduation was not an offer made to everyone; it was actually very unusual, and quite a compliment. My father could hardly criticise me for accepting an offer like that, one that was certainly not within his gift; and in fairness to him, when I told him about it in a letter, he replied immediately with warm words of congratulation. I was also very happy about the prospect of a career in academia. Legal scholarship came naturally to me, and I found it very satisfying. I also felt that there was much I could contribute as a teacher, not only in preparing students for the practice of law, but also in supporting the values for which WITS stood, which corresponded closely to my own.

When WITS was established in 1922, its principal and Vice-Chancellor, Jan Hofmeyr, ensured that its founding documents committed the University to equal treatment for all students, without regard to class, wealth, race, or creed. This made it inevitable that, as Verwoerd's hard-line, ideological approach to apartheid reached its zenith during the early 1960s, the University would come into direct conflict with the government. By 1964, that conflict had escalated to frequent large-scale and often violent student protests, policed by enthusiastic white officers spoiling to inflict some damage on anyone posing what they considered to be a threat to public order.

It was during one such protest that I saw the white officer send the black student to his death, with a single blow from the heavy metal baton he was carrying, the sound of which I have never since been able to put out of my mind. When it happened, right outside the Great Hall, I was standing a short distance away with Pieter. As a faculty member I was perfectly free to be present at demonstrations, though it was expected that I would stop short of any act the police might consider to be a threat to public order. That suited me very well. I am not a natural protester, and I had taken the same approach as a student, though I always wore an anti-apartheid badge depicting three people, white, black, and brown, holding hands. I still have that badge today. I remember being amazed that, after the student fell to the ground and lay there motionless, the protest, and the police response, seemed to continue around his lifeless body, as if nothing had happened. With that dreadful sound still ringing in my ears, I was rooted to the spot on which I stood. It was Pieter who had the presence of mind to react to the situation, and to call for an ambulance. When it arrived, he led me away from the scene.

Later in the day, I was with Amy in my rooms – as I had no home off-campus, the University had provided me with a pleasant suite overlooking the greenery of several rugby pitches. We had not yet undressed to make love. She was still shaken by her own experience of the protest, which had turned particularly violent all around her. I was holding her and stroking her hair as we lay together on the bed. Then, there was a knock on the door. Instantly alarmed, we both sat up, and she rolled off the bed on to her feet. The knock on the door represented danger. I had, of course, noticed that Amy was in the Cape Coloured category, and that our relationship was against the law in South Africa. But until she voiced it, I had allowed my passion for her to suppress my sense of danger. Since then, we had taken infinite pains not to be seen together in public, and to avoid any show of recognition. As far as I knew, we had succeeded. The only person I knew of who was aware of our relationship was Pieter. He had been with me when I first met Amy at the reception, and he knew me too well to miss the signs: there was no point in trying to deny it to him. I wasn't anxious about Pieter: I trusted him implicitly. But I could only hope that my feelings for Amy had not been equally obvious to others, and as day succeeded day, she and I were becoming increasingly aware of the dangers all around us in this hostile environment. The only course we had not discussed was giving the relationship up: danger or no danger, it was already too strong for that.

I gestured to her to hide in the bathroom while I went to see who was knocking. I walked through my living room and study to the door, and opened it a fraction, very tentatively. To my immense relief, it was Pieter. But the relief was short lived. He was clearly troubled. I had never seen Pieter without at least the suggestion of a smile on his face. But now he looked tense and fearful. As I opened the door, he almost pushed me aside, and strode agitatedly into the living room.

'Is Amy here?' he asked.

'It's OK, Amy. You can come out,' I shouted in the direction of the bathroom. 'It's Pieter.'

Amy made her way into the living room and sat quietly on the sofa, her arms crossed in front of her chest.

'You two need to leave,' Pieter said. 'Now. As soon as you can.'

We looked at him blankly, and were silent for some time.

'What do you mean, leave?' I asked eventually.

'I mean, leave.'

Amy and I looked at each other.

'I'm not following. You mean, leave my rooms, leave WITS, leave Johannesburg, what?'

He shook his head. 'Leave South Africa.'

I laughed aloud.

'You're joking.'

'Do I look like I'm joking?'

I collapsed on to the sofa next to Amy. Pieter seated himself in an armchair next to us.

'For God's sake, Pieter,' I said, 'what are you talking about?'

He sat up and leaned forward towards us.

'I had to give a statement to the police,' he replied, 'because that student we saw being attacked died, and I was the one who called the ambulance. These officers weren't the riot police; they were detectives investigating the death. After I'd given them my statement, they started getting friendly – one of them is a cricket fanatic, he'd seen me play, and he wanted to chat about it. After we'd talked about cricket for a while, and they were about to leave, they said this was the second time they'd been called to WITS in a week. The first time, they said, was because of a complaint about a member of the faculty getting too close to a coloured student. They didn't mention any names, Danie, but who else could it be?'

I held my head in my hands. 'Oh, God.'

'I don't understand,' Amy said quietly. 'We've been so careful.'

'You're here in Danie's rooms,' Pieter pointed out. 'Are you sure nobody saw you arrive? Look, you know what this place is like. You don't even need to be seen. The whole place is a hotbed of gossip. It doesn't take much to start a rumour, and a rumour of illegal sex is all it takes to get the police's attention – especially if it involves a member of the faculty.' He paused. 'I don't know how long you have before this gets really serious, but it may only be a matter of days. You know what's going to happen to both of you if you're arrested for this. You know what they're like. Rape, torture, they're capable of anything. You can't take that risk. You need to leave now.'

Again, we were silent for some time.

'And go where?' I asked.

'Wherever you can.'

'I have family in Salisbury,' Amy suggested tentatively. 'If there's a way to get across the border… separately, perhaps?'

Pieter shook his head. 'Rhodesia's no safer than here. South African police operate just as freely in Salisbury as they do in Jo'burg. And you could get your family in a lot of trouble if the police thought they were harbouring you.'

'My father has a friend in England,' I said, 'Sir John Fisk. He's the master of a Cambridge college. They met at some conference or other, years ago, and I guess they must have hit it off, because they've kept in touch ever since: correspondence mainly, though he and his wife came to Bloemfontein to visit us once, when I was fifteen or sixteen. He's a classicist or a philosopher, I think, but they have a daughter about my age called Harriet, who's reading for the Bar. They might be worth a try.'

'England would work,' Pieter replied. 'But there's no time for correspondence. Do you have a phone number?'

'No. My father has it, but obviously, I'd prefer not to have to explain why I need it.'

'International directory inquiries are bound to have his number at his College,' Amy pointed out.

'Yes,' Pieter agreed, 'but you shouldn't use the phone here. You don't know who may be listening in.'

'Oh, come on, Pieter...' I protested.

'What, you think I'm being paranoid? Danie, listen to me: at my dad's firm we've had employees arrested under the racial laws: men just like you and me, women just like Amy. They just disappeared into thin air one day, and we never saw them again. These people don't fool around, Danie. You think they wouldn't tap your phone if they thought they might overhear you and Amy whispering sweet nothings to one another? Trust me, if they have any suspicion at all, that's the first thing they'll do; and you know as well as I do, there's no law to stop them.'

I let out a long, slow breath. 'This can't be happening.'

'It is happening,' Pieter replied, 'trust me. Come to my place. You can call directory inquiries from there. Just you, Danie. Amy, I'm sorry, my love, I really am, but you will need to make your own way home for now.'

'I understand,' she replied. She hesitated. 'Pieter, how would we ever get to England? If they're already keeping watch on us, we can't just book ourselves a passage with Cunard or BOAC. It looks like we're trapped.'

Pieter smiled. 'There are some advantages in having a rich father,' he said. 'I called my dad as soon as the police let me go. You can use our private jet. It will make it to England, with one stop for refuelling, somewhere friendly. We avoid the major airports. We use a small field, where they know us. The runway is only just long enough for the aircraft, but it has the advantage of being quiet. There's some customs and police presence there, but nothing like Jo'burg. They all know my dad's plane, and they don't give us a hard time.'

'That may change if they see an interracial couple boarding,' Amy suggested.

Pieter smiled again. 'We thought of that too,' he replied. 'You look like you're about the same size as Jenna, one of our regular stewardesses. You can borrow one of her uniforms. No one's going to give a second thought to a Cape Coloured stewardess. We're ready to go, as soon as we have a destination.'

Amy and I looked at each other, and reached a silent agreement, in the time it might have taken us to agree what we would have for dinner. We agreed to commit our lives to each other in a foreign country, or be destroyed in the attempt, knowing that there was no way back.

She stood, walked over to Pieter, and kissed him on the cheek.

'Thank you,' she said. 'We won't ever forget.'

'You and your father are taking one hell of a risk for us, Pieter,' I added.

'You're my friends,' Pieter replied. 'What else are we going to do in this godforsaken place until sanity prevails?'

5

The next three days were frenetic. Three days wasn't enough time, but both Pieter and his father were adamant that any longer delay would be too risky. When I finally reached Sir John Fisk by phone from Pieter's house, he didn't hesitate for a moment. We should come as soon as we could. We should stay with them for as long as we had need; and they would do everything they could to help us build a new life in England. The die was cast.

We packed as much as we could take with us, which was whatever we could squeeze into two medium-size suitcases each. Everything else, however familiar and treasured, we abandoned: the books, records, pictures, photographs, mementos, clothes, the very fabric of our lives; all those personal accoutrements we take for granted, never knowing how much they mean to us until we are about to lose them. The loss included family and friends: there could be no question of saying goodbye until we had left South Africa. Apologies and explanations would have to wait. We were walking away in the dead of night, knowing that our lives, as we had known them, were lost to us; and that we might never again be free to celebrate them in the country of our birth. On the desk in my study I left my letter of resignation from the WITS Law Faculty, citing 'personal circumstances'. Only the joy of having each other made it bearable.

As Pieter had promised, the small airport from which we flew was quiet, and we aroused no real interest. I was impersonating a production manager in his father's company, en route to London for urgent talks with our British suppliers, while Amy gave an Oscar-class performance as an efficient and charming stewardess. The immigration officer who checked our details was well known to our pilots, who exchanged pleasantries with him and solicitously inquired after his family, while he signed off on us after a perfunctory glance at our passports and paperwork. With one stop to refuel, somewhere in Portugal, we had an uneventful flight into a quiet corner of Heathrow airport.

We were in England: where no one showed the slightest interest in the colour of our skin; or paid any attention as we walked together, hand in hand, to recover our suitcases. John and Annabel Fisk had driven to Heathrow to pick us up, and take us back with them to Cambridge.

These were acts of extraordinary generosity and kindness towards us, on the part of Pieter and his father, and on the part of John and Annabel, and even today I can't think of those days without tears in my eyes. Amy still has her stewardess uniform.

We lived with John and Annabel for about a month before we found a house to rent in Tenison Road, about half way between Mill Road and the railway station. It didn't take me long to marvel at how far John was willing to go to help a friend, and at how much benign influence he wielded, both within the University and elsewhere. Before becoming Master of his College, he had enjoyed a successful career in the diplomatic service, culminating in two ambassadorships in very tricky corners of the world; so the irritations of academic wrangling, the downfall of so many in his position, barely registered on his radar. John dealt with such matters with ease.

He allowed me only a couple of days to settle in, before taking me on a guided tour of the menswear shops of Cambridge to make sure, he explained in his best diplomat's manner, that I was not entirely dependent on the limited wardrobe I'd been able to bring with me. When I self-consciously broached the subject of money, he waved it away, assuring me that I could pay him back once I started work, which in due course, I did; though at the time, I was painfully aware that the pound sterling equivalent of the rand we had drained from our bank accounts in Johannesburg was not going to last long in Cambridge. But, as I was to discover, John's purpose was not so much to supplement my wardrobe as to shape it to ensure that I could look the part on every occasion: because he lost no time in taking me into College, introducing me to everyone he could find – Fellows, porters, the Bursar's staff, everyone – and taking me to dine as his guest at High Table. For all of this, I needed to look the part, and items such as the evening dress, suits and ties I had been obliged to leave hanging in the wardrobe in my bedroom at WITS, had to be replaced.

Fortunately, the Fellows took to me almost instantly. The College has always enjoyed a reputation as a haven for dissent. During the four hundred odd years of its existence, there have been many times when those in peril, during periods of political or religious turmoil, had found refuge within its walls, often at considerable risk to the College. There is a pervasive air of openness and tolerance about the place, which, after the genuine but constrained liberalism of WITS, came as a breath of fresh air. Within two weeks of my arrival, John had gained the unanimous agreement of his colleagues to award me a research scholarship, which in addition to the opportunities for writing and publishing, would bring in some welcome money from teaching at the undergraduate level within the College. When I asked John what subject I should choose for my research, he immediately insisted that it should be Roman law. I was genuinely surprised. I knew, of course, that at Cambridge, every law student was made to study Roman law for two of their three years. Still, I had been expecting John to suggest something different – commercial law, or international law, perhaps, something more in tune with contemporary England, so that I could show off my versatility and willingness to adapt. But John had, as he so often had, a deeper insight into the circumstances. He knew, as I came to discover, that Roman law was essentially the domain of a solitary aging don, Professor Jenkins, who was contemplating retirement. The Roman law team was in need of reinforcement. By 1967, I had been appointed a full Fellow of the College, and University lecturer in Law; in 1973 I would succeed Professor Jenkins as Buckland Professor of Roman Law in the University of Cambridge.

'It's a natural fit, dear boy,' John explained when we first discussed it. 'Quite apart from the pressing need for someone to teach Roman law, I'm told that the Law Faculty always has a number of South

African students in residence, and apparently, someone has to teach them a bit of Roman-Dutch law. Who else is going to do it? The trick is to make yourself indispensable.'

John is the only man I've ever known who could call someone 'dear boy' without sounding patronising.

John also saw to it that Amy was enrolled as an undergraduate at Girton to complete her law degree, and given a part-time administrative job in his own college's bursary office, which brought in a little more money. Harriet befriended her in another way. She was only a year into her practice as a barrister in London, and very busy, but she made time to show Amy round London, introducing her to Covent Garden and Oxford Street, and taking her to dinner in Gray's Inn, which persuaded Amy to read for the Bar herself after completing her degree. Amy, by then, was more inclined towards teaching than practice, but qualification as a barrister was more than useful to her when, in due course, she applied for her own fellowship.

The only efforts John made on my behalf that proved to be beyond even his diplomatic skills were his attempts to reconcile me with my parents. They could never accept my leaving South Africa, especially in the circumstances in which I did. John wrote to them several times over the years, but never received more than a formal acknowledgement of his letters. I wish I could truthfully say that I am devastated by their rejection of me, or indifference to me; but the truth is that, while I find it sad, it has had little impact on my life. Amy and I have become successful, and are very happy in our house in Tenison Road. We were married as soon as it could be arranged, a quiet register office affair, with John and Annabel as our witnesses, followed by a lovely dinner with the two of them, and Harriet, at the University Arms. We have two children: Sally, born in 1969; and Douglas, born in 1972. It would have been open to my parents to get themselves on a plane and come to England to see their grandchildren, as Amy's parents did. They could have demanded regular photographs, as Hilda and Pieter did. But they never approached us at all, and now they are dead, and there is nothing that John, or I, or anyone else, can do about it.

By October 1968, at the beginning of the academic year, Amy and I felt settled in our new lives. The memory of the abrupt ending of our old lives was beginning to recede.

That was before Art Pienaar appeared in my life.

6

Monday 7 October 1968

Sidney, the College's venerable Head Porter, put a friendly arm around the visitor's shoulder as he ushered him through the door of the porters' lodge and out into the main quadrangle. After the subdued lighting of the lodge, and the shadow of the covered passageway running between the quadrangle and the College's massive wooden gates, the sharp autumnal sunlight came as a shock. It made them both squint, and quickly raise a hand to shield their eyes.

'Straight across the quad, sir,' Sidney said, pointing, 'turn left, and when you pass the entrance to the chapel, N is the next staircase but one. You can't miss it. Mr du Plessis' rooms are on the first floor.'

'Thank you,' the visitor replied, smiling.

'You're very welcome, sir.'

Sidney did not return to the porters' lodge immediately. Instead, he leaned back against the wall, pulled the rim of his bowler hat down ever so slightly, folded his arms, and watched the visitor until he disappeared from view into N staircase. Why, he couldn't have said precisely. Perhaps it was the lack of hesitation with which the man followed the directions he had been given, almost as if he'd known the way all along, without Sidney's telling him. In fairness, as Sidney had said himself, you couldn't miss it – the visitor was in no danger of getting lost between the porters' lodge and N staircase.

All the same, there was something… it was just a bit too quick, a bit too assured for a first time, there was a hint of familiarity from some previous occasion. Or perhaps it was just the dark blue three-piece suit the man was wearing on such a warm afternoon.

After more than thirty years in the job, Sidney had developed a good porter's instinct for something not being quite right. Almost always, nothing of real concern came of it. Once in a while, he would become aware of an undergraduate drinking too much – drinking too much by undergraduate standards, that is – or experimenting with more exotic substances, or smuggling women into his room. Sidney dealt with such cases in accordance with the College's low-key tradition, with a quiet word in the ear. Only if there was a risk of things getting out of hand, despite the warning, would he report the matter to the student's tutor. Every now and then, too, his instinct had prevented some harm to the College, or to one of the Fellows, by enabling him to head off a theft of property, an act of vandalism, or even, once or twice, a potentially violent reaction to something said in a lecture or a debate, or written in a journal. In the visitor's case, there was probably nothing to it, but he would keep an eye on N staircase, and on Mr du Plessis, his newest Fellow, for a day or two, just in case.

For his part, the visitor was aware of being watched, but he had no intention of giving himself away by turning back to look. Instead, he briskly pulled the main doors of N staircase open and fairly bounded up the stairs to the first floor – as he had in fact done, as Sidney's instinct suggested, on a previous occasion some ten days earlier, before the start of term, when the College was quiet. On that occasion, his incursion had been covert and brief, and had been made for reconnaissance purposes to assess an unknown quantity before meeting him – a tip he had picked up from one of his clients. The incursion was simple, and fairly safe as such things go – the ancient lock was ridiculously easy to pick, and he knew that Danie du Plessis would be out for at least an hour, delivering a lecture to a group of foreign students. The only objective was to ascertain whether there were any obvious red flags – or, for that matter, any obvious green flags. It had not taken long. These were the rooms of someone who hadn't yet occupied them for long enough to leave his imprint on them. There were no pictures or posters on the walls. But the meagre handful of books were all legal, nothing political, the files, and notebooks likewise. The only item of any real interest – an anti-apartheid badge, depicting three people, white, black, and brown, holding hands – was lying on the desk for all the world to see, no attempt having been made to hide it. So far, so good, the visitor concluded.

Then, since he had time to spare, he had unscrewed the fittings of the telephone and lamp on the desk to check for listening devices – another tip from the same client. He found nothing. 'He's too new, I suppose; they haven't had time,' he concluded.

7

The visitor knocked, and opened the door just enough to poke his head inside the room. The man he had come to see was sitting at his desk, reading from a book open in front of him, and making notes. He was wearing a jacket, but the top button of his shirt was open, and his tie was lying, neatly folded, on the desk. His black academic gown was draped over the back of his chair.

'Mr du Plessis?'

'Yes.'

The visitor took this as an invitation to enter the room, and once inside, he took one or two tentative steps towards the desk.

'I hope I'm not disturbing you, Mr du Plessis. I can see you're busy, but I'd like to take a moment to introduce myself, if I may. Art Pienaar, a fellow exile from back home.' He smiled. 'Not that I need to tell you that, I'm sure – not with my accent. Fifteen years in

England, and it's as strong as the day I left Port Elizabeth.'

Danie returned the smile. 'Not to mention your name. There aren't too many places you can claim to be from with a name like Pienaar – or du Plessis, for that matter.' He stood and offered his hand, which Pienaar took. 'Have a seat. I don't remember seeing you around before. Are you with the College?'

Pienaar pulled up a small chair for himself in front of Danie's desk. He shook his head.

'Oh, good God, no. I've never been the academic type, I'm afraid. I scraped a degree, and just about passed my solicitor's exams, and that's about it for me on the academic front.'

He rummaged through the pockets of his suit jacket before producing two business cards to hand to Danie.

'Barnard, Pienaar & McFall, St John's Wood. We're in what you might call general practice. I have a client in Cambridge I had to see this morning, so I thought this might be a good chance to drop by and see how you're settling in – and, of course, to congratulate you on your fellowship: mustn't forget that, must we?'

'Thank you.'

'I hear they've got you teaching Roman law,' Pienaar continued. He laughed. 'Well, they would, I suppose, wouldn't they? Give Roman law to the South African. Nothing like being typecast, is there?'

Danie examined his visitor's face, but the laughter had died away almost as soon as it had appeared, giving nothing away.

'Mr Pienaar...'

'Art, please.'

'Art... I appreciate your interest; but it's a rather busy day, so perhaps you could...'

'Of course, Danie – I'll call you Danie, if I may. I didn't mean to intrude. It's just that I feel... well, a sense of responsibility for new arrivals, so to speak. Presumptuous of me, I know, but I can't help it. We exiles have to stick together, don't we? If it helps, you can think of me as a community ambassador.'

'A community ambassador?'

'Yes. We may live in different parts of the country, but at the end of the day, we South Africans are a community, aren't we? When one of us has a success – such as becoming a Fellow of one of Cambridge's oldest colleges – we should all celebrate it. It reflects well on all of us, and you've done us proud – well, you've certainly traded up from WITS, haven't you? It would be remiss of us not to congratulate you.'

'You seem to know a lot about me,' Danie observed.

Pienaar smiled. 'Nothing I couldn't find out in an hour at my local library. I keep my eyes and ears open, that's all. It's just a question of keeping up to date, getting to know who's here with us.'

'Really? So, what else do you know about me?'

'I know this: if you're a South African living in England and you're not working for the government, you probably have a very good reason for being in England, and for not being in South Africa. You're probably here because you have no choice, because you couldn't go back to South Africa even if you wanted to – because you've done something to offend the powers that be, committed some crime in their eyes. My crime was getting too close to the ANC, the African National Congress, and helping them to perpetrate a bit of mischief here and there, some of which, admittedly, got a bit out of hand. What was yours?'

'Falling in love with a Cape Coloured girl,' Danie replied, after some time.

Pienaar nodded. 'Now your wife, I understand; congratulations on that too, by the way. The only other thing I know about you is that you're not on the Bureau's radar yet – at least, I don't think you are.'

'What?'

'If I may...?' Pienaar reached into the inside pocket of his jacket and took out a screwdriver. 'I couldn't find any evidence when I was last here, but there's no harm in checking again, is there? They're bound to catch on to you before too long. Don't let it worry you. I can teach you how to do this for yourself. It's not complicated: it's just a matter of remembering to do it regularly.'

Danie pushed himself up, out of his chair.

'When you were last here? What do you mean, when you were last here? Why…? What the hell is going on?'

Pienaar shook his head, and placed his right forefinger over his closed lips. Reluctantly, Danie choked back a further protest and watched in silence as his visitor dismantled his phone and lamp in turn, finding nothing, and reassembled them.

'Do you have a tall ladder?' Pienaar asked.

'A ladder? No, I don't have a ladder. Why…?'

'I've got my eye on the chandelier. The audio quality wouldn't be as good from up there, but they might think it would be more secure. They might think no one's going to want to climb up there every other day, are they? It might be a good idea to have a tall ladder within easy reach, just in case. I'm sure the porters could oblige. Don't tell them why, obviously.'

Danie shook his head. 'All right, Mr Art Pienaar, or whoever you are, that's enough of your games,' he said firmly. 'Either tell me what you want, or get out of my room and let me get on with my work.'

Pienaar nodded. 'I need your help, Danie,' he replied. 'That's why I'm here: to ask for your help.'

Danie stared at him for some time. 'Help with what, for God's sake? How can I help you? You said it yourself: I'm a newcomer. You're the community ambassador, whatever that may mean.'

'There are some things only newcomers can do,' Pienaar replied. 'I'll be totally honest with you, Danie. BOSS, the Bureau for State Security, takes an interest in any South African living outside South Africa – don't be under any illusions about that – especially when you have a track record like yours, or mine. The only good news is that their resources aren't infinite: so they can't keep track of everybody; they have to pick and choose. As things stand now, they will check on you and your wife from time to time, as resources permit; but it will be very low-key – you probably won't be of any real interest to them. On the other hand, if you agree to help me, and they get any wind of it at all, that will change, big time. If that happens, you'll have to be careful – very careful. I can't speak more plainly than that. You're free to say no of course, for any reason, or for no reason. But I'd appreciate the chance to make my pitch.'

Danie thought for some time, then slowly resumed his seat.

'I'm listening.'

'Danie, you're a White man, married to a Coloured woman. You share a bed with her; you make love to her; you walk around Cambridge with her, holding her hand. You take her into a restaurant or a pub, and no one says you can't come in because it's for Whites only. And there are no police officers breaking your door down in the dead of night to arrest you for being in bed with your wife, to cart you off to jail and beat you half to death, and take her away to God only knows what hell-hole, where it will be open season on her for any of those thugs who want her. Danie, answer me this: don't you want there to be a South Africa, one day, in which everyone has the same freedoms you and I enjoy in England?'

'Yes, of course I do,' Danie replied, quietly.

'In that case,' Pienaar said, 'I need your help. Believe me, I wouldn't be asking if I didn't need you.'

'What exactly do you want from me?' Danie asked.

8

Pienaar glanced up at the chandelier.

'Let's go for a walk,' he said. 'Show me around the College.'

They emerged into the remains of the beautiful autumnal day, cooler now, the sun beginning to set, casting long shadows across the lawns, a breeze whispering in the ancient trees surrounding the quadrangle. The College was quiet at this hour of the afternoon, with only a handful of students in evidence.

'I assume you keep up with the news,' Pienaar said, 'in which case you will know that the ANC has been hit very hard.'

'Yes.'

'It's been outlawed; its demonstrations broken up using lethal force; its leaders dead; or forced into exile, like Tambo in Lusaka; or serving long prison terms, like Mandela and Sisulu on Robben Island. Morale is at rock bottom. The ANC is broken. No one believes any more. To all intents and purposes, the ANC is finished.'

They turned left from the main quadrangle into a narrow passage leading to a smaller quadrangle, this, too, surrounded by ancient trees, a reproduction of the main quadrangle with smaller proportions. There was a bench on the quadrangle's central lawn. Danie gestured towards the bench, and they sat down.

'Two clients of mine,' Pienaar continued, 'are convinced that they can make people believe again, and they have started a campaign designed to make it happen.'

'What kind of campaign?' Danie asked.

'I'm not going to tell you anything about them, except that they are white South Africans, legally in this country as graduate students, at a college whose student body has something of a reputation for supporting radical causes.'

Danie laughed. 'Answers on a postcard,' he replied. 'Don't worry. I have no interest in knowing who they are.'

'It will be the same with you.' Pienaar replied. 'They won't know who you are, or what you're doing.'

'Assuming I agree to help you.'

'Assuming you agree to help me. That's how I work. It's important for you to understand that. Now, to answer your question as to what they do: they recruit white students from the aforementioned radical student body – mainly men, but one or two women as well – who are prepared to travel to South Africa, using their own British passports, in the guise of tourists; and who are also prepared to carry with them certain materials.'

'Such as…?'

'Such as leaflets for mass distribution – propaganda basically –

to show the apartheid regime that the ANC is still a potent force, capable of operating both inside and outside South Africa. It's designed to offer the black population some hope, and to create an element of doubt in the minds of the Afrikaner community about how long they will be able to sleep peacefully in their beds at night. Some of these materials are sent on through the post, carrying a postmark from Jo'burg, or Durban, or wherever, to show them that the ANC still has the capacity to operate within South Africa. Others are released into the street using a clever device invented by one of my clients, which operates rather like a tiny bomb, with a miniscule amount of explosive – not enough to hurt anyone, but enough to make a bit of a bang and scatter the leaflets far and wide. There's a timer attached, so that whoever plants the device can give themselves time to escape.' He laughed. 'Believe it or not, there's even a plastic snake you can place on top of the device to deter anyone who finds it before it detonates. On one level, it all seems a bit childish, but it's having an effect. Those little explosions have attracted some attention. They've been covered in the press and on TV news throughout South Africa.'

'Your client is obviously an ingenious man,' Danie said. 'But how are they getting all this stuff into the country?'

'The recruits carry them in carefully modified suitcases, with false bottoms and hidden compartments.'

Danie whistled. 'That sounds pretty risky. They would be in serious trouble if they were caught carrying stuff like that.'

'It's very risky. The recruits are left in no doubt about what will happen to them if they get caught. My clients don't try to pull the wool over their eyes. But fortunately, it turns out that British tourists are a protected species. The boycotts are already starting to hurt the economy, and in addition to earning money, tourism proves that people like you: so the government is desperate to promote tourism – especially tourism from friendly countries.'

'Like Britain.'

'Like Britain. So Customs officers tend to wave British visitors through without asking too many questions. And once they're in the country – well, they're white, and they have English passports and English accents, so it's a case of make yourself at home. They can move around freely, as long as they're careful. So far, it's worked.'

'But you're not convinced their luck can hold?'

'That's my clients' problem,' Pienaar replied, matter-of-factly. 'I'm not involved with the operational side. My concern is with the money. My clients trust me to handle that side of things.'

They stood, and walked slowly around the quadrangle.

'What does that involve?' Danie asked.

Pienaar stopped for a moment.

'What my clients do isn't cheap to run. The recruits buy their own tickets, and get reimbursed; same for hotels and other expenses, once they're in South Africa. Plus, they need a fair bit of spending money, for internal travel, food and drink, and so on. They're supposed to be tourists, so to keep their cover they have to act like tourists, which involves spending money. It all adds up.'

He resumed his walk.

'But the real point is the recruits have also been carrying cash donations for certain individuals – funding for ANC cells and activists. It's getting to the point where I can't risk that anymore. The amounts are getting too large, and it's only a matter of time before we lose a large donation. The donors wouldn't like that. They're nervous enough about it as it is. Some of them don't like dealing in cash at all. They prefer to hand me a cheque, which rules out the recruits anyway. But not one of them likes the idea of their donations being entrusted to students they know nothing about. I need to find another way of doing it, and I think I have.'

'Where are the donations coming from?' Danie asked.

'There are a number of wealthy South African exiles who contribute, in this country, in Europe, and in America. They're people I've cultivated over the course of the past few years, and who trust me. But they depend on me to be discreet. Not even my clients know who they are – they don't need to; the money is my department.'

He stopped again.

'If you agree to help me, you and I will be the only two people who know who they are, and how much they donate. Interested?'

'It depends,' Danie replied. 'Tell me about this new plan you've come up with.'

9

'Imagine,' Pienaar said, 'that you're a wealthy aristo – a duke or an earl maybe – living somewhere near Cambridge in the thirteenth century.'

'What?'

'You get on well with the King; you've got a nice castle, a beautiful wife, all the trappings of wealth. Life is good. But the Bishop of Ely is making a nuisance of himself. He's persuaded you that, if you want to save your immortal soul, none of that matters. The only way to save your immortal soul is to join a crusade, and do your bit to liberate the Holy Land from the Infidel. It's not the way you'd planned to spend the next four or five years; but with your immortal soul at stake, what else can you do?'

Pienaar stopped in his tracks.

'But here's the point: it's only when you leave the bishop and get home to the castle, that you start to realise what you've signed up for. You can't go on a crusade without purchasing large quantities of supplies along the way. You also need men-at-arms, and assorted hangers-on, such as squires, cooks, men to look after the wagons and the horses, a priest, and so on. And it's a long way from Cambridge to Jerusalem. It's going to cost a lot of money. But you don't want to carry that amount of gold around with you, do you? God forbid some well-organised band of brigands, in unfamiliar territory somewhere in Europe, should ambush you, take you by surprise, and make off with it. If that happens, you're royally screwed. So, what do you do?'

Danie shook his head. 'I don't know.' He laughed. 'Take your cheque book, and make for the nearest branch of Lloyds, once you reach civilisation somewhere en route?'

'Close,' Pienaar replied. 'But for Lloyds, read the Knights Templar. By the time of your crusade, they're fabulously wealthy; but they started out as warrior monks dedicated to freeing Jerusalem. The whole crusade thing is their project, so they have a vested interest in making it easy for you. So, before you leave Cambridge, you deposit your gold with the Templars at the Round Church; they give you a certificate as evidence of the deposit; and when you get to Paris, or Rome, or any major city along the way, you call in at the Templars' branch office, produce the certificate, and they give you the equivalent in gold, or the local currency. Less a small commission to cover administrative costs and a small profit, of course: some things never change. And there you are: back in funds and ready to press on with the next stage of your journey.'

'So, the Knights Templar invented banking: is that what you're telling me?'

'I did read somewhere that the Chinese had something similar going on even earlier, but as far as the West is concerned yes, they probably did. The beauty of it is that it's value that moves, rather than money, so it's very secure. We like to think that our banking is more sophisticated today, but the Templars' system is still in use. In the Middle East and the Indian subcontinent, it's still the most popular way of doing business. They call it *Hawala*. But *Hawala* has its practitioners everywhere, including here in England. So, if I need to get funding to the ANC in South Africa, and I don't want to entrust it to a student…'

'You entrust the funding to a practitioner of *Hawala*, and ask him to contact his colleague in Pietermaritzburg and make the equivalent amount, less commission, available to the recipients there,' Danie said.

'Exactly. The business works because of the sheer volume of transactions going on at any given time. You're not the only client, England and South Africa are not the only countries, and these two practitioners are just a small part of a much bigger network, with members all over the world. The network has hundreds of deals, maybe thousands, going on every day, and they have constantly changing credits and debits with each other; so there are always local funds available, and the network settles all accounts every twenty-four hours. And it's all perfectly legal.'

Danie smiled. 'Are you sure about that? It sounds perfect for evading tax...'

'Or for breaking sanctions,' Pienaar said, 'yes. I know. But I don't inquire into my donors' tax affairs, Danie. I don't ask whether they're paying me out of gross income or after tax. That's their business. And the government of this country has consistently refused to support UN sanctions against the regime; so screw them – as far as I'm concerned, it's all above board, it's fair game.'

They had walked in a circle, and now found themselves standing again at the entrance to the main quadrangle.

'Do I take it that you have someone in mind?' Danie asked.

'There's a man called Balakrishnan, Indian, based in the East End, in Whitechapel. He has a cousin of the same name in Durban. You deliver the cash to him in person, but any cheques will have to be credited to one of a number of bank accounts in England and Scotland. Balakrishnan controls all these accounts under a number of aliases.'

'And this is still perfectly legal?' Danie asked.

'As far as I know; but in any case, there's no real choice if you want to be secure. Originally, *Hawala* was a strictly cash business, but nobody wants to keep huge wads of cash on the premises these days; so Balakrishnan has bank accounts here, as does his cousin in Durban. I can't see a problem if it's not being used to evade tax.'

Danie shook his head.

'Well, that's my theory, and I'm sticking to it,' Pienaar said. He turned to face Danie. 'I want you to handle this for me, Danie. I would stick out like a sore thumb, and BOSS will be watching. I have too much of a track record with the ANC. Your only crime, on the other hand, was to fall in love with the wrong girl. They're not going to approve of you, but neither are they going to suspect you of being in bed with the ANC. You can get away with it.'

They walked on to the entrance to N staircase.

'How would it work, exactly?' Danie asked.

'I will give you the details of the bank accounts. There are three in England and three in Scotland, so I'm afraid it will involve a trip to Edinburgh to deal with the Scottish accounts – this has to be done personally, no using the post. For the English accounts, you go down to London; don't use banks in Cambridge – it's a small town, too much risk of being recognised. Do the cheques first, then take the paying-in stubs and the cash directly to Balakrishnan in Whitechapel.'

'How often would this happen?'

'Three or four times a year,' Pienaar said. 'I will find a way to get the donations to you – not personally, but I will find somebody reliable to make sure they reach you.'

'That's all I would have to do?' Danie asked.

'That's all.'

Danie nodded. 'How would I get the receipt from Balakrishnan to you?'

'Balakrishnan doesn't do receipts,' Pienaar replied, smiling. '*Hawala* has always been an honour-based system.'

'But…'

'Balakrishnan is an honest man, Danie. They all are. They have to be – it's their code, it's a way of life, has been for centuries. If you're someone like Balakrishnan and you cross that line, you're out. Besides, you couldn't get away with it even if you wanted to. If there's any unaccounted-for shortfall or surplus anywhere in the accounts, the network's daily reckoning would be off. It wouldn't take the other members of the network very long to find out why, and they would come down on you like a ton of bricks. You would forfeit their trust. That would be the end for you.'

'I don't know,' Danie said, after some time. 'I need to think about it.'

'You need to do more than that,' Pienaar replied. 'You need to talk to Amy, discuss it with her – it is Amy, isn't it? This concerns her too. I need it to be a decision the two of you agree on.'

'That's – I'm not sure of the right word – impressive,' Danie said, 'that you would let me bring her into it…'

'It's the only possible way, Danie. You can't do something like this without telling your wife. Just make sure she understands that she can't talk about it with anyone else. When you have an answer, call me at the office. Use the name Stevens. If you decide not to help – and there will be no hard feelings if you do – just say that you've decided not to pursue the claim. If you agree to help, say that you want to go ahead with the case, and ask if we can take counsel's opinion.'

'When would I see you again?'

'You won't – not unless I have to tell you something really important. It would be insecure to meet regularly. Don't worry. If you really need to contact me, call the office as Stevens, and say you need advice. I'll find a secure way for us to talk. But don't do that unless it's really necessary.'

Danie walked to the main gate with Pienaar, and shook his hand as he left. He turned back to find Sidney standing at the door of the porters' lodge.

'Your guest found you without any trouble then, did he, Mr du Plessis?'

'Yes, thank you, Sidney.'

'He said he hadn't been to the College before, sir.'

Danie hesitated. 'I don't know. Not to see me, anyway.'

'You can always check with me if you need to, sir.'

'Thank you, Sidney. Oh… by the way, would we have such a thing as a tall ladder in College somewhere? I assume the staff must have one.'

'How tall a ladder did you have in mind, sir?'

'Well… let's say, tall enough to reach the chandelier in my room.'

'I'm sure Bert, our handyman, has one, Mr du Plessis. It's probably in his hut, behind W staircase. Is there a problem with your chandelier? If so, Bert will have a look at it for you, sir. You don't need to be climbing up there yourself.'

'No, of course,' Danie replied. 'It's fine at the moment, just thought I'd ask for future reference.'

'Of course, sir,' Sidney replied, filing the conversation away in his mind.

10

Danie decided to wait until after dinner to tell her. They had both had a long day, and the conversation they were about to have concerning Art Pienaar was not one to be had while they were tired and hungry. Amy had announced over breakfast that she was planning baked salmon and rice for dinner; so on the way home, he called into an off-licence, and found a nice bottle of Western Cape Chenin Blanc to go with it. They would both be in a far better mood after dinner. As she was about to clear away, poised to pick up a plate, he took her hand, and steered her away from the table. She tended to be compulsive about disposing of the evidence, once a meal was finished. But tonight, he insisted that she leave the dishes for him to deal with later, and he led her from the dining table to the sofa to finish off the wine. When they were settled, he started to talk to her about his day. She sensed at once that whatever was coming was important and listened attentively, eyes closed, as he relived for her his meeting with Art Pienaar. When he had finished, she swung her legs up on to the sofa and rested her bare feet in his lap. Some time went by.

'This is a lot to take in,' she said eventually. 'It feels like… like an intrusion into our lives. Part of me would prefer to ignore it, pretend it hasn't happened.'

'I understand that,' he said.

'I suppose, if I'm honest about it, I've been hoping that we would wake up one morning and find that we had somehow, magically, left South Africa behind us, once and for all.'

'I'm not sure that's possible, Amy,' he replied.

'No.'

'And I know what I've just told you sounds like something out of a James Bond film,' he admitted. 'But…'

'The part about the leaflets is true,' she said. 'My mother has mentioned them in her letters. She says they caused quite a commotion.' She smiled. 'She was quite indignant about it – she doesn't approve of people littering the streets, even if it is in a good cause.'

They laughed together.

'But that doesn't take us very far,' she said. 'What do we actually know about this man?'

'Well, according to the Law Society,' Danie replied, 'there is a solicitor by the name of Arthur Pienaar, and he is a member of the firm of Barnard, Pienaar & McFall in St John's Wood. I got that much just by picking up the phone.'

She nodded. 'So he probably is who he says he is,' she said. 'There wouldn't be much point in lying about that, would there?'

'No. The real question is: what does this Arthur Pienaar want with me?'

She was silent for some time, sipping her wine.

'Well, there are only two possible answers to that, as far as I can see,' she replied. 'Either he genuinely wants to recruit you to work for him, because he thinks you are the right man for the job; or he is trying to entrap you into saying you will work for him, which he can then use against you on some future occasion. In other words, it comes down to which side he's on, who he's working for.'

'What's your sense of it?' he asked.

'I don't have a sense of it,' she replied. 'But you do: you saw him and listened to him. What's your sense of him? Not forgetting that, the first time this man was in your room, it wasn't to talk to you, and it wasn't because you'd invited him in. He was in your room because he'd picked your lock and broken into your room, without your knowledge. What does that tell you?'

'But he did admit what he'd done, didn't he?' Danie pointed out. 'I would never have known if he hadn't told me. And it's not as though he didn't have a reason.'

'Sweeping the place for bugs?' she said. 'I'm not sure I find that particularly convincing.'

He laughed. 'You know what? On any normal day, it would strike me as too ridiculous to even take seriously. But today doesn't feel normal, and after everything else I've heard, it somehow doesn't sound so unreasonable. I can't help thinking back to what Pieter said when he told us we had to leave South Africa, the day of the demonstration. Remember? I needed John's phone number, but he wouldn't let me call directory inquiries from my rooms, in case the police were listening in. I had to go to his house.'

'I remember,' she replied quietly.

'So, we could take a charitable view, and assume that Pienaar genuinely wanted to check me out before he approached me, to be sure that he and I were playing for the same side.'

'I'm not sure how charitably inclined I feel towards Mr Pienaar yet,' she said. 'All right, I can understand that he would want to be careful. But he already knew why we left South Africa, didn't he? Why would he need to break into your room to find out which side you're on?'

'Amy, if half of what Pienaar says is true, he's playing a very high stakes game. In his shoes, I'd probably feel paranoid enough to question everybody and everything too.'

She nodded. 'Well, you've met the man.'

'My sense of him is that he's genuine,' he said.

11

'All right.' She paused. 'And we think this *Hawala* business is all legal and above board, do we?'

He shook his head.

'I've been going over and over it in my mind, and I can't shake this feeling that there should be something wrong with it – you know, it's against every instinct I have as a lawyer.'

'That's my first reaction, too.'

'But so far, I can't come up with a single solid legal argument against it; I can't think of any specific criminal offence I would be committing.'

'Neither can I, immediately,' Amy admitted. 'Maybe what I'm afraid of is the way it looks.'

'They can't prosecute you for the way it looks.'

'They can try. You remember Ben Schroeder, Harriet's room-mate in her chambers?'

'Sure.'

'Well, I had coffee with Harriet and Ben when I was in London last week. Harriet doesn't do crime, but Ben does; and he was saying that prosecutors are getting good at inventing new offences these days. Apparently, the trick is to make sure that the name of the offence begins with the word "conspiracy".'

Danie smiled. 'I get that. But according to Pienaar, *Hawala* is a common method of doing business all over the world, including in the Asian community here. Millions of pounds change hands every day. If people like Balakrishnan are doing this on a large scale, day in, day out, and the police aren't doing anything about it, doesn't that suggest that it's legit?'

'Maybe *Hawala* is legit, in itself,' she replied. 'Maybe the problem is what people use it for. As you pointed out to Pienaar, it's a perfect vehicle for tax evasion, if you're so inclined.'

'If you're so inclined, yes. But I have no evidence that anything like that is going on here. I don't know any of these people, the donors. I know nothing about them, or about what they do. If I agree to this, I wouldn't be dealing with them. Pienaar handles the donors himself. He made that clear. All I would do is make sure the donations find their way into Balakrishnan's hands. How would I know if some donor in America is trying to fiddle his taxes?'

She shook her head. 'God, Danie, for someone with such a brilliant legal mind, you can be incredibly naïve sometimes. It's not about what you know: it's about what they can reasonably assume you might know. If the authorities decide one day that they don't like what Pienaar is doing, they're going to pick on someone to blame for it – and as we both know, once that process starts, there's no telling who they might pick on. How many times have we seen that happen in South Africa? They're not going to care what you actually know or don't know. If they decide to charge someone with conspiring with Pienaar to do God only knows what, you would be the obvious candidate.'

'It doesn't work that way here,' Danie replied.

'Oh, really? How many times has someone run the "I didn't know what was going on" defence at the Old Bailey, I wonder? You wouldn't be the first, I can guarantee you that – and I'm willing to bet it doesn't have a great track record with juries.'

They were silent for some time.

'So, you're saying I shouldn't do it,' he said eventually.

'No,' she replied, firmly. 'I'm not saying that. I'm saying that there are risks, and we need to weigh those risks very carefully. I say "we" because, as Mr Pienaar was kind enough to point out, this does affect me, too. I'm pregnant with your child.'

'I know that, Amy.'

'I'm not saying we shouldn't do it.'

They were silent for some time.

'What are you saying, then?' he asked.

'If Pienaar is genuine,' she replied, 'how could we not do it? After what Pieter did for us? After what John and Annabel, and Harriet, have done for us? When we've been given this amazing second chance at life? How could we ever look at ourselves in the mirror in the morning if we don't do it?'

She brought her feet back down to the floor, leaned across towards him, and kissed him.

'Besides,' she said, 'I've always wanted to see Edinburgh.'

He grinned. 'What makes you think I'm going to take you to Edinburgh with me?'

'Do the dishes,' she commanded.

12

In the early evening of Monday, two weeks later, a Mr and Mrs Stevens checked into the North British Hotel in Princes Street, Edinburgh, where they unpacked the few things they had brought with them, enjoyed a cocktail in the hotel's bar, and dined in its restaurant. The only odd feature of the evening, to an alert observer, would have been that Mr Stevens carried his briefcase with him throughout, rather than leaving it unattended in his room.

On the following morning, at ten o'clock, Mr and Mrs Stevens paid their bill and checked out of the hotel, leaving their suitcase with the concierge for safe keeping, but Mr Stevens carrying his briefcase with him. They left the hotel together, and walked into the New Town area of the city, stopping here and there to admire the displays in the shop windows. When they arrived at George Street, they exchanged a kiss, following which Mrs Stevens went shopping on her own, while Mr Stevens, as duly authorised agent, entered the premises of the Bank of Scotland, where he deposited three cheques and two money orders, having a total value of £4,500, to the credit of Ecclestone Holdings Ltd, keeping a paying-in stub as evidence of the deposit. While Mrs Stevens continued to shop, Mr Stevens walked the short distance along George Street to the premises of the Clydesdale Bank, where in a similar manner he deposited five cheques, having a total value of £2,750, to the credit of the Albion Import and Export Company Ltd. Finally, Mr Stevens made his way to St Andrew Square to the premises of the Royal Bank of Scotland, where he deposited four cheques and one money order, having a total value of £5,000, to the credit of Falstaff Industries Ltd. As he emerged from the bank, Mrs Stevens joined him, carrying a bag from a celebrated ladies fashion house, containing the two blouses she had purchased there. Together, they returned to the North British Hotel, collected their suitcase, and gratefully allowed the red-jacketed porter summoned by the concierge to help them with it over the short distance to Waverley Station, next door.

Two days later, Mr Stevens made his way alone by train from Cambridge to London, and took a taxi to Waterloo Place, where South Regent Street joins Pall Mall. He entered the premises of Lloyds Bank and deposited three cheques, having a total value of £6,000, to the credit of Madras General and Commercial Enterprises Ltd, keeping a paying-in slip as before. Another taxi took him to the Midland Bank in Chancery Lane, where he similarly deposited four cheques and one money order, having a total value of £4,150, to the credit of Poulter Amalgamated Holdings Ltd. From there, he walked quickly to Barclays Bank in Fleet Street, where he deposited two cheques, having a total value of £5,800, to the credit of Morrison Stanley Investments Ltd. He then took a taxi to Whitechapel, in the heart of the East End of London.

It was only when the taxi dropped him off at the corner of Whitechapel Road and Fieldgate Street that Mr Stevens began to feel nervous. He had been watchful even in the lively bustle of Edinburgh, and remained so in the cheerful hubbub of Chancery Lane and Fleet Street. But the East End was different. There were not many people in evidence in Fieldgate Street, and the few men he saw during his walk down the street, huddled together in small groups, or lounging against the wall of some building, aroused his anxiety. It did not help that the sky had turned to grey, and it was starting to rain. Instinctively, he tightened his grip on the briefcase, until he almost cut off the flow of blood to his right hand, looking over his shoulder, feeling that he must by now be an object of interest to every robber and cut-throat in London. The street looked down-at-heel, an unprepossessing collection of grey brick buildings, all of which had seen better days; and to make matters worse, he was having trouble finding number four. By the time he eventually noticed the remains of the small number four painted on the door, which had been almost obliterated by the weather and the passage of the years, he was sweating profusely. Belatedly, he also noticed the name Balakrishnan, inscribed below the number four – just the name, without any elaboration such as a phone number, or any indication of the business in which Balakrishnan engaged. But there was also a button to push for a bell, and what looked like the outside of a sliding wooden panel to allow observation from within.

He heard the bell ring, and to his relief, almost immediately, he heard the sliding panel being pulled back, and saw a pair of dark eyes peer at him. There was some conversation in a language he didn't understand, and the door was pulled open by unseen hands. As he entered, he briefly had an image of a young woman clad in an orange sari, disappearing to his left. In contrast to the street outside, the interior of Balakrishnan's office was warm and cheerful, with bright lamps, and an appetising aroma of an Indian dish wafting through the air. To his right, an older woman wearing a yellow sari, and two younger women wearing red, all barefoot, sat at a long desk, surrounded by several piles of banknotes, notebooks and an abacus. One of the young women was making and taking calls incessantly, using two telephones. Behind them, at a smaller desk, sat a man in white kurta pyjamas, writing rapidly in a notebook, an abacus to his left-hand side. Behind him stood a younger man wearing a black T-shirt and blue jeans, doing nothing obvious except to keep observation on Mr Stevens. Mr Stevens approached gingerly.

'Mr Balakrishnan?'

The man looked up from his notebook.

'I am Balakrishnan.'

'My name is Stevens.'

For a second or two nothing seemed to register, but then the man smiled. He stood and offered his hand.

'Yes, of course. Mr Stevens. You are here for Mr Pienaar, yes?'

'Yes.'

'Yes, of course. Please, take a seat.' He snapped his fingers towards the desk in front of him. 'Arya, masala chai for Mr Stevens.'

The younger woman not occupied with the phone rose to her feet immediately, and made her way to the back of the room, where a large teapot and kettle stood on a table by the wall.

Stevens raised a hand. 'Please, don't go to any trouble on my account.'

Balakrishnan waved the objection away.

'It's no trouble at all. You look like a man in need of masala chai. It's very good for calming the nerves, you know. We have many clients who experience some anxiety when they come to see us, carrying money and such like, you know, perfectly understandable.'

Arya returned with a cup of masala chai for him, and one for Balakrishnan. Stevens drank, and found himself agreeing with Balakrishnan. The hot tea brought a welcome, soothing relief, and its rich, creamy aroma was delicious. Balakrishnan did not hurry him.

'Did you have any trouble finding us?' he asked.

Stevens smiled. 'Not once I saw the number,' he replied.

Balakrishnan smiled in return. 'Ah, yes. It can be difficult the first time you come. To be honest with you, Mr Stevens, it's a matter of benign neglect. You see, we have got used to how the building looks. Once you have found us, you will always be able to find us again. But it would be easier the first time if the number were clearer; that is true. One of these days we will repaint the whole place, when we have the time, you know. Now, what have you got for me?'

Stevens put his cup down on the desk, and reached for his briefcase. It contained two large brown envelopes.

'Paying-in stubs,' he said, placing them carefully in front of Balakrishnan, 'and cash.'

'How much in cash?'

'Exactly £6,500.'

Balakrishnan nodded and removed the cash from its envelope. He removed the elastic band that held the large stack of banknotes together, and ran a finger through them briefly. He snapped his fingers. The older woman came immediately, and took the stack from him. Stevens followed her with his eyes, and watched with fascination as she returned to her desk, and ran her fingers through the notes at lightning pace, pausing twice to make a calculation using her abacus. Satisfied, she nodded, stood and returned the notes to Balakrishnan. He divided the wad into two unequal parts. He handed the larger of the two back to the woman, with the word 'safe'. She immediately walked towards a huge vault at the very rear of the room. He handed the smaller part to the young man, with the word 'bank'. The young man nodded, pocketed the money, and left the room by a back door.

He looked at Stevens and smiled.

'I'm sure you are glad to get this over with, aren't you?'

Stevens picked up his cup and drained it, savouring the taste and warmth.

'Yes, I certainly am.'

Balakrishnan nodded. 'You'll get used to it. The first time is always the most difficult.'

'Will I be able to get a cab from here?' Stevens asked.

'Yes, of course. Not in this street, but if you go back to Whitechapel Road, you shouldn't have any trouble – not at this time of day.' He smiled again. 'But actually, you know, if you are still feeling nervous, there is a lot to be said for taking the tube – safety in numbers, you see, and less conspicuous than standing on the street waiting for a taxi. If you turn left on Whitechapel Road you will soon arrive at Aldgate East. Or you could turn right and go to Whitechapel. But I think you will prefer Aldgate East – more like the City, you know.'

He stood and offered his hand.

'In the end, it's all about what gives you the greatest peace of mind, you know.'

By the time Danie arrived home, it was after seven. They had agreed that dinner would be baked salmon with rice, accompanied by a bottle of Western Cape Chenin Blanc. It would become a tradition for them on these occasions.

13

Danie du Plessis

Amy couldn't always come with me to Edinburgh. Sometimes she had a lecture or a supervision to give, and once Sally arrived, it became increasingly difficult for her to leave home overnight. But we kept up the tradition of baked salmon with rice, and a Western Cape Chenin Blanc, whenever I returned from London.

By 1975, my anxiety about what we were doing had abated. The experience of having envelopes containing large stacks of banknotes, and a sizeable collection of cheques and money orders delivered to my home by an anonymous motorcycle messenger, usually with next to no notice, was unsettling at first. But I quickly got used to following my instructions – by immediately transferring all of it to a safe one of Pienaar's associates had installed for me in a vacant space under the stairs. I settled into the quarterly routine of becoming Mr Stevens, and visiting the Scottish banks in quick succession in less than an hour. I became known at the North British Hotel. Mr Stevens had developed a backstory as a businessman from Cambridge with interests in Scotland; and the concierge always inquired solicitously after Mrs Stevens if she was not with him. The London banks were always easy by comparison. I had become more and more convinced that *Hawala* was not unlawful in itself, and I was less inclined to look over my shoulder to make sure I wasn't being followed by some eager police officer.

For some time, feeling relaxed in Whitechapel was far more difficult, but that had nothing to do with the police. Eventually, I started to walk around the area when I was in London for some other reason, just to get to know it, to make friends with it. I frequented a few of the local pubs and talked to the regulars. I finally realised that the groups of men I had seen were simply part of the scenery of East London, and did not pose any threat to me, provided I stayed aware of my surroundings and developed a degree of respectful street sense. It wasn't too hard – it wasn't really all that different from some parts of Jo'burg I'd had to pass through in my student days. I found myself liking the East End, the people I met, the atmosphere of bustle and cheerful banter. I soon forsook the suit and tie Mr Stevens wore in Edinburgh in favour of a casual shirt and jeans. A large holdall replaced the formal briefcase. I learned how to walk past the groups of men confidently, as if I owned Fieldgate Street, occasionally venturing a cheery, 'All right, mate?' if someone made eye contact.

As time went by, Balakrishnan and I came to terms with each other too. I took him for an honest man, and I think he saw me the same way. He was always courteous and hospitable; and if I timed my visit to coincide roughly with lunchtime, I would sometimes be invited to join him and the family – as I learned the women and the young man were – for a bowl of delicious lentil dhal with chapattis, and the inevitable cups of masala chai.

Besides, it was only four times a year, and the rest of the time, life was going on normally. I was getting ever busier, developing my lectures on Roman and Roman-Dutch law, meeting with students in their small supervision groups, and individually, to comment on their essays. I was also roped in to help with the coaching of the College's first and second XVs. Once the word was passed around – I suspect by the Master – that I had 'played rugby in South Africa', no inquiry was made into the level at which I had played. South African rugby was rarely seen by then because of the boycotts and embargos, which naturally made it the stuff of legend in the eyes of rugby players elsewhere; and so the tacit assumption made was that I must have been an amazing player, a Springbok in waiting, cruelly deprived of my chance to play test match rugby only by my urgent need to flee the country – an assumption, I must admit, I was disgracefully slow in correcting. Amy finished her degree with first class honours, and went on to complete an advanced degree, the one year LLB in international law. At the same time, she passed her Bar exams, and after eating her dinners at Gray's Inn, she was called to the Bar. She was also elected to a research fellowship, with teaching responsibilities, at Girton.

In 1973, after I had been appointed Buckland Professor of Roman Law, Cambridge University Press approached me about writing a new student text on the subject. The leading text was the work of Buckland, the professor whose name my Chair bears. CUP asked for a version of Buckland that not only deals with the basic principles of Roman law, but also shows how they are applied today in the Roman law-based systems of continental Europe and South America, and in Roman-Dutch law in South Africa – in the hope, I think, of persuading students that Roman law has some relevance to their lives today, rather than only to life in Justinian's time. They found me a young research fellow at St John's to work with me. He's Swiss; his name is Johann; he seems to be well versed in the law of most western European countries – as well as speaking several of their languages – and he's as keen as mustard. I agreed immediately, and the project got underway.

In addition to all this, our two children, Sally and Douglas, came along, and of course, everything else in our lives then happened in that context also. John and Annabel are wonderful with the children, especially Annabel. They adore her. She and John became the grandparents they didn't have – or, at least, didn't have access to – and spoiled them rotten. Annabel was always willing to look after them when Amy and I were both swamped. There were all the usual decisions to take about their futures, looking into schools, and resources in case they should turn out to be musically or artistically inclined, and all the other things parents have to plan for. John and Annabel were amazing on that score too – a veritable mine of information about local schools and teachers of every description. We loved making plans for our children while they were still so young, even though we knew that every plan we made might have to change out of all recognition later, in the face of reality. It was fun.

The conversation I had with Amy about the children I remember most vividly was one that took me completely by surprise. When you know, or feel you know someone well enough, you can easily fall into the trap of thinking that you also know exactly how they will react in any given situation. But sometimes, it turns out that you have no idea. Once, when she was pregnant with Sally – who, she insisted, she always knew was going to be a girl – we were talking about schools. I made some off-hand comment to the effect that, at least our child wouldn't need to worry about speaking more than one language at home. I was speaking in the context of the pressure children could be under during early education, and I had absolutely no sense of saying anything contentious. If I'd thought about it at all, it had never crossed my mind that this was something we could possibly disagree about.

'You mean, you want to raise her to speak English only?' she asked.

'Yes, obviously.'

She took some time to reply.

'You don't want her to learn Afrikaans?'

I didn't. Afrikaans had been my first language, but Amy's had been English, and although we were both brought up to be bilingual, why should that be the case with Sally? For one thing, she would almost certainly never need to speak Afrikaans, so why expose her to all the baggage that came with the language? Which, of course, was what this was really about for me. I had told myself over and over that I didn't want her to be brought into contact with what, in my mind, Afrikaans stood for. What I meant was that I did not want that association in my own life anymore. It was my baggage that was haunting me, not hers; the ghost of my upbringing with my parents in Bloemfontein, not the upbringing she would have with Amy and me in Cambridge. I just didn't have the wisdom to see that then. Thank God, Amy did.

'Why make her life more complicated than it has to be?' I asked. 'A second language is just additional pressure – and it's pressure she doesn't need. The only language she needs is English. If her English isn't good enough because she's chatting away in Afrikaans at home half the time, it could harm her education.'

'It didn't do you any harm,' she observed.

'I didn't have a choice.'

She scoffed. 'Come off it, Danie. We South Africans are a nation of linguists, all of us. We have to be. You know that as well as I do. The secret is starting as soon as she's born. You speak Afrikaans to her, and I'll speak English. She'll learn Daddy's language and Mummy's language at the same time, and it will be effortless. Besides, she'll be speaking English all the time in school, and with her friends. There's no danger of her English not being up to scratch.'

'I don't want to bring up a little Voortrekker,' I replied, without thinking. Sometimes, the truth will out.

She stared at me for some time, then came to sit by my side, and took my hand.

'There's nothing wrong with being descended from the Voortrekkers, Danie,' she said. 'That's her heritage, part of it, anyway – and yours – and it's perfectly honourable. Afrikaans is part of that. Don't you want her to learn about her heritage?'

'I don't want that heritage for her, Amy. Why did we come here, to England, for God's sake, if it wasn't to get away from all that? Afrikaans is the language of Verwoerd and Vorster. It's the language of apartheid.'

'It's also the language of the man I love,' she said.

I didn't reply. I didn't know what to say. I bowed my head.

'Languages don't create horrors like apartheid, Danie,' she continued, after some time. 'People do that. The language those people speak is just an accident of history. When she goes to school, are we going to tell her she can't learn German because of the Nazis? Are we going to tell her she can't learn Spanish because of Franco? That she's not allowed to read Goethe or Cervantes, or listen to Beethoven? It's not about the language, Danie.' When I still didn't reply, she added, 'She needs to grow up knowing who she is.'

We were quiet for a very long time.

'*As u nie met haar Afrikaans praat nie, Danie,*' she said eventually, '*sal ek dit doen.*'

If you won't speak Afrikaans with her, I will.

She stood and left the room.

Sally and Douglas are both growing up with Daddy's language and Mummy's language, and they speak both fluently, appropriately for their ages. Not only that: Amélie, Sally's best friend at school, is the daughter of a French diplomat, and Amélie's language is coming along nicely, too.

14

Tuesday 4 March, 1975

'But Professor du Plessis, I checked carefully in Buckland, and I'm sure he was saying that...'

'He wasn't saying that third parties could never have any rights at all under *stipulatio*,' Danie replied, 'although you're correct – they were very limited, certainly until Justinian.'

The student was the persistent type, and had walked with Danie, uninvited, clutching his essay, from the Squire Law Library back to college, arguing that a comment Danie had made in marking the essay was wrong. There was a part of Danie that admired the student's enthusiasm; but his refusal to back down was sometimes irritating; it wasn't the first time, and today, enough was enough. Danie had delivered two lectures during the morning, and had barely had time to scoff a sandwich before the student descended on him. It was already after two o'clock, and he had work to do. It was time to bring the conversation to an end.

'Michael, look: your essay isn't bad. I'm not saying that. I'm just disagreeing with you on this one point. If you spend an hour or two in the Squire and go back over the sources Buckland refers to, I think you will see what I mean.'

'But Professor...'

Danie turned and unlocked the door to his rooms.

'Take a look at the sources, and we'll talk about it next week.'

He stepped inside quickly, and closed the door. He was so preoccupied with the manoeuvre that he did not immediately notice that someone was sitting in the chair behind his desk. It had been the best part of seven years since he had last seen the man, but he recognised Art Pienaar instantly. As Danie entered, Pienaar stood.

'Sorry to take your seat, Professor. Just keeping it warm for you.' He extended a hand. 'How are you, Danie? You look well.'

Danie stepped forward and took the hand. 'As do you.'

Pienaar sat down in a chair in front of the desk. Danie took off his overcoat and gown, threw them over the back of an armchair, put his file down on the desk, and reclaimed his chair behind it.

'I know the porters didn't let you in, so I'm not going to ask,' he said.

Pienaar smiled.

'Good God, no. That one chap – what's his name? Sidney – was looking at me most suspiciously when I passed the porters' lodge. We haven't seen one another for years, but I swear he remembers me as if I'd been here yesterday.'

'Count on it,' Danie replied. 'There's not much gets by Sidney.'

'Sort of chap we could use in South Africa. I didn't want him to find me loitering on N staircase, so I thought it would be more prudent to let myself in. I hope you don't mind.'

'Why should I mind?' Danie replied. 'Did you check for bugs while you were waiting?'

'As far as I could. I see you haven't acquired a tall ladder yet. But there's nothing at ground level. Let's go for a walk anyway, just in case.'

'A walk? It's freezing out there.'

'I told you to get a tall ladder, Danie,' Pienaar said. 'Relax: I know a place where it will be warm and we won't be disturbed.' He stood.

Reluctantly, Danie grabbed his overcoat and put it on. They walked together to the porters' lodge, where Pienaar could not resist giving Sidney a wave as they passed, and on to the majestic gates, where they left the College and took to the street. As Danie had said, the day was a very cold one, with a keen, icy wind blowing in from the Fens.

'Where are you taking me?' Danie asked, pulling his overcoat as tightly as he could around his neck, and regretting that he had left his College scarf in his rooms. Pienaar, wearing his three-piece suit, seemed oblivious to the weather.

'Great St Mary's. There won't be many people there at this time of day. We'll find a quiet corner there.'

The University church was, as Pienaar had predicted, almost empty. A priest was talking with a man wearing an academic gown near the altar, and a woman was polishing the brass railings around the choir stalls. Otherwise, the church was perfectly quiet. The doors to the balconies, near the entrance at the back of the church, were open. Pienaar led the way upstairs and immediately made for a corner, where they would notice instantly if anyone threatened to intrude on their privacy. They sat down next to one another on a pew.

'Family well?'

'Yes. Thank you.'

'Good. Oh, congratulations on the Chair, by the way, Danie. That's attracted quite a bit of attention within the diaspora.'

Danie nodded. 'I daresay it has. It's a fairly high-profile appointment.'

'That's what I mean. So, I need to ask. Have you been conscious of any increased attention from anyone, noticed anything unusual going on? You've never called the office, so I'm assuming you think everything is ship-shape, but I can't help asking – I'm a natural worrier.'

Danie shook his head. 'I haven't noticed anything out of the ordinary. And you do know that I've already held the Chair for almost two years now?'

Pienaar smiled. 'Yes. I know. But there's a reason why I'm asking you these questions now. So, bear with me. Nothing unusual on your last trip to Edinburgh, or Whitechapel?'

'No. Has that been going to plan? Have the recipients been receiving the funds? I have no way of knowing…'

'Oh, yes. Balakrishnan's very reliable. Like clockwork so far. So, nothing unusual going on? You're sure? Your wife hasn't noticed anything?'

'Not that she's told me. Neither of us has. I don't know what else to tell you, Art.'

'No. That's fine.'

'Good… Look, I assume after so long, you're not here just to…'

'No. I'm not. I'll come to the point in a moment. But before I do, Danie, I want to say thank you. That comes from my clients, as well as on my own account. We've achieved a lot over the past few years, and we couldn't have done it without you. So, thank you.'

'I'm glad to have been able to do it… Art, the clients still don't know who I am, right?'

'Correct. But they are grateful to whoever you are, and they wanted you to know.' He paused. 'So, to come to the point, Danie: the situation has been evolving quickly over the past few years, especially during the last twelve months or so. As a result, to put it bluntly, a decision has been taken to move what we're doing up to the next level.'

Danie raised his eyebrows. 'What next level?'

'I'll come to that. But the next level means we need more money. That's the main reason I'm here today. Not that I'm not glad to see you. But that's what's on the agenda for today.'

'Tell me about the next level,' Danie said.

15

'The propaganda campaign has run its course, Danie,' Pienaar said. 'It's been useful, but people have got used to it. They tune it out. It doesn't register. We haven't followed it up with anything more serious, so sadly the Afrikaner community sees it as an occasional nuisance rather than a real threat, nothing they have to worry about.'

'It's been going on too long?' Danie suggested.

'Probably. But that's not all, I'm afraid.' Pienaar pursed his lips.

'It's become too dangerous. The authorities have started to figure out where it's coming from. My clients have had three operatives arrested in the last year, at the airport on their way into the country.'

'They found the leaflets?'

'And the explosive devices.'

'Oh, my God,' Danie replied. 'What's happened to them?'

'One was a woman. They released her, for reasons best known to themselves. Maybe she gave them some information. We don't know. My clients haven't seen her since. But the two men have disappeared from sight. My clients have no idea where they are, what's happening to them, whether they've been charged with any offence, or anything else. It's like they don't exist anymore. So, the programme is in abeyance, as you might say.'

'I hear that,' Danie said.

'So we either give up, or we move to the next level,' Pienaar said. 'The next level involves warfare. The time has come to get rid of these fascist bastards once and for all – by force, since they don't seem inclined to go any other way.'

Danie stared at him. 'Warfare?'

'Obviously, I'm not talking about an army in the traditional sense, facing the foe across the battlefield, banners unfurled, buglers sounding the advance, cavalry charging, and all the rest of it. I'm talking about asymmetrical warfare – small groups of highly trained fighters based in neighbouring countries, making short incursions into South Africa to take down police stations or military installations, and maybe relieve them of a few weapons in the process. They could also carry money for cells inside South Africa.'

'Is that realistic?' Danie asked.

'It's starting to happen, Danie. The ANC has been rebuilding outside the country, in Tanzania, Botswana, Angola. Angola is a real mess, as I'm sure you know, with a civil war going on; but the word is that it will become fully independent by the end of the year. In the meanwhile, no one is too interested in what the ANC gets up to, and from there, you can find a way in through South West Africa. From Tanzania, there are potential routes through Mozambique or Rhodesia. And from Botswana, you can walk straight in across the border. Some routes are safer than others; it's a question of trial and error.'

He stopped abruptly as they heard two male voices apparently coming from the bottom of the staircase. But if the owners of the voices were thinking of coming upstairs to the balcony, they seemed to abandon the idea, and the voices died away.

'What have you noticed about the donations?' Pienaar asked.

'The amounts have been going up steadily,' Danie replied. 'When I started, we were turning over – what? – £25,000, £30,000 tops each time; but now, it must be three or four times as much, especially over the last couple of years.'

'We've recruited more donors,' Pienaar said. 'That's part of it. And, of course, we're not the only fish in the sea. There are other networks of donors. But the real point is, we're using the donations to buy more expensive things. Instead of leaflets and tiny explosive devices, we're funding sophisticated weapons, training camps, and vehicles you can use for military incursions. That's what I mean when I talk about the next level.'

'How does this affect me?' Danie asked.

'There's something I need to tell you,' Pienaar replied. 'I take it you'll recognise the name of Vincent Cummings, Vince to his friends and family.'

'Of course. He's a donor, came on the scene about three years ago – one of the bigger ones.'

Pienaar hesitated, and took a deep breath.

'That's the man. Danie, when I first approached you about working with us, seven years ago, or however long it's been, you were concerned about whether what we were asking you to do might be illegal. You had to think about it, and I assume your wife had to think about it also.'

'We both had to get it straight in our own minds. Neither of us thinks that *Hawala* is unlawful unless it becomes so by being abused. It's legit in its pure form, let's put it that way. But yes, we had to think about it.'

'Vincent Cummings may have changed the equation,' Pienaar said.

Danie sat up abruptly in his seat. 'What do you mean? Are you telling me Cummings is fiddling his taxes?'

Pienaar held up his hands. 'I don't know that, Danie. I don't know very much about him at all. That's the problem. I was introduced to him by a contact in South Africa, who hinted that he'd made a lot of money in business, and might be worth approaching. I was told that he was based here in Britain, but I'm not sure he's based anywhere for very long. He seems to be on the move constantly. He's hard to pin down: you meet him on his timetable, not yours.'

Danie fought to control a sense of rising anxiety. 'What business is he in?'

'My contact was a bit vague about that too,' Pienaar replied, 'as was Vince on the two occasions I managed to meet him. But recently, his name came up in connection with a purchase of arms by one of the ANC groups in Tanzania.'

'He's an arms dealer? On the black market?'

'It would seem so – in addition to supplying other commodities, in all probability.'

'What other commodities?'

'It's inevitable in this kind of situation. Training to kill or be killed is a stressful way of life. People are always looking for ways to take the edge off, so you'll always find drugs in the camps. It doesn't usually take the suppliers long to work out that they can increase their profits by diversifying and satisfying the demand. They often offer a full line of medical supplies, too – very useful if you're planning a guerrilla campaign a long way from the nearest hospital.'

'For God's sake, Art.'

'The other thing is that Vince probably has partners and associates I don't know about. The amounts he's throwing around seem on the high side for a sole trader. God only knows who they are, and what they have going on, but I have a strong feeling that they're out there somewhere.'

Danie shook his head. 'So, if it's not tax evasion, it's black market arms and drugs, and money laundering. And you're telling me about this now?'

'I didn't have anything definite to tell you until now.'

'You obviously had your suspicions. Why haven't you confronted him about it?'

Pienaar shook his head. 'You didn't listen to a word I said seven years ago, did you, Danie? The one thing you never do is ask a direct question. Once you do that, you know the answer, you can't un-know it, and your innocence is gone forever.'

They sat in silence for some time.

'We have to drop him,' Danie said.

'It's too late for that,' Pienaar replied, 'and in any case, he's too useful.'

'Well, let me restate that,' Danie said. 'If you want me to continue with this, you have to drop him.'

'It's too late, Danie. You've already been working with Vince for three years.'

'But I didn't know there was a problem, and as soon as I found out, I stopped.'

'So you say. But are you sure you didn't have suspicions of your own? You don't have to answer that. But try to see the situation through the eyes of a prosecutor. A prosecutor already has more than enough to ask you some hard questions. He may even have enough to charge you.' He paused. 'Look, Danie: running an armed rebellion isn't the same as running a university faculty. You're not dealing with scholars and bishops and merchant bankers. You're dealing with people operating on the fringes of the civilised world, people who think nothing of breaking the law, people for whom the law is an irrelevance. You're not going to find these people setting up their stalls in the market place across from the church here.

These people trade in the shadows, and if you want to trade with them, that's where you have to go.'

'So, you're saying that it's all right to deal with people like Cummings?'

'It's all right for some, and for others, it's not. But if you want to change South Africa, there's no other way to do it. When we started this, you told me that you wanted White men in South Africa to be free to fall in love with Coloured girls. If you really mean that, if you really want to bring that about, you may have to get your hands dirty.'

'According to you, I've got my hands dirty already.'

Pienaar smiled. 'Oh, cheer up, Danie. I haven't told you the best bit yet.'

16

'I can't wait.' Danie said.

'We've been here long enough,' Pienaar said, raising himself up just enough to view the church below over the top of the balcony. 'Let's walk. If we start to freeze, we'll drop in somewhere for coffee.'

They made their way downstairs. They resumed their walk through the market place, where the stalls, selling everything from food to books, jewellery, electronic devices, and records, seemed to be enjoying a brisk trade, despite the biting wind.

'Having had a taste of *Hawala* recently,' Pienaar continued, as they walked around the stalls and then doubled back towards King's Parade, 'our boy Vince now seems to think it's the best thing since sliced bread: the upshot of which is that he's willing to entrust us with the entire profits of the British and European end of his operation – in cash – in return for a handling fee of ten per cent. We're talking six figures, Danie, cash, at least three times a year.'

Danie stared at him. 'By "entrust us with", you mean he wants us to launder it for him.'

'Quite so.'

Danie shook his head. 'Well, of course he does. It's the best tax break he'll ever get, if he lives to be a hundred.'

'Again, Danie, I'm not assuming that to be his motivation.'

'What else could it be? Why else would he want to hide all his profits away in South Africa?'

'If that's what he's doing,' Pienaar replied. 'Actually, I doubt it is. Balakrishnan can put him, or his agent, in credit in any country, or combination of countries, he chooses. Remember, Balakrishnan handles thousands of transactions, all over the world, every day of his life. It's no big deal for him. All he needs is the money and the identity of the recipient, and his colleague in the country in question does the rest.'

'Cummings could take his money to Balakrishnan himself,' Danie pointed out. 'He doesn't need us to do that. The only reason he's giving us ten per cent is he wants us to act as his errand boys, to keep his name out of it.'

Pienaar smiled. 'Undoubtedly – but that in itself is not evidence of tax evasion.'

'It's evidence that he's up to something,' Danie insisted.

Pienaar laughed out loud. '"Vincent Cummings,"' he said, '"you are charged in this indictment with one count of being up to something. How do you plead? Are you guilty or not guilty?" Sounds just like South Africa.'

Reluctantly, Danie found himself laughing too. They had left King's College chapel behind, and were making their way slowly towards the Fitzwilliam Museum. It was barely teatime, but already the bright lights of the shops on the opposite side of the street were struggling to penetrate the encroaching dusk and a thin mist drifting in off the river. They walked on in silence for some time.

'And don't tell me you didn't know, Danie,' Pienaar said gently. 'You've always known.'

'You can say what you like, Art,' Danie said, as they approached the Fitzwilliam, 'but it's different this time. This time, it feels like you're asking me to become an outlaw.'

'There are times,' Pienaar replied, 'when life leaves you no choice.'

They stopped outside the museum.

'I'm not going to tell Amy about this.'

'I don't recommend secrecy between partners,' Pienaar replied. 'You know that about me.'

Danie shook his head. 'I can't. I have two children, Art. I can't put both their parents in peril. She must be able to say she never knew.'

Pienaar nodded silently for some time. 'Well, these are very personal decisions,' he replied finally. 'Danie, give me another two or three years: that's all I ask. By then, Vince's money will have made a huge difference, and with any luck, the war will be well underway. If that happens, and we have some successes, money will be pouring in from all over the place, and I won't need you anymore. You will have performed an extraordinary service for the new South Africa. I won't ask more than that of you.'

17

Danie was more than ready to leave his rooms in college and make his way home. He felt exhausted, and he needed to clear his mind. But just as he was putting on his coat, there was a knock at the door. The door opened, and Sidney's face appeared in view, as if detached from the rest of his body. Danie closed his eyes.

'Yes?'

'Sorry to disturb you, Professor du Plessis. I've got Mr Erasmus here, from South Africa. I understand you will be supervising him for his PhD. If you recall, I did make him an appointment to meet you at four o'clock, but when we came, you weren't in. But then I saw you coming back into college, so I thought we'd give it one more try.'

Danie ran a hand through his hair in frustration. 'Oh, God, I'm sorry, Sidney. Something came up, and I forgot all about it. It went completely out of my mind. Show him in, please.'

Sidney entered, accompanied by a tall, well-built man with blue eyes and a shock of red hair, formally dressed in a light grey suit with a red tie. Danie put him at late twenties or early thirties. He extended a hand.

'Mr Erasmus, I do apologise. It hasn't been my day. I had an unexpected meeting just after lunch, and it ran on and on. I'm afraid you slipped my mind. That won't be the rule, I assure you. I'm usually quite dependable.'

Erasmus laughed, taking his hand. 'That's quite all right, Professor. And it's Nick, by the way. I know how busy you are. I don't want to take too much of your time. I just wanted to introduce myself.'

'Will that be all, sir?' Sidney asked.

'Yes, thank you, Sidney.'

'Very good, Professor,' Sidney replied. 'Mr Erasmus.' He left silently, closing the door behind him.

'Come and have a seat,' Danie said, indicating a chair in front of his desk. 'Let me make some coffee.'

Erasmus held up a hand. 'Please don't bother, Professor. I'm sure you're anxious to get home. I just wanted to check that you received the proposal for my thesis. I haven't started work yet – I've been too busy getting a place to live, finding my way around town, and all the other things you have to do in a new city, so it will be a few days before I do anything useful. I just wondered if you had any preliminary thoughts about the proposal.'

Danie rummaged quickly through a stack of papers on his desk. 'Yes, I have looked at it. I've got it here somewhere… Yes, here it is.' He sat down behind his desk and scanned the first few pages.

'Yes. *The Evolution of the Distinction between Civil and Criminal Law in Roman Law, from the Twelve Tables to Justinian, and its application to the Modern Law of South Africa.* Well, it's an interesting subject, Nick. My only reservation is one of substance – whether there's enough there for a full PhD thesis. How are you going to approach it?'

'I'm aware that might be an issue, Professor, but I'm going to start with a thorough theoretical and jurisprudential analysis, and I suspect I'm going to go well beyond South Africa, look at the position in Europe, then compare and contrast with the Common Law countries.'

Danie nodded. 'All right. Well, let's see how it goes. I would think you'd have a pretty good idea of how the land lies in three months or thereabouts, so let's revisit it then. In the meanwhile, I would have thought a meeting every two weeks would be more than enough, don't you?'

'I agree, Professor.'

'But any time you need to see me, just give me a call, or leave a message with the porters. How are you settling in? Have you found yourself somewhere decent to live?'

'Yes, I've got a flat on Park Parade, my college found for me. It's in an older house, and it's not very big, but I'm sure it will be fine.'

'With a good view over Jesus Green, I hope?'

'Very nice view, yes. I seem to have fallen on my feet.'

Danie glanced down at the proposal again. 'I see you're originally from Pretoria?'

'Yes. My father was a civil servant. He passed away.'

'Oh, I'm sorry. And you did your degree at Witwatersrand.'

'Indeed so. Following in your footsteps, Professor.'

'Well, you'll have to come and have supper with us, once you're settled in. My wife started at WITS too, and I'm sure we will both enjoy hearing how the old place is doing.'

'That would be my pleasure, Professor.'

They shook hands, and Erasmus left. Wearily, Danie put on his coat once more, and made his way out of college. As he was passing the porters' lodge, Sidney emerged.

'If you don't mind my asking, sir,' he said, 'what's your impression of Mr Erasmus?'

Danie stared at him. 'I've only just met the man. He seems all right. Why do you ask?'

Sidney shook his head. 'Oh, I don't know, sir. It's just a feeling. You know how I am. He just doesn't come across as your average graduate student, that's all – and I've met a few of those during my time at the College, sir, as I'm sure you can imagine.'

Danie smiled. 'Well, if he starts acting strangely, Sidney, I'll report it to you immediately.'

'I'd appreciate that, sir. Have a good evening.'

18

Friday 8 October 1976
It was four o'clock in the morning, and Detective Inspector Ted Phillips was feeling his age. Being woken up in the middle of the night was not exactly unusual in his line of work as a CID officer, but it never got any easier, and today his body was telling him in no uncertain terms that it would have preferred to remain in the deep sleep from which it had been aroused. Reluctantly he forced himself to climb out of bed; walked sleepily to the bathroom; splashed copious quantities of warm water over his face; returned to his bedroom; got himself dressed; and made his way downstairs to his garage where his car awaited. As he approached the University Arms Hotel, Phillips switched off the flashing blue light, and allowed the car to glide to a halt just in front of the hotel's front entrance. He switched off the ignition, climbed out of the car, and made his way to the main doors, where a uniformed officer made a show of inspecting his warrant card before ushering him inside. A uniformed sergeant was standing

at a table just inside the doors, with a tall man wearing a suit and tie.

'Morning, sir,' the sergeant said confidentially. 'This is Mr Hargreaves, the hotel manager. Mr Hargreaves, DI Phillips.'

Phillips offered his hand. 'Good morning, Mr Hargreaves, Sergeant Foster.'

'It's room 224, sir,' Foster said. 'Stairs just ahead, to your left.'

Phillips nodded. 'Thank you, Sergeant.'

The sergeant hesitated. 'There is one other thing, sir, if I may… The coloured lady, Miss Whittaker, has been in charge until you arrived. She was duty CID officer, you see, and…'

Phillips rounded on him. 'Who? Are you referring to Detective Constable Whittaker, Sergeant?'

'Yes, sir.'

'Then call her Detective Constable Whittaker.'

Foster gritted his teeth. 'Yes, sir. Detective Constable Whittaker has ordered the hotel to be locked down, sir, no one in or out except police and scenes of crimes. No guests or staff are to be allowed to leave before being interviewed and giving a statement.'

'Good,' Phillips replied. 'See to it that it's done.'

'Yes, sir… it's just that… I'll need some reinforcements. I don't have enough officers, and those I do have been on duty for… well, they've had a long night of it already, and…'

'I'll take care of that,' Phillips replied. 'I'll be calling Superintendent Walker as soon as I've looked at the scene. In the meanwhile, see to it that DC Whittaker's order is carried out.'

'Yes, sir.'

'I'm sorry, Mr Hargreaves,' he added. 'We'll be as quick as we can, but we have to secure any evidence there may be.'

'I understand, Inspector,' Hargreaves replied.

Phillips took Foster aside. 'And if I ever hear you call her anything other than Detective Constable Whittaker again, I'll have your guts for garters. Understood?'

'Yes, sir.'

Fighting his fatigue, Phillips more or less ran up the four flights of stairs that separated him from room 224, where another uniformed officer was standing guard. As he was showing his warrant card, Detective Constable Connie Whittaker, wearing white plastic gloves over her hands and shoes, came to meet him at the partly open door. She had brought him pairs of the same gloves.

'Good morning, sir.'

He nodded. 'Morning, Connie. So, what's all this, then?'

She frowned. 'It's not good, sir – definitely not your Friday night on the town getting out of hand, let's put it that way. I take it you will be waking up Superintendent Walker before he hears about this on the news?'

'That's the plan.'

She opened the door, and ushered him inside. He stared at her for a moment, and they entered room 224 more or less together. She indicated the bed. What he saw removed any lingering feeling of fatigue, but replaced it with a sudden, violent sensation of nausea. There was blood everywhere, and a terrible smell. He tried to fight off the nausea by taking in the other details of the room, which were reassuringly unremarkable. Apart from the carnage on the bed, the room appeared to be in pristine condition, as if it had just been prepared for the next guest to take up residence – that is, if you ignored the two white-coated scenes of crimes officers who were methodically going over every inch of it. The excursion allowed him to regain control, but it wasn't long before his eyes were drawn back to the bed.

'What we've got is two white males,' Connie was saying, glancing down at her notebook, 'both with their hands tied behind their backs, and three bullet wounds each, two in the back, one to the back of the head. We'll know more about the weapon once scenes of crimes have recovered the shell casings, but whoever did this may have used a silencer – uniform canvassed the rooms on either side and opposite, and no one heard anything.'

Phillips nodded. 'Assassination? A professional hit?'

'Could be, sir.'

'What has he used to tie their hands? It looks like wire of some kind.'

'I'll ask scenes of crimes to run it down, if they can. They will go over everything with a fine toothcomb, of course. They're just waiting for us to get out of their hair. Dr Harris is over there.'

She waved to a man wearing a white clinical coat and gloves, standing on the far side of the room, talking quietly to a scenes of crimes officer. Seeing her wave, he walked over to them.

'Morning, Inspector Phillips.'

'Morning, Doctor. What can you tell me?'

'I can tell you the cause of death.'

'Thank you. I think I can work that one out for myself.'

'As to time, I'm going to stick my neck out, and say within the last four hours. I'll confirm once I've done the post-mortems, but I'd be surprised if they've been dead for much longer than that.'

'Who found them?' Phillips asked.

'One of the night porters happened to be passing,' Connie replied, 'and found the door open, so he came in to check. He's recovering, poor lad; we've put him in 228, which is unoccupied. He's a bit shaken and he's been throwing up, but he seems pretty sure about the time. He says it was one o'clock, give or take a few minutes. That's consistent with the 999 call, which was logged in at ten after one. Uniform were on the scene about ten minutes later, and scenes of crimes arrived at about two, as did Dr Harris and I.'

'Do we know who they are?'

'I found identification on both bodies,' Dr Harris replied. He walked to the far side of the room and removed two plastic exhibit bags from a sideboard. He returned and handed them to Connie.

'One has a driving licence in the name of Vincent Cummings,' she said, 'with an address in St Albans. The other has a business card in the name of Arthur Pienaar. He's a solicitor, with a firm in London, St John's Wood. Uniform are checking for information about next of kin.'

'St Albans and London?'

'Yes, sir.'

'Any evidence of drugs?'

'Nothing obvious,' Dr Harris replied. 'And I didn't detect any immediate signs of alcohol. I'll run a full set of tests once I've got them on the table, of course.'

'Both had wallets with money in them, sir,' Connie added, '£50 to £75, no suspiciously large sums – but it wasn't taken.'

'So, whatever else this was, it wasn't a robbery,' Phillips said. He paused. 'I take it there's no evidence of…'

'No. Nothing like that,' Dr Harris replied. 'There's no physical evidence to suggest it, and they're both fully clothed.'

Phillips shook his head. 'Well, is there anything at all to explain what these two men were doing together in Cambridge, in a room at the University Arms Hotel?'

'Nothing so far, sir,' Connie replied. 'I'll start making some calls later in the morning to see what I can find out about their movements.'

'All right, Connie,' Phillips said. 'There's nothing more we can do here. We're going to have a long day tomorrow.'

'Today, sir,' she pointed out.

'Today. Right. Well, let's get out of the way and leave the experts to get on with their work, shall we?'

'Are you going to try to sleep for an hour or two?' she asked as they walked downstairs.

'No,' he replied. 'I'm going to wake up Superintendent Walker and get Sergeant Foster some backup.'

She grinned. 'Rather you than me, sir.'

'He's probably going to want to know why we haven't got it solved by now, isn't he?' Phillips replied. 'What's taking us so long?'

They shared a welcome, relieving laugh.

19

'There must be some explanation for this,' Superintendent Jonathan Walker insisted. 'The Chief Constable wants to know why we've got Al Capone on the rampage in the University Arms. It's a reasonable question. This is Cambridge, for God's sake, not Chicago. What am I going to tell him?'

'Tell him we're doing all we can,' Ted Phillips replied, calmly. 'We're taking statements from everyone who was in the hotel at the time. Scenes of crimes have been all over the room. We should have their report by close of play today, tomorrow morning at the latest, depending on what they've found. I've asked Dr Harris to expedite the post-mortems. We're not expecting any great revelations in that area, but if there's anything to find, Dr Harris will find it.'

'Make sure I'm kept informed of any developments without delay,' Walker ordered.

'I will, sir,' Phillips replied. 'Look, if it's any consolation, I know this all seems a bit mysterious now, but my gut tells me this isn't a complicated case. There's a connection between these two men, and once we find that connection, the answer will be staring us in the face.'

'What's your take on it, Constable Whittaker?' Walker asked.

'I agree with DI Phillips, sir,' Connie added. 'There has to be a reason why two men with nothing obvious in common end up dead together in the same hotel room.'

'Were they men of good character?'

'Cummings had form for drug possession and obtaining by false pretences, sir,' Connie replied, 'down in London. It was a few years ago, and it doesn't sound all that serious, but it's worth a look. There might be something that fills in some of the blanks about him. I've put a request in to the Met for copies of their files.'

'Pienaar's clean, sir,' Phillips said. 'Well, he was a solicitor: that's what you'd expect. But it doesn't mean he wasn't involved in something dodgy. As soon as we've finished here, I'm going to take myself off to St John's Wood and talk to his partners. I want to know what kind of work he did, who his clients were, whether the firm was aware of anything untoward going on.'

There was a knock on the door.

'Come,' Walker shouted.

A uniformed constable came in.

'Sorry to disturb you, sir, but the firearms examiner called with a message for DI Phillips. Pienaar and Cummings were definitely both killed by bullets fired from the same weapon, a Browning 9mm pistol. He will send a full report, but he thought you'd want to know straight away.'

'Thank you, Constable,' Phillips said.

The officer nodded and left.

'Well, what can I do to help?' Walker asked.

'Just at the moment, sir,' Phillips replied, 'the best thing you can do is let us go so that we can get started.'

'I'm going to need regular reports.'

'I understand, sir.'

'Oh, and Constable Whittaker,' Walker said, as an apparent afterthought, 'I almost forgot. The Chief Constable has received a request from the *Cambridge News* for an interview.'

She stared at him. 'Again sir? About being the first black woman to make CID?'

'He wasn't specific, but I imagine so.'

'Just when I'm starting a murder inquiry, sir? I gave them an interview about that two or three months ago.'

'Perhaps they want to follow up, see how you're doing, and so on.'

'It's not very convenient, sir,' Phillips said. 'Can't we push it down the road, at least until we've got this case done?'

'It's good publicity for the force,' Walker insisted. 'The Chief

Constable is always on the lookout for a chance to have the press say something nice about us. God only knows, they're quick enough to criticise us whenever they feel like it. He calls it balancing the books. Besides, how long would it take? No more than an hour or two, surely?'

Connie took a deep breath. 'It's not just that, sir. After the last one, I got some really snide comments from our white male colleagues. Who do you think you are? Why should you be the Chief Constable's special girl? That kind of thing. Not only verbal: notes left for me on my desk, and, on one particularly memorable occasion, scrawled in lipstick on the mirror in the ladies. There are some people who don't like the idea of black officers, period, let alone a black woman; and the more attention I get, the more they resent me. I know there's nothing you can do about it, sir, and I'm not going to give in to them; but it doesn't make the job any easier.'

'Couldn't you have a quiet word, sir?' Phillips asked.

Walker nodded. 'All right. Leave it with me. I'll see what I can do.'

'Thank you, sir,' Connie said.

'What do you want me to do first, sir?' Connie asked, once they were outside Walker's office.

'Why don't you take a drive down to St Albans, and see what you can find out about Cummings? What was his business? Is there a Mrs Cummings? There must be someone who knows him, or knows of him. Let's start finding out who Vincent Cummings was.'

'Right you are, sir.'

20

'Mr McFall will see you now, Inspector,' the receptionist said.

Phillips did not respond immediately. He had assumed that the bustle in the office would be enough to stop him falling asleep, and he had closed his eyes, just for a moment. He had been mistaken. True, there was a lot going on. The death of Arthur Pienaar had thrown his law firm into disarray. There were files to review in case any urgent steps or deadlines were pending; clients to be notified; files to be reassigned – assuming that the clients were content to leave their cases with the firm. There was more than enough movement through the reception area to keep the average person awake, but at this precise moment, Phillips was not the average person – he was a very tired man. He had come to St John's Wood by train and tube, rather than trust himself to drive down to London from Cambridge and back again.

'Inspector?' she repeated.

This time, her voice registered with him, and he jolted himself awake.

'Sorry,' he said, yawning. 'Not enough sleep. Much the same with you, I imagine.'

'It's been terrible,' the receptionist confided. 'We were all called in early, and Mr Barnard told us what had happened. Ever since then, everybody's been running around like chickens with their heads cut off. The phones have been ringing off the hook. It's such a shame. He was such a nice man. Was he really murdered, sir? It's hard to believe.'

'Yes, I'm afraid so,' Phillips replied, following the receptionist along a dimly lit corridor. 'Do you know whether he was married, whether he had a family?'

'I don't think he was married,' she replied. 'He would bring a guest to the Christmas party and what have you – a woman, I mean – but it was never the same one twice. He was quite a private man, kept himself to himself, if you know what I mean. We did wonder whether he had anybody back home in South Africa.'

Phillips looked up. 'South Africa?'

'Yes. That's where he was from originally – although he'd been living in this country for years, of course. It's amazing how long you can know someone, and still know so little about them isn't it?'

She knocked on an office door and opened it.

'Mr McFall, Detective Inspector Phillips to see you, from the Cambridge Police.'

McFall stood and extended his hand. He was a youngish looking man, with red hair and a matching short beard. His tie was hanging loosely around his neck, and his eyes looked bloodshot. 'You look just like I feel,' Phillips said to himself. He sat down in front of McFall's desk.

'I'm sure this has come as a shock to you, sir,' Phillips began, 'and I know you have a lot to do. I'll keep this as short as I can, but you understand, I need to find out who did this, and why.'

'I understand, Inspector. How can I help you?'

'I'm trying to find out who Arthur Pienaar was,' Phillips replied. 'When we found him, all he had on him, apart from some money, was a business card – which is how we found out about you. There was nothing personal at all. I'm hoping you may be able to paint a picture of him for me, and perhaps even give me some idea of who might have wanted to kill him.'

McFall sat back in his chair and shook his head. 'I honestly can't think of anyone who would want to kill him,' he replied, after some thought. 'But even if there was, I'm not sure I'd know. He wasn't the kind of man who was easy to get to know. It's been ten years since we started the firm – we'd just qualified, all three of us, and we decided to go out on our own. It was a gamble, and it's been hard work. But with Art, it was always a strictly business relationship. He would come to the firm parties at Christmas, or when somebody joined the firm, or left; but that was about it – we rarely socialised outside work.'

'He wasn't married?'

'No. I'm sure I would have known about anything like that.'

'Where did he live?'

'He has – had – a flat in Hampstead. The receptionist will have the address. I've never been there.'

'He was originally from South Africa, I understand. How long had he been in this country?'

McFall raised his eyes, apparently contemplating the ceiling. 'Well, it must be fourteen, fifteen years, possibly more,' he replied. 'As I said, the firm has been going for ten, and before that, he did his law degree and his articles to become a solicitor. So, I would say, at least fourteen years.'

'Where did he do his degree?'

'Bristol, followed by the Law Society's professional training course at Guildford. That's where I met him, actually.'

'Did he ever talk about South Africa, about why he left?'

McFall shook his head. 'No. That was a closed subject. If you tried to ask him, he would shut you down straight away. I think we all assumed he must have had a good reason for leaving, shall we say, but he never talked about it.'

'What kind of cases did he handle?' Phillips asked.

'We all do much the same kind of work,' McFall replied, 'civil cases in the High Court and county courts, all the usual stuff – landlord and tenant, debt collection, commercial contracts, setting up companies and small businesses, a bit of bankruptcy. We don't do crime, and we don't generally do personal injury – too specialised. My partner Geoff Barnard does the odd one, but that's about it. Other than that, we do anything civil that comes through the door.'

'I'd like to look through his files, if you don't mind.'

'I'm sorry, Inspector,' McFall replied. 'I can't agree to that without a court order – legal professional privilege, you understand.'

Phillips thought for a moment. 'All right: let me ask you this. Is there anything out of the ordinary he was dealing with, anything that could have been particularly controversial, anything that could have stirred up particularly strong feelings?'

McFall looked directly into Phillips's eyes. 'I don't know about that. But now that you come to mention it, there is one file that's a bit strange.'

He stood, walked across to a side table covered by blue file folders, and removed one. He handed it to Phillips.

'I just found it this morning, when I was going through that lot to contact his clients. I don't see any reason not to show it to you. As you can, see, there's almost nothing in the file.'

Phillips glanced at the clients' names as recorded on the cover of the file, and smiled. 'Rosencrantz and Guildenstern?'

'I checked. They're on our books as clients. Obviously, Art didn't want to use their real names for some reason. I have no idea who they are, or why we don't know their names, or even why they need our services. But, as you can see, Art kept a detailed time sheet for them for several years, according to which they should have paid us thousands of pounds.'

'Do you know whether they ever paid anything?'

'I seriously doubt it. We all keep a careful eye on fees coming in, and I wouldn't have overlooked something like this. We're a small firm, and this would be a hefty chunk for us. So I'm pretty sure the answer is no, but I'll check for you, just to make sure.'

'Apart from the bill,' Phillips observed, 'all we have in the file is one sheet of paper, with two phone numbers: one for a Mr Stevens – a Cambridge number, interestingly enough – and the other a London number for someone with the initials BK. Nothing to indicate why the clients needed a solicitor, or even how to get in touch with them, except for these two phone numbers.'

'So it would appear.'

'Would you have any other information about Mr Stevens, or BK?'

'No. I'm sorry. These are Art's clients, and evidently he kept them to himself.'

Phillips copied the numbers into his notebook. 'All right, Mr McFall, thank you for your time. I will have to make further inquiries, after which I may have further questions for you. Please don't dispose of any of Mr Pienaar's files, and if anything comes to mind that we haven't covered, I'd appreciate a call. Here's my card.'

21

Ted Phillips fell into a deep sleep before the train even left the station, and it was only the happy circumstance that Cambridge was the train's final stop that prevented him from ending up unintentionally in some remote part of the country. The driver happened to notice him as he left at the end of his shift, and woke him before the driver coming on duty could remove the train from the platform to the sidings. He was surprised to find, on arriving home by taxi, that it was still comparatively early, only eight thirty. It felt more like two in the morning. But the short sleep had given him a second wind, and after making himself a large cup of coffee and a ham sandwich, he felt revived. He was suddenly curious to find out what Connie Whittaker had discovered, and decided to call her.

'If you're too tired, we can do this tomorrow,' he offered. 'I'm only awake because I've had a major shot of caffeine.'

She laughed. 'No, sir, I'm fine.'

'Tell me about St Albans, then.'

He heard her exhale heavily. 'Oh, God, what a mess, sir. I had no trouble finding the address. It's quite a large house in what I imagine is an expensive part of town. I thought at first there was no one home. I knocked on the door, and rang the bell several times – nothing. Finally, just as I'm about to give up, this woman answers: hair all over the place, stained blouse, no shoes, clutching a martini in one hand, unsteady on her feet, speech slurred, breath smelling to high heaven – three sheets to the wind. This is just after twelve noon, sir. She admits to being Mrs Vincent Cummings, and invites me in, without my even telling her who I am. She offers me a martini, which I decline. The whole place is a war zone. It hasn't been cleaned for months, by the look of things. Empty booze bottles everywhere – nightmare.'

'Did you interview her in that state?'

'I didn't need to interview her, sir. She started talking non-stop as soon as I was over the threshold, and wouldn't shut up for the best part of an hour. I know I'll have to go back and take a statement when she's sobered up – if she ever does sober up – but since we're in such a rush with this one, I thought I'd listen to what she had to say, get whatever information I could. I'm sorry if…'

'No. I would have done exactly the same. Presumably, she knew about her husband's death?'

'Yes, the local police had been round earlier in the morning. Not that you'd have known to listen to her – well, she didn't seem unduly distressed by the news, let's put it that way. She spent most of the time telling me what a waste of space he was. He only came home every few weeks, and didn't stay very long when he did come. It was bad enough when he was just doing what she called the normal drug business on his own…'

'"The normal drug business"?'

'Her very words, sir, I promise you. But when he got mixed up with, and I quote, "those bloody foreigners", selling drugs abroad, it got even worse. And the final straw was when he and his mates got mixed up with selling guns and such like to those "bloody blacks in South Africa" – and by the way, sir, she's looking straight at me when she says this – because, since he got involved with the "bloody blacks", she never sees him at all.'

'She mentioned South Africa?' Phillips asked. 'Specifically?'

'Yes, sir. Why?'

'Pienaar was South African,' Phillips replied, 'and according to his law partner, it's the one subject he would never talk about. Is it possible that South Africa is our link?'

'Well, maybe, sir. But we would be hanging our hat on the ramblings of an extremely drunk woman. I don't mind taking another crack at her when she's sober – if I can find out when that would be – but…'

'Still, *in vino veritas*, as they say,' Phillips replied. 'We'll bear the source in mind, but if South Africa's not our link, it's one hell of a coincidence, isn't it?' He thought for some time. 'There's something I'd like you to do on Monday.'

'Sir?'

'I want to know why Art Pienaar left South Africa. Start with the Home Office. Ask them what Pienaar's status was in this country – whether he had the right of abode and so on, and particularly, whether he ever made a claim for asylum, and whether he was ever implicated in any criminal activity in South Africa. See what you can come up with.'

'Right you are, sir. What else did you find out about him?'

'Not much. Apparently, he was something of a lone wolf, kept himself to himself; but true to form, he had a secret file.'

'A legal file?'

'Yes. Two clients using the names Rosencrantz and Guildenstern.' She laughed. 'Highly original, sir.'

'So Pienaar had a sense of humour. But what does it tell us?'

'That there was no secret about the secrecy, if you take my meaning.'

'Exactly. He was advertising that he had clients he couldn't, or wouldn't name, rather than trying to conceal it. He was telling his partners: "Keep out: this one's mine. No one else in the office gets to work on it."'

'What kind of case was he dealing with for Rosencrantz and Guildenstern?'

'We don't know. There's almost nothing in the file. There's a very large bill for professional services, which Rosencrantz and Guildenstern have never paid, according to Pienaar's partner – hardly surprising, since the bill gives no real information about what the services rendered actually were. The only other thing in the file is a single sheet of paper with two phone numbers, one for somebody called Stevens, and the other for a BK, presumably initials. I'll follow those up on Monday. Stevens is a Cambridge number.'

'So that may be another link,' Connie suggested.

'Quite possibly. Pienaar also had a flat in Hampstead. I'd love to take a look around. There was a set of house keys on the body, wasn't there?'

'Yes, sir.'

'I think I might borrow them and go down there tomorrow. I can take Steffie out for dinner in the evening. She's in London this weekend.'

'Do you want company, sir – for the flat, I mean, not dinner? Two pairs of eyes, you know.'

'Yes, I'd be glad of it, if you have nothing else on. It is a Saturday, you know.'

She laughed. 'I'm as free as a bird, sir. Should I pick you up at ten, or is that too early?'

'No, that would be fine. Thank you.'

'You and Steffie need to stop doing this, sir,' she said.

'Tell me about it.'

'You're both on the job, but with different forces? Does she really love the Met that much?'

'Or do I love Cambridge that much?' he replied. 'I'm sure it will work itself out.'

'I hope so, sir. See you tomorrow.'

22

The children were asleep, Amy had done her usual efficient job of clearing away after dinner, and they were sitting down with a glass of wine to watch the nine o'clock news on the BBC. The first item was about the effects of inflation on the forecasts for economic growth. It went on for some time, during which they became bored, and chatted about their day. Eventually, inflation gave way to the second item.

'...and the Prime Minister has agreed to make a further statement to the House about the economy next week.

'Police in Cambridge say that two men found dead in a hotel room in the city early this morning appear to have been the victims of an assassination. Both men had been shot in the back and in the back of the head, in a manner sometimes described as an "execution-style killing". Police say that the discovery was made in one of the hotel's bedrooms, at about one o'clock this morning. Dorian Robson has the story.'

The scene shifted to the grassy expanse of Parker's Piece, on the south side of the University Arms Hotel, where Dorian Robson, his coat and scarf pulled tightly around him to keep out the evening chill, was facing the camera.

'Kenneth, the University Arms Hotel is a much-loved institution in the ancient University city of Cambridge. Many of the great and good – royalty, presidents and prime ministers, stars of stage and screen – have stayed and dined within these walls during its long history. It's part of the scenery – as popular with locals and tourists as with those in high places. It boasts luxurious rooms, an award-winning kitchen, and a magnificent cellar. Events and functions held here are often very important locally, and the University Arms is rarely out of the news for long.

'But a grisly discovery by a night porter on the hotel's second floor early this morning, has brought this venerable hotel publicity of a different kind – publicity, as the manager, John Hargreaves, confided in me earlier, it could have done without. At about one o'clock, the young night porter noticed that the door to room 224 was open. When he went into the room to investigate, he found *the bodies of two men, both appearing to be in their late thirties, early forties, fully clothed, their hands bound behind their backs. Both men had been shot, execution style, with two bullets each to the back, and one to the back of the head. Police quickly sealed the hotel off, and no guests or staff were allowed to leave before being interviewed and giving a statement to a police officer.*

'The men have been named as Arthur Pienaar, a London solicitor, and Vincent Cummings, a businessman, said to be from the St Albans area. Why these two men were in room 224 at that time, police do not yet know. With me now is the officer in charge of the investigation, Superintendent Jonathan Walker.'

The camera caught Superintendent Walker, in his pristine uniform, walking into the shot, and taking up his position next to Dorian Robson.

'Superintendent, I know you've had a busy day, so thank you for your time. Is there anything you can add for our viewers? Do you have any clues about the possible motive for these killings, or why they took place at the University Arms?'

'Not as yet, Dorian. I can confirm that both men were shot in the manner you've described, and I can add that we also know, from forensic evidence, that they were killed using the same weapon, so it seems clear that both murders were committed in sequence, at more or less the same time. But why these men were killed, and why they were at the University Arms, we don't as yet know.'

'So, there's no clue as to the motive? Does the method of killing suggest an underground hit or execution?'

'That's certainly possible. But there are various other possible explanations, and at this stage, we have to keep an open mind. One thing we will be inquiring into is what connection there may have been between the two victims. We have a team of highly experienced CID officers conducting the inquiry, led by Detective Inspector Ted Phillips – who, you may recall, was closely involved with the recent

investigation into historic child sexual abuse at Lancelot Andrewes School, near Ely. I'm confident that once we find the link between these two men, the case will become much clearer.'

'I covered the Lancelot Andrewes affair for the BBC, Superintendent, and I remember that Inspector Phillips was widely praised for his work on that case.'

'Exactly, and what that shows is that the present investigation is in good hands. Like any murder inquiry, it will take time. We don't expect results overnight, but your viewers can be assured that we are doing all in our power to bring the perpetrator, or perpetrators, of these heinous crimes to justice, and to keep the people of Cambridge safe.'

The camera took Walker out of the shot and focused on Robson with a climactic close-up.

'Thank you again for joining us on such a busy night, Superintendent Walker. Well, Kenneth, tonight the second floor of the University Arms remains locked down, sealed off by long stretches of yellow police crime scene tape. The rest of the hotel is open again, inviting guests to stay the night, and visitors to enjoy dinner or a drink. But the sense of shock here is still very new, and palpable, and it may be some time before this famous old hotel returns to something approaching normality. For BBC News, I'm Dorian Robson, outside the University Arms Hotel in Cambridge.'

Danie switched the television off. They stared at each other, unable to speak for some moments.

'Is that *our* Art Pienaar?' she asked eventually.

He nodded. 'Yes. It has to be.'

'What was he doing in Cambridge? Did you know he was going to be here?'

Danie took a deep breath. 'He called me last week and said he might be coming up, and would I make time to meet with him. But

I didn't hear anything after that. I was waiting for another call. He didn't say why he wanted to see me.'

She looked at him, aghast. 'Danie, are you telling me that, if he'd gone ahead and arranged a meeting, it might have been you in room 224 of the University Arms instead of this Vincent Cummings?' She sat back in her seat on the sofa and held her head in her hands. 'Jesus Christ,' she whispered.

'Not necessarily,' Danie pointed out. 'When I'd met Art before we were in my rooms in college. He never struck me as the type to meet in hotels. He preferred a low profile. The UA might have been Cummings's thing.'

She lowered her hands to look at him. 'Oh, good – that's very reassuring. So you might have been shot in college instead of the UA. I feel much better now.'

'Come on, Amy...'

'And how would you know what Cummings's "thing" is? Do you know him, too?'

'I know who Cummings is – was. He was one of Art's donors – the biggest donor, as it happens. But I've never met the man, and I don't know why he was here. Art didn't say anything about bringing anyone with him.'

'Why didn't you tell me Art was coming?' she asked, quietly, after some time.

'I assumed it was just routine. I didn't see any need to bother you with it.'

She rounded on him. 'No. Don't you dare give me that crap, Danie. We agreed from day one that we were in this together, or not at all. We knew there were risks, but they were our risks. I could have lost you, Danie, without ever knowing why. I can't live like that. And what do you mean by "routine" anyway? How often was Art coming to see you?'

'He wasn't. Everything was going along smoothly.'

'Well, not today, apparently,' she pointed out. 'I think it's time you told me what's been going on.'

23

'Art came to see me about eighteen months ago.'

'Eighteen months?'

'Yes. Oddly enough, I remember the day because it was the same day Nick Erasmus came to see me to start work on his thesis. Art wanted to tell me that the donations were going to increase substantially, because they were now financing much more than just leaflets. They're now financing the ANC's military incursions into South Africa.'

'What, the raids from Angola and Mozambique?'

'Yes. They're funding weapons, training camps, military transport, you name it.'

'My God, Danie. That must be costing a fortune. We can't be sending that much.'

'No. That's not just from our network; there are any number of networks of donors now. But all of them, ours included, were being asked to handle much bigger sums.'

'How much bigger?'

'Six figures, every time.'

'And in our case, these greater sums were coming from…?'

'From Vincent Cummings, mostly. Cummings had already been a donor for about three years at that point, but he had offered to up the ante.'

'Meaning?'

'He was prepared to pay our network a fee of ten per cent to send the entire proceeds of his British and European business to God only knows where, via Balakrishnan.'

Amy shook her head. 'You're not serious.'

'I know. It's an obvious case of laundering, and Art didn't even know for sure what Cummings's business was. But he had found out that part of it involved supplying arms to the ANC on the black market. He strongly suspected that Cummings was in the drug business as well, but I don't think he had any actual proof of that – if he did, he didn't share it with me. He thought I ought to know.'

'He thought you ought to know that we've been laundering money for a drug dealer?'

'A possible drug dealer.'

'Really? And what about me, Danie? Did he think I ought to know?'

Danie closed his eyes and hung his head. 'He did, as a matter of fact. It was my decision not to tell you.'

'Unbelievable,' she said quietly.

'Amy, he asked me for two more years, after which we would have done our service and we would be off the hook. I agreed to do it. I didn't tell you because we have two children now: one of us has to be able to deny any knowledge of criminality.'

She shook her head. 'Well, that plan just went out of the window, didn't it?'

He reached out a hand towards, her, but she turned away. She made a huge effort to recover her composure.

'I can't tell you how angry I am about this, Danie,' she said.

'I'm sorry, Amy. The only reason…'

'No,' she said firmly. 'We will have that discussion at some point, but not now. Now, we have to deal with the reality of the situation. We're in danger, and we need to decide what to do about it. My vote is we go to the police.'

'The police? What are you talking about?'

She stared at him. 'For God's sake, Danie, can you really be that naïve? Wake up. We are a part of a network helping to finance an attempted coup against the South African government. The organiser of that network and its main donor have just been assassinated. They're taking the network down. They shot Pienaar and Cummings in Cambridge, Danie, on our doorstep. We're next.'

He held his head in his hands. 'Amy, we can't go to the police without telling them what's been going on,' he said.

'Well, to me, that seems like the lesser of two evils at this point. You said it yourself, Danie: we have two children now. Are you ready to risk their lives, as well as ours?'

'Amy, if Cummings is a drug dealer, what happened today could have been to do with his business. Drug dealers bump each other off all the time. It's their way of settling disputes. It may be nothing to do with the network. Art may just have been in the wrong place at the wrong time.'

'Are you willing to bet the lives of our children on that?'

Before he could answer, the phone rang. He walked out into the hallway and picked up.

'Danie du Plessis.'

'Hello, Professor… It's Nick… Nick Erasmus… Sorry to disturb you.'

'Oh, hello, Nick.'

'If this is a bad time…'

'No… well, yes, actually: is it something that could wait until Monday?'

'Professor, it's just that I'm very shocked by what happened at the UA. I'm sure you've heard about it?'

'We've just been watching the news.'

'Did you know either of these men?'

Danie hesitated. 'Why do you ask that?'

'Oh, nothing really… it's just that… there can't be all that many South Africans in Cambridge… and to lose one like this, you know… Do you think there's someone out there who's got it in for us? Do we need to be worried? Are there any precautions we should take?'

Danie tried desperately to focus, running a hand through his hair. 'Someone whose mission is to rid Cambridge of South Africans? No, Nick. I think that's very unlikely. It's far more likely that one or both of these men had got themselves mixed up in some shady business that ended badly for them. The police sounded fairly confident of solving the case quite quickly. I wouldn't worry about it.'

'But did you know them?'

Danie hesitated again. 'I knew Pienaar slightly. He was a solicitor. I met him once or twice. The other man, no. Now, if you don't mind, I need to get back to my wife.'

'Of course, Professor. I'm sorry to bother you. I'll see you on Monday.'

'What was that about?' Amy asked. She had been standing behind him in the hallway.

He replaced the receiver. 'That was Nick Erasmus, wanting to know if I knew Art Pienaar or Vincent Cummings.'

'Nick? Why would he...?'

'That's a good question. He said he was worried about there being some madman out there, trying to shoot every South African in Cambridge.'

'That doesn't make sense,' she replied.

'No, it doesn't,' he agreed.

They stood silently together for some time.

'Wait a minute,' she said, eventually. 'Didn't you say that the last time you saw Art was the same day you met Nick for the first time?'

'Yes.'

'How did that come about?'

'I'm not sure, really. Art and I had been walking around town, talking. I left him at the college gates and went back to my rooms; and the next thing I knew, Sidney was knocking on my door, with Nick in tow.'

'So, Nick had been around college while you were with Art?'

'It's certainly possible.'

'So, then, the question is: is it merely a coincidence that he's calling now, asking about Art, or is it something more?'

'I think it could be more,' he replied. 'And I think you're right.'

'About what?'

'About the police.'

24

'All pretty spartan, sir, isn't it?' Connie commented. 'More like a student flat than a solicitor's residence, if you ask me.'

Phillips nodded. 'It fits McFall's image of him, certainly, the man who kept himself to himself. He lived like a man determined not to leave a long shadow.'

Their first impression of Art Pienaar's flat remained unchanged after a careful, lengthy search of the living room, bedroom, kitchen and bathroom that lasted until late in the afternoon. The flat occupied the top floor of a tall, narrow Victorian house in Agincourt Road, Hampstead, roughly equidistant from the Heath and the Royal Free Hospital.

In the hands of someone with a little flair, a little vision – and a lot of money – Connie thought, the flat, and the whole house, could have been made into something special. But no one of that kind had lived there. The flat, and the house as a whole, had flaking paint in drab colours, and signs of untreated wear and tear. The small garden at the front was running wild, untended. Pienaar's furniture was cheap and garish. The single bookcase featured a collection of books about South Africa: its history, demographics, statistics, government reports, some in English, some in Afrikaans; there was no evidence of reading for pleasure. There was a small television, but no record player. A number of back copies of *The Times* and *Die Volksblad* lay on the dining table in a pile, next to a half-empty bottle of whisky. There was no sign of any cultural leaning, and scant evidence of pleasure of any kind. The food in the small refrigerator was plain and unappetising; and apart from the solicitor's professional suits and ties, the clothes in the bedroom wardrobe were pedestrian and lacking in any sense of style.

The main item of interest, and what had made the search worthwhile, was a hardbacked file folder found on the bottom shelf of the bookcase. They had left it on the dining table, to be examined once the overall search of the flat had been completed. At length, satisfied that they had found everything of interest there was to find, they took their seats at the table and opened the file.

'No markings on the outside,' Phillips observed. 'Inside… well, what do you know?'

He pointed to a handwritten inscription on the first page. It read: 'Rosencrantz and Guildenstern/Stevens/BK.'

'So, there is more to the mystery file, after all,' Connie said.

'It seems to be a ledger of some kind, doesn't it?' Phillips said. He turned over several pages. 'It has entries dating from 1968 to… well, just a few weeks ago.'

'He's recording sums of money for some reason,' Connie pointed out. 'Each amount is accompanied by initials – perhaps the person who gave, or received the money? We don't know whether these are funds coming in or going out, do we?'

'My guess is that it's money coming in,' Phillips said, 'but there's no indication of what happened to it. Was it banked, or sent on to someone else? And why was this money coming in? It can't all have been for Pienaar, can it? He must have been acting as an agent for somebody.'

'Well, at least he's helpfully added it up for us at the end of each column,' Connie said, 'and whatever this is about, it involves a lot of money. Some of these totals make your head spin.'

'It's a lot of money for a solicitor in St John's Wood to be handling,' Phillips agreed, 'unless he was investing, or buying property for his clients. But if he was doing something like that, why the secrecy, and why don't we have records of the transactions?'

Connie smiled. 'Maybe he was running an underground gambling syndicate.'

Phillips laughed. 'If he was, he had some well-heeled punters; but then, you'd expect money out, as well as in, wouldn't you? No, I don't think so. It's more complicated than that.'

They examined the document in silence for some time.

'The amounts get bigger as you go on,' Connie said. 'Just look at these figures for the past couple of years.'

'And just look at these initials,' Phillips added.

'"VC",' Connie said. 'As in Vincent Cummings, perhaps?'

'Possibly. The initials change over time. How far back does "VC" go?'

She worked her way backwards. 'A little over three years. I don't see anything before that.'

He nodded. 'We need to find out who these people are, Connie.'

'You have a number for Stevens, sir,' she reminded him. 'Do you have it with you?'

He smiled. 'Detective Constable Whittaker, you're surely not suggesting that I make use of Mr Pienaar's telephone, are you?'

She returned the smile. 'I don't think he'll mind, sir, in the circumstances.'

Phillips dialled the number the file had provided. Someone answered and wished him a good afternoon, a male voice. 'Good afternoon. I'm Detective Inspector Phillips. I'm with Cambridge Police. May I ask your name? Really… I see. I had been given this number for a Mr Stevens. Do you have anyone of that name in college? Are you sure, sir? No one on the academic staff, or the administrative staff? No student of that name? Well, it seems I was given the wrong number. Sorry to disturb your afternoon.' He replaced the receiver.

'Dead end, then, sir?' Connie asked.

'Looks like it,' he replied. 'It's a college number. I spoke to the head porter, one Sidney. Sidney says they had a student called Stevens a couple of years ago, but he graduated and went back home to Liverpool. Other than that, no one of that name.'

'It could be a code name, sir,' Connie suggested. 'After all, we are dealing with a man who calls his clients Rosencrantz and Guildenstern.'

Phillips nodded. 'I'm sure we'll get there. Connie, this makes it all the more important to find out about Pienaar's background in South Africa.'

'I'll get on to the Home Office first thing Monday morning, sir.'

'Good. I think we will take possession of this piece of evidence, if you wouldn't mind taking it back to the nick with you.'

'Certainly, sir.'

He hesitated. 'I suppose, as a matter of courtesy, we should tell the Met we've been here and seized an item of evidence. That's what we'd expect of them, if they turned up on our patch without telling us, isn't it?'

She smiled. 'You're having dinner with one, aren't you, sir? You could tell her.'

25

Monday 11 October 1976

Ted Phillips left home just before nine o'clock with the intention of driving straight to Parkside Police Station. But as he was waiting in traffic at a red light on his way into town, something occurred to him. He changed direction abruptly, and made his way directly to the city centre, taking the chance that a rare parking space would be available somewhere. It proved to be his lucky day. He left the car and walked the short distance to the College. He made his way to the porters' lodge. A man formally dressed in a black three-piece suit and a bowler hat stood behind the counter.

'Good morning,' he said. 'I'm Detective Inspector Phillips, with Cambridge Police. I called on Saturday and spoke to Sidney.'

'Yes, good morning, Inspector Phillips. I'm Sidney. How can I help?'

'Well, you remember, I asked you whether you had anyone in College called Stevens?'

'You did, sir, and I informed you that the last Mr Stevens we had graduated and returned home to Liverpool two years ago.'

'You did indeed. I should also have asked you a different question: do you have any South Africans in College?'

Sidney gave him a broad smile. 'We most certainly do, sir. One of our most distinguished Fellows, Professor Danie du Plessis. Professor du Plessis holds the Buckland Chair of Roman Law in the University. He's very highly regarded, sir.'

Phillips nodded. 'Might Professor du Plessis might be in College now?'

Sidney shook his head. 'No, I haven't seen him this morning yet, sir. I'm sure he will be in later. May I tell him you called and ask him to contact you?'

'That would be very helpful,' Phillips replied. 'Thank you. Here's my card.'

Sidney took the card, read it, and looked up. 'Excuse my asking, sir, but Professor du Plessis's not in… any kind of… is he?'

Phillips smiled. 'No, not at all. We think he may have some information that might assist us in an inquiry, that's all.'

'Oh? That wouldn't be to do with that nasty business at the University Arms on Friday, would it, sir? I understand one of the gentlemen who was shot had a South African name, and I did wonder…'

'I'm sorry, Sidney, I can't discuss the details of the inquiry.'

'No, of course sir. I understand. It's just that the name, Mr Pienaar, rang a bell. You see, if I'm not mistaken, Professor du Plessis did have visits in his rooms from a gentleman of that name from time to time.'

'Really?' Phillips said. 'When would this have been?'

Sidney affected deep thought. 'Well, I remember two occasions, sir,' he replied. 'The first time would have been several years ago. But more recently, we saw Mr Pienaar again, either during the current academic year, or last year – I don't quite recall, but relatively recently. Whether there were also other occasions, when I wasn't in College, I couldn't say.'

'I see,' Phillips said. 'Did Mr Pienaar have any connection to the College, or the University?'

'Not as far as I know, sir.'

'I'm sure you have a home address for Professor du Plessis?'

'I do, sir, but obviously... Is it an urgent matter, sir?'

'Extremely.'

Sidney took a directory from the drawer in a desk behind him, opened it to a particular page, and held it up for Phillips to see.

'I can't give it to you, sir.'

'No, of course.' Phillips wrote hurriedly in his notebook. 'Much obliged, Sidney. You've been very helpful.'

'You're very welcome, sir. Oh... the other thing I should probably mention is that Professor du Plessis is supervising a South African graduate student, a Mr Erasmus, Nick Erasmus.'

'Supervising?'

'Advising him with regard to his thesis for his PhD, sir. It's something all the Fellows do from time to time.'

'I see.'

'Mr Erasmus isn't a member of this College, sir – I think he's at Jesus. But I thought I should mention it, since you're asking about South Africans.'

'Thank you again,' Phillips said.

'You're most welcome, sir,' Sidney replied.

26

'Come on, Sally, Dougie, we're going to be late for school,' Amy called from the foot of the stairs. She repeated what she had said, in Afrikaans. 'Danie, are you ready? I left their lunches on the table.'

'Just coming,' Danie shouted in reply.

It was a normal weekday morning in their household, the frantic dash for the bathrooms, clean clothes and breakfast, followed by the frantic dash to the door to ensure that everyone was running according to schedule. But on this weekday morning, Danie had more than the schedule on his mind. The morning before, he had called the police, leaving a message for the officer in charge of the University Arms murder case, but no one had yet returned his call. He was trying to decide whether to call in at the police station personally, before making his way to college. He had even considered keeping everyone at home until he heard from the police, an option he had not yet completely dismissed. As he made his way downstairs, the doorbell rang. 'Oh, not now,' he muttered to himself.

'I'll get it,' he shouted. He opened the door. What he saw stopped him in his tracks. He recovered as quickly as he could, but not quickly enough.

'Nick,' he said. He tried to push the door shut, but Erasmus was prepared. He pushed back, and stepped inside the house with some ease. He was holding a pistol under his coat, and he made sure Danie saw it.

27

Having parked, Phillips made his way as quickly as he could to the CID office, where Connie Whittaker was scribbling notes on a pad.

'Morning, Connie,' he said. 'Any news?'

'Morning, sir. Yes. I just got off the phone with a very helpful lady at the Home Office. She told me that Pienaar didn't have form in South Africa, but that was more due to luck than judgement. He arrived in this country in June 1961, with almost nothing except the clothes he stood up in. When he applied to be allowed to remain, he was interviewed by immigration officers. He admitted to them that he'd been involved in some violent actions by the ANC, including a raid on a police station, in the north of the country, in the course of which two policemen were killed. He insisted that his role was confined to planning, behind the scenes; he wasn't present himself. In any case, he convinced them that, if he had to go back to South Africa, his life wasn't worth the proverbial plugged nickel. They allowed him to stay, and he's been here ever since.'

Phillips nodded. 'Well, he applied himself, got his law degree, became a solicitor. You could say he's made the most of his chance.'

'Yes. But there was a bit more to him than that. MI5 and Special Branch were keeping a discreet eye on him, because there were suspicions that he still had ANC connections. He was seen at the London School of Economics during periods of time when it was a pretty radical place, students demonstrating and taking action in support of all kinds of leftish causes.'

'I remember those days,' Phillips said. 'Did he have any professional connection to LSE?'

'Not as far as they know. According to MI5, he was trying to recruit white students to go to South Africa and cause havoc in different ways: small-time stuff at first, distributing propaganda and so on; but there were suspicions that later, he became interested in far more serious activities, including violent resistance.'

'So Rosencrantz and Guildenstern might be two of his recruits?' Phillips asked.

'Very probably, sir. It appears that in the end, he took on the role of soliciting funds, and dealing with the money as it came in, which would tally with the file we found on Saturday. If so, he must have other people working with him – such as Stevens and BK, perhaps.'

'I've found Stevens,' Phillips said.

'Sir?'

'His name is Danie du Plessis. He's a law professor, he's South African, and he lives at an address in Tenison Road,' Phillips said.

'Du Plessis?' she asked.

'Yes.'

She rifled through a stack of message pad pages on the desk. 'There was a message from a du Plessis over the weekend.' She found the page, and held it up. 'Sorry, sir. I haven't had time to get to the messages yet.'

'Don't worry about it. He's probably in College by now. I think we should go and talk to him, don't you?'

28

'Sorry to disturb you, Professor – or actually, I think I'll call you Danie today. Sorry to disturb you, Danie, but I need some information rather urgently. Let's go into the living room, shall we, and why don't you ask Amy to join us? Just be careful you don't say anything to make her do anything stupid.'

Danie went as far as the living room door. 'Amy,' he called. 'Can you come down, please? Leave the children upstairs.'

'Who is it?' she called back. 'Is it the police?'

'Can you just come down, please?' Danie said.

When she entered the living room, Erasmus was standing by the fireplace. He was no longer attempting to conceal the pistol. He was pointing it directly at Danie, who was sitting on the sofa.

'Danie, who…?' she asked.

'Good morning, Amy. Children safely upstairs, are they? We don't want to bring them downstairs unless and until they're needed, do we, and let's hope that won't be necessary.'

'What do you want?' she asked.

'Well, first you should remember your upbringing, girlie,' Erasmus said. 'You're a Coloured girl. Weren't you brought up to say "sir" when you speak to a White man?'

'Go fuck yourself,' she replied.

He laughed. 'Say that again for me, in Afrikaans. That would really be a turn on.'

She spat on the floor in front of her.

He laughed. 'Well, well, you have given yourself airs and graces after so many years away from home, haven't you, girlie? Never mind. Perhaps I can remind you of your manners. Perhaps you'll call me "sir" when I'm holding this fucking gun to your fucking daughter's head. But first things first. So, you called the police, Danie, did you?'

'Yes,' Danie replied defiantly, 'after your call on Friday night. You gave the game away, asking whether I knew Pienaar.'

'Clever of you,' Erasmus said. 'And the police are on their way now, are they?'

Danie did not reply.

'That's what I thought. So let me come to the point. I know all about your syndicate, or network, or whatever you call it, that you've been running with Pienaar. All I need from you are the names of the people who were supplying the money.'

'I don't know what you're talking about,' Danie replied. 'I told you. Pienaar was a solicitor. I met him a couple of times in connection with lectures he wanted me to give for the Law Society. That's it.'

'Don't waste my time, Danie,' Erasmus replied. 'We've had you under surveillance for over a year now.'

'We?'

'The Bureau, the Bureau for State Security, who else? I've followed you to London twice, including to Whitechapel. I know about the banks. I know about Balakrishnan, and I know what he does for you. I even had a colleague follow you to Edinburgh once. I couldn't risk doing that myself, obviously. If you'd seen me, I'd have no explanation for being up there, would I? We know how these networks operate, and what you've been doing fits the pattern exactly. So, I'll ask you again. I need the names of the people supplying the money.'

Danie stared at him. 'So, you've been here under false pretences all this time, masquerading as a graduate student, applying for a visa under false pretences, pretending to be a WITS grad, leading the University to believe that you were here to do your PhD?'

Erasmus smiled. 'Yes, shocking isn't it? But it wasn't all lies, Danie. As a matter of fact, I did get my law degree from WITS. What you didn't know is that I was already an officer of the Bureau before I started there. They do that kind of thing these days. They like to have a few agents with special qualifications. They even paid my way for all three years. And it's paid off for the Bureau. It gave me the perfect way of getting close to this particular network. Sorry if it offends your sensibilities. I know it's not cricket, as you English say, but it worked.'

Erasmus adjusted his grip on the gun. 'We'd known about Pienaar for years. He always was a troublemaker. He was involved in Black attacks on police stations. Just organising, of course – he wasn't going to put himself in harm's way, was he? But he did a lot of damage. He was lucky to get out of South Africa alive, and it hasn't been easy keeping track of him here. But everyone gets careless eventually, Danie, don't they? Including you: I mean, I shouldn't have been able to follow you all the way to Whitechapel without you seeing me, should I? I had my cover story all ready, but I never needed it.'

'You're the one who got careless on Friday night, though, Nick, aren't you?' Amy said. 'Why do you think we called the police? Asking Danie if he knew Art Pienaar, just a few hours after he was shot? You gave the game away. You told us right there you were the one who murdered Art Pienaar and Vincent Cummings. Every police officer in Cambridge is looking for you, Nick. How far do you think you're going to get?'

29

'How did you find Stevens, sir?' she asked, reaching for her coat.

'I asked Sidney the question I should have asked him on Saturday,' he replied. 'Did the lady at the Home Office have anything else to say?'

'Yes, sir. Since we were asking about Cambridge, they said MI5 had reported to them on a man called Nick Erasmus. He's a law graduate from South Africa, registered as a PhD student at the University.'

Phillips nodded. 'Sidney told me about him. I'm not sure why. But he's not at Sidney's college. He's at Jesus.'

'Well, MI5 suggested that the Home Office keep his visa under review.'

He looked up sharply. 'For what reason?' he asked.

'He's suspected of being under cover for the South African Bureau for State Security. I don't think they have anything concrete, but...'

'Oh, Christ,' Phillips said suddenly. 'Come on, Connie.' He ran at full tilt from the office, out into the corridor. She ran after him, pulling her coat on at the same time.

'Where are we going, sir?' she asked, as they continued to run.

'Either Tenison Road or the College. My money's on Tenison

Road. Let's hope I'm right, and that we're not too late.'

As they passed the duty sergeant's desk on the way out, Phillips stopped and scribbled the address on a sheet of paper.

'I need armed backup at this address,' he said to the sergeant. 'Now.'

The sergeant looked blank. 'Armed backup, sir? But that needs authorisation from…'

'I don't care how you do it, Sergeant,' Phillips shouted, as they ran towards the exit, 'just bloody do it.'

30

'Pienaar and Cummings had it coming,' Erasmus replied, angrily. 'And if you want to know the truth, they were just as stupid as your husband. Jesus, all I had to do was pose as a potential donor, and ask for a meeting at a fancy hotel. They didn't even ask for references, for God's sake. I had hoped they'd bring your husband with them. That was the only disappointment. I could have dealt with all of you at the same time. And, by the way, do you know that Cummings was a drug dealer, in addition to supplying Blacks with weapons to use against us? Trash. We're well rid of him.'

'Well, you're next, Nick,' Amy said quietly. 'There's no way out for you.'

Erasmus felt his finger tighten on the trigger, and made a supreme effort to control himself.

'If I get one more word out of you, girlie, I'll put a bullet in your fucking head right now. Do you think I give a damn about you? The Bureau doesn't waste its time chasing down people like you – a mongrel whore living with a White man, bearing his mongrel children. The Bureau's only interest in you is that you've been helping to pay for all those kaffirs at home who think they can wage war on South Africa, who think they will one day rule South Africa, and turn my homeland into the kind of corrupt mess every country in Africa has become under Black rule. We're not going to permit that. We're going to close people like you down. Now, Danie, one last time, give me the names of your donors. If you don't, the whore dies, and after that, if you still say no, your fucking mongrel children die, one by one, and finally you die. Now, is there any part of that you don't understand?'

'You're going to kill us anyway,' Danie replied. 'You can't let us live, knowing what we know.'

'I don't have to shoot the children,' Erasmus said. 'No need. I'm not totally heartless, Danie. That's up to you.'

Amy looked at Danie. 'We don't have a choice, Danie,' she said, slowly and determinedly. 'I'm going to give him the list.'

Danie did not reply. He had no idea what she was talking about. There was no list. Whatever she had in mind, she was gambling their lives on it. But there was nothing he could do.

'That's more like it, girlie,' Erasmus said, 'and be quick about it.'

Amy stood, and made her way to the fireplace and reached up to the mantelpiece.

'We keep it inside the frame of this picture,' she said, reaching for a picture of herself and Danie, with children, on holiday in Northumberland, two years before. 'We don't leave it just lying around.'

'Very clever,' Erasmus commented. 'Just get on with it.'

In what seemed to Danie to be a single movement, with one hand she allowed the picture to fall to the floor, breaking the glass of the frame. With her other hand, she seized the metal poker from the container in which it had stood inside the fireplace. Turning her body quickly through a full 180 degrees, she lashed out and struck him a single, ferocious blow with the poker, full in the face. Without a sound, Erasmus dropped the gun and fell to the floor, cracking his head against the fender.

Danie knew instantly that he was dead.

31

Phillips switched off the blue light, pushed the gear lever into neutral, killed the engine, and allowed the car to drift into position at the kerb, outside the du Plessis residence. They looked at each other.

'We should probably wait for backup, sir,' Connie said.

'We probably should,' he agreed.

They looked at each other again, and he took his personal radio out of the glove compartment. 'Come on,' he said.

They climbed out of the car and made their way cautiously to the front door. There was no obvious sign of anything amiss.

'Perhaps they've already left for work and school,' Connie whispered.

'I hope so,' he whispered in return. He gritted his teeth and knocked loudly three times, using the brass lion-shaped knocker. 'Police!' he shouted as loudly as he could. 'Open the door!'

After some moments, they heard footsteps. They seemed unhurried. A woman opened the door.

'Keep your voice down,' Phillips whispered to her. 'Are you safe?'

She nodded. 'Yes.'

Phillips sighed with relief, and allowed his body to relax. 'We'd like to speak to Professor du Plessis. I'm Detective Inspector Phillips and this is Detective Constable Whittaker, Cambridge Police. Is he here?'

'You'd better come in,' she replied. 'I'm his wife, Amy Coetzee. It's taken you long enough. We left a message for you yesterday.'

'I'm sorry. We just saw it this morning, I'm afraid.'

She led them into the living room. Danie was sitting silently on the sofa.

'This is Professor du Plessis,' she said. 'Danie, these are police officers, Inspector Phillips and Constable Whittaker.'

'And this, I take it,' Phillips said, indicating the body lying by the fireplace, 'is Nick Erasmus?'

'*Was* Nick Erasmus,' Danie replied.

'Well, I'm sure you won't mind if we verify that for ourselves, sir,' Phillips said. He searched in several places for a pulse, in vain. 'It seems you were right,' he conceded, eventually.

Connie had produced a handkerchief and taken possession of the pistol. 'Browning 9mm,' she said.

Phillips nodded. 'Apart from Erasmus,' he said, 'has anyone been harmed? Where are the children?'

'They're upstairs in their rooms,' Amy said.

Phillips switched on his radio. 'This is DI Phillips,' he said. 'Are you reading me?'

'Loud and clear, sir,' a voice replied.

'I've got an apparent fatality at this address. You can stand down the armed backup, but I am going to need an ambulance, scenes of crimes, and a photographer.'

'Copy that, sir,' the voice replied.

'Out,' Phillips said, turning the volume down low to hide the continuing crackle.

He looked at Amy and Danie in turn. 'Well, would anyone like to tell me what's been going on here? I suppose, given the circumstances, I'd better caution both of you that you're not obliged to say anything unless you wish to do so, but anything you do say may be put into writing and given in evidence.'

'He threatened to kill us,' Amy replied, 'Danie and me and the children, all of us, unless we gave him some information. As you can see, he had a gun. Actually, he said he might let the children live if we gave him the information, because he has a heart, or some crap to that effect. But Danie and I were dead either way. He admitted to us that he killed Pienaar and Cummings on Friday, and we were next. So I got close to him by pretending I was going to find the information he wanted, and I hit him as hard as I could with the poker. He fell and hit his head on the fender. I didn't intend to kill him. I just wanted to neutralise the threat to myself and my family. But I would have done whatever was necessary. Otherwise, we would all be dead now, and you'd still be looking for him.'

'That's exactly what happened, Inspector,' Danie added.

'I see,' Phillips said. 'And was the information he wanted related to the network Pienaar was running, in support of certain activities against the government of South Africa?'

Danie and Amy exchanged glances.

'We know all about it,' Phillips added. 'We searched Pienaar's flat in London over the weekend, and found his records.'

'We were transferring money for him, that's all,' Amy replied, 'using the *Hawala* system of transfer of credit. It's used all over the world, including in this country. It's not illegal.'

'I didn't say it was,' Phillips pointed out.

'That's all we ever did.'

'Did that, by any chance, involve anyone with the initials BK?' Connie asked.

Amy thought for a moment. 'Not initials; it might be an abbreviation. We use a man called Balakrishnan, in London, for the *Hawala*.'

'Do you have an address for this man?'

'Number four Fieldgate Street, in Whitechapel,' Danie replied.

'We left South Africa because we fell in love,' Amy said. 'Danie is White, and I'm what they like to call Cape Coloured. Our relationship was illegal. If we'd been caught, we would both have ended up in prison. I would probably have been raped, and we would both have been tortured. We left our friends and family behind, and we came with nothing except a few rand, and a change of clothing. We've tried our best to make a good life here for ourselves and our children. I'm very grateful to this country for the opportunities we've been given. But I'm not going to apologise for doing what little I could to try to put an end to apartheid.' She looked at Connie. 'I'm sure it's difficult for you to understand. Things are so much easier in England.'

'Not always,' Connie replied quietly.

There was a loud knock on the door.

'That will be the ambulance,' Connie said. 'I'll go.'

When she opened the door, the ambulance crew were just leaving the ambulance with their equipment. It was a woman who had knocked.

'Would you mind telling me who you are?' the woman asked. 'What's going on? Are Amy and Danie all right? Why is there an ambulance here?'

Connie flashed her warrant card. 'I'm DC Whittaker,' she replied, 'Cambridge Police. And you are?'

'Harriet Fisk. I'm a friend. Amy called me some time ago, and asked me to come urgently. I came as quickly as I could.'

Connie nodded. 'All right, come in. Amy and Danie are fine, as are the children. We'll have to take a break anyway to let the ambulance crew do what they have to do.'

'A break from what?' Harriet asked.

'From interviewing them,' Connie replied.

'I've arranged legal representation for them,' Harriet said, 'and I'd appreciate it if you would discontinue the interview until their solicitor arrives. He has to come from London.'

The ambulance crew had confirmed the death of Nick Erasmus, and after he had been photographed where he lay, had removed his body quickly and efficiently. The photographer and scenes of crimes officers had arrived hard on the heels of the ambulance crew, and had taken over the living room, so they had moved into the kitchen.

'May I have his name,' Connie asked, notebook in hand, 'the solicitor?'

'Barratt Davis. He will be instructing Mr Ben Schroeder, of counsel.'

Phillips smiled. 'I worked with Mr Schroeder recently on the Lancelot Andrewes child sexual abuse case. You'll be in good hands.'

'I would like to speak with Mr Davis before we say any more,' Danie said.

'I have to see to the children, too,' Amy added. 'They've been upstairs on their own for a long time. God knows, they must be frantic.'

'I'm happy to suspend the interview until Mr Davis arrives,' Phillips said. 'In fact, I suggest we continue it at the police station, if you will agree to report to the police station as soon as you've had an opportunity to talk to him.'

'Thank you, Inspector,' Danie replied. 'We will be there.'

'I do want to add, Miss Fisk,' Phillips said, 'just for the record, that I did caution them before beginning the interview, and that neither Professor du Plessis nor Miss Coetzee asked for a solicitor.'

'That's absolutely right, Harriet,' Danie said.

32

Wednesday 13 October 1976

John Caswell stood to welcome his visitors. He shook hands warmly with Ted Phillips.

'It's good to see you again, DI Phillips. You remember Andrew Pilkington, of course, senior Treasury Counsel.'

'Yes, of course, sir,' Phillips replied, as Pilkington also stood to shake his hand.

'You won't have met my colleague, DC Connie Whittaker, sir,' Phillips said.

'Officer,' John said, extending his hand.

'Sir,' she replied.

'Please, do sit down,' Caswell said. 'DC Whittaker, this is all new to you, I understand, but DI Phillips worked closely with Andrew and myself on that awful Lancelot Andrewes business, the child sexual abuse scandal, so he's used to it all. I'm sure he's told you what to expect.'

'He has, sir.'

'Which means I can be brief. What it comes to is this. The Director of Public Prosecutions very rarely involves himself with individual investigations. He can't possibly – the numbers alone dictate that; there are thousands of new cases every day. Besides, there's no need. The vast majority of cases are routine local matters, which cause no difficulties, so the Director doesn't interfere, unless he is asked to do so, for good reason. But every now and then, you get the exceptional case – a case that has particularly difficult legal issues, a sensitive or high-profile case, or a case that may have political implications. The Director has to take a more active interest in a case like that, because he may have to report to the Attorney General. Clear so far?'

'Yes, sir.'

'As Assistant Director, it's my job to advise the Director in those exceptional cases. I have to think about the law, and about such matters as how an investigation should be conducted, what charges should be brought, where a case should be tried, and so on and so forth. Fortunately, I have Andrew to call on for advice when it comes to the law.'

'I understand, sir,' Connie replied.

'By the way, there's coffee and water on the table over there. Help yourselves whenever you're ready. I know everybody's very busy, and I won't keep you longer than necessary. But in this case I need your help, because the Director has asked me what charges, if any, should be brought against Professor du Plessis, and Miss Coetzee, as I believe she prefers to be called.'

'She uses her maiden name, sir.' Connie said. 'It's not uncommon nowadays.' She stood and walked over to the table to fetch coffee for Phillips and herself.

'Quite so. The first and most obvious question is: what criminal charges should be considered arising from the death of this man Erasmus?'

Connie glanced up at Phillips from the coffee table, where she was about to add milk and sugar.

'We haven't concluded our investigation into Mr Erasmus's death yet, sir,' Phillips pointed out. 'We started to interview both Professor du Plessis and Miss Coetzee at the scene. Neither of them asked for a solicitor immediately, but it turned out that a friend had retained one on their behalf, Mr Barratt Davis.'

'Davis is a good man,' Andrew Pilkington said. 'He will instruct Ben Schroeder as counsel, if he's available.'

'Another Lancelot Andrewes alumnus,' Caswell commented, smiling. 'It's getting to look like what the Americans call Old Home Week.'

'I believe Mr Davis has already instructed Mr Schroeder, sir,' Phillips said.

'Well, they're a formidable team,' Pilkington noted. 'And in contrast to Lancelot Andrewes, John, we'll have them on the other side, not on ours.'

'Mr Davis's office is here in London,' Phillips continued, 'so we agreed to wait until they'd had a chance to talk to him before concluding the interview. We're expecting them at Parkside police station tomorrow.'

Caswell looked up at him. 'And you're confident they'll show up, are you, Inspector? They're not going to make a run for it?'

'They're both Fellows of Cambridge colleges, sir,' Phillips replied, 'and they have two young children. They're not going anywhere.'

'Certainly not back to South Africa,' Connie added, returning to sit next to Ted Phillips with the coffee.

'The officers are dealing with these people, John,' Pilkington said. 'I'm sure we can trust their judgement.'

'As you think best,' Caswell replied. 'Well, in any case, I've read your interim report, and apparently, they've already provided an explanation for what happened to Erasmus. What more is there to add?'

'Miss Coetzee did tell us the basic story, sir,' Connie replied, 'since she was the one who actually struck the fatal blow. It's simple enough, as far as it goes. Erasmus threatened to kill the whole family, he had a gun, and he clearly had every intention of carrying his threat out. She struck him with the poker while she was in fear for her life, and the lives of her family.'

'According to your report, he demanded information, and threatened to kill them if they didn't provide it.'

'He said he would spare the children if they gave him the information, sir. I don't think they gave that much credence. The parents were going to die anyway. They were part of Pienaar's syndicate, or network, which Erasmus was in the process of destroying. Besides, they knew too much. Erasmus admitted to them that he had killed Pienaar and Cummings at the University Arms hotel. There was no way out for them.'

'I see.'

'But, to answer your question, sir, we didn't have time to go into all the detail. There's still a lot of background we need to ask them about, for clarification, and we need to know more about Erasmus before we prepare our final report.'

Caswell nodded and looked at Andrew Pilkington. 'Well, be that as it may: it sounds to me like a classic issue of self-defence and defence of another. Doesn't it to you, Andrew? If what they say may be true, if the jury accepts their version, then it's a case of lawful defence, justifiable homicide: verdict, not guilty. If the jury doesn't buy their story, she's guilty of murder. It's your quintessential jury case.'

'Murder, sir? You can't be serious,' Connie asked incredulously.

'Excuse me, Officer?'

Phillips put a firm hand on Connie's arm. 'With all due respect, sir,' Phillips said, 'I have to agree with DC Whittaker. I've been doing this job for a long time now, and I flatter myself that I know a case of murder when I see one. This is not a murder case. It's as clear a case of self-defence as you could wish for.'

'Only if you believe their story,' Caswell replied.

'There's nothing to contradict it. Erasmus showed up in their house with a gun on a weekday morning, without any warning, while they were getting their children ready for school. They didn't go looking for him. It's obvious what he intended to do. What alternative did she have? And besides, what possible motive would either of them have for killing Erasmus?'

Caswell shrugged. 'Protecting whatever business they had going on with Pienaar and Cummings, and this man Balakrishnan, or whatever his name is.'

'This isn't about business, sir,' Connie said. 'These people are idealists. They had to leave South Africa with nothing, because it was a crime for them to fall in love. Apart from the law, and their children, their only interest is helping to bring about change in South Africa.'

Caswell was silent for some time.

'I'm not entirely insensitive, Officer,' he said at length with a rueful smile, 'though I must admit, I often do my best to create that impression. I see what you're saying, and in other circumstances, you might even persuade me round to your point of view. But the problem I have is that this case has a serious diplomatic dimension. You don't have to concern yourselves with such matters, but unfortunately, I do.'

'What matters would those be, sir?' Connie asked.

'Officer, the victim was an agent of a foreign state, a state with which the United Kingdom enjoys good diplomatic relations...'

'Victim?' Connie asked quietly.

Caswell ignored her. 'His death is going to be the subject of some awkward exchanges between London and Pretoria. The Foreign Secretary is going to ask the Attorney what the hell's going on, and the Attorney is going to pose the same question to the Director. I have to write the Director's script for him.'

'Sir,' Phillips said, 'with all due respect: may I remind you that Erasmus gunned down two men in cold blood in a hotel in Cambridge, while falsely posing as a graduate student? There was nothing diplomatic about the way he conducted himself: and if he were still alive today, we would be arresting him and charging him with two murders.'

'Based on what he allegedly told Professor du Plessis and Miss Coetzee?'

'No, sir. Based on the fact that the gun Erasmus had with him was the weapon used in the University Arms killings. It's a Browning 9mm. So was the gun used to kill Pienaar and Cummings. That's in our report. What isn't in our report, because we only got it this morning, is that our firearms expert has now matched Erasmus's gun to the bullets used in the murders. They were fired from that gun. Erasmus's gun is the murder weapon.'

'I have to agree with the officers, John,' Andrew Pilkington said, after a lengthy silence. 'As you know, the test I have to apply is whether there's a realistic prospect of convicting Miss Coetzee of murder. I don't see any prospect of a conviction at all.'

Caswell scoffed. 'Isn't that for a jury to decide?'

'There isn't a jury anywhere in the country that would convict her,' Pilkington replied. 'Most of them will think she's performed a public service and deserves a medal – and that's before you factor in that she will be represented by Barratt Davis and Ben Schroeder.'

'So,' Caswell said, 'what you're telling me is that we shouldn't prosecute anyone over the death of a South African agent in this country. Is that what I'm to tell the Director and the Attorney?'

'John, it's the best advice you'll ever give them. If they allow this to go to trial, they could end up facing huge embarrassment. The moment the jury returns the inevitable verdict of not guilty, not only will there be strong comment from the Bench, but there will also be a political firestorm. The Director and the Attorney will be pilloried in the House, and in the press, for allowing a coloured refugee from an odious regime to have her life ripped apart, for protecting herself and her family against an agent of that regime – an agent who had already murdered two people in this country. I wouldn't be surprised if the Home Secretary has a few questions to answer too, about what was done to check Erasmus's credentials, and how he was able to register as a PhD student at Cambridge without anyone noticing.'

Caswell nodded thoughtfully for some time.

'We've still got the money, John,' Pilkington added. 'Why don't we talk about that?'

33

'The money?' Connie asked.

'Even by their own account of things,' Andrew Pilkington said, 'they've been laundering money for years. I'm sure they believed it was in a good cause, but the fact remains.'

'All they did was transfer whatever money Pienaar gave them to South Africa,' Phillips replied, 'using Balakrishnan, and the *Hawala* credit transfer system. As far as I understand it, there's nothing illegal about that, in and of itself. They're both lawyers, and they certainly thought it was legal.'

'I'm sure they're right,' Pilkington agreed. 'If you have a man working in this country who wants to send money back to his family in Bangladesh, he goes to Balakrishnan, hands the money over to him, pays him a commission, and off it goes to Dhaka, where it's available to the family as a credit. Nothing wrong with that. The problem comes when you start laundering drug money.'

Phillips looked up sharply. 'We have no evidence that they did anything like that,' he said.

'Well, we do,' John Caswell said. He picked up a thick file from his desk, and pushed it forcibly down the table to Ted Phillips. 'You can read this at your leisure. The Met had been watching Vince Cummings for years. He started out as a small-time dealer, in and around Soho. The London drug trade was a pretty cut-throat business at that time. Vince wasn't the brightest light on the Christmas tree. You wouldn't have given much for his chances of making it to thirty. You'd have thought he'd go under, and end up being found dead in an alley somewhere early one Sunday morning. But somehow, he survived and thrived, and started to do business with bigger players, here and on the Continent. At the time of his death, he was running a multi-million pound drug business, which had just begun to expand into the sale of arms and ammunition – some of it to be used against South Africa, a state, as I said before, with which Her Majesty's government enjoys good diplomatic relations. It's all there in the file.'

They were silent for some time.

'I don't think you can prove that du Plessis or his wife knew anything about that,' Phillips said eventually.

'That's where you come in,' Caswell replied. 'Familiarise yourselves with the contents of the file, and see what comes up when you continue the interviews. I say "interviews" – plural – because obviously, from this point onwards, you will want to interview them separately. If evidence comes to light to suggest that they knew what type of business Cummings was running, then we will have to consider the appropriate charges. It's unfortunate that Pienaar is dead. The Met are convinced he knew all about it – again, see the file – and we would probably have had him bang to rights. He might even have rolled on the professors in return for a deal. But that's all water under the bridge now. So we need you to get the evidence for us. Do the best you can, and report back when you have something to report.'

'One thing in particular you might ask them,' Andrew Pilkington suggested, 'is whether they were aware of the sudden increase in the amounts of money Cummings was providing over the past year or so. It's all in the ledger, isn't it? When he started out as a donor, a little more than three years ago, it was a matter of £2,000, £3,000. I think the most he ever came up with was about £4,500. Then suddenly, out of the blue, without any explanation, he's hovering around the £100,000 mark every time. I must say, that would have got my attention. What changed, and why? These are intelligent people. They must have noticed something like that. Did they ask Pienaar what was going on, and if so, what did he tell them?'

'Yes, sir,' Phillips replied. He seized the file, and made himself ready to leave.

'The other thing you might do is this,' Andrew added. 'You'll see in the file details of a number of bank accounts held by Cummings at various banks here and abroad. It would be interesting to know whether there's any connection to any bank accounts held by Pienaar or Professor du Plessis, or his wife. Any transfers of money between them, or evidence of sending money to or receiving money from a common third party, would be most enlightening. DI Walsh can put you in touch with the Met's banking experts. They're absolute wizards at finding stuff like that, and I'm sure they'd be pleased to help.'

'I'll need a court order to gain access to the accounts,' Phillips pointed out.

'I'll get that for you,' Andrew replied.

Connie remained sitting perfectly still, her gaze down on to the table.

'Do you have a problem with any of that, Officer?' Caswell said.

'I was wondering, sir: do you want to prosecute them because Cummings was a drug dealer,' she asked, 'or because they're working against the government's friends in South Africa?'

'I'll answer that, John,' Andrew Pilkington said, 'if I may. As Treasury Counsel, I would never sanction a prosecution for political reasons, and I sincerely hope that no prosecutor in this country would do anything like that. I'm sure John takes the same view. But the law is clear. If it's proved that I've knowingly committed a criminal act, the fact that I may have committed that act with an idealistic motive, however praiseworthy, does not provide me with a defence. Professor du Plessis and Miss Coetzee are perfectly entitled to oppose the South African regime – and many of us might be cheering them on from the sidelines, even if we can't say so openly. But they have to obey the law: and helping a drug dealer to launder the proceeds of his drug dealing is against the law. As lawyers, they ought to know that better than most.'

'Besides, Officer,' John Caswell added, 'you must understand: the fact that the government may have good diplomatic relations with South Africa doesn't mean we approve of everything that goes on over there. But if we refused to talk to any country that behaves in some way we don't approve of, we would have a very short list of friends to talk to. Professor du Plessis and his wife must remember that this isn't South Africa. We don't have apartheid here, and coloured people are treated fairly.'

'So white people keep telling me, sir,' Connie replied.

'Thank you for your help,' Caswell said, brusquely. He stood to leave the room. 'Can you see yourselves out?'

Connie went ahead of them, as Ted Phillips lingered for a few moments at the door of the conference room to talk to Andrew Pilkington.

'How is DI Walsh – Steffie, isn't it?' Pilkington asked. 'I remember the two of you so well from Lancelot Andrewes. If I recall rightly, you started seeing each other just as the case was ending. How's it going?'

'It's difficult,' Phillips replied. 'She's still with the Met and I'm still with Cambridge, so we're commuting at weekends. I'm not sure what we're going to do about it, to tell you the truth.'

'Well, it could be worse: London and Cambridge aren't a million miles apart, are they?'

'Connie Whittaker keeps telling me we should find a place somewhere in the middle. Perhaps we will, but I'm not sure it's a real solution. We may just end up with a home we're never both in at the same time.'

'"The course of true love never did run smooth," as someone or other once put it,' Andrew Pilkington said, with a smile.

'That's the truth, and no mistake,' Phillips replied. 'I've got longer in the job than Steffie, so I'll probably go first. Strictly between us, I'd been thinking of hanging my hat up after Lancelot Andrewes, but the Super asked me to stay on for a while, mainly to mentor Connie, really. She hasn't had it easy, but she's bloody good, Andrew. If you ask me, she's going all the way to the top – if they'll let her.' He hesitated. 'I'm sorry if she upset John. I keep telling her not to wear her heart on her sleeve so much. I've warned her it won't make her any friends.'

Andrew Pilkington laughed. 'Oh, don't pay any attention to John. He can be a crusty old bugger sometimes. He means well, but he doesn't always engage the old brain before pontificating.' He turned to face Ted Phillips directly. 'Ted, you can tell Connie from me that she made one friend today,' he said, 'and I, for one, hope she doesn't listen to a bloody word you say.'

They laughed together.

'Thanks for your support on the murder charge, Andrew,' Phillips said.

'No problem,' Pilkington replied. 'You were right. It was as simple as that. John knew that: he was just playing hard to get.' He paused. 'But I can't help with the money laundering, Ted. The chips will have to have to fall where they may on that. You understand that, I'm sure.'

'I understand.'

They shook hands.

'Are you staying over in London tonight?'

'I wish. Too much work, I'm afraid,' Phillips replied ruefully.

'Have a good trip back to Cambridge, then,' Andrew Pilkington said.

34

Danie du Plessis
Something Art Pienaar said to me, the last time I saw him, sticks in my mind. *'The one thing you never do is ask a direct question. Once*

you do that, you know the answer, you can't un-know it, and your innocence is gone forever.'

You can have a lot of fun with a class of first-year law students – bright, eager, idealistic young men and women – by asking them to define the object of a criminal trial. I know this because I've done it any number of times now, and it never fails to amuse. Everyone wants to shout out an answer they clearly consider to be obvious, and it's not long before a general consensus emerges, something like: the object of a criminal trial is to establish the truth about what happened, or to get as close to the truth as possible. The look on their faces, when I tell them they're about as far from correct as they could be, is priceless. After I've enjoyed watching them squirm for a minute or so, I enlighten them. The object of a criminal trial, I explain, is: to establish whether the available evidence is sufficient to prove, beyond reasonable doubt, that a specific defendant, charged with a specific offence, committed that offence; or whether the evidence is insufficient for that purpose. No more, no less. Truth, even if we understand what that word means, doesn't necessarily enter into it.

Then, feeling somewhat guilty about letting the air out of all those youthful sails, I tell them not to be discouraged. There was a time, I remind them, when they would have been right. In the early days of our law, guilt or innocence was often judged by ordeal – tying a suspected witch to a chair and submerging her in water to see if she would drown; or making a suspected murderer pick up a piece of red-hot iron to see if his hand would blister. What does the class think of that, I ask? Again, there is an almost immediate consensus: stupid, they say, illogical, nothing more than primitive superstition, the whole thing. Again, I have to tell them they're wrong – except possibly, about the superstition. The ordeal was neither illogical nor stupid, if you understand the system of logic involved.

The logic underpinning the ordeal was a syllogistic system, which began with the basic premise that God exists, and exists in exactly the form taught by the Church. As this basic premise could not be challenged, it was an easy series of steps to the conclusion that: if the Church prescribed a ritual to divine the will of God, and that ritual was faithfully carried out under the supervision of a priest, God's will would inevitably be revealed. Legal questions could be resolved with certainty. Why the Church preferred the ordeal to something less destructive of the defendant, such as drawing lots, or flipping a coin, I tell the students, is a matter only theologians can answer. But never forget: these are the same people who brought you the Inquisition, so if they do offer some explanation, consider the source. When the ordeal was finally abandoned, it was abandoned not because of any fear of illogicality, but because, by then, the Church found it to be unseemly, and faintly embarrassing, to be seen to prescribe such rituals for use in court.

The demise of the ordeal and other primitive procedures had two seismic effects on the law. First, it instantly removed all hope that a court could ever be certain of the truth of a case. God's will no longer being known, certainty ceased to be attainable in human affairs. In attempting to reconstruct the facts of a case, it became necessary to deal in terms, not of certainty, but of probability; and to rely, not on revelation, but on evidence. Second, the law had to find a way to deal with criminal cases so as to reflect the impossibility of certainty as an end result.

We adopt a standard of proof, such as proof beyond reasonable doubt, because it represents the minimum degree of probability we are prepared to accept as a basis for allowing people to be convicted of crimes, and to be sentenced for those crimes. Our modern criminal trial is, or should be, a scientific inquiry into past events, the process being: to draw inferences from a forensic examination of the evidence; and to evaluate those inferences in the light of the standard of proof. The modern form of criminal trial did not rise fully formed from the ashes of the ordeal. Rather, it evolved very gradually and uncertainly, with many twists and turns, over the course of several centuries. This was not because lawyers and judges didn't understand about probability and standards of proof, or the process of analysing evidence, but because every age has its own superstitions, which affect the way it looks at evidence; and because, until we had an organised, consistent science of investigation, skilled people to carry out investigations, and efficient means of gathering, and preserving evidence, the raw materials were hard to come by.

Applying all this to my own state of mind *vis-à-vis* Vincent Cummings, what can I say? I return to the words of Art Pienaar, which now loom so large in my life. Is there anything about Vincent Cummings that I know, and cannot un-know? Is my innocence gone forever?

There are three words, I tell my students, they will have to contemplate a good deal in the course of their study of criminal law: knowledge; belief; and suspicion. Today, most crimes require proof, not only of an act or omission, such as an assault, but also an accompanying state of mind, such as intention, knowledge or belief. In the case I expect to be facing, the act is clear and easy to prove: clearly, I did cause money donated by Vincent Cummings to be deposited elsewhere, by means of *Hawala*. Leaving aside the fund's ten per cent, where Balakrishnan sent it, and to whom, I cannot know. But the prosecution are not required to prove that. It is sufficient for them to prove that I caused him to send it. But they must also prove that I knew that the money represented the proceeds of drug trafficking.

What I have to resolve in my own mind is this: in a post-certainty world, what does it mean to say that one 'knows' something? How does that differ from 'believing,' or 'suspecting' it? What did I know about Vincent Cummings? Did I become an outlaw?

PART TWO

35

'We are in an interview room at Parkside Police Station, in Cambridge. Present are myself – DI Phillips – DC Whittaker, Professor du Plessis, and Professor de Plessis' solicitor, Mr Barratt Davis. The time is just before ten o'clock. Mr Davis, could you please confirm that we rescheduled this interview of Professor du Plessis from last week, to enable you to have sufficient time to confer with the Professor?'

'I'm very happy to confirm that, Inspector, and I'm grateful for the time you've given us.'

'Are you now happy to proceed with the interview?'

'Absolutely. We'd like to get it over with as soon as possible.'

'Very good, sir. Professor du Plessis, we're here today because we have some questions to ask you, mainly about two things: first, about your relationship with Arthur Pienaar; and second, about your part in causing money to be sent to South Africa on his behalf, over a prolonged period of time. Obviously, I'm aware that you're a lawyer, and I know you understand these things, but it is my duty to caution you that you are not obliged to say anything unless you wish to do so, but anything you say may be put into writing and given in evidence. Do you understand the caution?'

'Yes, I do.'

'Thank you. Then, let's get underway. When did you first meet Arthur Pienaar?'

'It was in 1968, shortly after I'd become a Fellow of my College.'

'How did it come about that you met him? Did someone introduce you?'

Danie laughed. 'No. Actually, he just turned up in my rooms one day, out of the blue, and introduced himself. He said he was there as a community ambassador, or some nonsense to that effect.'

'An ambassador for the South African community?'

'I assumed that's what he meant. But you have to understand, Inspector, nobody made him an ambassador. It was a title he gave himself. He used it as an excuse to meet people like me – exiles – but I didn't pay much attention to it. I remember, I was quite busy at the time, and I didn't really want to talk to him. But he was a persistent man, and it became clear that he wasn't going to leave until I'd listened to what he had to say.'

'So it wasn't a purely social visit: "How are you finding England? Can we introduce you to other members of the community? Can we help you deal with these terrible locals?" that kind of thing?'

'No. He tried to dress it up that way at first. He congratulated me on my fellowship, asked me about Amy, and so on. But he'd done his homework. He knew who we were, and why we'd left South Africa, and it wasn't long before it turned political.' He laughed again. 'Actually, "political" doesn't really do it justice: it was more like "cloak and dagger". We hadn't been talking for five minutes before he told me he'd broken into my rooms a few days before to check me out, and to make sure BOSS hadn't planted listening devices. He checked for bugs again while we were talking.'

'He'd broken in to your rooms?'

'Picked the lock – not that it would take any particular skill to do that: it's falling apart. But he was quite open about it. He said he was looking for evidence of political leanings or affiliation: was I friend or foe? Apparently he concluded that I was a friend. At the time, I thought it was all a bit paranoid. But now, of course…' He allowed his words to trail away.

'Just for the record,' Phillips said, 'BOSS refers to the South African Bureau for State Security, is that right?'

'Correct.'

'If I may, sir,' Connie said, 'just to clarify. Professor, when we spoke previously, you told us that you left South Africa because you were classified as White, and Amy was classified as Cape Coloured; and under South African law it would have been illegal for you to get married, or indeed, have a sexual relationship. Is that right?'

'That's exactly right.'

'And Pienaar knew you'd escaped together, and were now married?'

'Yes. As I say, he'd done his homework.'

'Thank you,' Connie said.

'Following up on that,' Phillips said, 'did you get the impression that Pienaar intended to use your history against you in some way?'

Danie thought for some time. 'I only ever met Pienaar twice: the time we're talking about now, and on an occasion last year, which I'm sure we'll come to. I didn't know him all that well. I don't think he was threatening me, if that's what you mean. That wasn't his way. He certainly wasn't above a bit of moral pressure. "You have a good life here in England now. Don't you want people in South Africa to have the same freedoms you have? If so, won't you help me to change things back home?" That kind of thing. He could be very persuasive. But in fairness, he also said that there would be no hard feelings if I said no, and he insisted that I had to talk it over with Amy before agreeing to anything. Also, he was quite upfront about why he'd had to leave. He told me he'd got a bit too close to the ANC, and he'd become implicated in some serious violence.'

'Again, just for the record,' Phillips said, 'ANC refers to the African National Congress?'

'Sorry, yes.'

'Did Pienaar ask you to do anything specific, to help him to "change things back home"?'

'Yes. He explained to me that he had two clients, who recruited white students to travel to South Africa and foment a bit of trouble – nothing too serious, distributing anti-apartheid leaflets, mainly; but also carrying money and messages for ANC agents inside the country. Pienaar had nothing to do with the operational side of all that; his role was controlling the financing of the operation.'

'Did he tell you the names of his clients, or any of the students they recruited?' Connie asked.

'No…'

'Not Rosencrantz and Guildenstern, by any chance?' Connie asked, with a grin towards Phillips.

'What?'

'Sorry – Pienaar's private joke. That's what he called his clients in the file he kept in his office.'

Danie smiled. 'For all I know, they could have been called Rosencrantz and Guildenstern. Pienaar was obsessive about not telling you who else he was dealing with. I knew the names of some of the donors, because I had to, but he never told me a single name I didn't need to know. He kept my name confidential, too – well, that's what he told me, and I have no reason not to believe him.' He thought for a moment. 'I did work out that the students they recruited were probably from LSE – the London School of Economics – and he didn't deny it. But that was it.'

'Why would he need your help with the financing? Why you, specifically? Presumably, he wasn't asking you for money?'

'No. It was something he could just as easily have done himself, but he was afraid he was being watched. He thought I wouldn't attract as much attention as he would. I was a newcomer, I had a respectable position, and, unlike him, I had no history with the ANC.'

'He thought BOSS was keeping him under surveillance?'

'Yes. Again, at the time, it all sounded a bit James Bond to me. Now, obviously, I know differently.'

'What exactly did Pienaar want you to do?' Phillips asked.

36

'Four times a year, a courier would bring me a large amount of money, some in cash, some in cheques and money orders. My role was to deposit the cheques and money orders in one of six banks, three in Edinburgh, three in London; and then to take the proof of deposit, and the cash, to a man called Balakrishnan, in Whitechapel, number four Fieldgate Street. I was to use the name Stevens.'

'Why Stevens?'

Danie shrugged. 'Security, I suppose. That was his code name for me.'

'What was Balakrishnan's function?'

'Balakrishnan is a practitioner of *Hawala*. Are you familiar with…?'

'Yes,' Phillips replied.

'Pienaar told me that Balakrishnan had a cousin in Durban, also called Balakrishnan. Durban Balakrishnan would ensure that the equivalent of the funds provided by London Balakrishnan became available to whoever was supposed to receive them in South Africa. I have no idea who received them. Pienaar would never have told me that, and I would never have asked.'

'But it would be reasonable to assume that the funds were intended to be used for various subversive purposes – I'm not being critical when I say that; I just mean, they were being channelled to people involved in organised resistance to the government of apartheid South Africa,' Phillips suggested.

'Yes,' Danie replied. 'That would be a perfectly reasonable assumption.'

'With the understanding that Professor du Plessis has made it clear that he doesn't know who the funds went to,' Barratt Davis added.

'Understood,' Phillips replied.

'Professor,' Connie said, 'there's one thing I find strange in all this. You've made it clear that Pienaar was a very cautious man, very security-conscious. Yet he was prepared to let you walk around London and Edinburgh on your own, without any protection, carrying very large sums of money. Didn't that strike you as odd?'

'There is such a thing as hiding in plain sight,' Barratt Davis suggested, with a smile.

Phillips shook his head. 'That doesn't sound like Pienaar to me, based on what Professor du Plessis has told us. Why wouldn't he just use a security firm, and have done with it? Why take the risk? After all, there was a lot of money at stake, wasn't there? The expense would have been worth it, surely?'

'Pienaar didn't like to create records when there didn't have to be records,' Danie replied, 'and he was deeply distrustful of everyone. In his eyes, the simplest solution was always best.'

'He must have known that he was taking a huge risk,' Phillips insisted.

Danie nodded. 'In retrospect, knowing what I know now, I suppose I would have to agree – although actually, I don't know for a fact that I had no protection. It's possible that Pienaar was having me shadowed. If so, they were very good, because I never saw any evidence of them. But also, I was always very careful. I took taxis everywhere in London, and apart from Whitechapel, the areas I visited in London and Edinburgh were pretty safe, right in the centre of town, and I always went there in broad daylight.'

'You wouldn't be safe anywhere from a trained operative,' Connie said. 'If BOSS found out where the funds were coming from, they would be bound to pick up on what was happening, and who was involved, eventually, wouldn't they? As, apparently, they did: you told us previously that Nick Erasmus followed you to London, and had an accomplice follow you to Edinburgh – well, according to him, anyway.'

'And it wasn't just BOSS, was it?' Phillips said. 'There's always some risk of simply getting mugged, even in broad daylight, these days – certainly in places like Whitechapel.'

'I don't know why Pienaar did things as he did,' Danie replied.

'Did Amy accompany you on any of your runs?' Connie asked.

'Never to London. She came to Edinburgh two or three times in the very early days, but only to see the sights and shop – she never had any role in the operation. Once our daughter Sally came along, it wasn't easy for Amy to be away from home overnight. Most of the time, I was on my own.'

'Well, let's talk about your second meeting with Pienaar, and about Vincent Cummings, shall we,' Phillips said.

The door of the interview room opened, and a uniformed sergeant poked his head inside.

'Sorry to interrupt, sir, but there's an important call for DC Whittaker – the Home Office, apparently.'

Phillips nodded. 'All right, let's take a short break. We can get some coffee, and I think you know where the facilities are if you need them.'

'Excellent idea, Inspector,' Barratt Davis replied.

37

Phillips had retreated to his office with his notes and a cup of strong coffee. Some ten minutes later, Connie knocked, came in, and closed the door behind her.

'We have a problem, sir,' she began.

Phillips looked up wearily. 'What kind of problem?'

'The call was from Hilary Vaughan,' Connie replied, 'the very helpful lady from the Home Office I spoke to last week, the one who told us about Erasmus. Oh, and by the way, it seems that Nick Erasmus may not have been his real name…'

'Imagine that,' Phillips said.

'Yes, sir: which raises further questions about how he was able to come here on a student visa. But anyway...' Connie paused to consult her notebook. 'You remember the information about Erasmus came from MI5?'

'I remember.'

'Well, they called the Home Office again this morning. They think Professor du Plessis and his family aren't out of the woods yet. They think BOSS is going to take a second crack at them.'

Phillips looked up. 'What on earth for? To avenge their wounded pride? I know du Plessis was moving decent amounts of money at one time, but that's all ancient history now, surely? Erasmus closed the network down. How is du Plessis a threat to them now?'

'It may be they think Professor du Plessis and his wife are the only ones who can link Erasmus to the killing of Pienaar and Cummings,' Connie suggested. 'I'm sure the South African government would prefer not to be tagged with those two murders if they can get away with it. Without Danie and Amy, they may think they can bury it.'

'You may be right,' Phillips agreed. 'But it still seems like a lot of trouble to go to, to send another operative all the way from South Africa.'

'Apparently, they don't have to send anyone from South Africa,' Connie replied. 'MI5 says BOSS has had a sleeper in Cambridge for years – a long-term agent who stays hidden until activated for a particular mission.'

'Do they have any idea who it is?'

'No, sir. They think it may be someone outwardly respectable, someone who may have a responsible position somewhere: and the hardest thing is that he may not even be South African. If so, he's going to be hard to track down.'

'Unless there's some intel on him, it may be impossible,' Phillips agreed.

'BOSS seems to think there's more to Professor du Plessis than meets the eye. MI5 have intelligence that the sleeper has been activated, with instructions to succeed where Erasmus failed.' She looked directly at him. 'The family may be in danger, sir.'

Phillips shook his head. 'Wonderful. That's all we need.' He thought for a moment. 'Well, we have no choice, do we? We'll have to give the family round-the-clock protection.'

'Armed protection,' Connie added.

'Do you want to tell the Super, or shall I?'

She smiled. 'He really needs to hear that from an officer of the rank of DI or above, sir.'

'Thank you, Connie.'

'Actually, sir,' she said, 'it may not come to that. MI5's preference is to move the family to London, so that Special Branch can babysit them while they try to flush the sleeper out here. Hilary said someone from Special Branch will be calling Superintendent Walker about it this morning.'

As if on cue, Superintendent Walker entered Phillips's office without knocking.

'Make that "has called Superintendent Walker",' she added, quietly. 'Good morning, sir.'

'Good morning. I take it you've both heard the news?' Walker asked.

'I spoke with the Home Office a few minutes ago, sir,' Connie replied, 'and I was just briefing DI Phillips.'

'How far have you got with the interview?'

'We're making good progress, sir,' Phillips replied, 'but there's a long way to go yet. It's not going to finish today.'

'I'm afraid we'll have to postpone it for now,' Walker said. 'I don't see any alternative. The priority must be to make sure the family is safe. He's here. Where are the wife and children?'

'We'll have to ask him, sir,' Phillips replied. 'She's a Fellow of Girton, and I would think the children are in school, but he needs to tell us where, and what their movements are today.'

'Shall I fetch him, sir?' Connie asked.

'Yes,' Phillips replied, 'and bring Barratt Davis with you. We need him to be on board with all this.'

'Who's Barratt Davis?' Walker asked after Connie had gone.

'His solicitor. He needs to know what's going on.'

'Did DC Whittaker tell you that they want to move the family to London?'

'Yes, sir.'

'What do you think?'

'It might be for the best, sir. For one thing, it would be much harder for the sleeper to find them down there, and even if he does, he has to deal with Special Branch. They have far more experience of this kind of thing than we do, and they can arrange for armed officers without jumping through all the hoops we have to jump through.'

Walker turned to look directly at Phillips. 'Yes. Speaking of which, the Chief Constable wasn't exactly amused by your ordering up an armed escort on your own authority the other morning.'

Phillips shook his head. 'What? Oh, come on. You can't be serious, sir. With all due respect, DC Whittaker and I didn't know Erasmus was dead. As far as we knew, we were about to confront an armed killer. We didn't have time to…'

Walker shrugged his shoulders, with just the suggestion of a smile. 'You know the Chief – he can be rather old-fashioned when it comes to the regulations.'

'Which is the problem, sir, right there. The man did nothing but traffic and public relations his whole career, and he wants to tell us how to run a hostage situation? He thinks we should stop to make sure we've filled in all the forms in triplicate, when we have a family facing a villain with a Browning 9mm? For God's sake!'

The suggestion of a smile returned. 'I didn't hear that, Ted.'

Phillips took a deep breath. 'No, of course… thank you, sir.'

'You don't need to worry,' Walker said, 'I had a heart to heart with the Chief, and explained the facts of life to him.'

'Thank you, sir.'

'I even threw out the idea that you and DC Whittaker are due a commendation rather than a reprimand.'

Phillips smiled thinly. 'How did that go down?'

'Well, he raised his eyebrows at first, as he tends to, but actually, I think he'll come around to it in due course. We shall see.'

'Thank you, sir.'

'Well, then, I think we're agreed: Professor du Plessis and his family will be far safer with Special Branch down in London than they are here. Let's see what we can do. The other advantage of that, of course, is that du Plessis will be closer to the Old Bailey.'

'Sir?'

'I'd be very surprised if they decide to try him here, wouldn't you? Too much local interest. I think they'll ship him off to the Bailey for trial, and it will make it easier for everyone if he's already on the doorstep.'

'Assuming we decide to charge him, sir,' Phillips said.

Walker smiled. 'Yes, assuming that, of course.'

The door opened and Connie ushered in Danie du Plessis and Barratt Davis.

'May I ask what's going on, Superintendent?' Barratt asked. 'DC Whittaker said we may need to put the interview on hold for some time?'

'Yes, that's correct, I'm afraid, Mr Davis,' Walker replied. 'Professor du Plessis, would you please take a seat. A rather serious matter has arisen, and we need to talk about it without delay.'

38

Danie tried desperately to pull himself together and make himself focus. The news Walker had given him had shaken him to the core. He had images of Amy and the children alone in the city, with another Erasmus after them, images he could not shake off. He felt faint, there were beads of perspiration on his forehead, and he became conscious that his hands were shaking. He folded them across his body in an attempt to bring them under control. He fought off a wild urge to bolt from the police station there and then, to run like the wind until his legs gave out, to rescue Sally and Douglas, and Amy himself and to take them home to safety. But the problem with that was that home was no longer safe. Eventually, he became aware of the three pairs of eyes fixed on him. He took a deep breath, and forced his hands to do the only thing he could sensibly do – to write down the words that would tell the police where to find them.

'Amy's at Girton,' he said weakly, testing his voice. 'She has supervisions this morning. The children are in school, nursery school in Dougie's case. I'll write the addresses down for you.'

'We'll send uniformed officers to fetch them,' Walker said. He turned to Phillips. 'I suppose we should bring them here initially, while we decide what to do in the longer term.'

'Yes, sir.'

'Can't we all just go home?' Danie pleaded hoarsely. 'Please?'

Barratt Davis put a hand on his shoulder. 'The police are the experts here, Danie. You need to trust them. I'm sure the station is far safer for now, at least until they can assess the situation.'

'Mr Davis is right, Professor,' Connie agreed. 'We can't take chances with you or your family. At least we know they will be safe here for as long as necessary.'

'But we can't stay here indefinitely,' Danie insisted. 'We have to be out of here at the latest by the children's bedtime. Otherwise…'

'Let's see how things go,' Connie replied.

He stood abruptly, agitated. 'Look, if I could use the phone, I could contact Sir John Fisk, the Master of my College. He and his wife are good friends. We stayed with them when we first came to England.'

'Why would you want to contact the Fisks, sir?' Phillips asked.

'I'm sure we could stay with them again, at least until things quieten down a bit. No one's going to find us there, are they?'

'Professor, wherever you stay from now on,' Connie replied,

'there's no guarantee that someone won't find you, and you're going to have armed protection officers outside your door. That's a lot to lay on anyone, even if they are friends – and I imagine Sir John and Lady Fisk must be quite elderly.'

Danie smiled, suddenly feeling a little stronger, his hands a little more secure. 'Officer, before he became Master of the College, John Fisk was your ambassador to Jordan, among other places,' he replied, 'and Annabel was a diplomatic wife over there. They don't faze easily, believe me. They can tell you stories that will literally make your hair stand on end. I wouldn't put it past John to insist on picking up a revolver and taking his turn on watch.'

Phillips smiled in return. 'Use my phone, sir,' he said, waving Danie into his chair.

'John was at College,' Danie reported, hanging up after a lengthy call, 'but he's going home now to talk to Annabel. He wants us to stay with them, at least until we decide whether to move to London. They have a big house, so it won't be a problem for them to put us all up. The children won't understand what's going on, and they're bound to be very disturbed if we just drag them away from home for no apparent reason. But they've known John and Annabel all their lives – in many ways, they're their real grandparents. At least they would feel safe with them.'

'Well, the officer in charge of our armed unit will want to assess the address, sir,' Walker said, 'but if he's satisfied they can provide proper protection, I don't see why you shouldn't stay there, at least for a short time. It would certainly be safer than going home. Write down the address for me, please.'

Connie left with the addresses to brief the uniformed officers assigned to pick up Amy, Sally and Douglas.

'It shouldn't take long to round them up, Professor,' Walker said. 'As soon as DC Whittaker has finished her briefing, I'd like to suggest that we all go to the Fisk residence to wait for them. This will obviously come as a shock to your wife, and I'm sure she will be relieved to have you waiting for her when she arrives. Besides, the Fisks need to know that they are about to have armed officers stationed outside their house, day and night, and they need to hear that from me, in case they have questions.'

Danie nodded. 'Yes, of course,' he replied quietly.

Barratt Davis took Ted Phillips aside.

'Will you contact me about rescheduling the interview?' Davis said.

'I will, sir. There's nothing we can do until we know where they will be living, and things have settled down a bit. If they move down to London, we'll have to borrow an interview room at one of the Met's stations. I'll let John Caswell know what's going on. You did get the evidence we sent to your office, I hope – the copies of the ledger, and so on?'

'I did, thank you.'

'Good. If you have any questions about it, give me a call. We haven't put names to all of Pienaar's donors, as yet. We're working on it, but it's a slow process. They're elusive buggers.'

'I understand.'

'Well, let's go and find DC Whittaker, shall we?' Walker said. 'The sooner we get ourselves organised, the better.'

39

'So you're telling me we have to allow ourselves to be hounded out of our own home by these murderers?' Amy said angrily, not for the first time. 'No. There must be something we can do that doesn't involve capitulating to these people.'

Amy and the children had arrived in three separate police patrol cars within a few minutes of each other to find Danie waiting for them with his solicitor and three police officers. Amy was visibly alarmed; Sally and Douglas were noticing, and showing signs of agitation. Annabel had quickly appointed herself the children's companion for the afternoon, and had taken them upstairs with games and chocolate, leaving their parents to talk to the officers. By chance, Harriet Fisk was also there. Having finished a morning case at the Cambridge County Court, she had dropped in unannounced on her mother, whom she assumed would be at home alone, in hopes of scrounging a quick lunch before returning to her chambers in London – only to find both her parents at home, and preoccupied with matters far removed from lunch. She made herself a cheese sandwich in the kitchen, and decided to wait to see Amy.

'Again, I understand how you feel, Miss Coetzee,' Superintendent Walker replied. 'But I must repeat: this isn't the time to take risks. MI5 didn't have much to give us in the way of hard information about the sleeper, or any associates he may have; so at this stage, we're not sure exactly what we're up against. But one thing we do know is this: they know where you live; and if you stay at home now, you're offering them an easy target. I'm not even sure we could protect you there. I will have officers keep an eye on the house while you're away – I promise you that. Hopefully, it won't take too long to sort this out, but until we do, we need you to stay somewhere safe.'

'Such as here,' John Fisk added.

'If we stay here, John,' she said, 'we're putting you and Annabel in harm's way too. We can't do that.'

'Stuff and nonsense, Amy,' John Fisk replied. 'No one knows you're here, except for Harriet and the police. Besides, it's going to take more than a couple of Afrikaner bullyboys to intimidate Annabel and me. We dealt with far worse characters in Amman, and sent them packing. Ask Harriet: she'll tell you.'

Harriet grinned. 'They're a formidable team,' she said.

'In any case, Superintendent Walker will have armed police officers stationed outside. We'll be perfectly safe.'

She shook her head. 'Cambridge is a small town, John. It's not hard to find out who our friends are, who we work with. It's only a matter of time before they find us. These are ruthless people – believe me, I've seen them at work; and I don't want to have that experience again.'

'Amy's right, John,' Danie said. 'We can't take chances with this. The safest thing for everyone is for us to get away from Cambridge and go down to London for a while. They're not going to find us there.'

'But Danie, where will you stay?' Harriet asked. 'Do you have somewhere in mind?'

'Not yet. I'm not even sure where to start, to be honest. Maybe we could look for a small hotel somewhere.'

'They could stay at the house, I suppose,' John Fisk suggested, after a silence. 'That would be one possibility.'

'You mean the College house?' Harriet asked.

'Yes. Why not?'

Harriet's eyes lit up. 'Dad, that's a great idea,' she said. 'Amy, it would be perfect for you.'

'What's this, sir?' Superintendent Walker asked.

'The College has a house in London,' Fisk replied, 'a palatial old pile in Holland Park. As Master, I essentially have complete discretion about who stays there, and for how long. It's currently unoccupied, it's nice and quiet, and there's plenty of space.' He turned to Danie and Amy. 'If you want it, it's yours for the duration. Just give me a day or two to send the cleaners in.'

'And there's no problem about them being there for an extended period, sir?' Walker asked. 'At this stage, we have no way of knowing how long we may need it.'

'The house was bequeathed to us by a rich alumnus,' Fisk replied, 'almost a hundred years ago. According to the bequest, it was intended as a *pied à terre* for distinguished guests of the College, visiting academics and the like, who want to spend some time in London. But if we have no such guests, it's open to me, as Master, to let the Fellows loose in it. There's nothing in the bequest about how long for, so I assume that's also up to me.'

'And it could be ready in a day or two?' Walker asked.

'If I can get the cleaners in tomorrow morning, there's no reason why they couldn't move in tomorrow evening.'

Danie looked at Amy. 'It sounds good to me, Amy. Let's do it.'

'I think it's a very good idea,' Barratt Davis added.

Amy nodded reluctantly. 'I can't believe we're doing this,' she said, 'but I suppose, if we must, we must.' She walked over to kiss John Fisk on the cheek. 'Thank you, John.'

'If you wouldn't mind writing down the address and phone number for me, sir,' Walker said, 'I'll alert Special Branch. Anything else we need to talk about, DI Phillips?'

'Not that I can think of, sir, not for now.'

'All right, then, we'll get out of your hair, and let you get on with your day.' He handed Danie a card. 'You'll notice officers coming and going. Try to ignore them. They'll let you know if there's anything you need to know about. It's highly unlikely that anything will happen tonight, but if you're anxious, don't go outside: call the number on this card, and the officers outside will be alerted almost immediately. They will then check on you. They will knock four times, slowly. Don't open the door to anyone who doesn't do that. Got it?'

Danie nodded. 'Got it.'

'Danie, I'll call you tomorrow morning,' Barratt Davis said.

'That old house must be worth a few bob by now, sir,' Walker said as Fisk showed them to the door. 'It must be a temptation to put it on the market sometimes.'

Fisk smiled. 'Don't I know it? I've had to fight tooth and nail with the Bursar every couple of years to keep him from cashing it in – as, I'm told, did several of my predecessors.' He laughed. 'Fortunately, when I explain how much it's likely to continue increasing in value, he eventually agrees that we should hang on to it for a bit longer. Just as well: it's technically a charitable gift, and I don't want the donor's descendants trying to take it back because we haven't complied with the bequest. That would be a bore.'

Phillips turned to Barratt Davis, 'If you're going back to London, sir, I can give you a lift to the station,' he offered.

'That would be much appreciated, Inspector,' Barratt Davis said.

40

'Do you remember the first case we were involved in together,' Barratt Davis asked, once they were underway, 'you, me and Ben Schroeder?'

Phillips smiled grimly. 'I certainly do, sir. I'm not likely to forget that one, not if I live to be a hundred. It was Billy Cottage, the Fenstanton lock keeper: capital murder – one of the last of its kind, as it turned out.'

'Yes.'

'He raped Jennifer Doyce on that houseboat, the *Rosemary D*, near his lock at Fenstanton. He took a winch handle to both of them: left her for dead, and killed her boyfriend, Frank Gilliam. He had some kind of fixation about singing *The Lincolnshire Poacher* to himself, which was how we were able to identify him as the killer – well, that and the gold cross and chain he stole from her.'

Barratt nodded. 'Jennifer remembered him humming the tune. She recognised it because she'd heard someone singing it on the radio a few days earlier.'

'She did indeed, sir. She was a very brave girl, Jennifer. She got married, you know, when it was all over.'

'Really? I didn't know that. Good for her.'

'This was four or five years after the trial: Scottish chap, name of McHugh, a banker in Edinburgh. They've got a couple of children. The doctors didn't give her a prayer, just after it happened. They didn't think she'd survive, let alone give evidence in court. They didn't think she'd ever have children. But she did: she proved them all wrong.'

'I'm very glad to hear that,' Davis said.

They rode in silence for some time.

'They hanged Cottage for it... for Frank's murder.'

'They did.'

'...and if you ask me, sir – I mean, no offence, I know he was your client, and everything – but in my opinion, it was no more than he deserved. I know you're not supposed to say things like that anymore, but...'

'You can say whatever you want to me,' Davis replied.

'I'd only just been promoted to DI two or three weeks before we caught that case, and I was assigned to work with Tom Arnold – Detective Superintendent Arnold. Talk about being nervous. I felt completely out of my depth. Tom was a legend in the force, a real copper's copper, and there I was, doing a capital case with him. But he was brilliant, took total command of the case, told me exactly what he needed from me, put me completely at ease. I learned more from Tom in that one case than from anyone else in the whole of my career. He retired a couple of years after they hanged Cottage, and he was dead himself less than two years after that.' He smiled again. 'He probably died of boredom. He lived for the job.'

'I remember him well,' Davis replied.

'Of course, I've seen a lot of Mr Schroeder just recently, with the Lancelot Andrewes School case. You know all about that, sir, I'm sure. That priest, Father Gerrard, who'd been allowing his friends into the school to molest little girls for years – well, actually, for generations; our complainants were mother and daughter, and it had happened to both of them. He killed himself in the end, overdose of cyanide. There's another one for you. Good riddance to him, too.'

Davis nodded. 'I wasn't involved in that one. But I heard all about it from Ben. It was the first and only time he's been on the prosecution side.' He smiled. 'I'm not sure how much he enjoyed that experience.'

'Well, he did a fine job with it, sir,' Phillips replied at once, 'I'll tell you that. Of course, what we didn't realise was how deep the corruption went, how many very powerful people were involved, and how far they were prepared to go to cover it up.'

'But you put a stop to it, didn't you?' Davis replied. 'There have been several successful prosecutions.'

Phillips nodded. 'There are more to come, too. Of course, that's because we found out it had been going on in other schools Gerrard had been associated with. God only knows when it will end. It just seems to go on and on, doesn't it? I mean criminals, people like Cottage and Gerrard. I'm sure it's the same in your line of work, sir. You can never quite get them out of your head, can you?'

'No, you can't,' Davis replied. He paused. 'Can I ask you something, off the record?'

Phillips nodded. 'Yes, sir.'

'Do you think the people we've got now are criminals?'

'What, Danie and Amy?'

'Yes.'

'Off the record, sir?'

'Off the record.'

'No, I don't. I think Danie was bloody stupid to get involved with Pienaar in the first place. But I understand why he did it, and it's not an offence to be bloody stupid, is it?' He grinned. 'Just as well, too, if you ask me. I daresay we'd all have a bit of form if it was, sir, wouldn't we?'

Davis laughed. 'I daresay we would. When you say, you understand why he did it…?'

'I suppose I've had to think about things more since Connie – DC Whittaker – was assigned to me. I've had to see things more through someone else's eyes. They want me to be her Tom Arnold, you know, mentor her, and I'm more than happy to do it. But I see what she goes through, just because she's not white – actually, because she's not a white male, if you want the truth. It's shaken me up, sir, I don't mind telling you. I'd always assumed that we were basically fair to everybody in this country – that we at least respected people, regardless of the colour of their skin. But it's not true. I've seen the abuse and the snide comments she gets from officers who don't have a fraction of her talents. I've seen the efforts they make to sabotage her.'

'I'm sorry to hear that,' Davis replied quietly.

'I've seen it all through her eyes; and once you see things that way, through the eyes of the person being mistreated, you never see things the same way again. Obviously, this isn't South Africa…'

'No,' Davis replied quietly. 'We're a bit more subtle about it here, aren't we?'

'She's a bloody good copper,' Phillips said, 'probably the best I've seen coming up through the ranks in my time in the job. She's bright, she works hard, and she just has this feel for cases. It's hard to describe: she just has an instinct for them, and that's something you can't teach. If Connie was a white male, she'd be heading for the very top – Chief Constable material, I'd say, definitely Detective Chief Superintendent. I hope she makes it. Actually, I just hope she stays in the job long enough to give herself the chance. I'm not sure I would in her shoes.'

'So the two of you have some sympathy with Danie and Amy?'

He nodded. 'Connie did from day one, of course. These people have been through far worse than she has, haven't they? Living with apartheid; having to leave their country, just so they could be together. She saw how they felt immediately, and when I started to see it through her eyes, so did I. I mean, it's just not right, is it? If you'd been treated like that, why wouldn't you do whatever you could to change things in South Africa, if you got the chance – especially if all you had to do was move some money around?' He paused. 'But not everyone thinks that way. Did you know John Caswell wanted to charge Amy with murder?'

Davis turned to look at him. 'What? Over Nick Erasmus?'

'Yes, sir. Connie Whittaker talked him out of it – with some help from Andrew Pilkington and myself, admittedly; but she didn't pull any punches with Caswell, which is a pretty gutsy thing to do if you're a lowly DC.'

Davis exhaled audibly. 'Strewth.' He was silent for some time. 'Why is John Carswell pushing this so hard, do you think?'

'He's worried about it becoming a political issue. Well, I suppose it's his job to worry about things like that. He has people in that world above him to report to. But even so, I'm surprised he's been taking such a hard line.'

'Is there any chance we could talk him out of it, do you think?'

Phillips shook his head. 'I doubt it. The person you would need to convince is Andrew Pilkington. Caswell has a lot of respect for Andrew. If Andrew gave Danie the all-clear, my feeling is it would stop there. But when I last saw him, Andrew thought there was a case for Danie to answer. It's possible he might be persuaded otherwise. If you ask me, sir, the man to do that, if anyone can, would be Ben Schroeder.'

Davis smiled. 'Just what I was thinking,' he replied.

They were pulling up in front of the station. The car stopped, and they shook hands.

'Thanks for the lift,' Davis said.

'My pleasure, sir. And we have been…?'

'Off the record. Completely.'

'Thank you, sir. Please give my best to Mr Schroeder, won't you? Tell him I'm looking forward to seeing him again.'

Davis smiled. 'I will.'

41

Monday 25 October 1976

'If everyone's ready to go,' Ted Phillips began, 'why don't we make a start?'

There were nods around the table.

'Thank you. I'm DI Ted Phillips of the Cambridge Police. The time is now ten o'clock on the morning of Monday 25 October. With the kind permission of the Metropolitan Police, we're in an interview room at West End Central police station, for the purpose of continuing the interview of Professor Danie du Plessis, which began at Parkside Police Station in Cambridge a week ago, but had to be adjourned. Also present are DC Connie Whittaker of the Cambridge Police, and DI Steffie Walsh of the Met, who is our host here at West End Central.'

'I'm also available to coordinate any other assistance the Met can give in this investigation,' Steffie added.

'Yes. Thank you, DI Walsh. Professor du Plessis is present, with his solicitor, Mr Barratt Davis. Professor du Plessis, at the present time, you are living temporarily in London with your family, are you not? Can you confirm that you have had time to settle in, and that you are happy to have the interview proceed this morning?'

'Yes, thank you, Inspector. I'd like to go ahead and get this done.'

'We appreciate the time you've given us, Inspector,' Barratt Davis added.

'As before,' Phillips said, 'it is my duty to caution you that you are not obliged to say anything unless you wish to do so, but anything you say may be put into writing and given in evidence. Do you understand the caution?'

'Yes, I do.'

'When we spoke in Cambridge last week, Professor,' Phillips continued, 'you told us about the first time you met Art Pienaar, back in 1968: is that right?'

'Yes.'

'As a result of which, Mr Pienaar recruited you to assist in transmitting funds to anti-apartheid activists in South Africa, using the *Hawala* system of transfer of credit?'

'Yes.'

'And you indicated that the *Hawala* practitioner you used was a Mr Balakrishnan, who has an office in Whitechapel, in East London?'

'On Pienaar's instructions, yes. I didn't know Balakrishnan before then. Actually, I wasn't familiar with *Hawala* at all before that time.'

'And if I understood you correctly, the way it worked was: every so often, Pienaar would arrange for the funds to be delivered to you, some in cash, some in cheques and money orders?'

'Yes: not very often, three or four times a year.'

'You would deposit the cheques and money orders into bank accounts controlled by Mr Balakrishnan at banks in London and Edinburgh, and you would take the proof of the deposits to him at his office?'

'Yes.'

'Together with the cash?'

'Yes. He would do the rest.'

'Yes. And you understood that the funds you were entrusting to Mr Balakrishnan were provided by certain donors, wealthy expatriate South Africans known to Mr Pienaar, who, for obvious reasons, preferred to remain anonymous?'

'Yes. As I said before, Pienaar was obsessive about protecting the anonymity of everyone he worked with, myself included.'

'But you knew who they were?'

'In the case of the cheques and money orders, yes, because I needed to have the paperwork for the banks. But I didn't always know where the cash donations came from. With Pienaar, everything was on a strictly need-to-know basis.'

Phillips stretched out a hand to Connie Whittaker, who handed him a blue file folder. Phillips passed it on to Danie.

'Professor, I'm handing you a copy of what we've been calling the ledger, a document DC Whittaker and I found when we searched Mr Pienaar's flat in London after his death. I sent a copy to Mr Davis some time ago.'

'That's correct,' Davis confirmed.

'Have you had a chance to look at it with Mr Davis?'

'Yes, I have.'

'And are you happy for me to ask you some questions about it?'

'Yes.'

'Thank you, Professor. First of all, I realise that this isn't your document. You didn't write it. Had you ever seen it before Mr Davis showed it to you?'

'No. I had no idea it existed. I assume Pienaar would have kept records of some kind, but he never showed me any of them.'

'But would you agree with me that the ledger appears to be a record of amounts of money supplied by various donors, during the period of time after you took responsibility for taking the donations to Mr Balakrishnan?'

'Yes.'

'It records the donations received by reference to dates approximately three months apart, which corresponds with the intervals at which Mr Pienaar sent the donations to you to start the *Hawala* process: would you agree?'

'Yes.'

'And the donors are referred to merely by initials – their names are not given: is that right?'

'Yes.'

'One of the most consistent donors – by which I mean, one who apparently made a contribution almost every time – is someone referred to by the initials VC: yes?'

'Yes.'

'Do you know the identity of this donor?'

'I believe this donor was Vincent Cummings. It's not a name I associate with the cheques or money orders, so this is someone who donated in cash.'

'Yes. And in fact, the ledger itself seems to confirm that, doesn't it, because there are what appear to be bank account numbers, cheque numbers, and other details for certain donors, where applicable, but there are no such details provided for VC?'

'That's correct, yes.'

'Did you ever meet Vincent Cummings?'

'No. Never.'

'Professor du Plessis, you're aware, are you not, that in the early morning of Friday 8 October, just over two weeks ago, Mr Pienaar and Mr Cummings were murdered, found dead together in a room at the University Arms Hotel in Cambridge?'

'I'm very much aware of that.'

'Are you also aware that the evidence suggests that the killer was a man using the name of Nick Erasmus, who at the time had been accepted by the University as a PhD student, and assigned to you as his supervisor in your capacity as a professor?'

'Erasmus admitted…'

Barratt Davis held up a hand.

'Just a moment, Danie. Before Professor du Plessis answers that, Inspector, there are one or two things I would like to say, just to ensure they are on the record.'

'By all means, Mr Davis,' Phillips replied. 'Be my guest.'

42

'First,' Barratt Davis said, 'my understanding is that the man calling himself Nick Erasmus was an agent of the South African Bureau for State Security, known as BOSS, and that he was in this country in that capacity, and not as a *bona fide* graduate student. If that's also the prosecution's understanding, may it please be reflected in the record of the interview?'

Phillips thought for some time. 'The only reason I'm hesitating, Mr Davis, is that, while we have received certain information from the Home Office about Nick Erasmus, it's not something we're in a position to verify ourselves. The information would have come from the security services. So you'd have to ask the Home Office for any official confirmation.'

'My only concern is this,' Davis replied. 'I don't want to hear it suggested that Professor du Plessis knew about Erasmus's involvement with BOSS before it became clear to him in the light of the murders; or that he was involved in having Erasmus accepted as a student, or given a place at Jesus College.'

'No one is going to hear anything like that from us, sir,' Phillips replied.

'Trust me, sir,' Connie said, with a smile, 'no one suspects Professor du Plessis of working for BOSS.' Danie returned the smile.

Davis nodded. 'All right. Then, there's the death of Nick Erasmus. My understanding is that he showed up unexpectedly at the du Plessis home on the Monday after the murders, armed with the same weapon he used to kill Pienaar and Cummings, and threatened to kill the entire du Plessis family. It was in response to that threat that Miss Coetzee used force against Erasmus, not intending to kill him, but having that effect. Is there any issue about any of that?'

Phillips shook his head. 'DC Whittaker and I arrived at the scene very shortly after Mr Erasmus died,' he replied. 'Miss Coetzee immediately described the events to us in exactly those terms, and what she said was consistent with the evidence. I believe the Director of Public Prosecutions has decided not to bring any charges arising from the death of Mr Erasmus, and as the officer in charge of the investigation, I will add that I agree completely with that decision.'

'As do I, sir,' Connie added.

'Thank you,' Davis said.

'Now that we've clarified those points, Professor,' Phillips continued, 'let me ask you this. Did you know that Mr Pienaar and Mr Cummings were going to be in Cambridge on the day they were murdered?'

'I didn't know about Cummings,' Danie replied. 'I never met Cummings, and I never had any communication with him of any kind. Pienaar did call me a few days before the murders, to let me know that he was going to be in Cambridge, but he wasn't specific about exactly when.'

'Did he say he wanted to see you?' Phillips asked.

'He said he would call when he arrived, from which I assumed that he did intend to see me while he was in Cambridge. But I never heard from him again.'

'Mr Pienaar didn't tell you that he would be with Mr Cummings?'

'No. He did not.'

'If I may, sir,' Connie said, 'did he tell you that he would be staying at the University Arms?'

'No,' Danie replied, 'and if he had, I would have thought he was having me on.'

'Why do you say that?'

'Pienaar staying at the UA?' Danie said with a smile. 'No chance – far too public. Pienaar liked to be invisible. He wouldn't have been seen dead in the… Oh, God, I'm sorry, I didn't mean that.'

Connie and Steffie Walsh laughed out loud.

'All I meant was that the UA wouldn't have been his thing at all – it would have been the last place he would stay.'

'I understand,' Connie said. 'All I wanted to confirm was that there was no question of your meeting Pienaar at the UA.'

'There was no question of my meeting Pienaar anywhere,' Danie replied. 'As I said before, he never called me back.'

'If I could ask you to turn to page 32 of the ledger, Professor,' Phillips said, 'do you see there an entry for a donation by VC in the month of May of last year, 1975?'

'Yes. I do.'

'What, if anything, catches your attention about that donation?'

'The amount being paid,' Danie replied, without hesitation.

'What about the amount?'

'It's obviously far more than any of his payments before that time.'

'It runs to six figures, doesn't it, as opposed to the £2,000, £3,000 he had been giving before May 1975?'

'Yes.'

'And then his donations continue at the same higher level until shortly before his death, don't they?'

'His payments continue: yes.'

'Did that get your attention at the time?'

'Of course.'

'Did it come as a surprise? Did you call Mr Pienaar's office, using your alias of Mr Stevens, and ask him what on earth was going on with VC?'

'No.'

'Why not? Weren't you curious? After all, Professor, you were concerned about the legality of what you were doing, weren't you? As a lawyer, didn't it raise any red flags for you that this donor could suddenly afford to give Pienaar more than £100,000 every three months?'

'It didn't concern me: no.'

'It never once occurred to you that there might be some criminality involved in such large donations?'

'I wasn't concerned by the large payments, Inspector,' Danie replied, 'because I was expecting them.'

Connie's eyes opened wide. 'You were expecting them?'

'Pienaar had warned me to expect an increase of that order, and he had explained exactly why. I had no reason to doubt what he told me, and so I had no reason to be concerned.'

'Wait a minute,' Connie said. 'I've just noticed something, Professor. We've been talking about a large increase in his donations. But you've been talking about a large increase in his *payments*. Is that a distinction in your mind?'

'Yes, of course.'

'The donation isn't the whole £100,000, just part of it? Is that what you're saying?'

Danie smiled broadly. 'Well done, DC Whittaker,' he replied. 'You've got the point.'

'Well, I haven't,' Phillips said. 'Why don't you explain it to me?'

'May I, sir?' Connie asked.

Phillips sat back in his chair. 'Please,' he said. Steffie Walsh gave him a consoling smile.

43

'I told you before, Inspector,' Danie said. 'I only met Pienaar twice. The first time was the occasion we've already discussed, in 1968. The second time was in March of last year, 1975.'

'About two months before the Cummings payments started to hit six figures,' Connie observed.

'Exactly. Pienaar turned up in my rooms again, out of the blue, just as he had before.' He laughed. 'As a matter of fact, he picked my lock again, and he'd been checking for bugs while I was out.'

'What did he want with you this time?' she asked.

'It took him a long time to get to the point,' Danie replied. 'He seemed preoccupied, unusually nervous even by his standards. First, we had to walk to Great St Mary's church, and sit on the balcony there for a while. Then, we had to leave the church and walk around the market place, and then along King's Parade to the Fitzwilliam – and it was bloody cold, I don't mind telling you. We froze half to death – or at least I did: Pienaar never seemed to care about the weather.'

'What did he want?' she repeated.

'He started by telling me how his campaign had evolved over the years I'd been working with him. They weren't doing the propaganda – the leaflets, and so on – anymore. They weren't sending English students over to South Africa just to make trouble. They'd moved up in the world. They were playing in the big leagues – or at least, that was the ambition.'

'What did he mean by that?' Connie asked.

'That's my way of putting it, not his. What Pienaar told me was that the propaganda had outlived its usefulness – it wasn't effective anymore, because there was no real threat attached to it. So now it was time for something more direct. They were supporting ANC – African National Congress – groups outside South Africa, in Angola and Tanzania and elsewhere. These groups were setting up training camps; and making guerrilla-style military incursions into South Africa, hitting police stations and military bases. Essentially, they had declared war on the apartheid government.'

'Which required more money?' Connie asked, after some time.

'A lot more money.'

'Did Pienaar tell you where the extra money was going to come from?'

'It wasn't all coming from the Cambridge network, of course. By that time, there were many more donors than when I started, many more networks. Cambridge was only one.'

'But some of it had to come from Cambridge?'

'Yes.'

'And…?'

Danie took a deep breath. 'Pienaar told me he had reached an agreement with Cummings. The deal was that Pienaar would include all Cummings's earnings, in this country and in Europe, in the funds delivered to Balakrishnan, in return for a fee of ten per cent.'

'That would be ten per cent of his gross earnings?'

'I didn't say that. Pienaar didn't tell me whether this was before or after tax – if he knew himself, which I doubt.'

Connie looked at Phillips questioningly, raising her eyebrows. He nodded decisively.

'Professor,' she said, 'at this time, I'm going to remind you again of the caution. You are not obliged to say anything unless you wish to do so, but anything you say may be put into writing and given in evidence. Again, do you understand the caution?'

'Yes, I still understand it.'

'Referring to the May 1975 payment, did you take the entire one hundred per cent of Cummings's earnings to Balakrishnan, or just Pienaar's ten per cent?'

'All of it.'

'Where was the ninety per cent left after Pienaar's fee going?'

'Wherever Cummings wanted it to go. I have no idea. As long as our ten per cent ended up with the right people in South Africa, Pienaar wouldn't ask where the rest was going. It was none of his business.'

'Professor du Plessis,' Phillips said, 'what line of business was Vince Cummings in?'

'I don't know. As I said before, I never met the man, and I never had any communication with him.'

'Well, even so, surely it must have been obvious to you that some form of money laundering was taking place? Either Cummings was trying to evade tax, or he was washing his earnings from an illegal trade to make them look legitimate. Something was going on, wasn't it? What inquiries did you make to satisfy yourself that you weren't participating in a criminal enterprise?'

'I went to the only source I had: I asked Pienaar. Well, what else could I do? I could hardly go to the police, could I?'

'You could have told Pienaar you didn't want to be involved,' Connie suggested quietly.

Danie made no reply.

'We'll come back to that,' Phillips said. 'You say you asked Pienaar about Cummings. Was this during your meeting in March?'

'Yes.'

'And what did he tell you?'

'Pienaar told me that he'd only recently found out where Cummings's money was coming from, and it was purely by chance that he found out then. He was an arms dealer.'

'An arms dealer?'

'Yes.'

'And what chance was it that enabled Pienaar to make that discovery?'

'It turned out that Cummings was supplying arms to an ANC group that Pienaar was backing in Tanzania. He'd turned up in their training camp with a consignment of weapons. So, in a sense,

Pienaar had become one of Cummings's customers.'

'And you believed what Pienaar told you, did you?'

'I did, actually, yes. As I've said before, Pienaar was an obsessively cautious man. He would never have asked Cummings where his money was coming from. He wouldn't ask any of his donors where their money was coming from. He respected the privacy of everyone he dealt with.'

'Or perhaps he just didn't want to know,' Connie suggested.

'Maybe so. All I know is that Pienaar didn't ask questions like that – not just about money, about anything. With Pienaar, everything was on a need-to-know basis, and he applied the same rule to himself. He didn't want to know anything he didn't need to know.'

'Was Cummings also a drug dealer?' Phillips asked.

44

'I ask,' Phillips continued, 'because he has one or two drug-related matters on his criminal record – nothing too serious, I grant you, and all fairly old stuff. '

'Do you have a spare copy of the antecedents?' Barratt Davis asked.

'You can have this copy,' Phillips replied, sliding it along the table. 'In addition, there is the record of an investigation by the Met's Serious Crimes Squad over a number of years, which suggests that Cummings and his associates built up a considerable trade in hard drugs, both here and on the Continent. These materials suggest that Cummings would have had the kind of income needed to make the payments he did to Pienaar and Balakrishnan.'

'May I see what you've got?' Davis asked.

Phillips exchanged glances with Steffie Walsh. 'If Professor du Plessis is charged with an offence, we will give you whatever we can,' Steffie replied. 'I'm sure you understand Treasury Counsel will have to go over it first, just to make sure it's material we can release.'

'Excuse me?'

'To make sure it doesn't reveal the identities of other suspects, or undercover officers, or give away any investigative techniques. We'll give you everything we can on Cummings, which is quite a lot.'

'I take it you're not suggesting that Professor du Plessis could have had access to any of these records, or could have known what was in them?' Barratt Davis asked.

'No,' Phillips replied, 'but, Professor, let me ask you this: were you really unaware that Vincent Cummings was a drug dealer? Did that possibility never occur to you?'

Davis shook his head. 'I'm sorry, Inspector, but I'm going to advise Professor du Plessis not to answer the question in that form. What basis did he have for believing that Cummings was a drug dealer? It would have been sheer speculation on his part.'

Danie reached out a hand and touched Barratt Davis's arm.

'I want to be completely honest with you, Inspector. The only time the subject ever came up was during my meeting with Pienaar in March. After he'd told me about finding out that Cummings was an arms dealer, he did add that he might be involved with dealing drugs as well.'

'Did he?' Phillips asked. 'What did he say, exactly?'

'He told me that arms dealers often took drugs into the camps, because there was a market for them, and they wanted to take advantage of that market. But that was it. He didn't have any information that Cummings was dealing drugs, and he didn't accuse him of dealing drugs. I wasn't about to jump to any conclusions based on that.'

'So, you had a man who wanted to launder six-figure sums every three or four months, but it never occurred to you that he might be selling drugs?'

'No. Look, all the donors were wealthy men – that's obvious. You can't become a donor in this league unless you've got a lot of money. Cummings was no different from the others.'

'Except that he was prepared to pay Pienaar ten per cent of his income to have it securely laundered on a regular basis,' Connie pointed out. 'You didn't think that was suspicious?'

Danie raised his arms. 'Yes, I guess so. But I had no proof. What was I supposed to do?'

'Well, to return to DC Whittaker's earlier suggestion,' Phillips said, 'you could have walked away, couldn't you – told Pienaar you didn't want to have anything more to do with it?'

'Yes, I could have walked away.'

'Then why…?'

Danie suddenly pushed himself up on to his feet. 'Because South Africa has to change, and the only way it's ever going to change is if we make it change; which means that it has to be done by force; and force takes money. If people like Pienaar don't raise money, the struggle doesn't even get off the ground, and if I refuse to help because I'm squeamish about whether every last rand is clean and pure, then the failure of the struggle becomes my responsibility. There are times when you can't just walk away.'

'In your mind, would the struggle justify you in breaking the law here?' Connie asked after a long silence. 'Here, not in South Africa?'

'Don't answer that,' Barratt Davis advised.

'No. I want to answer,' Danie replied. 'How have I broken the law? What offence have I committed? What happened to the idea of *mens rea* – proof of the guilty mind? Is it enough now that you think someone you deal with may be acting suspiciously? Is that all it takes now to commit an offence?'

'No one's suggesting that,' Phillips replied.

Danie shook his head and sat back down. He was silent for some time.

'I confronted Pienaar directly,' he said, eventually. 'I asked him whether he was inviting me to become an outlaw.'

'Did he reply to that?'

'He said that sometimes there was no alternative.'

'What did you think he meant by that?'

'He meant that the work we were doing was too important to jeopardise just because he had suspicions about a donor.'

'Do you feel you've become an outlaw?' Connie asked.

'Again,' Barratt said, 'I advise you…'

'I had no knowledge that there was anything illegal about Vincent Cummings,' Danie replied.

When Danie and Barratt Davis had gone, they sat silently at the table for some time.

'Do we buy that?' Ted Phillips asked.

'The intelligence on Cummings confirms that he was expanding his operation into the arms trade,' Steffie said. 'So I'm prepared to believe that Pienaar told du Plessis about the arms he was supplying in Tanzania.'

'Is that enough?' Connie asked.

'The arms trade is a murky business at the level of training camps in Africa,' Steffie replied. 'I'm sure Cummings wasn't too meticulous about all the regulatory requirements. But that's all rather technical stuff. The question is whether it's enough to put Pienaar, or du Plessis, on notice that they were dealing with something illegal.'

'So, if there were drugs involved, that would make all the difference,' Connie replied.

'Yes. I can't see Cummings passing up the opportunity to sell some drugs in the camps, if it came his way. All the intel on Pienaar suggests that he was very well informed. If Cummings was dealing drugs in the training camps, I'd be very surprised if Pienaar didn't know about it.'

'On the other hand, if Pienaar knowingly accepted drug money, he'd be taking one hell of a risk, wouldn't he?' Connie said. 'He'd be giving the authorities here every excuse for closing his network down. Even if they'd turned a blind eye before, they could hardly ignore drug money, could they? Why risk everything he'd built up over all that time?'

'Because Cummings was offering a lot of money,' Phillips replied, 'and he needed a lot of money to fight his war against apartheid. Everyone has his price.'

'If Pienaar knew,' Steffie said, 'my money says du Plessis knew. He's not a stupid man, is he? He is a law professor, for God's sake. There's only so far he can turn a blind eye and ask us to believe him.'

'He knew,' Connie replied. 'The question is whether we can prove it – or whether we want to prove it.'

'Well,' Phillips said, 'let's focus on whether we can. What do we think? Let's have a show of hands.'

'Yes,' Steffie replied. 'It's not a sure thing, but we have enough to justify going ahead.'

'I'm not sure,' Connie said. 'We have no connection between du Plessis and Cummings, other than the money. There's no direct evidence that he knew Cummings was a drug dealer, and I don't think the arms dealing is enough without the drugs.'

Phillips nodded. 'It's a close call, but I have to go with Steffie. I think a jury could convict – not that they would, necessarily – but they could.'

'But do we really want to go after this man, sir?' Connie asked. 'Can't we take into account who he is, and why he was doing this?'

'Personally, Connie,' Phillips replied, after a silence, 'I agree with you. I don't want to go after du Plessis. But it's not up to us, is it? Ultimately, it's up to John Caswell. I don't see why we shouldn't tell him what we think. But at the end of the day, it's his decision.'

Connie nodded, and stood. 'I'll get them started on transcribing my note of the interview.' She walked to the door, but then turned back, smiling. 'By the way, sir, nice move, having Stef – DI Walsh – come in to coordinate the Met's involvement with the case.'

'My co-opting of DI Walsh was based on purely professional considerations, DC Whittaker,' he replied, 'and I'll thank you to remember that you're addressing two senior officers.' But he failed miserably in his efforts to suppress a smile.

'Of course it was, sir,' she replied. 'What did you think I meant?'

Steffie laughed, rolled a piece of notepaper into a ball, and tossed it towards Connie's head just as she disappeared through the door.

45

Amy had cleared away the remains of dinner, and they were sitting together with a glass of wine. But they were finding relaxation hard to come by. Not for the first time, there was a plaintive call of 'Mummy' from upstairs.

'Why don't I go this time?' Danie volunteered.

She smiled. 'A change of personnel may just do the trick,' she agreed. 'They haven't settled yet. Dougie is still young enough to tune things out; I think he's drifted off to sleep now. But Sally's very sensitive to her surroundings, and this is all very disturbing for her.'

'It's hardly surprising, is it?' he said, pushing himself up on to his feet. 'Suddenly, they're in a totally new environment, and we couldn't even give them any advance warning. They're not going to school, or seeing their friends any more. And I'm sure they must be picking up the anxiety we're feeling.'

'Sally's old enough to know that there's something wrong,' Amy said. 'She can put that much into words, but she doesn't know why. She knows the family is in trouble for some reason, and the fact that she can't articulate why must be making it worse for her. But I can't find the words yet to help her take it on board.'

'Children have a radar for bad news,' Danie said.

He left the living room quietly and made his way upstairs. He understood the children's discomfiture all too well. Even he felt uncomfortable and disorientated in the College's palatial pile; it seemed vast, cold and impersonal; it must have made the same impression on Sally and Douglas, but magnified many times when seen through their young eyes. There were four bedrooms on the first floor alone, and they were using only three of them. There were also two full bathrooms. On the floor above, there were a further three bedrooms, and another bathroom; and above the second floor were the attic rooms, with their creaking floorboards and crooked ceilings, small cells where the College benefactor's servants would have lived in times long gone. He looked in on Douglas, who was sleeping soundly, holding his teddy bear firmly to his side. Danie gently pulled his blanket up a little higher and left, leaving the bedside lamp on. In the next room, Sally was sitting up in bed. She seemed wide-awake, but her eyes betrayed her fatigue.

'*Wat is daar aan die gang, liefling? Het iets jou geskrik*?'

What's the matter, sweetheart? Did something frighten you?

She yawned, reaching out her arms to hug him. He held her close.

'Can we speak Mummy's language, Daddy – sorry, I mean English – can we speak English? I'm tired.'

'We can speak any language you like, sweetheart,' he replied, smiling, 'except French. You're far better at French then I am. I couldn't keep up with you.'

She laughed, but then went quiet. 'Daddy, I don't like it here. How long do we have to stay? When can we go home?'

He sat down on the bed, still holding her in his arms.

'I'm sure it won't be long.'

'That's what Mummy said yesterday.'

'Sally, all that's happened is that some very silly people are angry with Daddy. We're not even sure why. But you remember those nice policemen: they thought it would be better for us to come to London for a few days until it's all sorted out. Everything's fine at home, and we'll be back there very soon, I promise you. But isn't it interesting to see this old house? Do you know, it's over a hundred years old? Isn't it fun to explore a big old house like this?'

'I keep hearing noises,' Sally said, 'from upstairs. What if there's somebody, or something, up there?'

He kissed her on the forehead. 'There's no one up there, Sally. I've been up there myself. I've walked through all the rooms. I would have seen if there was anything there. All old houses have noises. It's just the way they were built, and the fact that they've been in the same place for so many years. Mummy and I hear the noises too. It's nothing to worry about. You know, Grandpa John wouldn't have let us stay here if there was anything to worry about.'

'Promise?'

'Promise.'

'Are Grandpa John and Grandma Annabel going to come to see us?'

'Yes, I'm sure they will. Now, you don't want to be tired in the morning, do you? Why don't you see if you can go to sleep?'

'I can't go to sleep.'

'I bet you can, if you try. Where's Sally bear?'

'I don't know. She's here somewhere. Under the blanket, I think, but I lost her.'

'I'll find her,' he said.

Danie retrieved Sally bear from the floor at the side of the bed. 'Here she is. Now, lie back down, and I'll pull the blanket back up for you.'

Reluctantly, Sally allowed him to lower her back down on to the bed. As he released his hold on her, her eyes finally closed, tentatively at first, then more confidently. He kissed her on the cheek. Leaving her lamp on, he left the room quietly, and made his way back downstairs.

'I think she'll sleep now,' he said. 'Oh, God, Amy, I'm sorry all this is happening. Sometimes I wish I'd never met Art Pienaar.'

'It doesn't work that way, Danie,' she replied. 'If it hadn't been Art Pienaar, it would have been someone else.' She turned to look at him directly. 'Danie, I'm not sorry about anything that's happened, except for the police taking such an interest in you. It's all such nonsense. I can't believe the DPP is even thinking about charging you with anything. How could you possibly have known about Cummings being a drug dealer?'

'It's new legal doctrine,' he said, 'the late twentieth-century version of the doctrine of *mens rea*. We are all deemed to have known anything that seems obvious to a police officer.' He reached out his arms and pulled her gently in to his shoulder. 'Don't worry about it, Amy. The DPP has access to very good legal advice. They probably won't even charge me, and even if they do, it won't stand up in court.'

'I hope you're right,' she replied.

'So, you're not embarrassed about being married to an outlaw?' he asked.

'Is that what you are?' she asked.

'Perhaps that's what I've become.'

'Well, if you have, I love you for being an outlaw, Danie du Plessis,' she replied, 'and I am very proud of you.'

He was about to reply, when there was a sequence of four slow, loud raps on the door.

'Our protectors,' he said, springing to his feet. 'I'll get it.'

'Evening, sir. You have two visitors,' the sergeant said. 'They say they're well known to you, but we have checked their IDs and checked them for weapons, just in case. Do you know them? Can they come in?'

'Yes, of course,' Danie replied. 'Thank you, Sergeant.' He ushered them in, shutting and bolting the door behind them. 'Harriet. John: what on earth brings you down to London so late?'

'I have some news to pass on,' Sir John Fisk replied, 'well, two pieces of news, actually; and I thought it might be as well to have Harriet here, in case we need her advice. Fortunately, she wasn't out to dinner, or otherwise gallivanting, this evening.'

Harriet smiled. 'Nothing so agreeable, I'm afraid: I was in chambers, working on a brief in the High Court tomorrow morning.'

Amy came over and hugged them both. 'It's good to see you. Let me take your coats.'

'Come and sit down,' Danie said. 'What about a glass of Chenin Blanc? We happen to have a bottle open.'

'Excellent idea,' John Fisk replied. 'South African, I hope?'

'Of course.'

'Not for me, thanks, Danie,' Harriet replied. 'Water would be great.'

'I had a call this morning from a friend of yours,' John Fisk said, once he was settled with his glass of Chenin Blanc. 'He gave me the name Pieter – sorry to put it like that, but with so much cloak and dagger stuff going on at the moment, you never know, do you? I didn't recognise the voice, of course, but wasn't he the chap who helped the two of you to escape from South Africa?'

'Yes, he was.'

'You were friends at university in Johannesburg; he runs one of the biggest engineering companies over there, family firm.'

'That's him. Did he say why he was calling you?'

'He'd tried to call you at home, but of course, he couldn't get a reply. He wondered if I could put you in touch. He knows about your current difficulties, Danie – apparently, there have been some reports in the press.'

'In the papers?' Amy asked. 'In South Africa?'

'Apparently. He said the papers are painting it in a rather different light there – the story is all about the death of that Erasmus fellow, nothing about the supposed network, or Pienaar. Just two exiles getting into a stupid fight that turned fatal, probably after having too much to drink. That refers to you and Erasmus, of course – no mention of Amy.'

'So, that's the government's spin on it?' Amy said. 'Danie, you need to call your parents, tell them what really happened.'

Danie nodded. 'Did Pieter say anything else?'

'Yes, he said he was going to fly over to see you, as soon as he can come up with a good excuse for coming to London. He also said that, if you are charged, he wants to pay for your legal expenses. I tried to explain to him about legal aid, but he didn't seem to have much faith in it. He would like to take care of it himself.'

Danie smiled. 'That's typically generous of Pieter,' he said. 'I couldn't accept, of course, but it's typical of him.'

'This is the number he gave me,' Fisk said, handing Danie a hand-written note. He paused. 'I'm afraid my second piece of news is less welcome.'

46

'I had a call from the Vice-Chancellor's office this morning,' John Fisk said, hesitantly. 'They want you to step down from the Buckland Chair until the "various outstanding matters have been resolved", as they put it.'

Amy sprang angrily to her feet. 'What? What the hell are they talking about? What "outstanding matters"?'

'They mean, until the DPP decides whether or not to charge me,' Danie replied, 'and if he does charge me, until the case is resolved one way or the other.'

'Exactly so,' John Fisk confirmed.

'These people are beyond belief,' Amy protested. 'Haven't they heard of the presumption of innocence?'

'In a case like this,' Harriet said, 'the institution typically argues that, regardless of whether there's a conviction, the mere fact of being charged, or perhaps even being the subject of an investigation, would tend to bring the institution into disrepute. Those are the magic words: "bring the University into disrepute".'

'What a load of… I can't believe I'm hearing this,' Amy said.

'I've been half expecting it,' Danie admitted. 'It's the usual knee-jerk reaction, isn't it – protect the institution at all costs?'

'Well, Danie's not going to play along with it,' Amy insisted. 'Why the hell should he?'

'That's what you have to decide,' Fisk replied, 'and that's why I thought it might be a good idea to have Harriet with us. She's had some experience with the law in this area.'

'I've done cases involving the managing director of a charity, and the manager of a football club,' Harriet replied. 'In both cases, we had an issue about whether the person accused should be forced to stand down pending whatever inquiry was going on.'

'But surely, you don't think Danie should stand down… do you, Harriet?' Amy asked.

'No – certainly not at this stage. They can't legitimately argue that the University is being brought into disrepute just because the police are making inquiries. There's no basis for asking Danie to stand down, unless and until the DPP decides to charge him.'

'What if he does charge me?' Danie asked.

'Then I would recommend that we have a conference with Ben, to get a feel for how he sees the criminal proceedings. At this point, we don't even know what offences they might charge you with, much less what evidence they think they have. We need Ben to give us a feel for all that, and then, based on his assessment, we can talk to the Vice-Chancellor's office about how we handle it.'

'Talk to them?' Amy asked. 'You're suggesting that we play ball with them?'

'I'm suggesting that we might want to be seen to be working with them, rather than having them chasing us. It all depends on the circumstances – there's standing down, and then, there's standing down. There are cases where standing down is an admission of defeat – where the person concerned expects to be convicted, and everyone knows it's all over bar the shouting. So for that person, in effect, "standing down" means resigning. That's not our case. We have every expectation that Danie will be vindicated, so, for Danie, "standing down" means something very different. It means stepping aside on a temporary basis. We might invite the Vice-Chancellor's office to issue a joint press release with us. Both sides agree on the best way forward. Danie agrees voluntarily to step down, in his best interests and the University's, until he is exonerated. Once he is exonerated, he will be reinstated immediately. There's all the difference in the world.'

Danie shook his head. 'Harriet, you're obviously already thinking of me as a client, which is very kind. But I can't… you understand… If I'm charged, I will have the criminal case to worry about. I'm not sure whether I can get legal aid, or whether I have to pay Barratt and Ben out of my own pocket, and I can't afford…'

'I could try pulling some strings with the College's solicitors,' John Fisk said. 'In a sense, it is a College matter. If Harriet would agree to…'

'I will waive my fees in your case, Danie,' Harriet said. 'After everything you've been through, it's the least I can do.'

'That's really sweet of you, Harriet,' Amy said. 'But you shouldn't have to do that, and neither should the College have to pay.' She looked at Danie. 'I think it's time to return Pieter's call.'

'I can't ask him…'

'You don't have to ask him,' she pointed out. 'He's offered – and knowing Pieter, he wouldn't have offered unless he meant it.'

'John, what's the position in College?' Danie asked. 'Is my Fellowship at risk?'

'No,' Fisk replied firmly. 'The College is my jurisdiction. The Vice-Chancellor's writ only runs in University matters – it doesn't run in College. I haven't heard any suggestion from the Fellows that they want to take any action, and I don't expect to hear any. And if I do, I will hold them off for as long as I have to.'

'Thank you,' Danie said.

'Danie,' Fisk said, 'it's your decision, of course. But I think Harriet is right. If you…'

He was suddenly interrupted by a loud shout of, 'Armed police! Stop!' This was followed by the sound of men running across the path in front of the house, a metallic dustbin falling over, loud cursing, and then the sound of a struggle. More shouting and screaming: 'Get off me!' 'Drop your weapon!' 'I won't tell you again!' 'Get the cuffs on him for God's sake!'. 'Check for any more weapons!' Then an officer was using his radio, calling urgently for back up. Danie and John Fisk instinctively ran towards the door. Harriet and Amy were screaming at them to stay inside, but Danie unbolted the door and opened it almost in a single movement. He and Fisk ran outside. They saw two police officers restraining a man, who was lying on his front on the ground. As they emerged from the house, one of the officers, a sergeant, waved a hand in their direction.

'Stay back, sir, please. It's all under control.'

'What the hell happened?' Danie asked.

The sergeant did not reply until he had ensured that the handcuffs he had just applied were tight enough. The man they had restrained was demanding, in vain, to be released. Only then did both officers get to their feet, breathing heavily, the second officer seizing what looked like a pistol from the ground just in front of the man.

'Browning 9mm,' the officer said to the sergeant. 'Very popular piece at the moment.'

'We were keeping observation from the shrubbery at the side of the house, sir,' the sergeant reported. 'We saw this character enter the driveway, and make his way towards the front door. Then we noticed that he was armed. We drew our weapons and ordered him to stop, which he showed no interest in doing, so we jumped him, which was what all the fuss and palaver was about. Sorry about that, but he won't be troubling anybody again this evening.'

'He left a can of accelerant down by the hedge, too,' the officer added, 'with a box of Swan Vestas. Talk about going equipped.'

'Are you taking him to the police station?' John Fisk asked.

'No, sir. MI5 want to talk to anyone we nick on these premises first, so our orders are to hold him here for collection by Special Branch. We have called them. They should be here in ten, fifteen minutes, I should think, traffic permitting.'

The man was still demanding to be released.

Danie turned to Fisk. 'John, perhaps I'm losing my mind – it wouldn't surprise me in the least, with everything that's going on – but I could swear I know his voice from somewhere.'

They both listened intently to the continuing protests.

'I'll be damned,' Fisk said. They both approached the man.

The sergeant held up a hand. 'Keep your distance, please, sir. We've got him under control, but we are treating him as dangerous.'

'I just want to see his face,' Fisk said. 'We may know who he is.'

The sergeant bent down and pulled down the black scarf the man had tied around his head, which had been covering his nose and mouth.

'Good God', Fisk said. 'Sidney? What the hell are you doing here, for God's sake?'

Sidney turned his heard towards them, to the extent he could while lying on the ground with his hands cuffed firmly behind his back.

'Good evening, Master,' he said, almost politely. 'Professor du Plessis.'

'What the hell…?' Danie said.

'So, you do know him, sir?' the sergeant asked.

'Yes,' Fisk replied. 'I'm John Fisk, the Master of the College that owns this house, and Professor du Plessis, who is under your protection, is one of our Fellows. This gentleman is Sidney Barton, the College's head porter. What he's doing here, I have absolutely no idea.'

'Well, perhaps he'd like to explain that to his Master,' the sergeant said. 'Can't do any harm to ask, can it? I don't suppose MI5 would object if we can pass on some information for them to work with.' He turned to the officer. 'Let's stand him up.'

'What's all this about, Sidney?' Fisk asked, once Sidney had been pulled to his feet, and stood facing him, held tightly on either side by the officers.

'Just doing my duty, Master.'

'Your duty?'

'Putting a stop to these white traitors trying to bring the country down, and hand it over to all those damned blacks. People like you, Professor,' he snarled. 'Somebody's got to do something about it. I did hope Mr Erasmus might deal with all of it, but he encountered a misfortune at the last moment. So I had to step in.'

'By "dealing with all of it" you mean, killing Pienaar and Cummings, and doing your best to kill me and my family?' Danie asked.

'You and your coloured whore, sir, yes. I would have burned you down in the house, with your chocolate-coloured children inside as well.'

'So you're BOSS's so-called sleeper?' Fisk asked.

'I've had the honour to be an agent of the Bureau for a number of years now,' Sidney replied defiantly.

Danie closed his eyes. 'Of course,' he said to Fisk. 'He would be one of the few people who could work out where we are. He would know about the College house.'

'Very good, Professor,' Sidney said. 'Yes. I checked your house in Cambridge, obviously, but when you weren't there, it didn't take me long to work out where they would have taken you.'

Fisk shook his head. 'I can't believe it. You've never given me any indication of feeling this way in all the years I've known you. What in God's name has brought you to this?'

Sidney looked down. 'No, well, you have to be discreet in my line of work, don't you, sir?' He looked down. 'But as it seems to be over now, I don't suppose there's any harm in my explaining myself. In fact, I'd rather like you to know.'

He took a deep breath.

'It started because of what happened to my brother, my older brother, Leonard. Leonard was an engineer, Master, a civil engineer. He was much brighter than me, needless to say. He wasn't going to spend his life being a porter, playing nursemaid to a bunch of idiot students who don't know which way is up, was he? Not Leonard. No, Leonard wanted a better future for himself and his family. So, he emigrated to South Africa. At that time, they were very short of skilled workers. They were advertising for people to move there from this country. He got himself a good job with an engineering firm in Port Elizabeth. Back in 1958, this was. He took himself out there with Jean, his wife, and his two little girls, Mary and Annie. They had a nice home, and a couple of servants; they were doing really well. I was planning to go out and see them. But because of what happened, I never did.

'A couple of years after they arrived, Leonard had to go out of town. He had to stay a hundred miles or so out in the country, to work on this big project they had going, building a new highway. He was away for a month or so, in all. And just before he got back, this gang of blacks broke into his house, stole whatever they wanted, and murdered Jean and the girls in cold blood. Just because they were white – they left a message written in blood on the wall, saying they were going to kill as many whites as they could. They used knives, machetes, killed them slowly, cutting bits off here and there as they went. God only knows how long it took them to die, and what they went through while they were dying. When Leonard saw what those blacks had done, he hanged himself.'

Sidney paused for breath, fighting off his scarf, which was trying to rise again towards his mouth.

'And already, then, there was talk about handing the country over to those savages. Bloody madness: we needed another fifty years to have any chance of civilising them. I mean, just look at the places in Africa we've handed over to the blacks. What's happened? Nothing but violence and corruption, and dictatorships. They've learned nothing from us. They say they want to kill whites, but if there are no whites to kill, they'll kill each other, won't they, someone from a different tribe? The thought that South Africa might go the same way was just too much for me. I knew then that I had to do whatever I could to stop it. So, a year or so later, I offered my services to the Bureau. They said I should sit tight and wait for instructions, and they would use me from time to time – which they have. You'll excuse me if I don't elaborate on that. And when I'm ready, they've promised me asylum in South Africa.'

He smiled at the sergeant.

'So, I don't think I'll be with MI5 for very long. I'll be in South Africa, enjoying my asylum.'

'The only place you'll be getting asylum is in Dartmoor, mate,' the sergeant replied, 'or Broadmoor, maybe.'

'I'm sorry you'll have to replace me with such little warning, Master,' Sidney said. 'But young Bernard is more than ready to take over from me. I trained him myself, you see. He will do you proud as head porter. Remember me to Lady Fisk, won't you, sir?'

Danie stepped forward angrily, his right hand in a fist. The sergeant held him back.

'I wouldn't advise that, sir. I understand how you feel, but with Special Branch involved, I can't look the other way on this one. Let's not make this any more complicated than it has to be.'

'Come on, Danie,' Fisk said, taking his arm. 'There's nothing we can do out here. Let's go back inside.'

47

Thursday 4 November 1976

'That sounds good to me,' Ben Schroeder said to the waiter. 'I'll have the mushroom soup and the braised steak, too.'

'Very good, sir,' the waiter replied. He looked at Andrew Pilkington. 'A bottle of the Club Claret, sir?'

'Why not, Ralph?' Andrew said. 'And a refill of our water too, please.'

'Very good, sir.' Ralph walked quietly away, towards the kitchen.

'This was a good idea, Andrew,' Ben said, smiling. 'After the week I've had, I'm not sure I could have lived through a meeting at the

Old Bailey, or the Director's office. This is much more like it. I've always enjoyed the Reform.'

'Why don't you join?' Andrew asked, reaching for his glass of sherry. 'I'll propose you, and we won't have any trouble finding someone to second you – the place is crawling with lawyers.'

'You know, perhaps I will,' Ben replied.

'I'll ask the Secretary to send you the forms,' Andrew said. 'And I know what you mean about having a bad week – although I've revised my definition of a bad week since Lancelot Andrewes. Somehow, they haven't been so bad since we finished with Father Gerrard and his pals.'

Ben nodded. 'There were days when it was hard to see any light at the end of the tunnel,' he said.

'You haven't prosecuted since Gerrard, have you?'

'No. Perhaps that was my one and only chance to represent the Queen.'

'I hope not, Ben. It would be a shame. You did a really good job in Gerrard. John Caswell was seriously impressed, I don't mind telling you. If your clerk dropped a hint that you might be interested, I'm sure he'd send some good work your way.'

'I haven't ruled it out, Andrew. Perhaps I'll give it a try with a less traumatic case – a nice civilised fraud, perhaps.'

'Now you're talking.'

'But I think I'd always come back to the defence side in the end.'

'Championing the underdog?'

'Something like that.'

Ralph returned with fresh water and a bottle of the Club Claret, which he proceeded to open. He looked questioningly at Andrew, who shook his head. Ralph poured each of them a glass before retreating again towards the kitchen.

'Club ritual,' Andrew explained. 'He has to ask if I'd like to taste it, but it would be bad form for me to take him up on it. The Club Claret is an institution not to be questioned.'

'I must remember that, for when I join,' Ben said, smiling.

'So, talking of underdogs,' Andrew said, 'I know you want to talk about Professor du Plessis. Are you going to try to persuade me that he's a fine, upstanding citizen, entirely innocent of the mysteries of the drug trade?'

'I'd like to persuade you to let him get on with his life,' Ben replied. 'I've read the note of his interview, and I'm not seeing any evidence of criminal wrongdoing.'

Andrew nodded. 'You're not the only one. The good professor has something of a fan club. You remember Ted Phillips – DI Phillips – from Lancelot Andrewes?'

'And from other cases, long gone. He's a good man.'

'He's a very persuasive man; and he's been doing his level best to nudge me in the same direction. I suspect that may be due partly to the influence of his admirable new DC. He's presented both sides of the case to me very fairly, but he makes no secret of it – he thinks we should give du Plessis a clean bill of health.'

'Good for him,' Ben said. He smiled. 'By the way, I couldn't help noticing that DI Walsh is now representing whatever interests the Met thinks it has in the case. I'm sure that's no coincidence. They're still together, are they?'

'Yes, and going strong, so I understand. One of the good things to come out of Lancelot Andrewes.'

'Yes indeed. Here's wishing them well.'

'Every happiness to them.'

They raised their glasses and clinked them together to drink the toast.

Ralph returned with their soup and a basket of bread rolls.

'Phillips sees du Plessis as misguided,' Andrew said as they started on the soup, 'and perhaps a bit naïve, but not someone who set out to run with the criminals.'

'I couldn't have put it better myself,' Ben said.

'The problem with that, Ben, is that he knew about Cummings. He told the police that Pienaar had laid it out for him. Cummings was prepared to pay a fee of ten per cent to have his income laundered, using Pienaar's network as cover. No great mystery about that is there? Who's going to go looking for drug money when you have a few idealistic donors raising funds to fight apartheid? You might question what Pienaar was doing for other reasons, but laundering drug money is the last thing you'd suspect. It's the perfect cover.'

'There's no evidence that du Plessis knew that Cummings was a drug dealer,' Ben replied. 'The only evidence you have is the Met's intel on him, which du Plessis never had access to. Cummings didn't even have form, except for some very minor stuff years ago. How is du Plessis expected to know?'

'Oh, come on, Ben,' Andrew said. 'He must have known something was going on, just from the amount of money involved.'

'"He must have known something was going on"?' Ben asked. 'Has something changed while I wasn't looking? Is that the standard for criminal liability now? When did that happen?'

'Pienaar told du Plessis he suspected Cummings of drug dealing.'

'He said arms dealers often took drugs with them to sell in the training camps. That's not quite the same thing.'

'Du Plessis is a law professor, Ben. He has to know this isn't a kosher deal. When someone is willing to fork over ten per cent to launder that much money, he knows damn well it's dirty money.'

They were silent, finishing the soup, for some time.

'Let me ask you something, Andrew,' Ben said. 'What exactly would you charge him with?'

Andrew smiled. 'Good question.'

'I assume you're not going to argue that *Hawala* is unlawful in itself? That would ruffle a few cultural feathers, to put it mildly.'

He laughed. 'Part of me says I should in the interests of the future health of the Inland Revenue and Her Majesty's Customs and Excise. But discretion being the better part of valour, no, I'm not about to open that can of worms just for Danie du Plessis. I'd need a much bigger fish to take that one on.'

'Well then, you're going to have to nail your colours to the mast, aren't you? You're going to have to tell the court exactly what kind of dirty money du Plessis was supposedly laundering. If you say drug money, you have to prove it was drug money; and you have to prove he knew it was drug money. Suspicion, or "there must have been something going on" isn't enough. Come on, Andrew, as a judge, with what you've got, you wouldn't let this case anywhere near a jury.'

Ralph appeared, and removed the remains of the soup. Almost immediately, a junior waiter joined him, and together they served the main course from a small trolley.

'Anything else, Mr Pilkington?' he asked.

'Not for now, Ralph,' Andrew replied. 'Thank you.'

'Thank you, sir.'

Andrew refilled their wine glasses.

'There are other issues involved in this, Ben,' he replied.

48

'Such as?' Ben asked.

Andrew tasted his braised steak appreciatively, then put down his knife and fork, and folded his hands under his chin.

'At the end of the day, this is the Director's call.'

'The Director will do whatever John Caswell recommends, Andrew. You know that.'

'He usually follows John's recommendations, that's true, but not invariably.'

'And John will do whatever you recommend.'

Andrew smiled. 'Again: usually, but not invariably.'

'You're senior Treasury Counsel, Andrew, and I've worked with you both long enough to know how much John respects your views.'

'He does. But as Treasury Counsel, I have to be careful where I tread when politics is involved. Political questions are outside my remit. I can talk to him about the law and the evidence, the strength or weakness of a case, until the cows come home; but I have to tread lightly when it comes to politics.'

'This is delicious,' Ben said, noting that Andrew was not eating. 'Don't let it get cold.'

Andrew smiled, and took another bite of his steak.

'Ben, the problem is this: John reports to the Director, who reports to the Attorney General, a member of the Cabinet.'

'Yes. And…?'

'Please understand: I'm not a student of foreign policy. I don't have the time, for one thing. I can only tell you what I'm getting from John. He tells me the government is walking a very narrow tightrope when it comes to South Africa.'

'How so?'

'There's a sense that apartheid's days are numbered. Economic sanctions, sporting embargos, are in the pipeline, if not actually happening. The South Africans don't have a lot of friends these days. Condemnation is flooding in from far and wide, and our government is under a lot of pressure to get on board. They've resisted so far, but it's getting more and more difficult to hold the line.'

'Why do we want to hold the line? Why aren't we joining in? What's the problem?'

'We have a long history with South Africa, Ben. We've been on friendly terms with them for a long time, and we're desperate to stay on friendly terms. The government is convinced that it's essential in our national interest. For one thing, we do a huge amount of business with them, hundreds of millions of pounds worth every year. But even more importantly, they have a perfectly situated naval base, to which we have full access, which provides us with the eyes and ears we need to track events on the other side of the world. It's like having our own private navy in the South Atlantic and the Indian Ocean. It's an asset you can't put a price on. The government would go to almost any lengths not to lose it.'

'But that doesn't mean we have to approve of everything that goes on in South Africa, does it?' Ben asked. 'It doesn't mean we have to condone apartheid.'

'We don't,' Andrew replied, 'if by "we" you mean the government. But according to John, the government is worried about being out of step with the people on this. If you ask the man in the street, the theory goes, you will find that he is well disposed towards South Africa, and has a certain sympathy for the idea of white rule. He might not say so in so many words, but there's part of him that thinks it wouldn't be a bad thing if we did the same here.'

'I don't believe that,' Ben said.

'Besides which, the man in the street resents being deprived of his cricket and rugby matches against people who, in his mind, are our kith and kin – and good chaps, to boot.'

'If the government are thinking that way,' Ben said, 'they need to get a grip. Times are changing, even here.'

'I've told John that,' Andrew replied. 'But he reckons it's a very personal matter for certain members of the Cabinet. South Africa was our colony – all right, we had to fight the Boers for it, but we were the dominant influence – and people have been emigrating there from Britain for more than two hundred years. They're family. Walk down any street in London, and you'll find people with relatives in Cape Town or Durban. They've also been very loyal to us. They fought on our side in both world wars.'

Ralph was hovering. Andrew signalled that he could remove the plates, which he did. He refilled their glasses.

'Would you like to see the dessert trolley, Mr Pilkington?'

'I'm sure we would, Ralph, but give us a few minutes.'

'Of course, sir.'

'Assuming all this, Andrew,' Ben said, 'I don't understand how it helps the government's cause to go after Danie du Plessis.'

'It shows we're serious about not opening this country up as a centre for subversion against the South African regime.'

'It also means that the man in the street is going to be reading the story of Nick Erasmus, in all its gory details, in his *Daily Mirror*, day after day, for the duration of the trial. They might even get wind of Sidney the Sleeper. It's not the kind of behaviour you expect from your kith and kin, is it: licensing their version of Agent 007 to carry out assassinations in England? How does John think that's going to reflect well on South Africa?'

'It doesn't. It reflects badly on them. But the point is: that's not our fault. Any bad publicity about all that is entirely of their own making. So they can't hold it against us, and meanwhile, we get the credit for doing the right thing – upholding the law, regardless of who may have broken it.'

'It would make far more sense just to drop it,' Ben said. 'They'd have every reason to bail out if Treasury Counsel tells them the case isn't going to fly. No one could criticise them for that.'

Andrew nodded. 'I'll put what you've said to John, but I can't promise you it will make any difference. He thinks it's a viable case, and he has people breathing down his neck from on high. The safe thing to do, in his mind, is to let it run; and as I said before, I have to tread very carefully when it comes to politics.'

He drained his wine glass.

'I'll tell you what, though, Ben, strictly *entre nous*: if du Plessis had kept his mouth shut at the police station, if he'd simply refused to answer any of their questions, I would already have told John to forget about it. We wouldn't have a case: the evidence would be too thin.'

'Tell me about it,' Ben replied.

'Well, anyway, shall we inspect the dessert trolley? And I think a glass of Sauternes might go down well. What do you think?'

'That sounds like a very good idea. By the way, is there any word on what's going to happen to Sidney the Sleeper?'

'Not as yet,' Andrew replied, signalling to Ralph. 'But my money would be on them cutting him loose, packing him off to South Africa, cancelling his passport, and telling him not to come back.'

'John wouldn't want to try him?'

'I doubt it. That's a trial that really could throw several very predatory cats among the pigeons. God only knows what names Sidney might be tempted to name if they force him to try to defend himself. I doubt the Attorney General would have any appetite for that. No. Let him go off to whatever meagre pension they give him, and whatever pokey little bungalow in the Eastern Cape he can find to spend the remainder of his days in, and good luck to him. He may find it's not quite what he was expecting – particularly if the South Africans do get around to having a multiracial democracy one of these days.'

49

Danie du Plessis

Apparently, it didn't take MI5, or Special Branch, very long to establish that Sidney had been working alone, and didn't have any maniacal co-conspirators waiting in the wings to take over from him when he was arrested. Within days of the arrest, it was agreed we could return home to Cambridge, subject only to Superintendent Walker's arranging for frequent drive-by checks on our house by uniformed officers.

It was a huge relief to be at home again, and, for me, at least, an even greater relief to reflect that BOSS hadn't commissioned anyone more competent than Sidney to track us down in London. What information they thought they had about his background when they appointed him their 'sleeper' in Cambridge, what it was about him that persuaded them that he was their man, I have no way of knowing. Perhaps it was just that no one else wanted the job. But with the benefit of hindsight, sending Sidney on a mission to assassinate someone looks like the stuff of comedy: a bit like putting Laurel and Hardy in charge of the relief of Mafeking. Even so, he could have got lucky on any given day, and I found the whole episode disturbing. I was haunted by another question too: how could I have missed so much hatred and bitterness for all those years?

I'd always thought there was something odd about Sidney. But I'd put it down to something you often see in Englishmen in a position like Sidney's – older men trapped in a form of servitude to those they see as their youngers and inferiors. They often adopt a rather ironic, patronising *fausse politesse*, designed to mask a deeply felt contempt. It wasn't something I particularly held against him. I could see how galling it must be: to have to act as a nursemaid for three years to immature young men who haven't been weaned from home properly, who react by drinking too much, wasting their time at university, and assuming airs of superiority to which they have no claim whatsoever; only to see those same men return to college for some gathering of alumni ten years later, apparently no more mature, but with enhanced airs of superiority, and flaunting the trappings of success in the City, the law, medicine, or engineering.

I understood that; and it didn't bother me at all that, as a young and untried Fellow, Sidney would treat me in much the same way. In due course, I reasoned, when I'd been around for a while and proved myself, he would begin to treat me as he did John Fisk and the more senior Fellows, with a more authentic show of respect. There was no way I could have known how he would feel towards a white South African with a coloured wife, or why he would feel that way. But I still find it hard to believe that he didn't give me some warning sign. If he did, I missed it completely.

Inevitably, he had become Erasmus's handler. He must have known that Erasmus was coming to Cambridge, posing as a graduate student, with the intention of killing me, Amy, and our children, and with the intention of destroying Pienaar's network in the city. He must have known when the time had come to execute the plan – though it must surely have been Erasmus, rather than Sidney, who discovered the convenient circumstance that Pienaar and Cummings would be in Cambridge together, opening up the possibility that the entire mission could be accomplished in one or two days. Looking back now, I recall a certain ambivalence, a suggestion of distrust on Pienaar's part, about Sidney. I recall his second visit to me, when he decided to break into my rooms again rather than wait for me outside on the staircase, where a roving porter might confront and question him. Pienaar never said anything to me, so it may be that he had nothing concrete to go on; but looking back now, I think he suspected that something wasn't quite right about Sidney. Pienaar had an instinct for such things, an instinct I presumably lack, because in all my dealings with Sidney over the years, I never saw him coming.

Despite everything, and although I hate and despise what Sidney did, I think I understand what drove him to it. There were, and still are, from time to time, ghastly atrocities perpetrated by blacks against whites in South Africa; and if his account of what happened to Leonard's family is true – which I have no reason to doubt – I can't imagine how anyone could simply put such loss, such horror, behind them and move on unscathed. It is his tragedy that he allowed it to consume his life. But it could so easily have been ours, too.

50

A few days after we arrived home, Pieter flew over from South Africa to stay with us. Pieter was married by now to a lovely woman, a clinical psychologist called Marieke. Although we'd exchanged letters and family photographs quite regularly, and shared the occasional phone call, we'd seen him only once since leaving South Africa. This was during a fleeting appearance in England in 1971, when he'd found himself in London for a day or two on his way to destinations in Eastern Europe in search of new business horizons.

Good as it was to see him, it was also frustrating to meet in the restaurant of his hotel, where we couldn't fully relax. Now, we had him to ourselves at home for several days. He came laden with gifts for the whole family, including some from Hilda. He'd tried his utmost to talk her into flying over with him at his expense. But flying was an experience too far for her. Although she was well and happy in her life, she was feeling her age, and wasn't confident that she could manage such a journey. We understood. The gifts and photographs were more than enough. Sally and Douglas took to Pieter immediately – in part because of the presents, of course – but also because he was a warm and friendly distraction from the bad memories they still had of the recent disruption to their lives.

On the second day of his stay, once we'd given him time to recover from the flight, we made a special dinner, accompanied by special wines, and we all ended up getting pretty drunk. Fortunately, Sally and Douglas were still making up for lost rest, and had started to sleep through the night again – something that had become a rarity for a while. We kept them up a bit too late, just to make sure, and as a result, we didn't need to go upstairs to comfort them during the evening. As we were relaxing after dinner with a very nice Cognac Pieter had found in Duty Free, he raised the question of his offer to pay my legal expenses. Immediately, Amy and I began to protest that we couldn't possibly accept. We meant it sincerely. It wasn't really about the money as such – Pieter was by now a very wealthy man, and we knew that our legal expenses would amount to little more than a blip on his financial radar. But we already owed Pieter more than we could ever repay – our very lives and freedom. Accepting his money seemed somehow too much. He listened patiently as we attempted to explain this.

'What people like you do, outside South Africa,' he said, once we had ground to a halt, 'is driving the resistance. You're doing important work, work those of us back home can't do. I have slightly more room to manoeuvre than most, because the firm is so important to South African national defence – especially now, with sanctions and embargos beginning to bite. Like my dad, I can probably say a few things in public that most people couldn't. But that's as far as it goes. And even that may not last. My dad knew Vorster well. I know Vorster pretty well, and we understand each other. But the word in my cricketing circle – which, as you know, is a pretty high-level, well-informed group – is that Vorster is on his way out. Botha is the man of the future, and he's an unknown quantity, at least to me. I doubt it's going to get any easier.

'My point is that back home, we can't support the struggle openly. Over here, things are different. Pienaar and others like him have worked wonders with money. They're financing a whole military campaign from outside South Africa. All right, it probably won't be enough to bring the regime down, in itself. But it serves to weaken the regime, and make it more vulnerable when the day finally comes for people to rise up in South Africa. It also weakens morale – it plants a seed of doubt in the regime's mind about whether they can hang on indefinitely. Along with the growing political pressure from different countries, it all has its effect.

'Look, Danie, Amy, you've sent a lot of money to the people who needed it over the past few years. And now, predictably, the regime has turned on you. Mercifully, they failed in their attempt to take you out by force, so now they're relying on the prosecutors here to do their dirty work for them. But that's something we can help with. We can make sure you have the legal representation you need, without having to worry about where the money is coming from. Compared to the money you've sent over to us, it's a drop in the ocean.

'What I'm trying to say is: it's not just about friendship – though your friendship is very dear to me, I hope you know that – it's also about standing up for you, and others like you in different parts of the world. It's about making sure you all know that we need you, and we won't abandon you.'

'But Pieter, what happens when they find out that you're paying for Danie's defence?' Amy asked.

Pieter smiled. 'Good luck to them, finding out,' he replied. 'You're not the only ones who know how to launder money.' We laughed. 'Unless you tell them, it won't come back to me.' He shrugged. 'And even if it did, what have I done wrong? I have an old friend from WITS who's been falsely accused of drug trafficking abroad. I don't know the details, but I have to do something, don't I? I'm not worried about it, Amy.'

I poured more Cognac for us all.

'So, what do you say?' Pieter asked.

'On behalf of your many outlaws throughout the world, Pieter,' I replied, 'we say "thank you".'

It was a week later, after Pieter had left to return home, that Barratt Davis called me with the bad news. After 'the most careful consideration' the Director of Public Prosecutions had decided to have me charged with aiding and abetting Vincent Cummings in trafficking controlled drugs of Class A – presumably heroin and cocaine. The fact that I had never met Vincent Cummings, much less seen him traffic drugs of any kind, apparently made no difference to the Director's assessment of the case. Mercifully, they had decided not to charge Amy. They hadn't even interviewed her after the day of Erasmus's death, so they would have had no case against her at all. At least we had one piece of good news.

Ordinarily, once the decision to charge me had been taken, officers would have come to the house to arrest me and taken me away in handcuffs. But DI Phillips had agreed that I should be allowed to attend the police station voluntarily at ten o'clock the following morning to be charged formally. Barratt arranged to meet me there. He explained that I would then be taken before the magistrates. The police had no objection to bail, and I would be released on my own recognisance as soon as a date had been set for the magistrates to commit the case to the Old Bailey for trial. The Director had decided that there might be too much local feeling in Cambridge about such a sensational case, and if so, that it might be difficult to find an impartial jury. Barratt agreed. Local feeling was too unpredictable, he cautioned – it could go either way – and we would be safer in the anonymity of London.

I picked up something in Barratt's tone. He was doing his best to be his usual diplomatic self, but there was an element of frustration in his voice. I knew why. He had advised me against submitting to a police interview. He had told me that Ben Schroeder agreed with him. The police had no real evidence against me, he said, except for the fact that I had taken money to Balakrishnan on behalf of a number of donors, one of whom had the initials VC. It didn't come close to being enough to convict me. If I answered the officers' questions, I might say something they could seize on to make it appear that I knew more than I did. I had nothing to gain from it, and I would be running the risk of giving hostages to fortune. I was fully entitled to remain silent, and no adverse inferences could be drawn against me if I chose to do so. It was a simple function of the presumption of innocence. I understood all that perfectly well. But I couldn't shake off the thought that if I remained silent, they would think I had something to hide; and if the officers could think that, so could a jury – even if technically they weren't allowed to hold it against me. I had nothing to hide. I had been acting in a just cause. Why shouldn't they hear the truth?

Now, belatedly, it occurred to me that the Director of Public Prosecutions had found, or thought he had found something in the interview that made a difference, and, in his mind, justified a charge. But I had never said I had met Vincent Cummings, and I had never said I knew he was a drug dealer. It was my case, my future at stake, and my decision whether to answer questions or to remain silent. It wasn't just the jury. I also had a Vice-Chancellor and others, who seemed determined to revoke my tenure of the Buckland Chair and ruin my career. It wasn't enough to be vindicated. I was a public figure, a Professor, and if I had become an outlaw, I had done so in a good cause. I wanted them to hear the truth. I needed them to hear the truth, and if they couldn't hear it from me, how would they ever hear it?

51

'So, remind me who we're meeting this morning,' Danie said.

They were walking through the market towards the Senate House, on their way to a meeting in the Old Schools building, which housed the University's administrative offices. Without slowing her pace, Harriet Fisk opened her briefcase, took out her blue counsel's notebook, stuffed it under an arm while she closed the briefcase again, returned the briefcase to her left hand, and with her right, flicked the notebook open at the page she wanted.

'Professor Clara Stein,' she replied, 'who I assume you know. She's a member of the Law Faculty, and a fellow of Newnham. She's the Deputy University Advocate.'

'What does that mean?' Danie asked.

'The Advocate is a bit like the DPP for the University. Professor Stein is his second-in-command. Under the University Statutes, the Advocate reports to the Vice-Chancellor. His function is to investigate complaints against members of the academic staff, and where appropriate he brings charges of misconduct against the person concerned, which are then heard by the University Tribunal.' She grinned. 'You should know all this. You're a member of Regent House yourself, for goodness sake. Don't you read your own Statutes?'

He returned the grin. 'I've been a bit remiss, I'm afraid,' he admitted. 'I never thought I would have anything to do with the Statutes and disciplinary proceedings. And that stuff is all so arcane.'

'What's your impression of Professor Stein?'

'Clara? I don't know her all that well. I see her at faculty meetings;

that's about it. I've always got on well with her, I think. She's always struck me as reasonable.'

'What's her area of law?'

'Commercial law, companies, that kind of thing.'

'We're also meeting a Professor Jim McVeigh, who is the Pro-Vice-Chancellor for Institutional and International Relations. He will be there to represent the Vice-Chancellor. He's an economist, apparently.'

'I don't know him at all.'

'I wouldn't expect him to take the lead. He'll stay in the background and leave it to Professor Stein to make the running, I would think. Danie, I know you'll be tempted to jump in, but I'd like you to leave the talking to me, if you can.'

'I'll do my best,' he promised.

The receptionist directed them to a meeting room overlooking Trinity Lane, where Professors Clara Stein and Jim McVeigh were waiting for them.

'Miss Fisk, this meeting is being held at your request,' Clara Stein began. 'What can we do for you?' Her tone was business-like, Harriet thought, slightly frosty.

'Well, as I said in my letter, we would like to take an agreed approach to Professor du Plessis' status within the University pending his trial. Professor du Plessis is prepared to step aside from the Buckland Chair on a temporary basis, until his trial has been concluded, and will resume his duties as soon as he has been exonerated. We would like to issue a joint press release to the effect that the Vice-Chancellor and Professor du Plessis have agreed that this is the most appropriate way of dealing with the situation. We're sure the University wouldn't want to risk prejudicing Professor du Plessis in the eyes of the court by removing him from his post unilaterally.'

Clara Stein opened a file she had in front of her on the table.

'I see he's charged with aiding and abetting the supply of Class A controlled drugs, the allegation being that he was laundering the proceeds of drug trafficking on behalf of a notorious international dealer. That's a very serious charge, and I assume the prosecution would not have brought such a charge unless there was evidence to support it.'

'Professor du Plessis has experienced criminal counsel, whose view is that the prosecution's case is extremely weak,' Harriet replied. 'Professor du Plessis never met the man in question, and never knew that he was a drug dealer. The prosecution has no evidence to prove otherwise. Professor du Plessis believed the man to be a donor, who contributed funds to an effort he was supporting, the aim of which was to undermine, and eventually end apartheid in South Africa. His College doesn't consider it necessary to take any action against him, and if the College takes that view, I'm not sure what basis the University has for taking a different view.'

McVeigh shrugged. 'The College is entitled to its opinion, but we have a duty to make our own evaluation of the situation on behalf of the University.'

Professor Stein nodded. 'Look, I know Professor du Plessis, obviously. We're members of the same faculty, and I'm familiar with his background. So I understand what you're saying.'

'Then you will understand that he has a complete defence to the charge.'

'Unfortunately, that's not for me to decide… Look, Miss Fisk, I agreed to see you today because Danie is a colleague, and also out of respect for your father, who is the Master of his College. But please understand: the Vice-Chancellor has expressed his grave concern about this case. It's a very serious charge, which has the potential to damage the University's reputation.'

'Not if he's acquitted.'

'If he is acquitted, then of course, we will reconsider the matter. But I should warn you that even then, the Vice-Chancellor believes that enough damage may have been done to the University's reputation to justify permanent dismissal.'

Jim McVeigh sat forward in his chair. 'The problem we have, from an institutional point of view, is that a charge of this kind, involving complicity in international drug dealing, possibly membership of a drug cartel of some kind, makes the University look very bad. It could easily affect our ability to raise funds, both in this country and abroad.'

'I understand that you're not a lawyer, Professor McVeigh,' Harriet retorted immediately, 'but no one, including the prosecution, has ever suggested that Professor du Plessis is a member of a cartel. You should think very carefully before repeating that suggestion to anyone.'

'He's charged with aiding and abetting,' Clara Stein said, 'nothing more. Let's stick to the facts.'

'I want to make one thing clear,' Harriet said. 'If Professor du Plessis is acquitted, as we fully expect, it would clearly be unlawful for you to dismiss him, and he would contest any such decision vigorously.'

'That's his right, of course, of course,' Professor Stein said. 'He's entitled to be heard in the University Tribunal, and he's entitled to be legally represented so that his case can be fully argued.'

'I'm not just talking about the University Tribunal,' Harriet replied. 'We will contest the case in the Tribunal, of course, and pursue an appeal, if we have to. But if that fails, we won't hesitate to go to the High Court. We're going to have this litigated out in the open, not behind closed doors in the University's own cosy forum.'

There was a long silence.

'There's no right of appeal to the High Court from the Tribunal,' Clara Stein said eventually. 'The Tribunal was established by the Statutes of the University. It has its own jurisdiction, and there's a right of appeal from the Tribunal to the *Septemviri*. But the courts have no right to interfere.'

'This isn't the sixteenth century, Professor Stein,' Harriet replied. 'The days when you could operate your own private court, and claim to be above the law, are long gone. The High Court has power to inquire into any potential abuse of power, even if it is under cover of some tame private tribunal. I don't need a right of appeal. I'll find a High Court judge who's prepared to take the lid off it, I promise you.'

'The Advocate will not be threatened, Miss Fisk,' Clara Stein said.

'I'm not threatening anyone, Professor. I'm simply being candid with you about my legal strategy, should the University dismiss Professor du Plessis unlawfully after he's been acquitted.' She took a deep breath. 'Hopefully, none of this will be necessary. All I'm asking is that you respect the presumption of innocence, and avoid prejudicing Professor du Plessis before his trial. All we can do today is make an interim arrangement. Work with me: let's do this by agreement, and we will both get what we want. The rest, we can deal with after the trial.'

There was another silence.

'The Vice-Chancellor will be issuing his own press release later today,' Clara Stein said, with an air of finality.

Danie rested a hand gently on Harriet's arm.

'I've had enough of this, Harriet,' he said. 'We're wasting our time. Let's go.'

'In a moment,' she replied.

'Is there something else I can do for you Miss Fisk?' Clara Stein asked.

'Yes,' Harriet replied, 'as a matter of fact, there is. I'll need a complete list of all the University's investments in South Africa, direct and indirect. I'm sure you understand what I mean by that.'

'What?'

'If you refuse, I'll do it the hard way, and make my own list. It will take me some time, but I will find your investments, and then I will make a scene about your refusing me access. The University is a public body. Its investments are a matter of public record. I imagine Professor McVeigh has exactly what I need in his office.'

'What have our investments got to do with anything?' Clara Stein asked.

'It's quite simple, Professor: I intend to demonstrate the University's bias against Professor du Plessis.'

'There is no question of bias. We…'

'The Vice-Chancellor wants to dismiss a member of the academic staff who is an idealist, and is working to put an end to apartheid. Some might argue that's a legitimate part of an academic lawyer's job, which the University should be protecting and encouraging. But the University has a vested interest in protecting its investments in South Africa, and so doesn't want to see South Africa embarrassed. It has an obvious motive for silencing Professor du Plessis. All I need to know is the scale of the investments, so that I can assess the extent of the bias. Let's see what damage that does to the University's reputation.'

'This is outrageous…' Clara Stein began.

But Jim McVeigh interrupted her. 'Would you give us a couple of minutes to confer in private?' he asked.

'Of course,' Harriet replied. 'Take all the time you need. We'll wait outside.'

Some ten minutes later, Jim McVeigh invited them back in.

'Do you have a draft of your proposed joint press release?' Clara Stein asked, through clenched teeth.

'As it happens, I do,' Harriet replied. She took the draft from her briefcase and laid it on the table.

'I will look at it overnight, and get back to you in a day or two,' Clara Stein said. 'You understand, it's not my decision: I'll have to put it in front of the Vice-Chancellor.'

'Of course,' Harriet said. 'I will look forward to hearing from you.'

'And even if the Vice-Chancellor agrees, it would be without prejudice to the eventual outcome.'

'Understood,' Harriet replied.

As they crossed King's Parade by Great St Mary's church, they finally exchanged grins.

'That was brilliant,' Danie said. 'Whatever made you think of asking for their investments?'

'I can't take any credit for that,' she replied. 'It was my Dad's suggestion. He says they're squeamish about a number of portfolios they've had for donkey's years, but which have recently become slightly toxic, politically speaking. They're not sure what to do about them, and the last thing they need while they're thinking about that is publicity. Dad thought it might be something to throw in as a last resort, if I couldn't get their attention any other way.'

'Apparently he was right,' Danie said, 'as ever.'

PART THREE

52

'We have just under a month to go before trial,' Ben Schroeder said, 'and we've received some further evidence from the prosecution, which may be very important – in fact, it may change the face of the trial to some extent. That's why I asked for a conference this afternoon. There are one or two important questions I need you to answer.'

'They've given us almost no evidence against Danie from day one,' Amy said, 'and now they're landing on us? They've had long enough. Why are they only coming forward with it now?'

'It's evidence I've been expecting,' Ben replied. 'They were bound to get their hands on it sooner or later. Perhaps they've been a bit slow, but it doesn't matter. It's here now, and we have to deal with it.'

He handed copies of a file to Danie and Amy, who were sitting in front of his desk in his room in chambers. Barratt Davis was sitting in an armchair to Ben's right.

'As you know, the prosecution sent us copies of Vincent Cummings's bank accounts, going back to 1968, as part of their original evidence. Most of those accounts were with foreign banks. The Met had been on his trail for a number of years, so they would have gradually tracked them down, and they would have been monitoring them during that time.'

'That's how they were able to follow the growth of his business,' Barratt observed.

'Yes, and very likely identify some of the people he was dealing with, or at least the markets he was operating in,' Ben agreed. 'It was through Cummings that they found out about Art Pienaar, and then it was only a matter of time before they started to look for his bank accounts too.'

Danie looked up, thumbing through the file. 'These are Art's accounts?'

'Yes. Assuming they found them all, it seems Pienaar wasn't very sophisticated for someone who was handling such large sums of money on a regular basis. There's a current account and a savings account with the Midland in St John's Wood. Those are his personal accounts. There's also a professional account with Barclays, which is his firm's bank, but there's nothing of interest there. They go back to 1968. I've been through them, and I'm not finding anything out of the ordinary. What do you think, Barratt?'

'Nothing to worry about, as far as I can see, considering he was a practising solicitor,' Barratt replied.

'What do you mean "nothing to worry about"?' Amy asked.

'Pienaar was a solicitor,' Barratt replied, 'so you'd expect a fair bit of activity on the account, with some pretty sizeable sums going in and out now and then. That doesn't suggest criminal activity. On the other hand, if you found regular large transactions, it would indicate business use, rather than personal. So then, the question would be: why wasn't this going through his firm account? Possible answer: he had some kind of business going on outside his firm's practice. If so, what business was it, what was the scale of the business, and is that enough to suggest it wasn't kosher?'

'But there was nothing like that,' Danie said. 'So, as you said, nothing to worry about.'

'Not in those accounts,' Ben replied. 'But there's one more. Page 152.'

Danie and Amy turned to the page.

'This is a foreign account,' Danie said, looking up.

'Algemene Bank Nederland,' Ben replied, 'a Dutch bank.'

'That's not surprising,' Amy said, turning over pages quickly. 'Art had donors in Europe. He had them in lots of places. Why shouldn't he have foreign accounts? I'm only surprised there aren't more.'

'Perhaps there are,' Danie suggested. 'Perhaps they didn't find them all.'

'Possibly,' Ben agreed, 'but the Met banking gurus are pretty thorough. It wouldn't have been hard. As I said before, for someone doing what he was doing, Pienaar wasn't very sophisticated.'

'Meaning?' Amy asked.

'You'd expect to find numbered accounts,' Barratt replied, 'in Luxembourg or Switzerland – no name or personal details: not impossible to trace, but guaranteed to slow the Met's experts down somewhat. Most of Cummings's accounts were of that kind.'

'Exactly,' Ben agreed, 'whereas in fact, what we have with Pienaar is a perfectly normal current account in his name with Algemene Bank in Amsterdam. What do you notice about it?'

Danie turned over a number of pages, and bit his lip. 'Regular payments in,' he replied, 'which look a bit on the large side. I don't know the exchange rate for the guilder, but…'

'They amount to between £1,000 and £1,500 a time,' Ben said, 'and the payer's reference number is identical to one of the Cummings accounts, based in Luxembourg.'

'Oh, God,' Amy said quietly.

'Which, the prosecution is going to suggest,' Ben continued, 'indicates that the relationship between Cummings and Pienaar was rather more complicated than just donor and beneficiary.'

'Art was taking a cut for himself,' Danie said. 'Cummings's fee to the fund was ten per cent, but he was actually paying a bit more, to include something for Art personally. It gives the impression that they were business partners.'

'Well, they obviously had some arrangement between them,' Ben replied. 'And I don't think Andrew Pilkington will have much trouble selling that idea to a jury. It puts Pienaar one step closer to Cummings than he was before, and unfortunately, because of your relationship with Pienaar, it puts you one step closer to Cummings too.'

'And he just paid it into this current account?' Amy asked,

'without any attempt to hide it – well, apart from the bank being in Holland?'

'Apparently,' Ben said.

'He could have run it through Balakrishnan,' Danie pointed out.

'He could have done any number of things if he'd wanted to hide it,' Ben agreed. 'That may be the only point in our favour. Why didn't he?'

'Lack of sophistication,' Amy said.

'Stupidity, more like,' Barratt replied. 'But let's face it: stupidity is how ninety per cent of criminals get caught. We may be able to paint Pienaar as an innocent abroad, but it's going to be tough, given the kind of contacts he had. It's going to be a hard sell.'

'It is,' Ben agreed, 'which is why I need to ask the two of you a couple of questions. You've already given us your current and savings accounts at Lloyd's in Cambridge. There's nothing untoward there.'

'Consistent with two academics with a family,' Barratt added.

Amy forced a smile. 'Broke all the time, you mean, living from hand to mouth?'

'But think very carefully,' Ben continued. 'Do you have any other accounts, anywhere in the world? Bank accounts, post office accounts, investment accounts, anything that might look like a bank account that you haven't told us about?'

They were silent for some time.

'No,' Danie replied. 'Nothing comes to mind. 'Our accounts in South Africa were closed years ago, not long after we came to England.'

Amy turned to him. 'There was that account my mother started for us,' she said. 'I'm sure it's been closed by now. It was just to handle a bequest in my uncle's will, but she set it up in my name in South Africa. My uncle left me about £5,000 – in rand, of course, that's the sterling equivalent – but the executors of his will paid it in instalments, as they gradually liquidated the estate, so there were several payments in.'

'When was this?'

'1970, 1971,' she replied. 'I'll check.'

'It shouldn't be a problem,' Ben said, 'but just in case, let us have any paperwork you have, and if you can't find any, ask your mother to have the executors contact Barratt.'

'I can't believe Art was on the take,' Danie said quietly. 'He was such an idealist. It just doesn't add up.'

'People are often full of contradictions,' Ben said. 'It doesn't mean he wasn't an idealist. From everything we know about him, that's exactly what he was.'

'It's not right,' Amy replied. 'Not if he was taking drug money for himself.'

'I understand why you're disappointed in him,' Barratt replied, after a silence. 'But, for what it's worth, I can't quite bring myself to condemn him outright.'

'Oh?'

'He was running a big operation, but it was one that could have blown up in his face at any time – as it eventually did. And, for all the money he was handling for other people, for the cause, he had nothing to fall back on – no security, no provision for his own future. I can't fault him too much for trying to make some hay while the sun was shining. All right, he must have known it was dodgy money, but still...'

'He had his practice as a solicitor, didn't he?' Amy said. 'He had that security, surely.'

Barratt laughed. 'If his secret life, his Rosencrantz and Guildenstern world, suddenly fell apart, and he was arrested? I don't think so, Amy. It would have brought his firm down with him, and I don't suppose his partners would have appreciated that very much.' He laughed again. 'I can just imagine if I did that to my firm. My partner, Geoff Bourne, would be enlisting Ben's services to have me thrown out on my ear, without a penny, before the week was out. No. I know you feel let down. But I think I understand why he did it.' He glanced at Ben. 'You don't approve.'

Ben smiled. 'I don't necessarily disapprove, Barratt. What I'm asking myself is: what a jury will make of it.' He paused for some time. 'Changing the subject, Danie, have you decided how you're going to manage the trial? We're going to need you to stay in London for the duration. We can't risk you commuting from Cambridge while you're on bail. All it would take is for the trains to be running late one morning, and the judge will revoke bail and remand you in custody.'

'John Fisk says I can have the College house in Holland Park again,' Danie replied. 'If I stay there, I can take the Central Line to St Paul's, for the Old Bailey.'

Barratt nodded. 'That will work.'

'I will be commuting to court,' Amy said. 'I have to be home at night because of the children. It's going to be bad enough for them having Danie away as it is, especially as I can't give them any explanation that makes sense without telling them the truth, which I can't bring myself to do, even if they were old enough to understand it. What I'm going to tell them if it all… goes wrong… God only knows.'

She brushed away a tear. Danie walked over to her chair, put his arms around her, and hugged her from behind.

'It's not going to go wrong,' he said. 'And our friend Pieter is coming back from South Africa. He will be at the trial with Amy every day, and he can help with whatever else needs to be done – in addition to being there to support everybody until it's over.'

'He's been a good friend to you,' Ben observed.

'The best,' Danie replied.

53

Monday 7 February 1977

Sarah Mulvaney

My name is Sarah Mulvaney. I'm thirty-six, and single. I live in Islington. I work as a librarian at Queen Mary College, a part of the University of London, in Mile End. And I'm about to serve on a jury. It's a new experience for me, and one I've been dreading. The jury summons dropped though my letterbox several weeks ago, so I've had a lot of time to think about it. I'm not a very gregarious person, and the thought of having to be closeted with eleven complete strangers for days on end, to have to argue with them, to have to decide somebody's fate in a court of law – just the sense of having that power, and the responsibility that goes with it – horrifies me. How am I supposed to know whether someone is guilty or not guilty? What if I get it wrong, and send some innocent person to prison? What if I release some violent predator back on to the streets? I hoped it might just go away. Surely, someone was bound to write or call me eventually to say that it was all a terrible mistake, that I wasn't the kind of person they needed on a jury after all. But no one wrote or called. So here I am.

When I arrived at the Old Bailey this morning, I had no idea what to expect. It's all so unfamiliar, with so many police officers milling around, and people – men mostly – wearing white wigs and black gowns, standing around, whispering together. My nerves were already jangling, and this great scrum of people wasn't helping. Mercifully, I didn't have much time to take it all in. Like everybody else – and I mean everybody: it felt as though most of the population of London must be arriving at the Old Bailey at the same time – I had to go through the security check, which involved opening my handbag, and taking off my coat and scarf. But when I told them I was a juror, and showed them my jury summons, it wasn't very long before they removed me from the general mêlée and escorted me upstairs to the jury assembly room, a large space with lots of chairs, and facilities for coffee and sandwiches and the like.

The gentleman who escorted me was Geoffrey, who told me that he was one of the court's most senior ushers, and a retired City of London police officer. I must say, he looks the part: the dark suit, starched white shirt and red tie, and over the suit, a long black gown with the City's coat of arms emblazoned on it. He might have been the inspiration for a piece of librarian humour. Librarian humour is something I resort to frequently when I feel stressed or nervous. Librarian humour is nothing to write home about, to be honest, and this example is no exception; but as I say, there are times when it helps to take my mind off something that's bothering me. So, what do you call an elderly man dressed in a formal suit, starched white shirt and red tie, who has a steady job and enjoys his cup of cocoa before bed? Answer: your average young female librarian's hot fantasy. I told you it was nothing to write home about.

I started to unwind a little in the comparatively calm atmosphere of the jury room, especially after treating myself to a coffee and a small packet of ginger biscuits. I even chatted with one or two of my fellow inmates about safe subjects: the weather, how expensive everything is now, how useless the government is. At nine thirty, one of the clerks of court, a balding man in his forties wearing a wing collar and bands instead of a tie, came in and gave us a lecture on the Old Bailey: its history; the kinds of cases we could expect to hear; why the court relies on juries to decide cases; what we could expect when we were taken down to court; the times of the court's sittings; and various other administrative details. The only reassuring moment of his talk came when he reminded us that all decisions are made by the jury, not by individual jurors, and that there is strength in numbers. If anything happened at any time to cause us concern, he added, we should notify the court usher immediately.

It was just after eleven when Geoffrey appeared in the jury assembly room again, this time with a list of twenty names, which he proceeded to read aloud. One of the names was mine. He asked us to follow him down to court five. I was reassured to make the journey with a familiar face. Court five is in the new extension to the building, which opened fairly recently in 1972. On the way, Geoffrey told us that the courts in the extension were of a more modern design, and in his opinion, looked much the same as new courtrooms in any court anywhere in the country: there was nothing to mark them out as Old Bailey courts at all. They certainly had nothing of the dramatic atmosphere of the four older courts in the main building, he added sadly. With their high ceilings and severe architecture, courts one and two, in particular, had witnessed the trials of Britain's most notorious criminals, so many of whom, after being convicted, had been taken away to a place of execution, to be hanged by the neck until dead. On the other hand, he added with a smile, everyone agrees that the new courts are a damn sight more comfortable.

When we entered court five, we initially remained standing in a corner, behind what I soon learned was the dock. We were all a bit afraid of doing something wrong, I suppose, and we didn't want to venture too far without being invited; though in fact Geoffrey was continually cajoling us to move further inside, so that all twenty of us could fit into the small space available. Eventually, I moved in far enough to have a good view of the courtroom. I saw a man in the dock, flanked by two prison officers, two barristers in the white wigs and black gowns, and the judge on the bench, resplendent in a magnificent red robe trimmed with ermine – who provided me with a second fleeting moment of reassuring librarian humour. Geoffrey had prepared us for that sight, telling us that the red robes identified him as a High Court judge, and that his name was Mr Justice Overton. Having a High Court judge, as opposed to one of the Old Bailey's regular judges, Geoffrey confided in us, meant that we were going to hear a very sensitive case. He knew what the case was about, of course, but he wasn't allowed to tell us: we would find out soon enough. Good judge, but can be irritable, was Geoffrey's brief verdict on Mr Justice Overton.

A man sitting in front of the judge, wearing a barrister's robes – the clerk of court, Geoffrey had told us – called for silence, asked the defendant to stand, and told him that we were the panel from which his jury would be selected, and that he had the right to challenge us. He then began to read out our names. If our name was called, we were to answer to it audibly and take a seat in the jury box. My name came out of the hat at number six. I answered audibly at my second attempt, while pushing past some of my fellow jurors and walking as fast as I could, which caused me to have a brief coughing fit just as I arrived at the jury box. Geoffrey was standing in front of the box and showed me to my seat at the end of the front row nearer to the dock. The box soon filled up, with twelve of us seated. The clerk turned towards the bench and bowed to Mr Justice Overton. Every eye in court was on him.

54

'Good morning, members of the jury in waiting,' he began. 'Ordinarily, at this stage, the learned clerk of court would proceed to swear in the jury. But in this case, there are a number of questions I need to ask the whole panel before we select a jury. These are questions which may seem strange to you, but we have to ask them, because they relate to the subject matter of the case before the court, and counsel for the prosecution and the defence have assisted me in compiling them. So please listen carefully to the questions. Initially, all the questions will be asked of the panel as a whole, and you will have to respond only if your answer to the question is "yes". If your answer is "no", you don't have to say anything. If anyone does answer "yes", then I will ask that person one or more follow-up questions. I hope that's clear to everybody, and if so, I will proceed.'

The judge paused to pick up his notebook and reading glasses.

'The defendant in this case, the gentleman in the dock, is Danie du Plessis, who is originally from South Africa, and is a law professor at Cambridge University. Does anyone know Professor du Plessis, or has anyone seen or heard his name mentioned in the press, or on radio or television?'

The man sitting next to me, a gentleman smartly dressed in a suit and tie, raised his hand. For some reason, I felt that everyone was staring at me, as well as him.

'Yes. I follow the news quite closely, and I seem to remember his name being in the paper. I can't remember why. This would have been several months ago, and I don't remember what the articles said about him, but I do remember seeing them.'

'Yes, thank you,' the judge replied. 'Mr…?'

'Gregory, sir.'

'Thank you, Mr Gregory. Would you please leave the jury box, and would the clerk please call another name.'

'Kenneth Avery,' the clerk called. Kenneth Avery replaced Mr Gregory in the seat next to me. I was pleased. I'd been chatting with Kenneth about how useless the government was just before we were called down to court, and he seemed very nice.

'The second question,' the judge continued, 'is this. Is any member of the jury panel originally from South Africa, or does anyone have a family member or close friend living in this country who is originally from South Africa?'

No one responded to this.

'Does anyone have family members or a close friend currently living in South Africa?'

Two men outside the jury box had relatives who had moved to South Africa some years ago, and still lived there. In reply to a further question from the judge, one added that he had spent several weeks in the country, visiting his family there, three years ago.

'Finally, members of the jury in waiting,' Mr Justice Overton said, 'may I take it that everyone knows what the word "apartheid" means, in relation to South Africa? Is there anyone who does not understand that word? I'm not asking you what you think about it, simply whether or not you understand the word. Please don't be shy about speaking up. No one knows everything, and there's no need to be embarrassed about it at all. But it is important for us to know.'

No one responded, though there was a certain awkward shifting in one or two seats, and on the floor behind us, that suggested that there were some who weren't too sure about it. Perhaps they didn't agree with the judge about the question of embarrassment. It occurred to me to wonder why, if it was so important, the judge didn't just tell us what apartheid meant. Then we would all have known.

'Thank you. Now, I want to make this clear: I'm not asking you what your opinion is about apartheid, and I don't want you to tell the court what it is. But does anyone have such a strong opinion about apartheid, whether positive or negative, that you would be unable to consider evidence that involves apartheid objectively? In other words, if you had to hear a case in which apartheid may play a significant role, is there any reason why you would be unable to consider the case fairly and impartially?'

After some time, and I suspect, just as the judge was about to move on, a man in the row behind me raised his hand.

'Thank you, Mr…?'

'McAlister.'

'Mr McAlister. Would you please leave the jury box, and would the clerk please call another name.'

'Marjorie Bloom,' the clerk called. Another small sigh of relief: I was not going to be the only woman on the jury, after all.

We then stood, one at a time, to take our oaths as jurors, swearing to return a true verdict according to the evidence. Those members of the jury panel who had not been selected then left the courtroom with Geoffrey.

The clerk stood once again, asked Professor du Plessis to stand, and turned to face us, holding a document.

'Members of the jury: you are all sworn. Members of the jury, the defendant, Danie du Plessis, is charged in this indictment with one count of aiding and abetting the supply of controlled drugs. The particulars of the offence are that he, between about May 1975 and October 1976, aided and abetted, counselled, and procured Vincent Cummings to supply controlled drugs, contrary to section four of the Misuse of Drugs Act 1971. To this indictment he has pleaded not guilty, and it is your charge, having heard the evidence, to say whether he be guilty or not.'

The clerk turned towards the bench again, bowed, and sat down.

'Members of the jury,' Mr Justice Overton said, 'before we begin the trial, I have one or two more things to say to you. First, it is important that you do not discuss the case with anyone outside the twelve of you. I know there will be a temptation when family and friends ask you about your jury service, but you must resist that temptation. Otherwise, your view of the case may be influenced by something said by someone who is not following the evidence, and is in no position to express an opinion. It is your opinion of the facts that counts, and only yours. Second, you may not do any of your own research, or try to conduct any investigation of your own. Your verdict must be based on the evidence you hear in this courtroom, and only on that evidence. You are free to discuss the case among yourselves, of course, but only when all twelve of you are together in the privacy of your jury room, where no one can overhear what you say.

'Bear this in mind, too: the key to reaching a true verdict is to listen carefully and quietly to the evidence, and to ask yourself where it leads you.

'Finally, I don't expect there to be any problems of this kind, but if anyone should approach you in connection with the case, or if anything should happen to cause you any concern at all, you must report it to me at once through the clerk or the usher. Don't discuss it with anyone else, but report it to me immediately. I hope all that is clear. I will now ask Mr Pilkington to make his opening speech on behalf of the Crown.'

I take comfort from what Mr Justice Overton said about listening to the evidence carefully and quietly. I understand that perfectly. I live in a world of quiet. The silence of the library allows time for contemplation, and its very quietness does help you to focus on what matters and what doesn't. And there's something – I've never been able to describe this properly – but there's something reassuring about being quiet, surrounded by those huge, silent floor-to-ceiling bookcases. The bookcases are full of dark tomes and can seem utterly impenetrable. But you know, too, that all the books are precisely catalogued, in long lines of filing cabinets stuffed with vast numbers of reference cards: one for each book. Somehow, you feel that every question can be answered if you listen in the quiet, surrounded by knowledge, and I've always found that deeply comforting.

55

We decided to take our lunch sandwiches into our jury room, rather than sitting in the cafeteria, so that we could start to get to know each other. My new friend Kenneth Avery rather took charge of things, as everyone else seemed reticent, and he did a good job of it, I thought. When we were sitting around the table, he suggested that we all introduce ourselves in turn. I was sitting to his right. Mercifully, he started with the person to his left, which meant that I would go last. We were a diverse bunch.

Marjorie Bloom, my prized other woman, was a retired

bookkeeper who lived in Golders Green. Most of the male jurors were white, but Mohamed Khan, a businessman from Peckham, and Winston Beckett, a musician from Wandsworth, were of Asian and Jamaican heritage respectively. I remembered the judge's question about apartheid, and wondered whether that would have any effect on us. The other men came from various walks of life. My new friend, and likely foreman-in-waiting, Kenneth Avery, was a stockbroker living in Hampstead; Steven Wainwright was an accountant; George Kennedy had a managerial role with the London Transport Executive; John Lacey was a teacher in Hackney, while Edward Brown had retired after a career as a surveyor. Jeff Simons was the landlord of a pub in Camden Town, immediately nominated as the prospective venue for our post-verdict party. Phil Ackroyd was a car salesman from Battersea. Joe Henley was a plumber from Lambeth, and no shrinking violet.

'What did you think of the prosecutor's speech, then?' he asked us. 'What was his name again? Pilkington, was it?'

'Andrew Pilkington,' Kenneth confirmed.

'He's good, isn't he?' Joe continued. 'He certainly didn't pull any punches. When are we going to hear from the defence geezer, what's-his-name, Schroeder?'

'They didn't say, did they?' Phil replied. 'Perhaps he's on after lunch. But the judge didn't mention him.'

'No. Mr Pilkington said he was going to call a witness after lunch,' Steven pointed out.

'Why don't we ask Geoffrey?' Mohamed suggested.

This was unanimously hailed as a good idea, though Geoffrey is outside our number, and I did wonder whether it was something Mr Justice Overton had told us not to do. I didn't say anything, though.

'I don't know what Schroeder can say, really,' John Lacey observed. 'I mean, if Cummings was dealing drugs on the scale they say, and Pienaar was working with him. And they know Pienaar and the professor were working together...'

'That's just what Mr Pilkington says, though, isn't it?' Marjorie reminds him. 'We haven't heard any evidence yet.'

'Still...' John insists. 'No smoke without fire; that's what I always say.'

56

'I swear by Almighty God that the evidence I shall give shall be the truth, the whole truth, and nothing but the truth.' She turned towards the bench. 'Stephanie Walsh, Detective Inspector, attached to West End Central Police Station, my Lord.'

'Inspector Walsh,' Andrew Pilkington began, 'this investigation was begun by the police in Cambridge. But you have been appointed the liaison officer for the Metropolitan Police, is that right?'

'It is, my Lord.'

'And have you been designated to give evidence about a Metropolitan Police investigation of a man called Vincent Cummings that continued over a number of years?'

'I have, my Lord.'

'Thank you, Inspector. If you would please look at the file I'm about to hand you.' He stretched out both hands to summon Geoffrey. 'Do be careful, it's rather heavy. Don't want any injuries on our first day, do we?' Several jurors chuckled.

'Inspector Walsh,' he continued, after Geoffrey had gingerly balanced the thick tome in front of her on the witness box, 'does this file contain an account of that investigation, which has been agreed between the prosecution and the defence?'

'Yes, sir.'

Andrew turned towards the bench. 'My Lord, may this be Exhibit one? I believe there is no objection. There are copies for your Lordship and the jury.'

'No objection, my Lord,' Ben confirmed.

'Very well,' the judge agreed. 'Exhibit one.'

There was a lengthy pause while Geoffrey distributed the copies, solicitously warning the jury several times about the weight of the exhibit. The copies were balanced rather precariously on the edge of the jury box, and having handled such exhibits many times before, he was anticipating picking those on the front row up from the floor at some stage in the proceedings, probably more than once.

'Now, Inspector, if you would turn to the first page, please, and, members of the jury if you would follow along...'

'My learned friend is free to lead the witness,' Ben said. 'There's no dispute.'

'I'm much obliged. Inspector, are pages one and two a copy of Mr Cummings's antecedents? Do they show that he was born in London on 8 March 1931, making him forty-five years of age at the time of his death last year?'

'Yes, sir.'

'And are there four previous convictions recorded against him?'

'That's correct.'

'But, in fairness, Inspector, were they in his early years; were the drugs offences to do with personal consumption; and would it be fair to say that they have no real connection with his subsequent career?'

'I would agree with that, my Lord, yes.'

'Thank you. Then, moving on, on page three, do we come to a series of reports dated between 1951 and 1956, authored by a DS Mitchell?'

'Yes, sir.'

'The jury will be free to look at them later at their leisure. But could you summarise for us, please, what is recorded in these reports?'

'Yes, sir. Police first became aware of Mr Cummings early in 1951, when it appeared that he was an associate of underworld figures in Soho, dealing in drugs, and arranging gambling and prostitution.

He didn't occupy any kind of leadership position at that time. He was more of a runner and enforcer, working for those higher up, so he wasn't the main focus of the investigation at that point. Even so, as we can see on pages 15 and 16, there are occasions when he seems to be dealing some drugs on his own account – low-level stuff, smallish quantities of cannabis mainly, not much money involved. It probably wasn't encouraged by his superiors, so there wasn't anything more than that at that time.'

'Yes. But in 1957, do officers notice the beginnings of some change? Page 32, members of the jury.'

'Yes, sir. Early in 1957, a prominent Soho gangster called Mo Rippon was murdered. Mr Rippon was the leader of a syndicate that dealt mostly in prostitution in Soho, but they also had a sideline in hard drugs. Another officer, DS Lamont, had taken over the reporting by then, and in his first report, DS Lamont indicates that a number of Mo Rippon's associates were suspected of having had something to do with his death; so there was some doubt about the initial reports that he had been murdered by a rival syndicate. I don't think that ever became totally clear, either way. No one was ever arrested for it. But in any case, one of Mr Rippon's associates, Reg Worley, seems to have taken over as syndicate leader, and all of a sudden, Mr Cummings starts to show up as Mr Worley's right-hand man. From that point, police interest in Mr Cummings increases considerably.'

Andrew paused and thought for a moment.

'Yes. Inspector, perhaps this might be the time to ask you this: other than the four minor matters mentioned in the antecedents, Mr Cummings was never convicted of any offence, was he?'

'No, sir.'

'Was he ever arrested?'

'No, sir.'

'The jury might be curious about why not. By 1957 he was already showing signs of rising through the ranks, and as the jury will hear, he seems to have eventually taken command of his own syndicate. Do you know why he was never arrested?'

DI Walsh smiled. 'It does seem strange, I know. It's important to understand that the decision to arrest someone in a leadership role in organised crime is always a difficult one. If it goes wrong, the villains find out we've been watching them, and it can cause all kinds of problems.'

'When you say "goes wrong", what do you mean by that?' Mr Justice Overton asked.

'If it turned out that we had insufficient evidence to hold him, my Lord, or we couldn't mount a successful prosecution against him.'

'Yes. I see. Thank you.'

'What kind of problems might result from that?' Andrew asked.

'Once they know we're on to them, the villains will take new precautions to secure their operation, and shield themselves from our view. We've probably wasted a lot of valuable police time, and our intelligence is now out of date. Also, once we move in, we risk exposing innocent individuals, and we risk endangering any undercover officers and informants who may have supplied information.'

'Why might evidence be a problem when you arrest someone higher up in the chain of command?' Andrew asked.

'As someone moves up through the ranks, he generally becomes less and less involved with the day-to-day business of the syndicate. He tends to leave that to those under him. We can arrest street dealers all day long – it's easy – but that doesn't have any real impact on the business. There are always others to take their place. So we keep watch on the leadership and hope they'll make a mistake: that we might catch them handling the product, or running a high-stakes game, or arranging prostitutes for friends, or even being seen in the wrong company – an associate whose operation police are about to shut down. We do catch one or two that way, but it's relatively rare. I can only assume that the officers in charge never felt confident enough of the outcome in Mr Cummings's case to take the risk.'

'And that would not be an unusual view for an officer to take?'

'Not in the least, no.'

57

'Thank you, Inspector,' Andrew said. 'Then, with that in mind, let me ask you how things developed between 1957 and 1960. Page 62, members of the jury.'

'By 1960, Mr Cummings seems to be running his own syndicate. He seems to have split from Mr Worley late in 1959 – apparently amicably: certainly there are no reports of any violence. That may be because the Worley syndicate was never that interested in drugs. Gambling clubs and brothels were more their thing. They may have been happy to hive that part of the business off to Mr Cummings – no doubt in return for a piece of the action.'

'A piece of the action, Inspector?' Mr Justice Overton asked.

Steffie had to bite her lip to avoid smiling. 'In return for some monetary consideration, my Lord.' The jury sniggered.

'Do we see him looking to expand his business?' Andrew asked.

'Very much so. He has an ever-growing number of people working for him in Soho, many of whom we arrest – runners, street dealers and the like – but who are always replaced quickly. He's also branching out into other parts of London, and sometimes outside London. And more significantly, he starts showing up on the Continent, mostly in Belgium and the Netherlands, meeting with known high-ranking figures in the drug world.'

'Did that lead the police to expand their coverage of Mr Cummings?'

'Yes. Actually, when he started going into Europe, he became a person of interest there too. Interpol contacted us about him, and we agreed with Interpol to share intelligence: so we were starting to build up quite a dossier on him. We were also tracking down his bank accounts by then, so we were able to keep track of his financial progress.'

'Yes. Inspector, the jury will see that they have extracts from five sets of bank accounts in their file. Pages 125 to 278, members of the jury. They are quite voluminous, I'm afraid, but they are there simply to give the jury a flavour of his financial development, which we can do without going over them line by line, would you agree?'

'I would, sir. If the jury look at the closing totals for each month of the account, they will see a steadily increasing positive balance from late 1962, early 1963 onwards.'

'And by the time of his death last year, does it appear that he was running a business worth several million pounds annually?'

'Yes, sir.'

'And does the intelligence suggest the nature of that business?'

'All the available evidence, based on his movements, his associates, and other factors, indicate that Mr Cummings had by then become a major player in the international drug trade.'

'Is it also right that, of these five accounts, only the first is what one might call a normal bank account – a current account with a branch of the Midland Bank in London – the remaining four being numbered accounts, with no name attached, held in two banks in Luxembourg and two in Switzerland?'

'Yes, sir.'

'And what you do you notice about the Midland account?'

'There are no large sums coming in or going out. There's nothing at all to raise any suspicion. It seems that Mr Cummings used this account for normal, everyday purposes in this country, and used the foreign accounts for business purposes.'

'Inspector, is there any information, in any of the reports the jury have before them, to suggest that Mr Cummings may have been making his money from legitimate employment, or self-employment?'

'We have no record of Mr Cummings having any legitimate activity, either as an employee or as a self-employed person, with one exception. Such tax returns as he filed – which was not every year – claimed that he had a business as a market trader in Dalston, his declared income from which was, shall we say, modest.'

'Not in the million-pound range?'

'Nowhere close.'

'Pages 280 to 304, members of the jury. Thank you, Inspector. Now finally, more recently, did police receive information about Mr Cummings branching out into a different line of work?'

'Yes, sir. From 1973, he seems to have involved himself in a limited amount of dealing in arms, military weapons and hardware. There is evidence of appearances by Mr Cummings and associates of his in Africa – primarily in Tanzania – in the company of known arms dealers, selling arms in training camps.'

'These training camps being associated with the African National Congress, a militant organisation dedicated to the overthrow of apartheid in South Africa?'

'Yes, sir.'

Andrew turned to the bench. 'My Lord, I shall be calling an expert witness in due course to deal with the question of apartheid generally. Unless your Lordship thinks I should, I don't propose to explain apartheid to the jury now, beyond saying that it refers to the system of government in South Africa, based on white supremacy in government and the segregation of the population along racial lines.'

'Is there any difficulty with that, Mr Schroeder?' the judge asked.

'None whatsoever, my Lord,' Ben replied.

'I'm obliged,' Andrew said. 'Inspector, is just anyone entitled to set himself up as an arms dealer without jumping through certain hoops?'

'Certainly not. You would have to apply for a licence, which would only be granted if you show that you are of good character, and that you understand the law relating to firearms, and undertake to follow the law. If you want to trade abroad, of course, there are also rules to be followed in whatever country you are trading in;

and you would require an export licence from this country, which involves further forms to fill in.'

'Is there any record of Mr Cummings holding any licence as an arms dealer?'

'No, there is not.'

Andrew paused. 'Thank you, Inspector. Now, I'd like to turn to a different subject and ask you some questions about a man called Arthur Pienaar.'

58

'Was Arthur Pienaar born in Port Elizabeth, South Africa, on 4 January 1940, making him thirty-six years of age at the time of his death last year?'

'Yes, sir.'

'Was he a man of previous good character? In other words, is it right to say that he had no convictions recorded against him?'

'Yes, sir.'

'And indeed, he was a practising solicitor, a partner in a firm in St John's Wood: is that right?'

'It is, sir.'

'And in their bundle, do the jury have records supplied by the Home Office, dealing with Mr Pienaar's presence in this country?'

'Yes, sir.'

'Page 315, members of the jury. Do these records tell us that Mr Pienaar left South Africa and came to this country in 1961?'

'That's correct sir.'

'Under what circumstances?'

'The circumstances are based almost entirely on Mr Pienaar's own account of things. He told the Home Office examiners that he was passionately opposed to apartheid, and that he had worked with the African National Congress in a number of operations – raids on police stations and the like – although he insisted that he was involved only in planning, and had not personally committed any acts of violence. The Home Office had no information to contradict that, though it is right to say that in at least one such raid there were casualties on both sides, including one or two fatalities on the police side. It was also clear that if Mr Pienaar had remained in South Africa, he would have been arrested, and in all likelihood, charged with very serious offences.'

'Yes. As a result of that, Inspector, was Mr Pienaar allowed to remain in this country?'

'He was, sir.'

'And, to all intents and purposes, did he get on with his life? Did he take a law degree at Bristol University, and then become a solicitor practising in London?'

'He did, sir.'

'But did the Home Office continue to keep a close eye on him?'

'Yes, sir.'

'Why was that?'

'He had a number of associates at a college in London known for its rather radically inclined student body, and it appeared that he was involved in recruiting students at that college for undercover propaganda operations directed against the government of South Africa. The Home Office were concerned about it because it had the potential to affect relations between this country and South Africa, and also because they wanted to be aware of any evidence that Mr Pienaar was in some way abusing the leave to remain in this country they had granted to him.'

'In fact, the Home Office did not find any reason to question Mr Pienaar's right to remain, did they?'

'No, sir, they did not.'

'And is it right to say, Inspector, that there's no suggestion that Mr Pienaar was committing any offence against the law of this country in his association with the students in question?'

'As far as I'm aware, that's correct, sir.'

'And as time went by, did it become clear that Mr Pienaar's role changed somewhat? Instead of being involved with the operational side of things, does it appear that he became responsible for raising money to support the operations?'

'Yes, sir.'

'Responsible to whom: do we know?'

'No, sir. That's something of a mystery. It would make sense that he was working in conjunction with someone in South Africa, but I'm not aware of any evidence about who that might have been. He obviously had a good number of associates in this country also.'

'How did Mr Pienaar go about raising funds?'

'He identified donors, rich expatriate South Africans, in this country and abroad, who agreed to make contributions on a regular basis.'

'Yes. Now, Inspector, I'm not going to ask you about the details of this. I'll get those from DI Phillips, the officer in charge of the case, when I call him. But are you aware generally that after Mr Pienaar's death, DI Phillips searched his flat and found a long document referred to as a ledger, that appears to record Mr Pienaar's receipts of contributions from his donors? Page 325, members of the jury.'

'Yes, sir.'

'And taking this briefly, does the ledger suggest that Pienaar was receiving donations from Vincent Cummings for a number of years?'

'Yes, sir.'

'Did you also find a bank account in Mr Pienaar's name with a Dutch bank, Algemene Bank, in Amsterdam? Page 340, members of the jury.'

'Yes, sir.'

'And are there payments into that account, on what appears to be a regular basis over the past two years, in the region of £1,000 to £1,500 every quarter; and do those payments match payments out of one of the Cummings accounts in both amounts and dates?'

'That's correct, sir.'

'Does it appear, then that, for whatever reason, Mr Cummings was making regular payments to Mr Pienaar personally, in addition to making his contribution to the fund as a donor?'

'It does seem so, sir, yes. There's no indication in the paperwork of why exactly those payments were made, but they were credited to Mr Pienaar's personal bank account at Algemene Bank.'

'Yes, thank you, Inspector. Now, finally, on Friday 8 October of last year, 1976, were police called to the University Arms Hotel in Cambridge, where they found the bodies of Vincent Cummings and Arthur Pienaar in one of the hotel's rooms; and had both men been shot dead, in the manner sometimes referred to as "execution style" – that is to say, being shot in the back of the head?'

'That is correct, sir.'

'Did the Cambridge Police open an investigation into the murders, led by DI Phillips?'

'That's correct, sir.'

'And I will ask DI Phillips more about that. Thank you, Inspector. Wait there, please.'

Ben stood.

'Well, Inspector, dealing with that last matter first: the murders of Vincent Cummings and Arthur Pienaar were not related in any way to the drug trade, were they?'

Steffie hesitated. 'I'm not the officer in charge of the investigation, sir. It might be better…'

'You've spoken to DI Phillips about it, haven't you, Inspector?'

'Yes, sir, but…'

Andrew stood. 'My Lord, the Inspector is quite right. It would be better if my learned friend directed his questions to DI Phillips, rather than to this witness.'

'I think that must be right, Mr Schroeder, mustn't it?' Mr Justice Overton said.

'In that case, my Lord, my learned friend should have waited to ask DI Phillips about it, rather than bringing it up with this witness. The problem is this: DI Walsh's evidence has been devoted to proving that Vincent Cummings was a drug dealer. If she then gives evidence, without any further explanation, that Cummings and Pienaar were murdered "execution style", it invites the jury to jump to the conclusion that the murders were drug-related. But both the witness and my learned friend know perfectly well that they were not drug-related, and it would be wrong to leave the jury with the wrong impression until such time as DI Phillips is called.'

The judge nodded. 'Very well. I will allow you to ask enough to establish that point, but anything further will have to await DI Phillips.'

'Much obliged, my Lord. Inspector, Vincent Cummings and Arthur Pienaar were murdered by a man using the name Nick Erasmus: that's right, isn't it?'

'Yes, sir.'

'And it is within your knowledge, is it not, that Nick Erasmus was an agent of the Bureau for State Security, sometimes known as BOSS, an agency of the South African government that undertakes covert operations on behalf of the State?'

'That's correct, sir.'

'And on the following Monday, the third day after the murders, Nick Erasmus forced his way into the home of my client, Professor du Plessis, and his wife, in Cambridge, threatened them with a gun, and announced that he was going to kill them and their two children unless they cooperated with them. That's right, isn't it?'

'I believe that is what the evidence suggests, sir, yes.'

'Yes. What Erasmus demanded was a list of Pienaar's donors, wasn't it? He believed that the Professor and his wife, Miss Coetzee, had such a list because they had been assisting Mr Pienaar in the handling of the donations. Yes?'

'Yes.'

'But fortunately, with extraordinary courage, Miss Coetzee took matters into her own hands, didn't she? She used force against Erasmus, which resulted in his death?'

'Yes, sir.'

'Which the Director of Public Prosecutions accepted was an act of lawful self-defence, and defence of others, against the threat of deadly force.'

Andrew stood again. 'My Lord, this witness has no knowledge of what the Director of Public Prosecutions may have decided,' he protested.

'The Director decided not to charge Miss Coetzee with any offence arising from the death of Nick Erasmus,' Ben said. 'That's right, Inspector, isn't it?'

'That is correct, sir.'

'Thank you. Let me move on. I only have one other matter. You've been asked about a number of reports dealing with the undoubted fact that Vincent Cummings was a drug dealer. Until they were produced for the purposes of this trial, these were all confidential police records, weren't they?'

'Yes, sir.'

'There is no possible way that Professor du Plessis could have had access to any of them, could ever have seen them, or could even have been aware of them, is there?'

'No. I accept that, sir.'

'Thank you,' Ben said, resuming his seat. 'Nothing further, my Lord.'

59

Sarah Mulvaney
After we'd heard from DI Walsh, there wasn't much time left before the end of the court's afternoon session. I think the judge would

have liked to call it a day then, but Mr Pilkington had his apartheid expert, a Dr Morrison, available and wanted to call him so that he didn't have to come back tomorrow. The judge obviously felt he couldn't object to that, but he did make a bit of a show of looking at the court clock and fidgeting in his chair, which had a few of us in the jury box looking down at the floor from time to time to avoid giggling.

But for most of the time Professor Morrison was giving evidence, giggling was the last thing on our minds. Mr Pilkington was the model of patience, and let Dr Morrison, a professor of African history at Edinburgh University, tell the story of apartheid in his own words. And what a story it was. I had thought I knew about apartheid; but I was shocked to learn that what I thought I knew – mainly gleaned from my reading of newspaper and magazine articles – was only the tip of a very unpleasant iceberg. By the time Dr Morrison had finished his evidence in chief, having given us his full, unedited account of the horrors of the White government's treatment of the Non-Whites, I think everyone on the jury – even some of the men, who liked to pretend that nothing shocked them – were feeling deeply disturbed. Some of our faces were distinctly pale, and I suspect mine might have been one of them.

Mr Schroeder did a great cross-examination. I know: who am I to say that? What do I know? But I thought it was brilliant, anyway. It couldn't have lasted for more than fifteen minutes. But in that time, he told Dr Morrison the story of Professor du Plessis' romance with his Cape Coloured wife, Amy Coetzee, and got him to confirm that the horrible story of their having to leave South Africa, literally to run for their lives just because they loved each other, would have been exactly the experience they had endured. A number of us glanced over towards the dock, and gave the Professor a sympathetic look. I tried to include Amy in my look too. We'd all noticed her sitting opposite us, in the public gallery, ever since the trial started. She was with a man, who I assume was a member of the family, or family friend, and although she tried to put a brave face on things, it was obvious that the experience was deeply distressing for her. The sympathetic look had nothing to do with the case; it was just a human gesture. But I, for one, ended up understanding completely why Professor du Plessis would try to strike a blow against this horrible system of apartheid, once he was safely in England. I couldn't blame him for that at all. Mr Schroeder had taken me all that way in fifteen minutes.

After court ended, we gathered in the jury room to collect our coats and other belongings. We were a pretty subdued bunch. Even the chatty ones among us, Steven, Joe and Winston, who could usually be relied on for a cheerful word, didn't say very much. We wished each other a good evening, and left the jury room empty in a matter of a minute or two. I went to catch my bus. I was in luck. I jumped on a bus straight away and was home in under half an hour.

I opened my front door using my key as usual. And there it was, lying on my doormat. I had no regular post: only this envelope someone had pushed through my letterbox. I opened it without really thinking about it.

So; a man walks into a library carrying a library book. He walks up to the desk and says to the duty librarian: 'I've come to return this.' The librarian examines the book, and sees that it's almost twenty-five years overdue. 'Why are you only returning this now?' she asks, horrified. 'We're redecorating,' the man replies, 'and it doesn't go with the new wallpaper.'

All right, I admit, it's pretty bad, even by the standards of librarian humour. But that's what came to me as I was lying on the floor, with my back to my front door, sobbing and gasping for breath, and looking at what someone had chosen to infiltrate into my house, my home, my sanctuary. It was a single piece of white notepaper, and written on it, in green ink, was the single statement: 'The verdict is Guilty.' Enclosed with the note was a single live matchstick. It was a Swan Vesta – it's strange what you notice when your mind is spinning out of control somewhere between your body and the ceiling.

After some time – which felt like several hours, but was probably closer to twenty minutes – I calmed down enough to get back up on my feet, and take the note and matchstick into the kitchen, where I was able to pour myself a glass of wine before sitting down at the table to ponder what had happened, and what I should do about it. Strangely, the one thought that never came to me was the possibility of doing what the writer of the note wanted, to predetermine a verdict before I had heard all the evidence. All my thoughts were devoted to ways not to comply with the demand – which, looking back on it now, was remarkable, given how frightened I was. As my rational mind began to return to me, it occurred to me to wonder whether whoever wrote this note had heard of majority verdicts. In this day and age it isn't enough to get to one juror, is it? You would need at least three to ensure that there couldn't be a majority. Was it just me he was trying to intimidate, or had he approached some of my colleagues, or even all of us? Apparently, it wasn't a problem for him to learn our names and discover where we lived.

None of this shed much light on the problem of what to do. But it came to me quite quickly that I couldn't keep it to myself. My first instinct was to call the police. But what if he was watching the house when they came? And in any case, what could the police do about it tonight? Besides, I wasn't supposed to talk to anyone outside the jury about the case: which left the obviously sensible option of showing the note to Geoffrey the following morning, and asking him to take it to Mr Justice Overton. I had no idea what would happen then. But I couldn't worry about that for now. One step at a time.

When I went to bed, I switched on every light in the house, double-locked the door, and put a couple of chairs up against the doorframe. None of that made me sleep any better. I got up early the next morning and left home almost an hour earlier than usual. I wanted to talk to Geoffrey before I saw any of the other jurors. I closed and locked my door, and made my way down my short path to the small gate leading out on to the street. I stepped out into the street. As I was closing the gate, a man dressed in a light raincoat, the collar pulled up high around his neck, brushed by me, almost walking right into me. 'Don't forget,' he whispered. He didn't stop, but continued walking quickly. I looked after him, and did my best to see something about him I might be able to identify. I couldn't see anything.

As I stood waiting for my bus, I noticed that I was shaking.

60

Tuesday 8 February 1977

'Well, what should we do about this?' Mr Justice Overton asked.

As soon as Geoffrey had showed him the note, he had given the usher two urgent orders. The first was to keep Sarah Mulvaney apart from the other jurors in a separate room with a female security guard to watch over her. The second was to find Andrew Pilkington and Ben Schroeder, prise them away from their coffee, and bring them to his chambers as soon as possible. As good fortune would have it, Geoffrey was able to carry out the judge's instructions without undue difficulty. It was still early, no other members of the jury had yet arrived at court; and Andrew and Ben were having coffee together in the Bar mess, talking over the evidence to be given that day.

'The first thing, Judge, must be to hear from the juror herself,' Andrew suggested. 'We need to find out who she's told about this, and what effect it's had on her.'

'I agree,' Ben said.

The judge nodded to Geoffrey. 'All right, usher, let's have her in, please.'

As Geoffrey showed Sarah into the judge's chambers, judge and counsel stood, and Miles Overton ushered her solicitously into a chair in front of his desk.

'Now then, there's no need to be nervous, Miss Mulvaney,' he began, in what she found a surprisingly avuncular tone. 'Would you like some coffee?'

'No, thank you, sir,' she replied.

He handed her the note. 'This is the note you found, is it?'

'Yes, sir.'

'Someone had dropped it through your letterbox?'

'Yes, sir: in that envelope, with a single Swan Vesta matchstick – a live matchstick.'

'Yes, quite. And is this the first time anything like this has happened?'

'Yes. But then, a man approached me this morning as I was leaving my house. He almost bumped into me, and said, "Don't forget". Then he just walked away, as if nothing had happened.'

'I see,' the judge said. 'Now, it's very important that we know this, Miss Mulvaney. You're not in any trouble, I promise you. Quite the contrary. You've done exactly the right thing in telling me about it. But it's important that you answer truthfully. Have you told anyone else at all about what has happened?'

'No: no one, until I told Geoffrey when I arrived at court this morning.'

'You haven't spoken to any other members of the jury?'

'No, sir. I went out of my way to make sure that I didn't run into anyone.'

'If I may, Judge,' Geoffrey said, 'I did check. No other members of the jury had arrived at court when I took Miss Mulvaney to her separate room. No one else knows anything about it.'

The judge nodded. 'Good.' He glanced at counsel. 'Is there anything else we should ask?'

'Miss Mulvaney,' Andrew said, 'I would like to ask what effect this has had on you. I imagine it must have been very frightening to come home to find something like this waiting for you.'

'It was, sir. I must admit, I didn't get much sleep last night. I'm feeling better this morning, but I'm still a bit shaken up.'

'Of course. I suppose what I really want to ask is whether you feel able to continue as a member of the jury, or whether you feel it wouldn't be safe for you. Would you prefer to ask the judge to discharge you?'

She looked up sharply. 'No. I want to stay and hear the case. Besides, it wouldn't help, Mr Pilkington, would it? He's told me he wants a verdict of guilty. If I drop off the jury, I'd be in just as much danger then, perhaps more. He knows where I live.'

'We can make sure you get police protection,' Andrew replied, 'whatever you decide to do. Judge, if the usher would kindly call down to the police room, I'm sure DI Walsh will be there. Perhaps she should join us.'

'By all means,' Miles Overton said, gesturing to Geoffrey to use his phone.

'You don't mind if Steffie organises this, do you, Ben?' Andrew asked quietly. 'She's finished giving evidence.'

'No problem,' Ben replied. 'Miss Mulvaney, may I just ask you this? I don't know quite how to put it. But has this incident had any effect on your view of the case? In other words, do you still think you can be impartial as between the prosecution and the defence? Do you think you can give Professor du Plessis a fair trial?'

'I'm more determined than ever to be fair to him,' Sarah insisted. 'I know I can't allow this to get to me. I take it seriously being on the jury, and I want to make sure I play my part in reaching the right verdict.'

'You're not feeling any pressure to return a guilty verdict?' Ben persisted. 'No one would blame you if you did. It's only natural.'

'No. I'm not going to give in to his threats, whoever he may be.'

'Miss Mulvaney,' Miles Overton said, 'if I can allow you to continue as a member of the jury, would you agree to say nothing about this to any of the other jurors? I mean, nothing about the note, or the Swan Vesta matchstick, and especially nothing about this meeting we're having now. It really would be of the utmost importance. I know it wouldn't be easy. Do you think you could do that?'

Sarah smiled. 'I'm a librarian, sir,' she replied. 'I don't say much at the best of times, and I wouldn't want to talk about this.'

They laughed together.

'I'm going to assign you a shadow, Miss Mulvaney,' Steffie Walsh said, once Andrew had briefed her about what had happened.

'A shadow?'

'An officer trained in surveillance. I have someone in mind. She will pick you up as you leave court and follow you home. We'll have a night guard outside your house, and your shadow will pick you up when you leave home to come to court tomorrow morning; and we will go on like that for as long as we have to. You won't notice her, but she will be there, I promise you; and if there's any trouble, she will have backup available.'

'But we don't know when he may appear again,' Sarah pointed out. 'What if he keeps himself hidden for weeks, months even?'

'I promise you, that's very unlikely,' Steffie replied. 'But we will keep up the security until we're satisfied that it's no longer necessary. And meanwhile, we will be making inquiries.'

'Inquiries?'

Steffie took the note and the envelope from the judge's desk. 'You don't mind if I hang on to these, do you, Judge?'

'I suppose not. Why?'

She smiled. 'They're evidence. We'll start with fingerprints and see where we go from there. With any luck we may even be able to find out who we're dealing with before he shows himself again.'

'Does either of you want me to discharge the jury?' Miles Overton asked, when everyone had left chambers except the two counsel. 'If either of you does, I don't think I would have any choice about it.'

'I'm sorry to say this, Judge,' Andrew replied, 'but I think you have to. It's too dangerous. There's no way to know what may be said in the jury room. And besides, I know Miss Mulvaney's putting a brave face on it, but this must have come as a terrible shock. The poor girl must be scared out of her wits.'

'I don't see any need to discharge the entire jury, Judge,' Ben replied. 'You could discharge Miss Mulvaney, and continue with the remaining eleven. We can tell them that she's not feeling well – which isn't too far from the truth. But I'm going to suggest that you don't even need to go that far.'

'But Mr Pilkington's right about the risks, surely, isn't he Mr Schroeder? We can't predict what might be said in the jury room. How do we know this won't taint the verdict?'

'Or that we know the whole story,' Andrew added. 'We don't know that other jurors haven't been approached too.'

Ben shook his head. 'If anyone ought to be worried about Sarah Mulvaney, Judge, it's me,' he said. 'She's been put under pressure to see to it that there is a guilty verdict. But I'm not worried about her. I think she's absolutely sincere in her belief that she can continue, that she can try the case fairly, and I think we should let her. In any case, she's only one voice among twelve. Even if she comes down against me for the wrong reason – which I don't think she will – she can't convict Professor du Plessis all on her own.'

'But we don't know whether whoever wrote the note has approached other jurors,' the judge pointed out.

'Well, we can't know that unless either someone else comes forward, or we ask them directly,' Ben replied, 'and I would be against asking them. That would really open up Pandora's box. Even if no one else has been approached, they would all start murmuring and speculating, and it would make Miss Mulvaney's position impossible – she would almost have to tell the others then, wouldn't she? And if that happens, you would have to discharge the entire jury. Judge, you directed them very clearly at the beginning of the trial to come forward if anything like this happened. Let's trust them to follow your directions.'

Miles Overton nodded thoughtfully for some time.

'All right. Let's continue with the trial with all twelve jurors for now. But let's keep our eyes and ears open. If anything else develops, I may have to change my mind.'

61

'DI Phillips,' Andrew began, once the Inspector had taken the oath and introduced himself, 'are you the officer in charge of this investigation?'

'I am, my Lord.'

'Inspector, I've been told that there is no dispute about the bulk of your evidence, and so, if my learned friend doesn't object, I will lead you much of the way.'

'No objection,' Ben confirmed.

'I'm obliged. Inspector, in the early hours of the morning of Friday 8 October 1976, were you called to attend the University Arms Hotel in Cambridge in response to a report that two men had been murdered there?'

'I was, sir.'

'On arrival did you make your way to room 224?'

'I did, sir. My colleague, DC Whittaker, was already on the scene, and pointed out to me the lifeless bodies of two men, who I now know to have been Vincent Cummings and Arthur Pienaar, lying on the bed. Both men had been shot more than once in the back, and to the back of the head. I discussed the case briefly with the medical examiner, and with DC Whittaker, before leaving the hotel to inform my superior, Superintendent Walker, of the events, so that we could set up the investigation.'

'Jumping ahead slightly, did you quickly establish that the murders had probably been committed at about one o'clock that morning, and that the same weapon, a Browning 9mm handgun, had been used in both murders?'

'That is correct, sir.'

'Tell the jury how the investigation proceeded from there.'

'Later that morning, after a meeting with Superintendent Walker, I asked DC Whittaker to drive down to St Albans to interview Mr Cummings's widow, while I visited the law firm of Barnard, Pienaar & McFall in St John's Wood, where Mr Pienaar had been a partner. I spoke to his partner, Mr McFall, for some time. He supplied me with one of Mr Pienaar's files, which appeared to relate to clients of the firm, referred to only as Rosencrantz and Guildenstern.'

'From which you no doubt deduced that these clients were operating under stage names,' Andrew said with a smile. The jury chuckled.

Phillips returned the smile. 'I did, sir, yes. The file had very little information in it, but it did refer to two people, a Mr Stevens, and someone using the initials BK. It later became clear that both names were in some way associated with Mr Pienaar's fundraising activities. I was also given the address of Mr Pienaar's flat, which I searched the following day together with DC Whittaker.'

'During that search, did you find the document we've been calling the ledger, which the jury have in their bundle?'

'We did, sir, yes.'

'And did you later ascertain that Mr Stevens was a name used by the defendant, Professor du Plessis, while he was helping Mr Pienaar to deal with the donations recorded in the ledger?'

'Yes, sir.'

'What about the person known as BK?'

'We later established that this referred to a Mr Balakrishnan, a practitioner of *Hawala*, who has an office in East London.'

Andrew looked up to the bench. 'My Lord, I don't propose to ask the Inspector any more about *Hawala* now. I'm sure it sounds rather mysterious, but I will be calling Mr Balakrishnan next, and everything should then become clear.'

'Let us hope so, Mr Pilkington,' Mr Justice Overton said, exchanging a surreptitious smile with the jury.

'Inspector, did you also ascertain that Professor du Plessis had been asked to supervise a South African man using the name Nick

Erasmus, who claimed to be a PhD student at the University, in the preparation of his thesis?'

'Yes, sir.'

'But did it later transpire that Nick Erasmus was in fact not a *bona fide* graduate student, but was working covertly as an officer of the South African Bureau for State Security, and that he was the person who had murdered Vincent Cummings and Arthur Pienaar?'

'That's correct, sir.'

Andrew paused for some time. 'Inspector, on the morning of Monday 11 October 1976, just three days after those murders, did you have occasion to go with DC Whittaker to the home of the du Plessis family in Cambridge?'

'Yes, sir.'

'Why was that?'

'Based on certain intelligence to which we had access, we had reason to believe that Professor du Plessis and his family were in danger from the man calling himself Nick Erasmus. We weren't sure whether the family were at home, or had left home for the day, but we decided that we needed to find them.'

'Inspector, I'm going to lead you through certain events now, because I want to emphasise them to his Lordship and the jury. My understanding is this: you and DC Whittaker were not armed. Before rushing to the du Plessis home, you requested armed backup. But because of the urgency of the situation, you approached the house and knocked on the door before that backup arrived, knowing full well that Nick Erasmus might be in the house, and that he would be armed. Is that what happened?'

Ted Phillips looked down modestly. 'Well... yes, sir.'

Andrew looked up to the bench. 'My Lord, I know that DI Phillips would prefer me not to say this, but I'm going to say it anyway. It is the view of the prosecution, and I believe of the defence also, that DI Phillips and DC Whittaker displayed conspicuous courage on that day, and I invite your Lordship to consider at the end of the trial, whether it would be appropriate to commend both officers for that courage.'

Ben stood immediately. 'My Lord, I agree entirely with my learned friend, and I would wish to be associated with what he has said to your Lordship.'

The judge nodded. 'I will certainly consider it, Mr Pilkington,' he replied, to one or two approving nods from the jury box.

'My Lord, I'm much obliged. Now, in fact, Inspector, by the time you arrived – not that you had any way of knowing this – but by the time you arrived, Miss Coetzee had already struck Nick Erasmus a fatal blow with her poker: is that right?'

'Yes, sir. Miss Coetzee told us immediately what had happened, with complete frankness. It was clear that Mr Erasmus, who was indeed armed – with the same Browning 9mm handgun he had used to kill Cummings and Pienaar – had threatened to kill the entire du Plessis family. Our recommendation to the Director of Public Prosecutions was that no charge should be brought against Miss Coetzee, as she was clearly acting in defence of herself and her family, and that recommendation was followed.'

'Yes. Inspector, let me move on to your interviews of Professor du Plessis.'

62

'Did you interview Professor du Plessis, together with DC Whittaker, in the presence of Professor du Plessis' solicitor, Mr Barratt Davis?'

'Yes, sir.'

'Did the interview begin on 18 October 1976 at Parkside Police Station in Cambridge?'

'That's correct.'

'But there was a second session on 25 October, at West End

Central police station here in London: is that right?'

'Yes, sir.'

'What was the reason for the change of venue?'

'During the first interview at Parkside, we received intelligence that, despite the death of Nick Erasmus, there was an ongoing threat against Professor du Plessis and his family, and that they might be in immediate danger. In those circumstances, Superintendent Walker and I determined that the safest course would be to move the family straight away from Cambridge to London, on a temporary basis, so that they could have specialised protection from armed units of the Metropolitan Police. This meant that we had to adjourn the interview until they were settled in their temporary home. This was all arranged at the London end by DI Walsh, who offered West End Central as a venue while Professor du Plessis was living in London.'

'Yes. And in fact, for the sake of completeness, the intelligence proved to be accurate, did it not? A man was arrested outside the family's temporary home, who was armed and appeared to intend them harm?'

'That's correct, sir. For reasons I won't go into, once that man was arrested, we were reasonably sure that the threat had passed. But we remained vigilant, of course.'

'Inspector, at the outset of both sessions of the interview, was Professor du Plessis cautioned?'

'He was, my Lord.'

'Please tell the jury the words of the caution.'

'The words of the caution are: you are not obliged to say anything unless you wish to do so, but anything you say may be put into writing and given in evidence.'

'Did you question Professor du Plessis to confirm that he understood the caution, and, of course, did he have his solicitor, Mr Davis, present throughout?'

'Yes, sir.'

'Inspector, there is a transcript of both sessions of the interview, and the jury have this in their bundle, beginning at page 370. I understand there is no dispute?'

Ben stood. 'No objection, my Lord. But I do point out that, although my learned friend describes it as a "transcript", the interview was not recorded and then transcribed. What the jury have is essentially the notes taken by the officers, mainly DC Whittaker, during the interview. We don't dispute the substance of what was said, and we have no objection to the jury having the notes – as long as it is understood that it may not be one hundred per cent word for word.'

'That's quite right, my Lord,' Andrew agreed. 'I shouldn't have used the term "transcript". I'm obliged to my learned friend. Inspector, the jury will be able to read through the whole of the notes at a later time, so I'm simply going to ask you to give us a summary of what was said. Dealing with the first session, the Parkside interview on 18 October, what did Professor du Plessis tell you?'

'He told us that he only ever had two meetings with Mr Pienaar, the first in 1968, when he had just settled in England and had become a Fellow of his College; and the second last year – but we only dealt with that during the second session. Actually, the full picture of what he had to say only became apparent at the end of the interview as a whole.'

'I understand. Let's stay with the first session as far as we can, but fill in if you need to.'

'Yes, sir. He told us that Mr Pienaar came to see him unannounced, in his rooms in the College. After making conversation for some time, he invited Professor du Plessis to help him in dealing with donations he had solicited from wealthy expatriate South Africans, with a view to financing operations directed against the government of South Africa.'

'At this stage, these were not military operations, were they?'

'No, sir. At this stage, they were essentially propaganda exercises, the distribution of pamphlets against apartheid, and so on. The operations were carried out, as I understand it, by students recruited by Mr Pienaar's clients, referred to in his file as Rosencrantz and Guildenstern. Mr Pienaar was not directly concerned with the operational side: his job was the financing of the operations.'

'What did Mr Pienaar want Professor du Plessis to do?'

'He wanted him to ensure that the value of the donations reached those who were intended to receive them in South Africa. Professor du Plessis explained to us that Pienaar was a very cautious man, and never disclosed to him exactly who the money was going to.'

'And as I understand it, Inspector, you and DC Whittaker were disposed to believe that: is that correct?'

'We were, my Lord. From everything we know about Mr Pienaar, it does seem that he operated on a strictly need-to-know basis, and DC Whittaker and I accepted that.'

'What was Professor du Plessis' exact role to be?'

Ted Phillips hesitated. 'I understand that you will be calling Mr Balakrishnan, sir. Essentially, Professor du Plessis' job was to get the money to Mr Balakrishnan in Whitechapel, in the form of cash, or receipts for deposits of cheques he made in banks in London and Edinburgh into accounts controlled by Mr Balakrishnan. Mr Balakrishnan would then put the recipients in credit with his opposite number in Durban, using the *Hawala* system.'

Andrew smiled. 'Don't worry, Inspector, I'm not going to ask you to deal with that in any detail.'

'I don't mind taking a crack at it, sir,' Phillips replied, 'with the understanding that I won't be as thorough as Mr Balakrishnan will be.'

Judge and jury laughed.

Andrew stretched out a hand. 'By all means, Inspector.'

'What it comes to is that if you supply Mr Balakrishnan with £100, plus his commission, he will then create a credit of £100 with his counterpart in Durban, so that the intended recipient of the funds can pick it up from the Durban office in the local currency, again paying commission. That's it, basically.'

The jury were smiling.

'Thank you, Inspector. And is it your understanding that the practice of *Hawala*, in itself, is perfectly legal and above board.'

'As far as I'm aware, it is, sir, yes.'

'Did Professor du Plessis agree to undertake this role, and did he visit Mr Balakrishnan with donated funds three or four times a year between 1968 and 1975?'

'He did, sir.'

'Let's move on to his second meeting with Mr Pienaar.'

63

'At the start of the second session, at West End Central on 25 October, did you caution Professor du Plessis as before, and was Mr Davis once again present?'

'Yes, sir.'

'What did Professor du Plessis tell you about on this occasion?'

'In the second interview, Professor du Plessis dealt with his second and last meeting with Mr Pienaar. He said that once again Mr Pienaar came to see him with no advance warning. This was in March 1975. He seemed nervous, and took Professor du Plessis to Great St Mary's Church, the University Church, and then for a walk through the city, because he was suspicious that his rooms in College might have been bugged.'

'What was the subject of their discussion?'

'Mr Pienaar explained that more money was needed because the operations had now moved to the stage of military strikes against government buildings in South Africa. These attacks were being launched from training camps in neighbouring countries, including Tanzania, so the funding now had to cover the upkeep of the camps, and the weapons and ammunition used. It was an expensive business. Many more donors had been recruited since the time of the first meeting in 1968, but Cambridge still had to play its part.'

'Did Professor du Plessis indicate that one particular donor had a significant part to play in the raising of more money?'

'Yes, sir. There was a donor listed in the ledger using the initials VC, which, Professor du Plessis told us, referred to Vincent Cummings. Looking at the ledger, it was clear that Mr Cummings's donations had increased very considerably, and we were concerned to ask Professor du Plessis what he knew about that. If I may, sir, may the jury look at the notes of the interview at this point?'

'Certainly, Inspector. Page 402, please, members of the jury. Inspector, it may be slightly more interesting for the jury if you and I read it aloud. Why don't you read the lines for yourself and DC Whittaker, and I will read the lines for Professor du Plessis and Mr Davis?'

'Yes, sir.'

DI Phillips: If I could ask you to turn to page 32 of the ledger, Professor, do you see there an entry for a donation by VC in the month of May of last year, 1975?

Professor du Plessis: Yes. I do.

DI Phillips: What, if anything, catches your attention about that donation?

Professor du Plessis: The amount being paid.

DI Phillips: What about the amount?

Professor du Plessis: It's obviously far more than any of his payments before that time.

DI Phillips: It runs to six figures, doesn't it, as opposed to the £2,000, £3,000 he had been giving before May 1975?

Professor du Plessis: Yes.

DI Phillips: And then his donations continue at the same higher level until shortly before his death, don't they?

Professor du Plessis: His payments continue: yes.

DI Phillips: Did that get your attention at the time?

Professor du Plessis: Of course.

DI Phillips: Did it come as a surprise? Did you call Mr Pienaar's office, using your alias of Mr Stevens, and ask him what on earth was going on with VC?

Professor du Plessis: No.

DI Phillips: Why not? Weren't you curious? After all, Professor, you were concerned about the legality of what you were doing, weren't you? As a lawyer, didn't it raise any red flags for you that this donor could suddenly afford to give Pienaar more than £100,000 every three months?

Professor du Plessis: It didn't concern me: no.

DI Phillips: It never once occurred to you that there might be some criminality involved in such large donations?

Professor du Plessis: I wasn't concerned by the large payments, Inspector, because I was expecting them.

DC Whittaker: You were expecting them?

Professor du Plessis: Pienaar had warned me to expect an increase of that order, and he had explained exactly why. I had no reason to doubt what he told me, and so I had no reason to be concerned.

DC Whittaker: Wait a minute. I've just noticed something, Professor. We've been talking about a large increase in his donations. But you've been talking about a large increase in his payments. Is that a distinction in your mind?'

Professor du Plessis: Yes, of course.

DC Whittaker: The donation isn't the whole £100,000, just part of it? Is that what you're saying?

Professor du Plessis: Well done, DC Whittaker. You've got the point.

'Did you then ask some further questions,' Andrew asked, 'and did Professor du Plessis explain the distinction he had made between donations and payments? Page 407, members of the jury.'

'Yes, sir.'

'I will begin five lines down on page 407.'

Professor du Plessis: Pienaar told me he had reached an agreement with Cummings. The deal was that Pienaar would include all Cummings's earnings, in this country and in Europe, in the funds delivered to Balakrishnan, in return for a fee of 10%.

DI Phillips: That would be 10% of his gross earnings?

Professor du Plessis: I didn't say that. Pienaar didn't tell me whether this was before or after tax – if he knew himself, which I doubt.

DC Whittaker: Professor, at this time, I'm going to remind you again of the caution. You are not obliged to say anything unless you wish to do so, but anything you say may be put into writing and given in evidence. Again, do you understand the caution?

Professor du Plessis: Yes, I do.

DC Whittaker: Referring to the May 1975 payment, did you take the entire 100% of Cummings's earnings to Balakrishnan, or just Pienaar's 10%?

Professor du Plessis: All of it.

DC Whittaker: Where was the 90% left after Pienaar's fee going?

Professor du Plessis: Wherever Cummings wanted it to go. I have no idea. As long as our 10% ended up with the right people in South Africa, Pienaar wouldn't ask where the rest was going. It was none of his business.

DI Phillips: Professor du Plessis, what line of business was Vince Cummings in?

Professor du Plessis: I don't know. As I said before, I never met the man, and I never had any communication with him.

DI Phillips: Well, even so: surely it must have been obvious to you that some form of money laundering was taking place? Either Cummings was trying to evade tax, or he was washing his earnings from an illegal trade to make them look legitimate. Something was going on, wasn't it? What inquiries did you make to satisfy yourself that you weren't participating in a criminal enterprise?

Professor du Plessis: I went to the only source I had: I asked Pienaar. Well, what else could I do? I could hardly go to the police, could I?

DC Whittaker: You could have told Pienaar you didn't want to be involved.

[No reply.]

DI Phillips: We'll come back to that. You say you asked Pienaar about Cummings. Was this during your meeting in March?

Professor du Plessis: Yes.

DI Phillips: And what did he tell you?

Professor du Plessis: Pienaar told me that he'd only recently found out where Cummings's money was coming from, and it was purely by chance that he found out then. He was an arms dealer.

DI Phillips: An arms dealer?

Professor du Plessis: Yes.

DI Phillips: And what chance was it that enabled Pienaar to make that discovery?

Professor du Plessis: It turned out that Cummings was supplying arms to an ANC group that Pienaar was backing in Tanzania. He'd turned up in their training camp with a consignment of weapons. So, in a sense, Pienaar had become one of Cummings's customers.

DI Phillips: And you believed what Pienaar told you, did you?

Professor du Plessis: I did, actually, yes. As I've said before,

Pienaar was an obsessively cautious man. He would never have asked Cummings where his money was coming from. He wouldn't ask any of his donors where their money was coming from. He respected the privacy of everyone he dealt with.

DC Whittaker: Or perhaps he just didn't want to know.

Professor du Plessis: Maybe so. All I know is that Pienaar didn't ask questions like that – not just about money, about anything. With Pienaar, everything was on a need-to-know basis, and he applied the same rule to himself. He didn't want to know anything he didn't need to know.

'Inspector,' Andrew asked, 'did you then question Professor du Plessis further about what he knew about Vincent Cummings? Page 415, members of the jury.'

'We did, sir.'

'Second line down on page 415.'

DI Phillips: Professor, let me ask you this: were you really unaware that Vincent Cummings was a drug dealer? Did that possibility never occur to you?

Mr Davis: I'm sorry, Inspector, but I'm going to advise Professor du Plessis not to answer the question in that form. What basis did he have for believing that Cummings was a drug dealer? It would have been sheer speculation on his part.

Professor du Plessis: I want to be completely honest with you, Inspector. The only time the subject ever came up was during my meeting with Pienaar in March. After he'd told me about finding out that Cummings was an arms dealer, he added that he might be involved with dealing drugs as well.

DI Phillips: Did he? What did he say, exactly?

Professor du Plessis: He told me that arms dealers often took drugs into the camps, because there was a market for them, and they wanted to take advantage of that market. But that was it. He didn't have any information that Cummings was dealing drugs, and he didn't accuse him of dealing drugs. I wasn't about to jump to any conclusions based on that.

DI Phillips: So, you had a man who wanted to launder six-figure sums every three or four months, but it never occurred to you that he might be selling drugs?

Professor du Plessis: No. Look, all the donors were wealthy men – that's obvious. You can't become a donor in this league unless you've got a lot of money. Cummings was no different from the others.

DC Whittaker: Except that he was prepared to pay Pienaar ten per cent of his income to have it securely laundered on a regular basis. You didn't think that was suspicious?

Professor du Plessis: Yes, I guess so. But I had no proof. What was I supposed to do?

DI Phillips: Well, to return to DC Whittaker's earlier suggestion, you could have walked away, couldn't you – told Pienaar you didn't want to have anything more to do with it?

Professor du Plessis: Yes, I could have walked away.

DI Phillips: Then why...?

Professor du Plessis: Because South Africa has to change, and the only way it's ever going to change is if we make it change; which means that it has to be done by force; and force takes money. If people like Pienaar don't raise money, the struggle doesn't even get off the ground, and if I refuse to help because I'm squeamish about whether every last rand is clean and pure, then the failure of the struggle becomes my responsibility. There are times when you can't just walk away.

DC Whittaker: Would the struggle justify you in breaking the law here? Here, not in South Africa?

Mr Davis: Don't answer that.

Professor du Plessis: No. I want to answer. How have I broken the law? What offence have I committed? What happened to the idea of mens rea *– proof of the guilty mind? Is it enough now that you think someone you deal with may be acting suspiciously? Is that all it takes now to commit an offence?*

DI Phillips: No one's suggesting that.

Professor du Plessis: I confronted Pienaar directly. I asked him whether he was inviting me to become an outlaw.

DI Phillips: Did he reply to that?

Professor du Plessis: Not directly. But he said that sometimes, there was no alternative.

DI Phillips: What did you think he meant by that?

Professor du Plessis: He meant that the work we were doing was too important to jeopardise just because he had suspicions about a donor.

DC Whittaker: Do you feel you've become an outlaw?

Mr Davis: Again, I advise you…

Professor du Plessis: I had no knowledge that there was anything illegal about Vincent Cummings.

'Wait there, please, Inspector,' Andrew said. 'There may be further questions for you.

64

'During the course of this investigation, Inspector,' Ben began, 'you came to know Professor du Plessis and his wife, Miss Coetzee, quite well, didn't you?'

'Yes, sir, that would be fair to say.'

'Not only because of the interviews you conducted, but also because you helped them through the times when they were under threat from Nick Erasmus, when they had to move temporarily to London, when there was still the possibility that Miss Coetzee might be charged in the death of Mr Erasmus?'

'Yes, that's correct.'

'You became familiar with the circumstances in which they had left South Africa, where they would have been prosecuted simply for falling in love and having a relationship, and where marriage and children would have been out of the question for them?'

'Yes.'

'Would it be right to say that Professor du Plessis has strong feelings about their experiences, and indeed about the whole subject of apartheid?'

'He has very strong feelings about it.'

'I'm sure the jury remember how he described his decision not to walk away from Mr Pienaar, as DC Whittaker had suggested, as recorded in the notes of interview, which you and my learned friend Mr Pilkington read to them. He had a very strong reaction to that suggestion, didn't he?'

'Yes, he did. It's not in the notes, but I remember that, during that part of the interview, he stood up and he appeared to be quite agitated. Mr Davis was trying to offer advice and get him to sit down, but he seemed determined to tell us how he felt about it all.'

'And in summary, how he felt about it was this, wasn't it: he felt that he had a duty to help to bring about a South Africa where people of all racial backgrounds have the same rights and freedoms they enjoy in this country?'

'Yes.'

'And that helping Mr Pienaar to deal with the donations, to make sure that the funds reached the proper people in South Africa was the very least he could do?'

'Yes, I would agree with that.'

'Did you have some sympathy with his position, in the light of his experiences?'

'I think it's fair to say that both DC Whittaker and I had a good deal of sympathy for Professor du Plessis and Miss Coetzee, sir.'

'Now, Professor du Plessis is a lawyer, of course. Was it also obvious to you that he was concerned about the legality of what he was being asked to do?'

'Very much so, yes. The question of whether *Hawala* is legal and above board was always very much on his mind. He and Miss Coetzee were both very careful to impress on us that they had devoted a good deal of thought to that question. They believe that the practice of *Hawala*, although it can be abused for the purposes of tax evasion and the like, is perfectly lawful in itself. I have no reason at all to doubt the sincerity of that belief.'

'And indeed, that is the position taken by the prosecution in this case, is it not?'

'It is, sir, and I must say, I agree with it entirely.'

'Thank you, Inspector. When he was made aware, after some years of taking money to Balakrishnan, of the greatly increased payments made by VC – Vincent Cummings – Professor du Plessis was also concerned about the legality of accepting those payments, wasn't he? Even then, he was concerned to keep his activities within the law?'

Phillips hesitated. 'He admitted to us that there was something suspicious about it, sir, and he had been made aware of the possibility that those payments represented the proceeds of the sale of drugs.'

'Pienaar's belief that arms dealers were developing a sideline, taking drugs into the camps in addition to the arms and ammunition? Is that what you mean?'

'Yes.'

'Pienaar never claimed to know that Vincent Cummings had done that, did he?'

'No: he did not.'

'He never told Professor du Plessis that Cummings was a drug dealer, did he?'

'Not that I'm aware, sir.'

'And Professor du Plessis told you that he challenged Pienaar about it, didn't he? He asked him whether he was being asked to become an outlaw?'

'Yes.'

'So the question of legality was still in his mind, wasn't it?'

'I'm sure it was, sir.'

'Inspector, let's be frank about this: what Cummings was doing was clearly suspicious, wasn't it? Asking Pienaar to transfer his entire income to places unknown by means of *Hawala*, in return for a fee of ten per cent, is something that would arouse anyone's suspicions, isn't it?'

'It is, sir.'

'And Professor du Plessis admitted as much, didn't he?'

'He did.'

'But he insisted that he didn't know where the money came from, didn't he?'

'Yes.'

'Do you agree with DI Walsh that there is no possible way Professor du Plessis could have known about the long-running police investigation of Vincent Cummings?'

'Yes, of course: there was never any possibility of that.'

'And indeed, there was no evidence available to Professor du Plessis that the money he was sending to Pienaar was drug money, was there? The payments could have been suspicious because Cummings was trying to evade tax, or because he was trying to hide the proceeds of an illegal trade in arms, or for that matter, because of some fraud we know nothing about. That's right, isn't it?'

'Yes, sir.'

Ben paused. 'Inspector, Professor du Plessis attended both sessions of the interview voluntarily, by agreement, didn't he? He hadn't been arrested.'

'That is correct, sir.'

'You cautioned Professor du Plessis at the beginning of each session of the interview, didn't you? You reminded him that he was not obliged to say anything?'

'I did, sir.'

'If he had remained silent and refused to answer your questions, you would have known nothing about the conversations he had with Pienaar, would you?'

'That's absolutely correct, sir.'

'You would never have heard Pienaar's theory about all those drug-trafficking arms dealers?'

'No, sir.'

'You wouldn't have had a case against Professor du Plessis, would you?'

Andrew was on his feet. 'That's not a proper question to put to this witness, my Lord,' he complained.

But Phillips did not wait for a reaction from the bench.

'No, my Lord, we would not. I would not have arrested him and had him charged in those circumstances.'

'If you had your way, would you have had him charged at all, even after the interview?'

'That is completely improper, my Lord,' Andrew said, more loudly and insistently, this time.

'That must be right, Mr Schroeder...' Mr Justice Overton began.

But Phillips pretended not to hear.

'If it had been up to me, sir? If it was up to me, I would have read the pair of them the riot act for being stupid enough to dabble in matters they didn't understand and couldn't control: but then I would have sent them on their way.'

'Thank you, Inspector,' Ben said. 'Nothing further, my Lord.'

'Well, that may be a suitable moment to break for lunch, members of the jury,' the judge said. 'Two o'clock, please.'

After the judge and jury had left court, Andrew turned to Ben.

'Bit naughty, Ben, the last couple of questions, don't you think?' He was smiling.

Ben returned the smile. 'Appropriate to the occasion, Andrew.'

Andrew shook his head. 'Sometimes I don't know why I bother. You've even got my witnesses on your side, telling the jury to acquit.'

'I did offer you a way out when we had dinner at the Reform.'

'So you did. Did you fill in the form to join, by the way?'

'Yes. I haven't heard anything back yet, though.'

'It takes a while sometimes. I'll find out from the Secretary where we are, and we'll find you a seconder.'

'They won't turn me down for asking naughty questions, will they?'

Andrew laughed. 'Certainly not. Club tradition, asking naughty questions. It's not called the Reform Club for nothing.'

65

'My Lord,' Andrew began when court reassembled at two o'clock, 'I have DC Whittaker available. Her evidence would be essentially the same as that of DI Phillips, and as his evidence was not disputed, I don't propose to take up the court's time examining her myself. But if my learned friend wishes to cross-examine, I'm very happy to call her.'

'I'm obliged to my learned friend,' Ben replied, 'but there's no need as far as I'm concerned.'

'In that case, my Lord,' Andrew said, 'I will call Mr Balakrishnan.'

Balakrishnan, wearing his best white kurta pyjamas, a black Indian waistcoat, and black sandals, made his way slowly to the witness box. It would have been difficult to guess his age. His face, adorned by a short, well-groomed beard and moustache, and light, thin, hardly-noticeable spectacles, gave little away. But he had an unmistakably dignified bearing about him, and every eye in court was on him as he entered the witness box. He looked around him, joined his hands and offered the *Namaste* greeting to everyone in court, in a series of slight movements of his head and hands.

Geoffrey approached him.

'Which book would you like to be sworn on, sir?'

Balakrishnan turned towards the bench. 'My Lord, all religions originate in the same source. Accordingly, it does not matter on which book I am sworn; but in order to avoid giving offence to anyone present, I would prefer simply to make an affirmation, without any book, if the court will permit it.'

'Certainly,' Mr Justice Overton replied.

Geoffrey handed Balakrishnan a card. 'Read the words on the card aloud, please, sir.'

'I do solemnly, sincerely and truly declare and affirm that the evidence I shall give shall be the truth, the whole truth, and nothing but the truth.'

'Mr Balakrishnan, please give the court your full name,' Andrew began.

'My name is Balakrishnan, my Lord.'

'Just Balakrishnan?'

'Just Balakrishnan. It is enough for me.'

'Yes. I see. Mr Balakrishnan, please tell my Lord and the jury: what is your profession, or occupation?'

'My Lord, I am a practitioner of *Hawala*.'

'For how long have you been engaged in that practice?'

'For more than thirty-five years, sir. It is our family business, so to speak. My father led the business before me, until his death. His father, before him, was a practitioner in India also. It was his generation of our family that came here from India, from our ancestral home in Himachal Pradesh, and on his arrival, he established the business in Whitechapel. We have been there ever since.'

'Mr Balakrishnan, the court has been waiting for this moment with bated breath.' There was general laughter in court. 'We have been waiting for an expert to tell us exactly what *Hawala* is, and how it works. Would you please explain that to my Lord and the jury, and to me, as simply as you can?'

'Well, my goodness, I am sorry to hear that you have been kept waiting, my Lord,' Balakrishnan replied. There was more laughter, much louder this time, but all of it benevolent. The jury were warming to this disarming witness. 'I will do my best to explain it simply.'

He adjusted his spectacles several times. 'My Lord, if you would please imagine that you wish to send a sum of money – let us say £1,000 – to your friend, Mr Pilkington, who happens to be, shall we say, in Shimla, in India. It may be inconvenient for you to travel to India yourself to present him with the money, and indeed such a journey might involve more expense than the amount itself – to say nothing of the perils of brigands along the way. Nor would you necessarily wish to entrust such an amount to the post, because in this case also it can be stolen.'

'I fear that Mr Pilkington might have a long wait for his money in those circumstances, Mr Balakrishnan,' the judge replied, to renewed laughter.

'Indeed, my Lord. But that is where *Hawala* comes in. If you were to deliver the sum of £1,000 to my office in Whitechapel, I would then notify my counterpart in Shimla, my cousin Balakrishnan, that I have received this money, and I would request him to make the equivalent amount in rupees available to Mr Pilkington on his request. So you have transferred the money without any physical transfer of notes or coins, if I can put it in that way.'

'Mr Balakrishnan,' Andrew asked, 'do I take it that *Hawala* goes back a long way?'

'Oh, my goodness, yes. No one knows exactly when and where it originated, but certainly before the advent of modern banks it was practised all over the civilised world for many centuries – and this remains true today, even though we have banks now.'

'One thing we may have some difficulty in understanding, Mr Balakrishnan, is this: in your example, his Lordship has provided you with £1,000 and I have received the equivalent amount in rupees in Shimla; but the £1,000 is not yours to dispose of, is it, because it is credit you owe to your cousin Balakrishnan in Shimla? How does this provide you with your income?'

Balakrishnan nodded and adjusted the spectacles again. 'In order to understand that, my Lord, you must also imagine that this transaction is only one of many, and that my cousin Balakrishnan in Shimla is only one of many practitioners with whom I deal. There are many syndicates, if I may call them that, all composed of many practitioners. In my case, I am a member of a syndicate of some two hundred practitioners, based in more than one hundred countries around the world.'

'So the transaction his Lordship brings you is not the only one you're dealing with?'

'Oh, goodness me, no. Sometimes, we may deal with hundreds of them during the day. You see, if you look at his Lordship's transaction in isolation, it seems that it has left me with only a debt to my cousin. But it may well be that, earlier in the day, he has asked me to provide his contact in England with £2,000, so he is in debt to me, and when his Lordship comes to see me, I am already in sufficient credit with my cousin.'

'And, of course, you have been trading with people other than your cousin,' Andrew pointed out.

'Yes. Please understand, they are not all my cousins – only some of them are my cousins.'

The jury laughed again, as did Andrew.

'Yes. You also have a cousin Balakrishnan in Durban, I believe, in South Africa.'

'Indeed, yes: also in Sydney and Hong Kong.'

More laughter.

'But your point is,' Andrew said, 'that you are constantly building credits and debits, and if you have a credit, you can treat that money as yours, subject to your obligation to honour any debits you may have.'

'Exactly so,' Balakrishnan replied. 'But also, and I omitted to say so before, his Lordship is also paying me a modest commission for my services, and you are paying a modest commission to my cousin Balakrishnan in Shimla for his services.'

'Yes, I see,' Andrew said. 'Are there any other matters to mention?'

'Yes, sir. It is important to mention the two basic principles on which the syndicate is constructed. The first is that all the daily debits and credits are calculated and accounted for in each period of twenty-four hours. In my syndicate, this is done with reference to eleven o'clock in the evening precisely, Greenwich Mean Time, and its equivalent around the world, regardless of things such as daylight savings time. At that time, it must be known precisely what the state of credit and debit is between each pair of practitioners who have traded with each other during the day. This forms the basis of the next day's trading. If there is a serious imbalance in favour of one practitioner and against another, they are at liberty to agree whatever resolution of that they wish, but in most cases, you can wait for the imbalance to change with the next day's transactions.'

'What is the second principle?' Andrew asked.

'The second principle is that *Hawala* depends above all on the integrity and honesty of every practitioner in honouring his debits promptly, and dealing in an honest and straightforward manner with colleagues and clients alike. This is fundamental, and any member who fails to live up to this principle must expect to be expelled from the syndicate immediately. Any dishonesty affects everyone, so it cannot be tolerated. Fortunately, such a thing is very rare.'

'Mr Balakrishnan,' Andrew said, 'thank you for that clear explanation. I want to ask you now about your dealings with a man known to you as Mr Stevens.'

66

Balakrishnan turned towards the dock in the *Namaste* posture. Danie smiled, joined his hands, and returned the greeting.

'Yes. I recognised Mr Stevens when I came into court, of course.'

'I daresay it came as a surprise to you to learn that Mr Stevens is not his real name, and that he in fact is Danie du Plessis, a law professor at Cambridge University?'

Ben thought about objecting, and pushed himself up slightly, but sensed that Balakrishnan would deal with it better than he could, and allowed himself to sink back down into his seat.

'Why should this surprise me?' Balakrishnan asked quietly, looking directly at Andrew.

Andrew paused, looking rather bemused. Ben smiled.

'You don't find it surprising that one of your clients has been using a false name?'

'To be truthful with you, Mr Pilkington,' Balakrishnan replied, 'the names of my clients do not concern me as much as their honesty. I am sure that many of my clients have some reason to use a different name when engaging my services. It is of no concern to me, as long as they are acting honestly with me.'

'How do you know whether they're acting honestly or not?' Andrew asked.

He sounded flummoxed. Once again, Ben thought about

objecting, but his instinct again told him to leave it to Balakrishnan.

'When someone comes to me and entrusts me with money on a regular basis, Mr Pilkington, it is difficult for him to conceal his true motives for long. I observe him. He spends time in my office, with myself, my wife, and my children, who are equally observant. Sometimes he will take refreshment with us. My wife prepares the most wonderful lentil dhal with chapattis.' The jury laughed. 'Over time, when we look into a man's eyes, when we eat and drink with him, we will discern whether or not the man is honest. Mr Stevens is an honest man, whatever name he may use in my office.'

'I didn't ask you for your opinion about Mr Stevens, Mr Balakrishnan,' Andrew said. He was sounding testy now, frustrated.

'No, you did not. This is true. But I am giving it to the court in any case.'

Andrew exhaled audibly and allowed several seconds to pass.

'Do you ask questions of your clients about the purpose of their sending money using *Hawala*? How can you tell whether a client may be using you to evade taxes, or launder money?'

Balakrishnan took a deep breath. 'Do I assume from your question that if his Lordship comes to me and says to me, "I wish to make £1,000 available to my friend Mr Pilkington in Shimla," I am to question a High Court judge about whether he is laundering money? My answer is no. I do not question the client. But also, it is unnecessary for me to do so.'

'Explain, please,' Andrew said, making an effort to recover his composure.

'Clients always tell me why they wish to set up a credit, whether I ask them or not. You know: their mother needs money for her eye surgery, or their sister is getting married, or their younger brother wants to go to university. For some reason they think they owe it to me to explain this, although in fact, they are under no obligation to do so. No one comes to my office and says to me, "Mr Balakrishnan, I would like your help in evading my taxes, or laundering the proceeds of my crimes." But when you listen carefully to the reason they give, it is sometimes obvious that this is exactly what they are planning to do.'

'What do you do if you reach that conclusion?'

'In this case, I advise the client, without assigning any reason on my part, that I will have no further dealings with him.'

Andrew nodded. 'How did you first encounter the man you knew as Mr Stevens?'

'At that time I had a client, Mr Arthur Pienaar, who brought me money every quarter, with the request to establish credit for certain parties in South Africa. I was able to do this through my cousin Balakrishnan in Durban. There came a time, and my records indicate that this was in the year 1968, when Mr Pienaar advised me that he would no longer be dealing with this account personally, and that a Mr Stevens would be assuming this responsibility for him.'

'What amounts of money were involved at that time?'

'At that time, the amount was reasonably small, anywhere between £5,000 and £15,000 each time, usually four times a year.'

'Did Mr Pienaar behave as your other clients did? Did he explain the intended purpose of this credit?'

'He did. Mr Pienaar explained that the money was being sent for charitable purposes, for the benefit of the disadvantaged black and other non-white communities in South Africa, who were suffering because of apartheid.'

'Did you accept that explanation?'

Balakrishnan smiled. 'Yes and no. I think "charitable" was a not inaccurate term, given the circumstances in South Africa, but I assumed that there was a political motivation also. But none of this troubled me, and it did not seem to trouble my cousin Balakrishnan in Durban.'

'But you assumed that there might be more to it than met the eye. Was Mr Pienaar being honest with you?'

'Certainly,' Balakrishnan replied. 'Honesty may consist of telling someone truthfully as much as it is wise to tell them, and no more.'

'And eventually Mr Stevens took over the handling of the account?'

'Yes.'

'Did he give you the same explanation for the credits?'

'Actually, no. He just confirmed that the credits were to continue exactly as before. That was all the information I needed.'

'How did Mr Stevens bring the money to you?'

'It was a combination of cash and receipts for deposits into bank accounts I control in England and Scotland.'

'Why use banks both in England and Scotland?'

'I have no idea. It was an idiosyncrasy of Pienaar's, which served no useful purpose that I could see. He was a very cautious man in his demeanour, and it may be that he thought it served some purpose of security.'

'Why do you have bank accounts in Scotland?'

'Because I have clients in Scotland,' Balakrishnan replied, with a smile. The jury smiled too.

'Was there any change in the amount of money involved when Mr Stevens took over?'

'Not at first, but over the course of time, it did increase, yes.'

'Was there a noticeable increase about two years ago, in 1975?'

'Yes. The amount went up very considerably, so that I was sometimes processing more than £100,000 on each occasion.'

'Was this a problem for you?'

Balakrishnan shook his head. 'No, not at all. It is not unusual for me to undertake credits in such an amount. If there is a problem the other end, my cousin will advise me, but I think it is quite normal for him also. He did not indicate any problem to me.'

'Did you ever know the identities of the donors who supplied the money for Mr Pienaar's charitable causes?'

Balakrishnan looked genuinely surprised. 'If they paid by cheque, then I would have a record of the names. But I had no other information about them. If they paid in cash, I would not know the names. There would be no reason for me to know.'

'So you would have no real information about the sources of the money brought to you by Mr Pienaar or Mr Stevens?'

'That is true.'

Andrew nodded. 'That's all I have, Mr Balakrishnan. Thank you. Wait there, please.'

Balakrishnan turned towards the bench. 'You see, my Lord, Mr Stevens often took refreshment with my family and myself. He spent much time with us.'

'Yes, thank you,' the judge replied. 'Mr Schroeder?'

'My Lord, I only wish I had questions to put to Mr Balakrishnan,' Ben replied. 'I think it would be a most enjoyable experience. But sadly, my learned friend has covered everything.' The jury laughed quietly. 'So I will not take up the court's time unnecessarily.'

'My Lord,' Andrew said, 'that is the case for the prosecution.'

'My Lord,' Ben said, 'in that case, there is a matter of law, which I would like to raise in the absence of the jury.'

Mr Justice Overton nodded, and glanced at the clock.

'Yes. I imagine it will take some time, Mr Schroeder?'

'Yes, my Lord. It may be that, rather than keeping the jury waiting, your Lordship would prefer to release them for the day now.'

'Yes, very well. Members of the jury, as you've heard, there's a matter of law I need to discuss with counsel. You're not concerned with questions of law. You are the judges of the facts, but it's my job to deal with the law. It seems unlikely that we can take the trial any further this afternoon. So, rather than keep you sitting around doing nothing, I will let you go for the day now. Ten thirty tomorrow, please, members of the jury. Don't forget what I've said about not talking about the case with anyone outside your number.'

The jury filed quickly out of court.

'Yes, Mr Schroeder,' the judge said.

67

Sarah Mulvaney

Everyone was pleased by the prospect of a slightly early afternoon, but strangely, rather than rushing off straight away in the direction of our respective homes, we lingered in the jury room for some time after the judge had dismissed us. Everyone wanted to talk about Mr Balakrishnan. I'd never seen all twelve of us smiling so much at the same time. I couldn't stop myself, even if I'd wanted to. Mr Balakrishnan was a breath of fresh air, one of those people who seem to lift the gloom simply by being in the same room, and I felt a mysterious surge of energy flowing through my body.

'He was a character, and no mistake,' Steven Wainwright said, 'that Mr Balakrishnan, wasn't he? I don't think the judge or Pilkington knew what to make of him.'

'He had Pilkington tied up in knots, didn't he?' Phil Ackroyd agreed.

We all laughed.

'He was funny too, wasn't he?' Marjorie Bloom said. 'But it wasn't as if he was trying to score points off anybody. He just has a lovely way of putting things. And he's obviously very intelligent – well, you can tell, can't you? You only have to listen to him.'

'I'm going to give this *Hawala* a try,' our musician, Winston Beckett, said. 'I still send money to my family back in Jamaica. If he has a cousin in Kingston, I'm going to see him and ask him to handle it for me. I'm tired of messing around with money orders and transfers and what have you. *Hawala* sounds far easier.'

'He seems to have cousins everywhere, doesn't he?' Marjorie said. 'All called Balakrishnan.'

We laughed again.

'I may do the same,' Mohamed Khan said. 'I think my family used to go to a family who did *Hawala* in Lahore, going back several generations, you know, when we were still in Pakistan. I do a lot of business with the Subcontinent, and Mr Balakrishnan might be a very useful contact – as long as his fees aren't too unreasonable.'

'Just don't approach him before the case ends,' Kenneth Avery, by now our undoubted foreman-in-waiting, advised. 'You don't want to get in trouble with the judge, do you?'

'Balakrishnan almost got into trouble with the judge, himself, didn't he?' John Lacey said. 'Saying that du Plessis was honest. He shouldn't have said that, should he? Pilkington looked like he was ready to kill him.'

'I don't see what was wrong with that,' Jeff Simons replied. 'I mean, Pilkington brought the subject up, didn't he? He asked him how he knew whether people were being honest with him. He'd known du Plessis for a long time by then. Why shouldn't he say what he thinks of him?'

George Kennedy was nodding. 'They often call character witnesses in trials, don't they? It's no different from that, surely.'

'We can all make our minds up for ourselves about how honest he is, can't we?' Joe Henley said. 'We don't have to take Balakrishnan's word for it. And Balakrishnan didn't know anything about Cummings, did he, because they never told him who was giving them the money? So he doesn't know whether du Plessis was giving him drug money to launder, or not. It looks like he was, and that's not very honest, is it?'

'Well, we haven't heard all the evidence yet,' Kenneth pointed out. 'We've only heard the prosecution's case. We shouldn't jump to any conclusions before we've heard the whole story. Let's wait and see what du Plessis has to say for himself when his turn comes.'

We began to drift away shortly after that. I was still very anxious about going home. As soon as I stepped off the bus and started the walk to my house, my nerves started jangling, and I had to suppress the urge to look around me in the hope of seeing my shadow, thinking how reassuring it would be if she gave me a friendly nod of recognition. DI Walsh had made it clear that wasn't going to happen. The shadow would be out there somewhere, but I wouldn't know who or where she was. It was better that way, for her and for me.

I steeled myself, kept my eyes firmly in front of me, and arrived home without incident. I locked and double-locked the door, and caught myself in the act of carrying two chairs to pile against the door as I had the previous evening, as, I imagined, some sort of last-ditch defence against invasion. I stopped and stared at the chairs for some time, before removing them and replacing them in their accustomed places. If someone forced my double-locked front door open, I realised belatedly, two light chairs leaning against it were not going to deter them for long. If anything, they were more likely to slow me down if I needed to leave the house urgently. I would have a police presence throughout the night. I had to trust that it would be enough to keep me safe.

And strangely, when I thought about Mr Balakrishnan again, which I did often during the evening, and in the waking hours of the night, I felt safe.

68

'My Lord,' Ben said, 'my submission is that there is no case for Professor du Plessis to answer, and I would invite your Lordship to withdraw the case from the jury at this stage.'

Out of the corner of his eye, Ben saw John Caswell quietly enter the courtroom, and take a seat behind Andrew. Mr Justice Overton looked up at Ben, his face suggesting some surprise.

'You're saying that a jury, properly directed, could not legally convict – not that they would be unlikely to convict, but that they could not legally convict – based on the evidence the Crown has presented?' he asked.

'My Lord, yes: and even if there is some evidence to support the prosecution's case, I say that it is far too weak and tenuous to allow the jury to convict. It would not be safe to leave the case to them.'

'You're going to have to explain that to me,' the judge said.

'My Lord, the Crown has charged Professor du Plessis with the specific offence of aiding and abetting the supply of controlled drugs. In order to prove that charge, the Crown must prove two things beyond reasonable doubt. First, they must prove that the money donated by Vincent Cummings to Pienaar's fund represented the proceeds of drug dealing. My Lord, for the purpose of this submission, I am content to concede that they have met that burden.'

'There can't be any doubt about that, surely?' the judge asked.

'It's a matter for the jury, if the case goes further, my Lord,' Ben replied. 'But as to the second essential matter, the Crown has offered no evidence whatsoever. The second matter is that Professor du Plessis *knew* that the money donated by Vincent Cummings represented the proceeds of drug dealing. DI Walsh took us at some length through the Met's long-running investigation of Cummings, but at the end of it, she had to concede that there is no possible way Professor du Plessis could have known anything about that. The Crown has not attempted to prove that Professor du Plessis and Vincent Cummings ever met. So what the evidence comes to is this: Pienaar told the Professor that certain arms dealers were also dealing drugs in the training camps in Tanzania, and suggested that Cummings might have been one of them. It's hearsay at best, and in reality, it's pure speculation.'

'But it's not an unreasonable supposition, is it,' the judge asked, 'given what we know about Cummings, and given the fact that he was in fact selling arms at one of the training camps?'

'Well, it's certainly supposition, my Lord,' Ben replied. 'There's no evidence at all to support it. It is sheer speculation. It provides no basis whatsoever for an inference that Professor du Plessis knew that Cummings was dealing in drugs.'

'That's a matter for the jury, surely, Mr Schroeder.'

'With respect, my Lord, it would be very dangerous to leave the case to the jury in that state, because, having sat through the whole of DI Walsh's lengthy evidence, it may be difficult for the jury to remember that the Professor knew nothing about Cummings's history as a drug-dealer, and to put all that evidence to one side when they consider the question of what he knew.'

The judge thought for some time.

'The fact remains, though, Mr Schroeder, that Professor du Plessis was suddenly faced with a huge increase in donations from "VC" – whom he knew to be Vincent Cummings. Pienaar even told him that Cummings was entrusting his entire income to them, so that they could whisk it away, using the magic of *Hawala*, in return for a fee of ten per cent. Why is the Crown not entitled to say that he must have known that there was, to say the least, a strong probability that the Cummings money was the proceeds of crime?'

'It's not enough for the Crown to say that,' Ben replied at once. 'The prosecution have nailed their colours to the mast – as they had to. It must be proved beyond reasonable doubt that it was drug money, and that Professor du Plessis knew that it was drug money. Nothing else will do.'

The judge nodded. 'Very well. Mr Pilkington, what do you say about it?'

Andrew stood. 'My Lord, I have Mr Caswell, the Deputy Director, with me in court. If your Lordship would allow me to confer with him for a moment, it may be that we could save some time.'

'Yes, very well,' the judge agreed. 'Do you want me to rise?'

'I don't think so, my Lord. If I may have a moment, and turn my back…?'

'By all means.'

Andrew turned behind him, and they spoke in whispers.

'I got your message, Andrew. So, you think the game's up, do you?'

Andrew nodded. 'I think so. We ran a good case, and we do have some evidence. But Ben's right. I'm feeling queasy about leaving this to the jury, when they know far more about Cummings than du Plessis could ever have known. There is a serious risk that they may convict for the wrong reason.'

'No smoke without fire, you mean?'

'Exactly. I had hoped that DI Phillips would let me make more of what du Plessis said during the interview about becoming an outlaw. That could have done some real damage. But I needed Phillips to help me to make the point, and to be honest with you, Phillips didn't want to know. He wants du Plessis to walk, and he said as much to the jury.' He smiled ruefully. 'Even Balakrishnan ambushed me. He insists that du Plessis is an honest man.'

John sniggered quietly. 'Phillips was never with us on this, was he?'

'No.'

John nodded decisively. 'All right, Andrew. Let it go. I can square it with the Director.'

'You're sure?'

'Yes.

Andrew nodded, and turned back towards the bench.

'My Lord, I'm grateful for the time to confer with Mr Caswell. Having done so, and having listened carefully to my learned friend's submissions, I have decided that it would not be right for me to oppose his application.'

The judge looked up in apparent astonishment.

'You're agreeing with Mr Schroeder that I should stop the case now?'

'Yes, my Lord. There is some evidence to support a conviction, but it has not emerged as strongly as I had hoped, and I agree with my learned friend that it would not be safe to ask the jury to infer that Professor du Plessis knew that the money was specifically related to the drug trade. He certainly had his suspicions – he admitted as much – and perhaps he did know; but proving that beyond a reasonable doubt is another matter. As a prosecutor, I have a duty to consider not only the prospect of a conviction, but also the wider interests of justice, and the importance of ensuring a fair trial. Having considered those matters, I find myself constrained to agree with my learned friend.'

'Well, I'm afraid I don't agree at all,' the judge replied.

There was a lengthy silence.

'Do I take it from that,' Andrew asked, 'that your Lordship proposes to leave the case to the jury, despite what I have just said?'

'I take the view that it's an eminently suitable case for the jury, Mr Pilkington.'

Andrew brought both hands down hard on the bench in front of him. 'My Lord, in my submission, it would be highly unusual, perhaps even unprecedented, for a judge to leave a case to the jury when invited to withdraw it both by experienced defence counsel and by senior Treasury Counsel.'

Mr Justice Overton shrugged. 'Something is only unprecedented until someone does it for the first time, Mr Pilkington. I shall leave the case to the jury. Ten thirty tomorrow morning.'

The judge left the bench abruptly.

Andrew raised both hands in the air, and turned to John Caswell and Ben in turn.

'What is wrong with this man?' he asked. He shook his head. 'I'm sorry, Ben. I tried.'

They gathered outside court. Danie was furious.

'Who does this judge think he is?' he demanded. 'What gives him the right to ride roughshod over us like this?'

Ben held up a hand. 'Not here,' he replied. 'Let's go back to chambers. We need to talk this through, and it may take some time.'

69

'Where am I? What am I doing here?' Tony Moran demanded loudly, almost, but not quite getting to his feet, as she entered.

'You're in an interview room at West End Central Police Station,' Steffie Walsh replied, taking her seat at the table facing Tony, 'as I'm sure the officers who brought you here explained to you. They're just outside in case I need them, so don't get any ideas, will you?'

She switched on the small tape recorder on the table. 'It's Tuesday 8 February, the time is five forty pm, and present are Anthony Roy Moran, generally known as Tony, and myself, DI Walsh. I have some questions to put to you, Tony.'

'Am I under arrest?' Tony asked.

'Not yet. But I would say it's only a matter of time.'

'I want to leave, or if I can't leave, I want to see my brief. I know my rights.'

'Yes, I'm sure you do, Tony,' Steffie replied. 'And I also know mine. If I have reason to believe that the life of a member of the public may be in danger, and that you have information that may assist police in preventing harm to that person, I'm entitled to question you about that without your solicitor being present – just to reduce the risk that he may try to warn accomplices or destroy evidence.'

'What are you talking about?'

Steffie laid some documents on the table in front of her.

'You've been round the block a few times, Tony, haven't you? But it's been relatively low-level stuff up to this point, hasn't it? Non-residential burglary, obtaining by false pretences, theft by finding – railway signalling wire, that was, wasn't it, lying at the side of the tracks? Theft of lead from church roofs, going equipped for burglary, public nuisance: and so it goes on. But nothing for violence, except that one common assault back in 1965. What was that about? Domestic, was it? Slapped the old lady around a bit, did you?'

'She asked for it.'

'Really?'

'Yeah. She was drunk, wasn't she, and she was saying I couldn't get it on any more in the sack, if you take my meaning.'

'Unfortunately, I do,' Steffie replied.

'Yeah, well there you go, then. She asked for it.'

Steffie shook her head. 'Well, you've left your common assault days behind you, haven't you, Tony? You're playing in the first division now. What did you get for slapping the old lady around? Conditional discharge, wasn't it? Well, you're not getting a conditional discharge for conspiracy to pervert the course of justice. And if a hair of her head is harmed, I'm going to do you for conspiracy to commit GBH, or murder, as the case may be. Do I have your attention now?'

Tony was staring at her. 'I don't know what you're talking about.'

Steffie picked up another sheet of paper and banged it down hard on the table.

'Don't waste my time, Tony. Your fingerprints are all over this. I'm talking about the original, obviously – this is a copy. Plus, the original is in green ink, very similar to the pen the officers found in your jacket pocket, which our forensic lads are looking at as we speak. My bet is it's going to be a match. I'm surprised at you, Tony. You're getting careless in your old age.'

The document read: 'The Verdict is Guilty.'

Tony shifted uncomfortably in his chair. 'What do you want?'

'Information. I don't think you came up with this caper on your own. You'd have no reason to, that I can see, and no disrespect, Tony, but this is out of your league. The lady you gave this to, by pushing it through her letterbox, is a juror in a case at the Old Bailey. Threatening a juror, trying to influence her vote, is a very serious offence. You're going straight inside, for a long time, for this. What I want to know is: who put you up to it, and whether you also threatened any other members of the jury. If you level with me now,

I'll tell the judge you cooperated, and that may reduce the sentence. If you don't, I'm going to assume that I've been underestimating you, and that you dreamed this up all on your own. I'm going to arrest you for attempting to pervert the course of justice. You won't have a prayer for bail – not with an ongoing threat to the juror – and then you're going down for the full stretch. It's up to you, Tony.'

There was a long silence. Steffie waited patiently.

'I met this geezer in the pub, didn't I?' Tony replied, eventually. 'How he knew about me, I don't know. But anyway, he said there was this other geezer, who was being tried at the Bailey, and all I needed to know was, he needed to go down for whatever he was charged with. All I had to do was post an envelope through a letterbox, and he'd make it worth my while.'

'Meaning what?'

'A hundred quid. Plus another hundred if I waited for her outside her house in the morning, and told her, "Don't forget".'

'Which you did?'

'Which I did.'

'Did you meet this man again to get your money?'

'Yeah. He paid me fifty quid as, like, a down payment, then I had to meet him again in the pub at lunchtime to collect the rest.'

'Did he give you a name?'

Tony shook his head. 'No.'

'I need your full cooperation, Tony. This woman is still in danger.'

'I'm telling you: he didn't give me a name.' He hesitated. 'But there was one thing…I don't know whether it means anything, but…'.

'Go on.'

'When he paid me at lunchtime, he had the money in a briefcase, and he opened the briefcase to take the money out. He didn't open it very wide – obviously, he was trying to make sure no one else saw what he was doing – but I did notice the corner of a letter, or something. It had a flag on it.'

'A flag?'

'Yeah, printed on it. It was the South African flag.'

'What?'

'Three horizontal boxes, orange, white and dark blue. The white box has a miniature Union flag, plus two other miniatures to the right – I forget the details, local references.'

Steffie stared at him. 'You are kidding me. How in God's name would you know what the South African flag looks like?'

'It was my old man, when I was growing up. He was obsessed with national flags, wasn't he? God only knows why, something to do with signals when he was in the Navy, apparently. Anyway, all of us in the family had to study his book of national flags. He would test us on them while we were trying to eat our supper. Bloody hundreds of them, there were, and he knew every bloody one of them, and he expected us to know them as well. We spent hours on them. Even now, I can't get them out of my head. It drove my sister away from home. She got herself pregnant because of it, and it did my head in, too. To be honest, I think that may be why I drifted into crime.'

'Let's not get carried away, shall we,' Steffie replied. 'Can you describe this man?'

'About thirty, thirty-five, tall, about six foot, light brown hair, blue eyes, clean-shaven, nice, smart suit and tie. Will you tell the judge I cooperated?'

'One more thing: was she the only one, or did you threaten other members of the jury?'

'She was the only one.'

'Are you sure about that, Tony? This is no time to be modest.'

'On my mother's grave.'

'All right. Can you tell me anything else? Did the man say anything about other people delivering other envelopes? Did you see any other envelopes in his briefcase?'

He shook his head. 'No. That's all I know. Will you tell the judge?'

'Yes, I will,' Steffie promised.

70

'Barratt and I both had dealings with Miles Overton before he became a judge,' Ben said, 'when he was in Silk. He could be very difficult then when the mood took him, and it seems that he hasn't changed very much with his new job. But still, I'm surprised he reacted the way he did in this case. I didn't expect that, and Andrew Pilkington didn't expect it either.'

They were sitting in Ben's room in chambers, drinking strong instant coffee hurriedly prepared by Ben's clerk, Alan.

'He always was a difficult bugger,' Barratt agreed. 'Once he got an idea in his head, you couldn't talk him out of it, even if it was total nonsense. But still, I've never known a judge to refuse to stop a case when both counsel told him that was the right thing to do. Have you, Ben?'

Ben shook his head. 'Never.'

Not for the first time, Danie stood, and started pacing around the room, still visibly agitated.

'That's all very well, but I should be a free man tonight, celebrating my freedom with my family after my acquittal. And I would be, except that we have this out-of-control judge behaving in a totally arbitrary way, as if he hasn't even been following the case.'

'Oh, he's been following the case,' Barratt replied. 'Make no mistake about that. He could probably quote you most of the evidence word for word, if you asked him. He had one of the best brains at the Bar, and the Bench hasn't turned him senile yet, as far as I can tell.'

'I know it's frustrating, Danie,' Ben said. 'But hopefully, it will only delay things by a day or two. I'm pretty sure the jury will do what Overton should have done and acquit you.' He paused. 'But the good news is that, if they don't, Overton has handed us a lifeline – which, I'm sure, is the last thing he intended to do, but he has.'

'What do you mean?' Danie asked.

'He's handed us a get-out-of-jail-free card to play in the Court of Appeal, if we should need it,' Barratt replied, smiling.

Ben nodded. 'The point is that Andrew would have to support us on appeal. Having told the trial judge that he agrees that a conviction would be dangerous, he would have to say the same thing to the Court of Appeal. That would be the end of it. The Court would allow the appeal without even thinking about it.'

'Assuming that Pilkington is as good as his word,' Danie replied.

'That's not in doubt,' Ben said. 'I had a case in which Andrew did exactly that a few years ago. I've known Andrew for a long time, Danie, and I can assure you that he is totally honest and ethical. You don't get to be senior Treasury Counsel unless the courts can rely on your word.' He paused. 'But there is one condition, one precaution we need to take.'

Danie returned to his seat. 'What's that?'

'When the trial resumes tomorrow, we open and close our case at the same time. You can't go anywhere near the witness box.'

Danie's jaw dropped, and he stared at Ben silently for some time.

'You're saying I shouldn't give evidence?' he asked in due course.

'I'm saying, you can't give evidence,' Ben replied.

'But… juries want to know what a defendant has to say for himself, don't they?' Danie asked. 'All right, I don't have your experience in the criminal area, but surely it's common sense. If the defendant hides in the dock, and doesn't give them his side of the story, what are they going to think? I know what I'd think.'

'You're forgetting about the burden of proof, Danie,' Barratt pointed out. 'You don't have to prove your innocence. The prosecution have to prove your guilt. Otherwise, you walk.'

'That may be true in theory, Barratt,' Danie replied, 'but would you want to bet the rest of your life on it? That's not the way people think, not the kind of people who serve on juries, anyway.'

'That's not the point,' Ben said. 'The reason why you can't give evidence is that you would give Andrew the chance to bring his case back to life.'

'What do you mean?'

'If you give evidence, he can cross-examine you, and then he can claim that his cross-examination has done so much damage to your story that his case has suddenly become much stronger. It happens all the time, Danie. The low point of any prosecution case is the moment when the prosecutor closes his case. Once the defendant starts giving evidence, it improves by leaps and bounds, because then he gets to take the defence case apart, piece by piece. If the defendant calls witnesses, it can get even better, but usually just the defendant giving evidence is all it takes to turn it around.'

'I'm not your average defendant, Ben. I can look after myself.'

'Really?'

'Yes, really.'

'All right, then. Let's pretend I'm Andrew. Answer me this: what did you mean when you asked Pienaar whether he was asking you to become an outlaw?'

Danie hesitated. 'It was just a term I used…'

'A term? What does that term mean, Professor du Plessis? Doesn't the word "outlaw" refer to someone who is prepared to, and does break the law?'

'I was just making sure that nothing illegal was going on.'

'Were you? Didn't Pienaar say that sometimes, one had no choice but to become an outlaw?'

'Yes, but…'

'And didn't you yourself tell Pienaar that you would stop helping him unless he stopped taking money from Vincent Cummings?'

'I did say that, but…'

'But you didn't stop helping Pienaar, did you?'

'That doesn't prove that I knew Cummings was dealing drugs,' Danie insisted.

Ben raised his hands. 'No, of course, it doesn't. But it puts the issue right back on the table. It lets Andrew off the hook. Suddenly, he's not stuck with such a hopeless case. He's got some wind in his sails.'

'But the jury know all about that already from my interview,' Danie replied. 'They're not hearing anything new.'

'They're hearing it in a different way,' Ben replied. 'Look, Danie, I've already told you, I've known Andrew Pilkington for a long time, and I've had a lot of cases against him. He is one of the best cross-examiners at the Bar. The way he does it is to be very reasonable, very understated, never arguing with you, just leading you on, one question at a time, until you suddenly realise you're completely stuffed – and the worst thing is, you have no idea how it happened. Trust me, I've seen him do this to very intelligent, confident witnesses; and I assure you, when he starts in on you about being an outlaw, you're not going to come out of it well in the jury's eyes.'

There was silence for some time.

'But it must be a risk not to give evidence,' Danie insisted, but without conviction.

'There is some risk,' Ben replied immediately. 'I very rarely advise a client not to give evidence. But in a rare case, it's the best thing to do, and in a very rare case, it's the only thing that makes sense. I can explain to the jury why you're not giving evidence, when I make my closing speech. Why should you? There's no evidence that you knew Cummings was a drug dealer. You have no case to answer. You told your story to the police, the jury have heard it, and you have nothing to add, because the prosecution haven't been able to disprove it. Besides, Barratt is right. Overton has to direct the jury that you don't have to prove your innocence; it's for the prosecution to prove you guilty. He won't like it, but if he doesn't explain that to them, we have a walkover in the Court of Appeal, even without Andrew helping us. Judges direct juries about the burden of proof every day of the week, and in my experience they understand it. There is a risk, but it's not a big one, and it's not a reason to throw away our get-out-of-jail-free card. It's your choice,

Danie, not mine. But my strong advice is, stay out of the witness box.'

'I agree with that, Danie,' Barratt said.

Danie smiled ruefully. 'Well, I got myself in hot water through not taking your advice at the police station, didn't I?'

'Yes, you did,' Barratt replied.

'So I suppose it would be foolish of me to make the same mistake twice. Very well. I shall remain mute.'

'Good,' Ben replied. 'Try not to worry, Danie. It's going to take a bit longer than it should have, but we will get there.'

71

Wednesday 9 February 1977

Sarah Mulvaney

It was comforting to get home rather earlier than usual yesterday evening. I felt much calmer, and didn't even entertain the thought of barricading my door with chairs. It got even better at about eight o'clock, when I got an unexpected call from DI Walsh. She was very guarded as she had to be as a witness in the case I'm sitting on. But she told me she had some really good news, and that she had approached Mr Justice Overton privately for permission to speak to me, which he had granted, as long as we didn't discuss anything else. The good news was that they'd recovered some fingerprints on the note, and had arrested the man who had pushed it through my letterbox and had threatened me in the morning. He has a criminal record, and they were able to trace him easily enough. He had confessed to what he had done, and officers had matched the green ink on the note to a pen he had on him when he was arrested. So it seems to be an open and shut case. DI Walsh added, however, that this man is a low-level criminal, and was hired and paid by others to do what he did. She wasn't free to tell me any more about that, except that he had been able to identify those others sufficiently to enable action to be taken, although it was action that had to be taken above her pay grade, as she put it. She was confident that the threat would now be removed. She was going to leave my shadow in place until the end of the trial, just in case, but she didn't think I would have any further problems. I thanked her profusely, and celebrated with more than one glass of wine, after which I slept better than I have for some considerable time.

When we took our places in court this morning, things took a rather unexpected turn. Mr Pilkington reminded us that he was closing the prosecution case. When the judge turned to Mr Schroeder, he announced that the defence would not be calling any evidence, and closed his case also. So suddenly, the evidence was all over. Mr Justice Overton explained to us that all that remained was for counsel to make their closing speeches, he would sum the case up to us, explaining the law, and then we would be free to start work on our verdict. But even that shortened schedule didn't last for long. Mr Pilkington announced that he didn't intend to make a closing speech, and handed over to Mr Schroeder. I sensed a real feeling of shock in the jury box. I think we could have done with a few minutes to digest the news, which wasn't at all what we'd been expecting, and I know we would have appreciated some answers to the questions running through our minds; but the court seemed oblivious to any reaction we might be having, so on we went without delay.

Mr Schroeder was really good. He didn't take too long, and everyone was listening carefully. He held me, at least, spellbound. He began by painting a picture of Danie du Plessis for us, his history of having to flee from South Africa, abandoning his family, his career, his whole life there, to be with the woman he loved. They had settled in this country, established new and distinguished careers as academics, and had a family. They were people of excellent character, respected and well liked both within

Cambridge University and in their community. Whatever he had done, Professor du Plessis had acted out of the altruistic motive of contributing to the eventual overthrow of apartheid. Mr Schroeder reminded us of the evidence we had heard about apartheid, and invited us to say that overthrowing apartheid was a worthy cause, or at the very least, that it was obviously so in Danie du Plessis' mind. There was no suggestion that he had acted for personal gain, or had received any personal gain, in anything he did.

The prosecution did not suggest that the *Hawala* system is unlawful in itself. As Mr Balakrishnan (smiles all round again) had shown, it is a perfectly respectable system for handling money by transferring credit, which has been used for centuries, perhaps millennia, and which depends on the honesty of all involved. Danie du Plessis had done nothing wrong under English law in helping Arthur Pienaar to fund anti-apartheid activities in South Africa. The only question was whether any of that changed when Vincent Cummings – the VC named in the ledger – increased his contributions to the fund by such a large amount in 1975.

Mr Schroeder was completely candid about that, which in my eyes bought him, and his client, a good deal of credit. He did not dispute that Vincent Cummings was a major international drug dealer, who was using Arthur Pienaar to launder some of the proceeds by including them with the money delivered to Balakrishnan, in return for a fee of ten per cent – obviously a good investment if it concealed the origin of the money, and at the same time, evaded tax. It was an open question, Mr Schroeder conceded, how much Arthur Pienaar knew about Cummings, and how far he went along with this scheme, knowing that drug money might be involved. The fact that he had received personal payments from Pienaar into his Dutch bank account was suspicious, but again, that did not necessarily have anything to do with drugs. It might have been suspicious that the two men were murdered together at the University Arms Hotel in Cambridge; though it seems clear from the evidence that their deaths were linked to covert activities by an agent of BOSS, the South African Bureau for State Security, rather than to any question of drugs. But the important point was that Danie du Plessis did not know about Cummings, and that the prosecution had no evidence to suggest otherwise.

The prosecution conceded that Danie du Plessis could have had no knowledge of the long Met Police investigation into Cummings, or indeed, of his old and undistinguished criminal record. All they had was Danie's own admission that Pienaar had told him about Cummings supplying arms and ammunition to an ANC camp in Tanzania, and speculating that some arms dealers were dealing drugs at the same time. Speculation was all it ever amounted to. Pienaar did not provide any evidence that Cummings had dealt drugs, and the prosecution would never even have known about that conversation if it hadn't been for Danie's honesty in telling the police the whole story during his interview. He hadn't been under any obligation to answer their questions, but he did, and he did so truthfully.

Was Danie du Plessis suspicious about Cummings? Of course he was. Anyone would be suspicious, wouldn't they, seeing such a huge increase in his contributions? And when it became clear that the 'contributions' were being laundered, with only ten per cent benefitting the fund, anyone would be suspicious, wouldn't they? Danie himself was honest enough with the police to admit that he questioned Pienaar about whether he was becoming an outlaw. But that isn't enough. The prosecution has charged Danie with the very specific offence of aiding and abetting Cummings in trafficking in controlled drugs. There was no evidence of that whatsoever. There was no suggestion that the two men ever met, or contacted each other; and if Danie had reason to suspect illicit money laundering by Cummings, as he surely did, the reasonable assumption for him to make would have been that it had to do with trading in arms, not drugs. That would not prove the offence charged in the indictment. In any case, at the end of the day, suspicion is not enough. The prosecution must prove knowledge, if we are to convict.

That was why Mr Schroeder was not calling Danie as a witness. He had already told his story in full. The jury have a full note of it, and we can read it as many times as we wish. There was nothing more he could add. In our system of law, as the judge would explain to us when he came to sum up, a defendant does not have to prove his innocence. In fact, he doesn't have to prove anything. It is up to the prosecution to prove the case against him beyond reasonable doubt. Nothing less than that will do. Even if we feel some suspicion, even if we feel that he possibly, or even probably committed the offence charged, that would not be enough. Mr Schroeder was confident that the prosecution's case didn't rise even to that level, and he invited us to say that the only possible verdict was one of not guilty.

I agree with him.

72

Mr Justice Overton began by doing exactly what Mr Schroeder had said he would do. He explained carefully that the prosecution had the burden of proof, and had to prove the case beyond reasonable doubt. The defendant did not have to prove his innocence; he was fully entitled not to give evidence, to rely on his interview to the police. We were not allowed to hold that against him, or take it into account in deciding whether or not to convict him. We had to rely exclusively on the evidence we had, and not speculate about evidence that had not been given. All that seemed clear enough, so I found it surprising that the judge returned to the point several times during his summing up. In fairness, on each occasion he emphasised that Danie du Plessis had been under no obligation to give evidence, and that we must not hold it against him; but it somehow seemed unnecessary, and slightly over the top, to keep

going on about it. I'm sure we'd all got the point the first time –
and watching Mr Schroeder, I saw him getting a bit irritated by the
repetition. The librarian in me was reminded of Mark Anthony
telling the Roman Plebeians, also more than once, that Brutus was
an honourable man.

The judge then took us through the indictment, explaining that
aiding and abetting simply meant playing some role designed to
help Vincent Cummings in an offence of trafficking in controlled
drugs. We could ignore the two other words 'counselling' and
'procuring', which were old pieces of legal language, on which the
prosecution did not rely in this case. The precise role Danie agreed
to play was not of great importance. It would be enough if he agreed
to assist Cummings to conceal and launder the proceeds of his drug
trafficking, by including them in the funds delivered to Balakrishnan.
Neither Mr Schroeder nor Mr Pilkington looked entirely happy with
that direction. I'm not sure why. But obviously, we have to rely on
what the judge tells us about the law: that's his job, after all.

It was important, Mr Justice Overton added, that Danie must have
known that he was dealing with the proceeds of drugs, and not the
proceeds of other crimes. So, if he may have thought he was dealing
with the proceeds of illegal arms dealing, reprehensible as that
might be, it was not covered by the charge in the indictment, which
relates solely to drugs, and the verdict would have to be not guilty.
Counsel, Mr Schroeder, was right about that. But then he added
that if, as reflected in his concern about becoming an outlaw, Danie
knew perfectly well what was going on because of information he
had been given by Pienaar, then the jury could assume that he knew
what any reasonable person, much less a trained lawyer, would have
known in his position. At this point, Mr Schroeder asked whether
he might raise a point of law, to which the judge agreed rather
grumpily, sending us out for coffee while they dealt with whatever
it was in our absence. When we returned, fifteen minutes later, the
judge did not modify his directions at all, and everyone looked to
be in a thoroughly bad mood.

The judge reminded us of the evidence quite quickly, and sent us out to start work just before lunch. He told us that, at this stage, we had to reach a unanimous verdict, and that we should begin by electing our foreman, who would return the verdict in due course, and would be responsible for sending him a note if we needed any further help with the law.

Geoffrey had foreseen that we would be sent out just before lunch, and had kindly placed orders for sandwiches, soft drinks, and coffee to be brought to us in our jury room; because now we were under his supervision as jury bailiff, and were not allowed to disperse, or mix with anyone outside our own number while we were deliberating. The canteen was out of bounds from now on, and he advised us to bring a packed lunch with us until the trial ended, although he added that he would pick up a sandwich for anyone who couldn't do that.

So, there we were. As expected, Kenneth Avery was elected foreman by acclamation. He sat at the top of the table, and we took our places all around him. I took the seat immediately to his left. The judge had not spent much time on the evidence during his summing up, and it soon became clear that we all wanted to read through some of the materials in our bundle, especially, of course, Danie's police interview. We agreed to devote the afternoon to reading, and not to begin a discussion before everyone was satisfied, even if that meant postponing it until tomorrow morning. But we did decide to take an initial vote, to see where we stood. After all, if by some happy chance we were all agreed, then we could return a verdict immediately. But I think we all knew that wasn't going to happen. I wrote down the votes as they were given.

Guilty

Joe Henley, plumber
Phil Ackroyd, car dealer
John Lacey, teacher

Not Guilty

Kenneth Avery, stockbroker (foreman)
Marjorie Bloom, retired
Steven Wainwright, accountant
Mohamed Khan, company director
Winston Beckett, musician
Jeff Simons, publican
Edward Brown, retired surveyor
George Kennedy, Manager, London Transport Executive
Sarah Mulvaney, librarian

Nine to three: not enough for a majority verdict. The judge hadn't told us about majority verdicts – deliberately, I'm sure, because the courts prefer juries to be unanimous, as they had to be until the law was changed fairly recently. But it's amazing the odd pieces of information you pick up when you work in a library, and somehow or other, I happened to know that, to be acceptable, the majority had to be either eleven to one, or ten to two. So far, then, we did not have any verdict, let alone a unanimous one. Only after I had compiled the list, did I notice that I had included the jury's occupations. Typical bloody librarian: never happy until we've catalogued everything.

I was more relaxed walking home from the bus stop this evening. DI Walsh had said that dealing with whoever had organised the threat to me depended on action above her pay grade, but she sounded confident about it, and if it was going on at such a high level, surely everything would be all right. Besides, I still had my shadow, for now.

73

Thursday 10 February 1977

This morning we returned to court only long enough for the judge to send us out again with a terse instruction to 'deliberate further'. No one asked us whether we might by any chance have reached a verdict during yesterday afternoon. I suppose they assumed we would have told Geoffrey if we had, and besides, we hadn't had much time as yet.

Kenneth took charge again in his calm, charming way. He began by suggesting that there might be one or two issues we could deal with, and put behind us, so that we could narrow the questions down to those that really mattered.

'For example,' he said, 'does anyone feel that Professor du Plessis did anything wrong just by getting involved with Pienaar and Balakrishnan in the first place? Do we accept that he was acting out of principle, not because he wanted something for himself?'

'Can we call him Danie rather than Professor du Plessis?' Marjorie asked. 'It's less of a mouthful.'

This was agreed to. No one seemed inclined to challenge Danie's attitude in general, except for Joe Henley – and even he sounded less than enthusiastic.

'I don't know why he had to get involved,' he replied, noncommittally. 'I mean, what did it have to do with him? Even if he didn't like what's going on in South Africa, he got out, didn't he? And, all right, he might not agree with everything they're doing over there, but at least they're keeping some law and order going, aren't they? Look what's going on in other places in Africa.'

Winston Beckett jumped in immediately. 'So what? Does that mean they have to tell white people and coloured people that they can't marry each other? What's that got to do with law and order?'

'I'm not saying that,' Joe protested. 'All right, they may be going too far with certain things. All I'm saying is, at least they're keeping the country stable, which is more than you can say for most of them.'

'Are you married, Joe?' Marjorie asked.

'Yeah. So?'

'So what if the government had said to you, sorry, you can't marry your wife?'

'Why would they say that?' Joe asked. 'We're both white.'

'Suppose they passed a law that people who marry each other have to have the same colour hair, or they have to be the same height. Just try to imagine what he and his wife went through, Joe.'

'That would just be stupid, if it was just the colour of the hair,' Joe insisted.

'Exactly my point,' Marjorie replied.

'And it's not as though Danie volunteered, is it?' Jeff added. 'It was Pienaar who approached Danie, not the other way round. Danie wouldn't have got involved otherwise, would he?'

Joe nodded. 'All right, look, I agree he wasn't in it for the money. He was trying to change things in his own way. But I still think he crossed the line over the money from Cummings.'

'Ah, well, that's the main point, of course,' Kenneth replied soothingly. 'But can we put the question of his motive to one side? Can we focus on what he actually did, and what he actually knew?'

Nods all round.

'Good. Well, perhaps the best thing would be to ask someone from each side to explain why they think Danie is guilty, or not guilty, as the case may be, so that we've got the basic idea of how both sides are thinking. Then everybody can join in. Is everyone all right with that?'

Everyone was. I felt instinctively that it was going to be interesting to see who stepped forward as the leader on each side, and on the guilty side, it certainly was. I would have put money on Joe thrusting himself into the role of cheerleader. But the conversation about Danie's motives seemed to have drained him. He was sitting quietly, showing no inclination to re-enter the fray just yet. My next wager would have been on Phil Ackroyd, who had also made quite a few remarks during the past couple of days along the same lines as Joe. But I was wrong on both counts. If I'd been betting in real life, I would have found myself ruefully counting my losses.

'I think the judge explained it best,' our teacher, John Lacey, said. 'Look, let's assume that everything was above board until sometime in 1975. Apparently, this *Hawala* thing is all right as long as you use it properly, and Danie didn't do anything wrong at first, not that I can see, anyway. But then you have this massive increase in funding from Cummings. Any way you look at it, there was something not right about it, and Danie had to know that.'

'Yes,' Edward Brown interrupted, 'but…'

'No, let him finish, please,' Kenneth said. 'You'll get your turn later – everybody will get their chance, but let's hear one from each side first.'

'What I was saying,' John continued, 'is that the judge put his finger on it. Obviously, Cummings wasn't going to come out and say, "I'm a drug dealer; help me launder my money." He was just looking for a way to do it – and he found one, because by keeping quiet and pocketing their ten per cent, Danie and Pienaar let him get away with it, until he got himself killed and it all came to a grinding halt. I mean, it's all very well for Danie to say he didn't know, but who comes up with that kind of money? Nobody except drug dealers. Pienaar as good as told Danie, didn't he? He may not have spelled it out in so many words, but he as good as told him that Cummings was a dealer. As the judge said, anyone with a bit of common sense would have worked it out in no time. Danie's a lawyer. He must have known, mustn't he? That's what the judge said they had to prove. You can argue all you want about knowing something, but you can't cut somebody's head open and see what they knew. You've got to judge by what they do. Danie knew it wasn't kosher, of course he did.' He shrugged. 'Conclusion: he's guilty.'

Kenneth nodded. 'Thank you, John. That makes it very clear, I think. Who would like to go on the not guilty side?'

I would have recouped at least some of my losses at this point. My bet hadn't said very much yet, but you could see him taking it all in and weighing it up. I wasn't surprised that he was ready to speak out now.

'The most important point the judge made,' George Kennedy said, 'was the same one Mr Schroeder made. The prosecution have to prove the case beyond reasonable doubt. That's what this case is about, and nothing else. They have to prove that Danie knew it was drug money, not just that it wasn't kosher – which could mean anything, or nothing. As Mr Schroeder said, it would have been more logical for Danie to assume it was money for weapons and ammunition, rather than drugs. But the real question is: has the prosecution proved he knew it was drug money, or is it just because we heard so much about Cummings from, what was her name…?'

'DI Walsh,' Marjorie reminded him.

'DI Walsh, right. Remember, Danie knew nothing about all that – couldn't have, could he? He didn't know who Cummings was from Adam. Obviously, it's suspicious. But that's not the same as proof beyond reasonable doubt, is it? The judge said that; and so did Mr Schroeder, so they agreed on that. I think that other officer said it best, DI Phillips. He said he thought Danie had been stupid to get in over his head when he didn't understand what he was dealing with, but that was all it was. Mr Pilkington didn't like him saying that – you could tell – he wanted Phillips to say he was guilty. But I think Phillips got it exactly right. Danie might have been stupid, but he's not guilty of drug trafficking – or, at least, if he is, they haven't proved it, not to me, not beyond reasonable doubt.'

Kenneth then threw the discussion open to the floor, and the atmosphere soon got much more lively, with interruptions, people talking over each other, and the occasional flash of temper. But I couldn't see any evidence that any minds were changing, and before we knew it, it was lunchtime. We agreed on a truce for an hour, so that we could digest our sandwiches in peace. The conversation shifted to football, and the government, and what was on TV, and what the plans were for our post-verdict party – none of our differences of opinion were going to affect that.

74

After lunch, before discussions resumed, Kenneth asked whether anyone had thought about changing their vote in the light of what they had heard during the morning. No one moved.

'Well, back to work, then,' he said, as cheerfully as he could.

'What's the point, Ken?' Phil Ackroyd asked. 'If nobody wanted to change their minds after this morning, what difference will it make to go over it all again? Me and Joe reckon he's as guilty as sin. So does Mr Lacey. You lot think he's done nothing wrong. That's it. We're flogging a dead horse, if you ask me.'

'The judge said we had to continue deliberating,' Edward Brown pointed out. 'He'll tell us when he wants us to stop, won't he?'

'The judge isn't stuck in here, getting nowhere and wasting his time, though, is he?' Phil replied. 'We've all got better things to do than sit around and argue with each other when we've all made our minds up.'

Marjorie looked to our foreman for guidance. 'Couldn't we tell Geoffrey we have a majority verdict, Kenneth? We do have a majority, don't we? Why don't we tell him, and see what happens?'

'I suppose we could,' Kenneth conceded quietly.

And then I heard myself speak.

'No, we couldn't, actually,' I said.

I couldn't have imagined the reaction to this innocent remark in my wildest dreams. It was as though the tension in the room had suddenly melted away. Suddenly, everyone was looking at me, and laughing out loud, and there was a spontaneous round of applause and one or two ironic cheers. I'm sure I must have turned a bright shade of red. I stared at them.

'What?' I asked, eventually.

'We didn't think you were ever going to say anything,' Marjorie said.

'We've been waiting all this time,' Steven Wainwright added, 'but not a dicky bird.'

'Mystery woman of the jury,' Winston said, 'creepy.'

'You haven't said anything about the case at all, Sarah,' Mohamed pointed out. 'You chat with us at lunchtime, but you haven't said a word while we've been arguing.'

I realised belatedly that they were right.

'Sorry,' I said.

'You've just cost me a fiver,' Joe said. 'I had a bet on with Phil that you wouldn't say anything until it was all over.'

'Sorry,' I said again, but this time, I found myself laughing with everybody else. It felt good.

'So, Sarah, now that you've broken your vow of silence,' Kenneth asked, 'tell us: why can't we tell Geoffrey we have a majority?'

'Because our majority is nine to three,' I replied. 'The court can't accept a majority unless it's eleven to one, or ten to two.'

'How do you know that?' Kenneth asked. 'The judge didn't say anything about it.'

'I'm a librarian,' I replied. I realised as soon as I'd said it that it didn't make sense. My mind started racing, and I desperately sought out my usual refuge. So; a lawyer, a priest and a librarian walk into a bar. The barman says... But I couldn't remember what the barman said, and somehow, the librarian humour didn't seem the right place to go in my mind just then. And then, an amazing thing happened. I remembered, and felt, all the fear I had been experiencing ever since the trial started: my threatening note, the Swan Vesta match, having to put my trust in my invisible shadow and an unbarricaded door. And I suddenly decided. Sod it. I wasn't going to be afraid anymore. I looked John Lacey full in the face.

'John, may I ask you a question?'

'Of course,' he replied. 'Fire away.'

'What do you teach?'

'History, and a bit of English if we're short-staffed.'

'How old are the children you teach?'

'I teach sixth form mostly, some fifth form.'

'So, they're on the verge of becoming young adults, about to go on to university in many cases?'

'Yes.'

'So, when you teach history, do you try to give them a sense of right and wrong? I mean, I know you have to represent all sides of a question, but do you try to teach them how to develop their own system of values?'

'What do you mean?'

'Well, for example, if you cover the Second World War, you wouldn't tell the story from a Nazi perspective, would you?'

'No,' he conceded at once, 'of course not.'

'So what will you tell your class, when they ask you about apartheid?'

John thought about it for some time.

'I'd tell them it was wrong, that I was opposed to it.'

'Would you tell them that they would be right to fight against it if they could, just as their parents fought against the Nazis?'

'Yes, I suppose I would have to,' he replied.

I turned to the room as a whole.

'You see, I think we all – or almost all – believe that apartheid is wrong,' I suggested. 'We all heard that terrible evidence Dr Morrison gave, and we all heard what happened to Danie du Plessis and his wife. So, this is the question I have: even if Danie knew he was using drug money to fund the fight against apartheid, why does it matter? Wouldn't that at least be putting dirty money to good use?'

There was a long silence.

'But you can't look at it that way, Sarah,' Kenneth protested. 'Drug dealing is illegal.'

'So is dealing in arms and ammunition without a licence,' I countered. 'But Mr Pilkington admitted that, if Danie thought he was using arms money, he wouldn't be guilty.'

'That's true,' Winston said, after another silence.

'Good point,' Jeff Simons agreed.

Kenneth stared at me.

'Sarah,' he said, 'just so I've got this clear. Danie is charged with aiding and abetting drug dealing, by laundering money. Are you suggesting that, even if he did launder drug money, we ignore that, we ignore the law, and find him not guilty?'

75

'I don't believe they've come close to proving that he knew it was drug money,' I replied. 'I think it's more likely he didn't. But either way, yes: I suppose that's what I am suggesting. I just can't find it in my heart to blame him for wanting to do whatever he could to bring apartheid down, not with everything he'd been through, even if it did mean closing his eyes to some wrongdoing. I still think it's the best possible use of drug money I can imagine.'

'It goes against the indictment, and the judge's directions,' Kenneth said. 'We'd be breaking the law.'

'No,' I replied. 'We'd be making the law do what it's supposed to do – to do justice in a good cause. Does anyone really want to send Danie to prison for what he did?'

'The judge wouldn't be very pleased about it,' Marjorie suggested.

'The judge would never know,' I replied. 'He's not allowed to inquire into how we reach our verdict. No one can.'

Kenneth was shaking his head. But I was watching John Lacey.

His eyes hadn't left my face for a moment. A thought came to me, and on impulse I decided to go for it before I could talk myself out of it.

'Have you asked yourselves,' I asked, 'how Danie came to be in this mess? I mean, who would want him to be convicted and sent to prison after all we've heard? I want to tell you something. It's something I'm not supposed to tell you, and I'll get into trouble if you repeat it. But I'm going to trust you. I'm going to tell you, and I'm going to trust you to keep it to yourselves.'

Every eye in the room was fixed on me.

'I received a threat at the start of the trial,' I said. 'A note was pushed through my letterbox with a Swan Vesta matchstick telling me that I had to vote guilty. And the next morning, a man bumped into me, accidentally on purpose, as I was leaving my house to come to court. He said, "Don't forget".'

There were audible gasps from around the table.

'Oh, you poor dear,' Marjorie said.

'Sarah, you should have told the judge,' Kenneth said.

'I did, Kenneth. Of course I did. He told me not to tell anyone else. But he asked DI Walsh to provide me with police protection, which she did, and they arrested the man who threatened me. They found his fingerprints on the note. But the point is, this man told them he had been hired to threaten me by some people DI Walsh said were above her pay grade. Apparently, she was able to take care of it – she doesn't think I'm in any danger now. But who do you think would do such a thing, threaten a juror, just to get Danie convicted in a case like this?'

'The South Africans,' George Kennedy replied.

'Oh, come on, George,' Phil Ackroyd said.

But everyone else remained silent.

'Think about it,' I said. 'These people murdered Vincent Cummings and Mr Pienaar in cold blood just to stop the funding coming from Cambridge. Their man – Erasmus – was going to do the same to Danie, and his wife, Amy, and their two little children.

He would have shot them down in their own home if Amy hadn't been so brave and determined. They're not going to think twice about having Danie convicted if they can, are they? They want to make an example of him to discourage others who may have the same idea. Danie was trying to stop these people if he could, and I, for one, think he was right. This is a weak case anyway. But even if it wasn't, I say, let's stand up for him. He's been through enough. Let's send him home to his family.'

This time, the silence seemed to go on forever.

'We would have to be completely united to do something like that,' Kenneth said, 'and can I please remind everyone that we still only have a majority of nine to three to find him not guilty.'

'No,' John Lacey said. He hadn't taken his eyes off me all this time. 'Actually, it's now ten to two.'

'Oh, for God's sake, John,' Phil complained. 'I thought you were on our side.'

'It's not about being on anybody's side, Phil,' John replied quietly. 'It's about doing the right thing. And for me, next week, when I go back to school, I need to be able to look my pupils in the face – and look myself in the mirror, and tell myself I did the right thing.'

Around the room I saw our majority nodding.

76

'This is where I like to come for a wake at the end of a case,' Steffie said, smiling. 'It's nice and cheerful, the food's good, and it's far enough away from my patch that there's not much risk of running into anyone who knows me.'

It was seven o'clock, they were in the Mille Pine, a small, noisy, brightly lit, bustling Italian family restaurant in Bloomsbury, and were on their second glass of the house Chianti.

Connie Whittaker smiled. 'Is that what this is, ma'am, a wake?'

Steffie pointed a finger, shaking her head. 'No ranks or titles allowed at wakes, Connie. Them's the rules. It's Steffie.'

'And Ted,' Ted Phillips added.

'And, in answer to your question, yes, we've just lost a case, so it is a wake. But that's no reason not to enjoy ourselves. These things happen. We win some, we lose some, just like everyone else. We have a wake, and we move on to the next one. But this one's not just a wake. It's also a celebration. It's not every day two of my colleagues get a commendation for bravery from a High Court judge – and absolutely bloody well deserved, too.' She raised her glass. 'I'm proud of you both.' She pointed a finger at Ted. 'But if you ever pull a stunt like that again, I may have to kill you myself.'

Both Ted and Connie blushed, but they also laughed.

'The verdict wasn't exactly a surprise, was it?' Connie said. 'There was no way we were ever going to get du Plessis. We just didn't have the evidence.'

'We could have done without prosecution witnesses telling the jury he ought to get off,' Steffie said, throwing a fake punch at Ted's arm.

They laughed.

'I was under oath,' Ted replied. 'I had to tell the truth, didn't I? But come on, Steffie, Connie's right. No jury was ever going to buy that case. Danie du Plessis isn't a drug dealer.'

'One or two of them bought it, though, didn't they?' Steffie pointed out. 'It was a majority verdict.'

'There must have been an element of sympathy for him, too,' Connie suggested. 'Of all the characters the jury heard about, he was probably the least blameworthy, but he was the only one on trial.'

'The other candidates were both dead, weren't they?' Ted said. 'Danie was the last man standing. So yes, of course they had some sympathy for him, and so they should.' He raised his glass. 'Here's to the jury, that's what I say.' They clinked glasses and drank.

The waiter approached with a large tray full of antipasto, which they attacked with a vengeance.

'So, Ma... Steffie, what happened about the juror who was threatened?' Connie asked. 'Did that get sorted out?'

'It did, actually, to my amazement. We nicked the bloke they paid to threaten her, no problem. He was just a small-time villain doing a job. But he tipped us off that the job was coming from South Africa House. So I called John Caswell and explained the situation, and asked him to help. He was brilliant. He got in touch with someone at the Home Office, and they fired a warning shot across the embassy's bows – threatened to start expelling people if they didn't behave themselves – and apparently it did the trick. John said they'd received an assurance that the dogs had been called off.'

'What a nightmare for her, though,' Connie said.

'Yes – not to mention that it could have derailed the trial if the judge hadn't given me a free hand to protect her.' She drained her glass. 'There's something else, too. I didn't say anything during the trial, because I thought we had enough going on as it was. But it turns out that the judge, Mr Justice Overton, has a South African wife. Second wife, apparently; the first one died suddenly some years ago. He asked the jury all sorts of questions about friends and relatives from or living in South Africa, didn't he? But I don't remember any mention of his wife. The usher told me, just after I'd given evidence. For some reason he'd read the announcement in *The Times* at the time, and it rang a bell with him during the trial. He's a retired City of London copper, apparently, and he takes an interest in his judges.'

'I can't believe the judge didn't disclose it himself,' Ted said, 'at least to Andrew Pilkington. Andrew, or Ben Schroeder, may have wanted him to recuse himself. Surely he must have mentioned it to them, in chambers perhaps?'

'If so, I would have expected Pilkington to tell us about it on the QT,' Steffie replied, 'wouldn't you? To see what we thought about it?'

'Yes, I would,' Ted agreed.

'What are you going to do with this, Steffie?' Connie asked. 'Are you going to pass it on? There must be people who need to know.'

'I've been thinking long and hard about that,' Steffie replied. 'Now that du Plessis has been acquitted, I'm inclined to let it drop. If he'd been convicted, I would have told both counsel quicker than you could say apartheid. I don't know whether I'm doing the right thing or not, but...'

'I think I'd do the same,' Ted said. 'Let sleeping dogs lie. Actually, I don't think you need to do anything. I'd be amazed if it's passed unnoticed. Some of his friends must be judges. They would have to know about the wife, wouldn't they? They've probably put two and two together by now, and if so, you can bet it's in somebody's notebook somewhere.'

'Oh, the hell with it,' Steffie said. 'Let's change the subject. I don't want to hear any more about South African agents, or about Danie bloody du Plessis, or about *Hawala*, or the cousins Balakrishnan, or Mr Justice bloody Overton, or any of the rest of it. Let's talk about something else, for God's sake.'

The antipasto was succeeded by the main course of veal chops with roast potatoes, and a fresh supply of the Chianti. In the wake of this, talk of dessert was put on hold, and they sat quietly for some time, sipping the wine.

'Actually, Connie,' Steffie said, 'there was something I wanted to talk to you about. Ted knows what I'm going to say; I'm not going behind his back.'

'All right,' Connie said.

'I want you to think about coming to work with me.'

She looked up. 'What?'

'Look, this case is a one-off for me, as you know. I'm officially attached to the Met vice squad. We work out of West End Central.'

'Yes. I know.'

'We're snowed under,' Steffie went on. 'It's not just about prostitution and dirty movies anymore. Nowadays we have to deal with drugs, and God knows what else, at the same time. The workload is off the charts, and we just don't have enough officers to tackle it. We need to expand, quickly, but we have to expand in the right direction. It's not like fraud, or even traffic, where you can have the same old white male faces staring at the punters all the time. We deal with all kinds of characters, and we need all kinds of officers. We need female officers – and a good non-white female officer would be worth her weight in gold.'

Connie stared at Steffie for some time.

'I don't know what to say,' she replied.

'My Super will give me a lot of room on this, Connie,' Steffie continued. 'He's told me I can pick my own people, within reason. And it would come with a promotion to DS.'

'Wow. But – the vice squad?' Connie said. 'I've never done anything specialised like that. All my work has been standard CID.'

'It's the same for everyone when they start out,' Steffie replied. 'You'll soon pick it up if you're half the copper I think you are.'

'You don't know that much about me, Steffie,' Connie said cautiously.

Steffie smiled. 'I know that Ted brought you up, and I know he thinks you're the bee's knees, and that's good enough for me. Behind that kind, benevolent exterior,' she reached out and touched his arm, and they all laughed, 'he's a hard man to please when it comes to young officers. You don't get his seal of approval unless you're good and you work your socks off. If Ted says you're OK, that's all I need to know – and he says you're much better than OK.'

Connie turned to Ted.

'What do you think, sir – I mean, Ted, sorry?'

He sipped his wine for some seconds.

'You'd be a real loss to Cambridge,' he replied, 'and personally, I'd hate to see you go. But we're so bloody provincial in Cambridge. You know how hard it's been for you just coming this far, just making CID, and it's not about to get any easier trying to climb up the ranks, however good you are. There's bound to be more room in the Met. So when Steffie asked me if I'd mind her trying to poach you, there was only one answer. It's a great opportunity, Connie. In your shoes, I'd go, and I wouldn't look back.'

'But I'd still get stick for being a coloured woman, even in the Met, wouldn't I?'

'Some,' Steffie replied. 'I get it myself, just as a woman. You'd get it in the house generally, but not within the squad. We can't afford to tolerate that attitude in the squad, and we don't. On the rare occasions it shows its head, the Super stamps on it, hard.' She glanced down at the dessert menu. 'You don't have to tell me now,' she said. 'Take a few days to think about it.'

'I'll call you tomorrow,' Connie replied.

77

Friday 11 February 1977

The knock on the door of Sir John Fisk's rooms in college came exactly on time. His visitor was punctual, and that was good.

'Come,' he called from his desk.

The door opened, and a young man, wearing his undergraduate gown over his suit and tie, opened the door and stepped tentatively inside.

'Oliver Marchant, Master. I got a message that you wanted to see me.'

Fisk stood. 'Yes. I do. Good of you to come. It's nothing to be alarmed about. There's something I wanted to chat with you about, that's all. I see you're wearing your gown. You're dining in hall, I take it?'

'Yes, Master.'

'Good. Well, I won't keep you long. Take a seat. I daresay a glass of sherry wouldn't go amiss before dinner, would it? Do you prefer dry or amontillado?'

'Dry, please, Master.'

'Very good. A man after my own heart. Amontillado's for the tourists, and they're welcome to it.'

Fisk poured sherry for them both. Instead of returning to sit behind his desk, he took his seat in the armchair opposite Oliver.

'I haven't seen you for a while, Oliver,' he said. 'Archaeology and Anthropology, isn't it? If I recall rightly, you got a decent two-one last year?'

Oliver smiled. 'Thanks to some last-minute revision, Master.'

Fisk laughed. 'But of course – how else does one get a decent two-one? Tell me: how's your father? I follow his progress with great interest, of course. He's been blazing a few trails since he won his seat, hasn't he? I hear there may be ministerial office in his future.'

'There are rumours, Master, but he's not counting on it. He is a bit on the radical side for some people's taste.'

Fisk laughed. 'Indeed he is. I've known him for a long time, as you know.'

'Yes, Master.'

'Long before he turned into a radical backbencher. We worked together very closely at one time. I don't know whether he told you. It was while I was ambassador in Amman.'

'He did mention it, yes, but he was very tight-lipped about it all. The impression I got was that it was a bit hush-hush.'

'It was indeed. Some of it was highly sensitive, can't talk about it even now. Your father was brilliant – a real tower of strength, competent, reliable and discreet.' Fisk paused and reached for the bottle on the table between them. 'Let me freshen you up.'

'Thank you, Master.'

'I'm sure you're wondering where all this is leading, and I don't want to make you late for dinner, so let me come to the point. What I want to know is whether you're a chip off the old block, so to speak?'

'Master?'

'If I were to take you into my confidence about something important, could I rely on your discretion, as I could on your father's?'

Oliver looked up. 'Yes, of course. I certainly hope so.'

Fisk nodded. 'I understand that, when you're not immersed in the wonders of archaeology and anthropology, you can sometimes be found promoting the odd radical cause of your own – like father, like son, I suppose. The odd demonstration here and there?'

'I must admit, it has been known, Master.'

'Well, why not? No harm in that. It's what students should be doing, making a nuisance of themselves in a good cause – as long as it doesn't interfere too much with work, of course.'

Oliver looked at Fisk closely. 'May I ask what you have in mind, Master?'

Fisk poured more sherry, without asking.

'A sensitive operation, Oliver, rather like the ones your father used to get up to with me in Amman. But this time, it's your turn. Interested?'

Oliver smiled. 'I'm intrigued.'

'Students against apartheid,' Fisk said. 'That's one of your good causes, isn't it?'

He nodded. 'I'm the Organising Secretary, Master.'

Fisk nodded. 'So I understand. And if you're interested in apartheid, I assume you've been following the case of Professor du Plessis?'

'Yes, of course. We all have. We heard the jury found him not guilty. It's wonderful news. He's something of a hero to us, obviously. Well, he's a Fellow of our College, apart from anything else. We were wondering about throwing a party for him to welcome him back.'

Fisk smiled. 'I'm sure he'd enjoy that. But the fact is, Oliver, he's not completely out of the woods just yet.'

'Master?'

'As you may know, in addition to his Fellowship, he holds a university lectureship. The University seems to think that he's brought it into disrepute just by getting himself charged and hauled into court, regardless of whether he's been acquitted or not.'

'You mean he's still under threat of being dismissed?'

'That's exactly what I mean.'

'What? Even though he's been found not guilty? That's outrageous.'

'I agree entirely, Oliver,' Fisk said. 'But the fact is, he's been summoned to appear before the University's disciplinary tribunal to answer the charge, and to show cause why he should not be dismissed from the University's employment. We will make sure that he's legally represented, of course. But between you and me, the disciplinary tribunal isn't exactly the Old Bailey. They don't always observe all the legal niceties, I'm afraid. In fact, it has something of a reputation for being a kangaroo court, and I'm not sure the legal approach is guaranteed to yield the right result. So, I've been giving the matter some thought, and it has occurred to me that there might be another way of approaching it, a way to boost our legal defence, if you will. And that's where you come in, if you're up for it.'

'Just tell me how, Master,' Oliver said.

Fisk stood, and walked back to his desk. He picked up a blue file folder, and handed it to Oliver.

'This is for you,' he said, 'on the strict understanding that you didn't get it from me. I need your absolute discretion on that. Do I have it?'

'Yes, of course. What is it?'

Fisk handed the file to him.

'This,' Fisk replied, 'is a complete list of all the University's investments, direct or indirect, including subsidiaries and business partnerships, in South Africa, the South African government, South African companies, anything and everything connected in any way to South Africa. It's been meticulously compiled, I assure you. As you will see, the amounts involved are very considerable – well, they certainly got my attention. You'll see the grand total in the summary on the first page. Simply put, it seems that the University is making a small fortune from investing in South Africa.'

Oliver turned to the first page and his eyes opened wide.

'From investing in apartheid,' he said quietly.

Fisk smiled. 'Exactly so,' he replied. 'It also suggests that, when the University accuses Professor du Plessis of bringing it into disrepute by taking up the fight against apartheid, it has a rather obvious conflict of interest: don't you think? I would like to bring that to their attention, preferably publicly – embarrass them a bit, make them think twice about what they're doing.'

'What can I do?' Oliver asked.

'The hearing is less than two weeks away,' Fisk said, 'on Monday the twenty-first of this month. We could ask for an adjournment, I suppose, but I'd rather not drag it out. I'd prefer to knock it on the head as soon as we can. It occurred to me that, if you were to share the contents of the file with your fellow radicals, they might perhaps be moved to express themselves in some way before the hearing.'

'In the form of a demonstration perhaps?' Oliver asked.

'One or two spontaneous demonstrations in support of Professor du Plessis,' Fisk replied, 'around the Old Schools building and the Senate House, over the weekend before the hearing, shall we say, and perhaps at one thirty or so on the Monday, an hour before the time fixed for the hearing. Being spontaneous, the demonstrations would have no overt connection to the College, or to Professor du Plessis, but it would show the depth of feeling there is within the student body about his case.'

Oliver smiled. 'I could see that happening, Master.'

'And, of course,' Fisk added, 'no doubt there would be some modest expense involved in making banners and what have you for the occasion. I'm sure we could reimburse you covertly for that kind of thing.'

Oliver drained his glass. 'Thank you for the sherry, Master. I should be making my way to hall for dinner.'

'Of course, Oliver. I must be on my way too. I'm not dining tonight. We're having a small gathering for Professor du Plessis and his wife at home. Remember me to your father when you talk to him, won't you, and let's talk again in a day or two, shall we?'

'We will.' He suddenly laughed. 'I probably shouldn't tell you this, but I've just remembered something my father used to say about you, and I've just realised how right he was.'

Fisk raised his eyebrows. 'Nothing too terrible, I hope.'

'He used to say you were a cunning old fox, Master.'

'Did he indeed?' Fisk replied. 'How kind of him to say so.'

78

Monday 21 February 1977

'I have the University's press release here,' Barratt Davis said. 'Shall I read it?'

There was a loud chorus of approval. They had gathered at John and Annabel Fisk's house for an impromptu celebration as soon as they received the message, confirming that the presence of Professor Danie du Plessis before the University disciplinary tribunal at the Old Schools building was no longer required. The Fisks had raided their cellar for champagne, to be accompanied by a selection of delicious hors d'oeuvres conjured up in no time by Annabel, who had paid attention during her long career as a diplomatic wife, whenever her domestic staff were called upon to produce fare for an impromptu embassy party with almost no notice. Annabel was now as adept as any of her former chefs at that particular form of fast food.

Professor Danie du Plessis, Buckland Professor of Roman Law, is no longer the subject of any intended proceedings before the University disciplinary tribunal, following his acquittal at the Central Criminal Court of a charge of aiding and abetting trafficking in controlled drugs, the Vice-Chancellor's office has announced. Professor du

Plessis, who had stepped aside voluntarily pending the outcome of the proceedings at the Old Bailey, pursuant to an agreement with the Vice-Chancellor's office, is now free to resume his privileges and duties as Buckland Professor. The announcement was made at the Old Schools this morning by Professor James McVeigh, Pro-Vice-Chancellor for Institutional and International Relations. The verdict ending the trial was delivered on Friday 11 February. Professor du Plessis had been on bail while the proceedings were pending, and throughout the trial.

The prosecution had alleged that Professor du Plessis, a native of South Africa, had knowingly accepted money from a drug dealer as part of his fundraising activities on behalf of anti-apartheid interests in South Africa. But by its verdict, the jury rejected that allegation, and it was not suggested that Professor du Plessis' activities were in any way unlawful, in the absence of any involvement with drug money.

'The Vice-Chancellor has been advised by the University Advocate that the verdict of not guilty returned by the jury at the Central Criminal Court entitles Professor du Plessis to be considered as wholly innocent of the charge brought against him,' Professor McVeigh said. 'Accordingly, it would be wrong, as a matter of law, for the University to pursue any further proceedings against him, in the absence of evidence of misconduct unrelated to the case at the Old Bailey. The Vice-Chancellor is not aware of any such evidence, and accordingly, the matter will now be regarded as closed. Professor du Plessis' terms and conditions of employment will continue as before.'

Professor Clara Stein, Deputy University Advocate, confirmed the Advocate's advice. 'The presumption of innocence is among the most important rules of law in our democratic society, as it is in any democratic society,' Professor Stein said. 'Professor du Plessis was given the benefit of that presumption before his trial, and now that he has been vindicated by the jury's verdict, no further action against him is warranted.'

Both the Vice-Chancellor and the University Advocate downplayed any suggestion that a series of demonstrations over the past several days by students involved in the 'Students against Apartheid' group had played any part in the Vice-Chancellor's decision. 'Professor du Plessis is an excellent teacher, as well as a noted academic,' Professor Stein said. 'He is very popular among our undergraduates, and it's only natural that they would want to support him as far as they can. We fully respect the right of our students to voice their concerns that he should be dealt with justly. But we made our decision because it is the right thing to do, and not as a result of any pressure arising from the demonstrations. No considerations of South African politics played any part in the decision, which was based entirely on the legal merits of the case.'

The reading ended with cheers and applause.

'All the same,' Harriet said, with a glance in John Fisk's direction, 'I can't help feeling that it was a happy coincidence that so many students turned out all around the Old Schools and the Senate House just before the hearing.'

'Yes, remarkable. Their timing was spot on, wasn't it?' John Fisk replied.

Danie put an arm around Amy's shoulder and raised his glass.

'Well, however they arrived at their decision,' he said, 'Amy and I would like to thank you all, our dear friends, for sticking with us throughout this terrible period in our lives. Ben, Barratt, I don't know what we would have done without your advice, and the brilliant way you dealt with the case in court. I know I gave you some grief over whether to follow your advice at times, but you didn't give up on me, and we came through it. I know the case was never a simple not guilty, no matter what the police officers thought. You two made that happen. Thank you.'

'We've had less cooperative clients,' Barratt said as the toast was drunk, 'haven't we, Ben?'

'One or two,' Ben replied.

'Thank you, too, Harriet. I will never forget how you stood up to the disciplinary tribunal – and how you dealt with all those investments the University has in South Africa, which of course played no part in their decision.'

Harriet shook her head. 'It's a mystery how that got so much publicity,' she said. 'Inquisitive students burning the midnight oil and spreading the word, I suppose.'

'Must have been,' John Fisk agreed.

'Pieter, I can't tell you what it's meant to me to have you over here during the trial, and to have you looking after Amy every day. And, of course, all the other things you've done for us, which I won't go into now.'

Pieter walked over to Danie and Amy and embraced them.

'It's friendship,' he replied simply. 'You'd do the same for me. I'm glad it's over.'

'And our hosts, John and Annabel,' Danie concluded. 'You've made us welcome ever since we came to England all those years ago, and you've been such an important part of our lives.'

'It's been our pleasure,' Annabel said.

'You've both added so much to Cambridge,' John replied. 'And now, happily, there is much more to come.'

They raised their glasses in a toast, and there was a silence for some time.

'There is one slightly concerning development,' Barratt said. 'I've told Danie and Amy already. I don't think it's in any way disastrous, but we will need to keep an eye on it. The Home Office called me this morning. They got word that charges of crimes against the State have been filed against Danie and Amy in South Africa – details unclear at this point; they're trying to find out more. They also say there's a warrant out for their arrest.'

'Oh, my God,' Annabel said.

'Will they try to extradite them?' Harriet asked.

Ben shook his head. 'No. These are obviously political charges, and besides, the present government won't extradite anyone to

South Africa now. It's one effect of the international pressure that has hit home.'

'I agree,' Barratt said. 'But what it does mean is that you can't go back to South Africa – not that you were thinking of that, anyway, I'm sure, but doubly so now. And you will have to be careful if you travel. You'll have to check to see if you're going to, or through, a country that has less scruples about extradition than we do. South Africa still has a few friends.'

'We'll be looking over our shoulders forever, won't we?' Amy said quietly.

'No, I don't think so,' John Fisk replied. 'They have other things to worry about. Yes, you're in the spotlight now because the trial has just finished, and I'm sure the press in South Africa have been all over it. But a month from now, they'll have forgotten all about you.'

'Are you sure?' Harriet asked.

'Yes, of course. Danie and Amy are small fry. The South Africans have an armed insurrection going on, right under their noses. They have the ANC blowing up police stations. Two money launderers in England aren't going to occupy centre stage for long. We saw the same thing happen time and time again when we were in the diplomatic service, didn't we, Annabel? They'll lose interest eventually.'

'I'm sure that's true,' Barratt agreed. 'But as long as the charges are on file, there's always the risk that you may end up in the wrong place at the wrong time. So you have to be aware. But I can work with you on this, with the Home Office. It doesn't have to take over your lives.'

'It feels like it already has,' Amy said.

79

Danie du Plessis

It's strange what goes through your mind, what conversations you have with yourself, while you're sitting in the dock in a criminal court. There's a school of thought that docks should be abolished as a relic of a bygone, more judgemental era, an era in which, if you were charged with an offence, there was a tacit assumption that you were probably guilty. Otherwise, why would the police have charged you? So what harm could there be in making you sit on your own in a box, guarded by a prison officer, while other people got on with your trial all around you? True, in law, you were entitled to the presumption of innocence; but that was a theoretical matter, designed to address the rare case in which the police might have made a mistake and charged some innocent person. The practical reality was that you were probably a felon, and the court and public should be protected by having you locked up at a safe distance. That's not how we think today, the argument goes, so perhaps it's time to consign the dock to history, and allow the defendant to sit in the well of the court with his counsel, as is the case in other countries.

Whatever the merits of that debate, I, for one, am grateful that we still have docks. Uncomfortable as it is to surrender to your bail each morning, and allow the prison office to take you into custody and lock you in the box, it shields you, at least to some extent, from the constant gaze of judge and jury, and curious members of the public. I imagine that I would have felt very exposed sitting behind Ben in the well of the court. I imagine I would have felt like a living exhibit in some macabre exhibition of the human condition. I was always conscious of Amy's presence, and Pieter's, in court.

Their eyes turned in my direction frequently, of course, but theirs was a benign gaze, which brought comfort. I would have felt very differently about being under the constant scrutiny of strangers, of curious onlookers wondering what my story was, and what combination of circumstances had brought me to the Old Bailey as someone on trial for a crime. I needed some privacy, some relief from that scrutiny, during those interminable days of the trial, days that seemed to stretch endlessly into the distance. I needed the privacy of the dock because those were exactly the questions I was asking myself.

It was not the narrative I was born to, not a narrative I could ever have imagined as a child in Bloemfontein. According to that narrative, I should have been a veritable pillar of society, a loyal descendant of the Voortrekkers, a lawyer like my father, and perhaps later a judge, also like him. I might even have become a lay reader at our Dutch Reformed Church. I would certainly have spoken Afrikaans, unless compelled to resort to English for some business purpose. Perhaps I would even have approved of apartheid – not out of any malice towards differently coloured people, naturally, strictly out of my sense of duty, as a White man, to safeguard and guide them until they evolve to become capable, at some distant time, of full citizenship and participation in the political process. Until that time, obviously, racial degradation through sexual mingling must not be allowed. Who knows, perhaps I would have married a woman who got off on thinking about Hendrik Verwoerd, and screamed his name when she came.

Even when I broke away from the claustrophobic grip of my life in Bloemfontein, and took myself off to study at WITS, with the more liberal outlook Hilda had inculcated in me, my expectation for my life was a respectable one as a lawyer or academic. At no time during that young period of my life did it occur to me that I might end up on trial for my freedom in a criminal court. Not once did it occur to me that I might become an outlaw.

Perhaps it was something nameless that grew inside me

during the demonstrations; or perhaps it was something I sensed instinctively the first time I found myself naked in bed with my beautiful Coloured lover, becoming a man at last, and realising that with manhood came a more complex series of choices; realising that nothing was as simple as it had been an hour earlier, before our differently coloured bodies had combined in such a wonderful outpouring of passion. Perhaps I knew in those moments when we finally sank into each other's arms, in those moments of exquisite exhaustion, when our lives had changed forever – when we had changed our lives forever. Perhaps, from those moments, it was only a matter of time.

Certainly, I suppose, after Art Pienaar entered my life, the idea of becoming an outlaw was in my mind on some level. It was something that occurred to me the moment he propositioned me to assist in his money laundering enterprise. If it had not, I would not have spent so much time delving into books on criminal law, examining what he had asked me to do from every angle, to see whether it might involve me in the commission of a criminal offence, endlessly analysing the practice of *Hawala* to allay my lawyer's ingrained suspicion that such a convenient device, even if sanctioned by usage over millennia, must somehow be legally questionable. I was anxious not to cross the line, and I was anxious to protect Amy from suspicion of crossing the line, and that anxiety could not have afflicted me unless I was all too aware of the existence of a line that I might be in danger of crossing.

And then came Vincent Cummings. Much as I protested to Art about the legality of accepting Cummings's money, I also understood why he had decided to do a deal for ten per cent of the stash he was going to launder. The only difference between us, at that stage, was that Art had reconciled himself to the idea that what he was doing was more important than the risk of infringing the law by helping Cummings to conceal his earnings from the drug trade. That was a step I hadn't taken, probably more because of fear than because of any question of principle, because by then my hatred of apartheid had hardened, and I was pleased to be playing a part, however small, in bringing it down. I understood where Art was coming from. If you are financing people who put their lives on the line by mounting armed raids on police stations, you probably feel that a touch of money laundering is small beer by comparison. I understood that. But there remained a part of me that balked at breaking the law.

Until, that is, Amy told me that she would support me, and that in her eyes, it was a heroic thing to become an outlaw in a greater cause. It was always Amy who kept my eyes on the goal, and who reminded me, mostly silently, why I cared about what I was doing. She made it possible for me to embrace an idea that ran contrary to the way I had been brought up, and to every natural instinct I had.

I honestly believe that I am right in saying that I did not know that Vincent Cummings's money represented the proceeds of drug dealing. As a lawyer, I maintain that there is a clear difference between knowledge and suspicion, and because the law requires knowledge to sustain a conviction, I have always believed, and believe now, that I was not guilty of the offence with which I was charged. But, sitting there in the dock during the trial, there were many moments when I doubted that the clear difference in my mind would be just as clear to the jury, or even to the judge. As the evidence unfolded, the circumstantial case about my state of mind – the question of what anyone in my position surely had to know – would not go away; and despite Ben's wonderful closing speech, and the prosaic legal direction given by Mr Justice Overton, there was the constant fear that the trial would end badly.

If it ended badly, Ben had told me, I was staring at a custodial sentence, probably somewhere in the region of two or three years. We had a very good chance on appeal, he added, to cheer me up; but it was a bleak prospect, nonetheless. Any such sentence, in addition to the dreadful spectre of such a long separation from Amy and the children, would be the end of my career and the end of my life as I knew it. I had to face up to the consequences of becoming an outlaw. I knew, of course, that there were many in South Africa who had faced up to that reality, and had paid an even heavier price for becoming an outlaw for their cause. I could only hope that I would not meet a similar fate. When the verdict came, it was by a majority of the jury. One or two of them had wanted to convict me, had been convinced beyond reasonable doubt that I was an outlaw. It was a disturbing thought, but at the end of the day, I walked away unscathed.

Now, ironically, I am unquestionably an outlaw. If they ever get their hands on me and take me back to South Africa, that will be a formality, and it won't be a question of two or three years. The same applies to Amy. Facing charges in South Africa has made us seem even more heroic in the eyes of many of our friends, and our students. But it is a notoriety we would prefer not to have, if we had a choice. I think John Fisk is probably right – in time, with the incessant disorder and violence on the borders, the erosion of their internal security, and the long-term threat to the apartheid regime, the authorities will probably be preoccupied with more significant outlaws, and forget about us. They don't have unlimited resources, and those they have will be focused on more immediate threats. We will just be names in a file gathering dust. If we avoid putting ourselves in harm's way by travelling to the wrong place, there's no reason to suppose that we will ever end up in a court in South Africa.

But that's the one thing about becoming an outlaw that had not occurred to us: that it might end, like the world in T S Eliot's poem, not with a bang, but with a whimper. Not with a concrete result, but with the constant, and apparently endless fear of the future: a life spent looking over our shoulders, waiting for some new Nick Erasmus to track us down; worrying at night when the children are late coming home; dreading the possibility that some future government may decide that allowing extradition to South Africa may be a price worth paying for continued access to the naval base. In all probability, none of this will ever happen. But when you become an outlaw, it seems there's no escape from the fear.

Author's Note

Writing *To Become an Outlaw* has been a new experience for me in a number of ways. For one, it was written during the first Covid-19 lockdown of 2020, in circumstances that permitted few distractions, and, therefore concentrated the mind. This was probably just as well, because this book represents another departure for me. In the past I've tended to write mainly about things and places I know, which is an axiomatic piece of good advice for any author. This time, I had to take a risk and branch out.

I have never been to South Africa, and my conversations with South African friends about the apartheid era are now some distance in the past. Although *To Become an Outlaw* is not set in South Africa in any significant way, it is a book about South Africa at a certain time, as well as about the workings of the English courts when confronted with the reality of that time. I have had to do my best to understand the mentality of those ruling South Africa during the apartheid era, now happily consigned to history. I have also done my utmost to see into the minds of those who resisted, and fought to destroy that evil system, often as exiles forced to live abroad. It will be for others to say how far I have succeeded.

I am grateful to two invaluable sources: Leonard Thompson's monumental and authoritative *A History of South Africa* (Fourth edition, revised and updated by Lynn Berat, Yale University Press, New Haven and London, 2014); and *London Recruits: The Secret War against Apartheid* (compiled and edited by Ken Keable, The Merlin Press Limited, Pontypool, 2012). The latter provided me with a rich background for my depiction of the much under-reported activities of those dedicated to the overthrow of apartheid working in Britain. I hope my book makes it clear that I emerged from *London Recruits* with nothing but admiration for everyone involved in that courageous struggle, and that there is no suggestion of anything I would class as wrongdoing on any of their parts. On the contrary, everything they did was, to my mind, not only lawful, but completely justified. For the avoidance of any doubt, my book is a novel; my characters were drawn from my imagination, and any apparent resemblance to any person, living or dead, is unintended and coincidental.

I am grateful, as ever, to Ion Mills and Claire Watts at No Exit Press, for their continued faith in my work; to my tireless agent Guy Rose; and to my wife Chris, my companion in a lonely journey through lockdown, who has always supported me in my writing, but whose support in this instance means more than ever.